Linda Finlay lives on the Devonshire coast and is the author of ten novels. From lacemaking to willow weaving, each one is based on a local craft which, in order to write authentically and place herself firmly in the shoes of her heroines, she has learned to do herself. However, it is people and their problems that make for a good story and, with so much interesting material to work with, it is easy for Linda to let her imagination run as wild as the West Country landscape which has inspired her writing. *Farringdon's Fate* is her eleventh novel.

Also by Linda Finlay

Farringdon's Fate

Linda Finlay

ONE PLACE. MANY STORIES

HQ
An imprint of HarperCollins*Publishers* Ltd
1 London Bridge Street
London SE1 9GF

www.harpercollins.co.uk

HarperCollins*Publishers*
1st Floor, Watermarque Building, Ringsend Road
Dublin 4, Ireland

This paperback edition 2021

1
First published in Great Britain by
HQ, an imprint of HarperCollins*Publishers* Ltd 2021

ISBN: 9780008392673

MIX
Paper from
responsible sources

FSC
www.fsc.org FSC™ C007454

This book is produced from independently certified FSC™ paper
to ensure responsible forest management.

For more information visit: www.harpercollins.co.uk/green

This book is set in 10.9/16 pt. Sabon by Type-it AS, Norway

Printed and Bound in the UK using 100% Renewable Electricity at
CPI Group (UK) Ltd, Croydon, CR0 4YY

To Pern,

my rock during lockdown

Chapter 1

Edwin Farringdon had much to consider as with faithful black Labrador Ellery by his side, he made his way down the sunken lane where frost still gathered in pockets. His meeting with Quarry Manager, Tom Wakeley, had not gone well. Not only were the workers demanding an immediate increase in wages, they wanted him to pay for the tallow candles they used to light their way underground, which, at five each per day, would be no mean amount. He conceded their point that the cost of living was spiralling, but wasn't it for everyone? Whilst there'd been a resurgence in both the building of churches and renovation of the older ones and the order book looked healthy, customers took time to settle their bills. However, priding himself on being a fair employer, he'd agreed to give the matter serious consideration.

With these problems weighing heavily on his mind, he found himself back on the estate before he realised. Nettlecombe Manor nestled in the shelter of surrounding hills at the head of a long combe that led down to the sea. Yet today, even the sight of the elegant symmetry and tall chimneys of the Jacobean building, its grey stones and mullioned windows bathed in the rosy glow of the setting winter sun, failed to lift his spirits. In truth, since marrying his second wife Charlotte, he no longer found his home the haven it had once been. Keen to show off her standing in society, she was forever changing the layout of the house, purchasing new furnishings and fripperies which were not to his taste but also unnecessary. And whilst he loved his eldest daughter Louisa May dearly, her forthcoming betrothal would necessitate yet more expense.

'Oh Beatrice, why did you have to leave?' he cried. Ellery, recognising the name of his dear departed mistress, peered up at him through his one good eye and whined. 'I know, old boy, I know,' he sighed, ruffling the dog's silky ears and noting with sadness the increasing number of grey hairs around his chin. As if sensing his master's misery, the dog gave another whimper and brushed against his leg.

'I guess we're both past our prime,' Edwin murmured, pulling his woollen coat closer as a gust of wind cut through him. His monthly inspection of the great subterranean caverns didn't usually affect him, but today it had left him weary and chilled to the bone.

'They say there's no fool like an old fool and I've certainly proved that, haven't I?' As his loyal friend barked in agreement, Edwin recalled the events that had changed his life seven years previously.

Whilst on business at the Inns of Court in London, he'd been introduced to the beautiful Charlotte Calveleigh, daughter of his solicitor. She'd flirted and flattered him, and being much younger at twenty-four to his forty-three years, her attraction to him had gone to his head. Bereft after his cherished wife's sudden death, he'd succumbed to her charms and, on a mad impulse, had proposed only a few months later and brought her home to Nettlecombe in East Devonshire.

From that moment, she'd become quite capricious and he never knew what mood she would be in when he returned home. She seemed to think that owning a manor house meant he had unlimited funds when, in truth, its upkeep took almost all the income the estate and quarry brought in. Once when he'd endeavoured explaining, she'd waved such talk away as if it was distasteful and carried on purchasing as if it were her right, adding friction to their already strained relationship. It hadn't helped that she'd failed to give him the male heir he so desperately needed to ensure that Nettlecombe remained in the family. Now he had five daughters to provide for and, whilst he adored them all, it seemed the curse the gypsies bestowed upon the Farringdon dynasty had come true.

Then, like an arrow piercing his brain, realisation hit him and he stopped abruptly, causing Ellery to stare back at him in surprise. When had he last paid a visit to her chamber? Whilst she was always obliging when he did, it had to be admitted such occasions were inevitably followed by demands for some new acquisition or other. Clearly things needed to change. Tonight, he would go to her room and then, if the luck of the gods was with him, he'd sire a son.

Feeling happier, he hurried along the wide driveway lined with magnificent lime trees that would soon be bursting with buds of new life, on past the manicured gardens that spread out on each side. It might only be January and freezing cold, but he could almost smell spring in the air. A time of hope and renewal, he thought, mounting the granite steps and entering through the studded front door.

'Her ladyship is waiting for you in the Ruby Room, my lord,' the butler announced, taking his cane, gloves and outer clothes from him.

'Thank you, Ferris,' he replied, resigned to the fact that, in her endeavours to outclass Lady Connaught who referred to her rooms by the colour of their furnishings, Charlotte had insisted theirs be named after precious stones.

Purposefully, he strode along the hallway flanked by elaborate oak panelling, the sound of Ellery's paws cushioned by the recently laid plush Axminster carpet. His ancestors seemed to frown down at him from their ornate frames and with every step he felt responsibility for the future of Nettlecombe settle heavier on his shoulders. As he shook his head to dispel more dismal thoughts, his attention was caught by something glinting on the marble table.

'I don't remember that clock being here before,' he said, turning to the butler.

'No, my lord, it was delivered this morning soon after you left. I believe her ladyship commissioned its design.' Glowering at the garish domed timepiece surrounded by grinning cherubs, Edwin entered the room he still thought of as the parlour.

'There you are at last,' his wife greeted him impatiently. She was reclining on the chaise longue that was drawn up in front of the fire, the bright flames tinting her fair hair golden. 'Nanny has already taken Sarah and Maria for their tea.'

'I'll go up and see them later, my dear,' he assured her, but she wasn't to be placated.

'How many times must I tell you not to bring that creature in here?' she remonstrated, glaring at Ellery as he flopped down on the rug beside the hearth.

'Don't be beastly, Step Mama,' Bea cried. At seventeen, she had the same sense of fairness as her papa and was never afraid to voice her thoughts. 'I expect you're worn out from that walk up the lane, aren't you, old boy,' she crooned, springing out of her chair to stroke the dog's coat. Edwin smiled, for like her mother, the youngest daughter from his first marriage loved all animals.

'I don't know why you had to go and see that wretched man when your eldest daughter has just become betrothed and there is much to plan.' As Charlotte continued her rant, Edwin couldn't fail to notice the emphasis she placed on the word 'your'.

'What is the point of employing a quarry manager if you still have to oversee the work yourself?' Her disparaging look emphasised the lines of discontent etched around her mouth, and again Edwin found himself making unfavourable comparisons between her and his first wife. Mild in manner, Beatrice had always listened to his problems, considering them at length before offering words of support and encouragement. He couldn't understand why memories of her were plaguing him today for he was a loyal man and, despite everything, he was still fond of Charlotte. Turning to his two older daughters, Louisa, who was twenty, and Victoria, eighteen, who were sitting together on the burgundy button-backed sofa, dark eyes staring sympathetically at him, he gave them a surreptitious wink.

'You must be excited, Louisa,' he said, trying to inject some cheerfulness into the proceedings.

'Captain Beauchamp is so handsome,' Bea cried, throwing her arms around herself and making them laugh.

'He is,' Louisa agreed, a flush creeping up her cheeks. 'And yes, Papa, I am excited. Except, Step Mama wishes to hold a grand ball for my betrothal.' Louisa's expression told him quite clearly what she thought of that idea.

'Indeed, I do. Such an occasion should be celebrated in style, do you not agree, Edwin?' Charlotte asked. Although this was phrased as a question, it was clear his wife considered it a fait accompli. 'A notice should be placed in *The Times*. Society needs to be informed of the betrothal of your eldest daughter to Captain Henry Beauchamp of Woolbrooke House. Goodness, we shall have to commission a special console table on which to display all the presents people will send and—'

'Aren't you getting a little ahead of yourself, my dear?' Edwin interrupted. 'Captain Beauchamp only spoke with me last evening.'

'Henry is visiting his parents today,' Louisa added, smiling gratefully at him. 'I am invited to luncheon on Saturday and will spend the weekend meeting his wider family.'

'Then I shall need to accompany you,' Charlotte cried.

'Actually, Step Mama, I thought I'd take Vanny to help me dress and see to my hair. You know I'm all fingers and thumbs when I'm nervous,' Louisa said quickly, looking at Edwin for support.

'Good idea to take your maid along,' he agreed. 'You will understandably wish to look your best, although you have nothing to worry about on that score,' he added, patting his daughter's shoulder reassuringly. Her dark hair neatly coiled at the nape of her neck emphasised her fine bone structure and he couldn't help but admire her composure as she sought to make her wishes clear, in that quiet yet steely determined way she had. 'And of course, Vanny will see you come to no harm.'

'Henry said his parents will issue a formal invitation for you to join them at Woolbrooke very soon, Step Mama. They like to do things properly,' she added as Charlotte opened her mouth to protest.

'I'm pleased to hear it,' the woman murmured, somewhat mollified. 'However, it is important you establish what alterations you require made to the building so they can be carried out before you take up residence. Of course, I am best placed to assist you there for I well remember when I first saw this old place...'

'Really, Charlotte, I don't think there is any need for Louisa to worry about such things now,' Edwin interjected. 'I was given to understand there will be an engagement period of at least a year.'

'Yes, but Victoria is to make her London debut this May and I will be required to present her at Court.' Edwin turned his attention to his second daughter who raised her brow and shrank back in her seat. Pretty, with chestnut curls framing her heart-shaped face, she was the least confident of his daughters and had no interest in society matters. Edwin could tell the idea didn't fill her with joy and vowed to speak with her in private, for the happiness of his family was paramount.

'It will necessitate us being fitted for an entire new wardrobe,' Charlotte continued.

'I am sure we can ask the dressmaker to visit,' Edwin agreed, trying not to think of the cost.

'Hardly, Edwin. It will be necessary to have a whole collection of couture clothing,' Charlotte continued, barely able to suppress her exasperation. 'Ladies in the city dress à la mode and there will be all manner of balls and parties to attend. My dear sister Emmeline has offered to accommodate us for the season. It is vital Victoria be introduced to as many eligible titled gentlemen as possible in order to make a suitable marriage.'

'Good heavens, Step Mama, you can't wait to get rid of us, can you?' Bea exclaimed, jumping to her feet in dismay.

'How can you say such a thing?' Charlotte whispered, her hand going to her heart. 'I only want the best for you.'

'Yes, that was quite out of order, Bea,' Edwin remonstrated, although privately he agreed with her. He'd felt for some time that his wife favoured her two daughters and it did seem as if she was planning for the precipitate departure of his own. 'Apologise to your step mama.'

'I apologise for not thinking of the outcome my words would have,' Bea murmured and Edwin had to turn away to hide his smile. Undoubtedly, his youngest possessed a better command of the English language than his wife, for, placated, Charlotte nodded.

'Apology accepted. Although by now you should be better able to control your emotions. In fact, your outburst merely goes to show that you need further schooling.'

'Oh really? And no doubt you have something in mind?' she demanded, blue eyes deepening to navy as she stood, hands on hips, glaring at her stepmother.

'Indeed, I have. An academy for young ladies will teach you to manage that wilful temper and acquire the finesse and etiquette befitting a young lady. Then, perhaps you too can make a suitable marriage.' Seeing Bea about to explode, Edwin thought it prudent to intervene.

'Why don't we put plans of the future aside and enjoy a family evening together?' he suggested. As his daughters nodded their approval, a pang shot through him for he was suddenly aware how grown-up they had become. Soon they would be living their own lives and gatherings such as this would be a thing of the past.

'But we need to discuss ball gowns and suchlike,' Charlotte protested, her lips set in a disgruntled moue.

'Well, never having worn one myself, I don't think I'd be much authority on the subject.' Edwin grinned, endeavouring to lighten the mood. As he'd hoped, the girls giggled, making facetious remarks and outrageous suggestions.

'When you've all quite finished,' Charlotte cried, spots of anger burning her cheeks. Knowing the evening would degenerate if he didn't intervene and remembering his earlier resolve, Edwin held up his hands.

'You're right of course, my dear,' he acceded. 'Time to change for dinner, girls. I understand Mrs Cookson has prepared a special dessert.'

'You spoil them, Edwin,' his wife sighed as, with squeals of delight, they hurried from the room.

'And why not?' he smiled. 'Ah good, it's that time,' he added, as Ferris silently appeared and went over to the drinks cabinet. Like all good butlers, he was well trained and prided himself on anticipating his employer's needs.

As they sipped their pre-prandial drinks, Edwin felt a frisson of excitement as he waited for a suitable time to raise the subject uppermost in his mind.

'I really should go and change,' Charlotte stated finally, beginning to rise to her feet.

'Later, my dear, if you feel you must, for really you look quite lovely as you are,' he told her. 'As you always do, of course.'

'Oh, do you think so?' She beamed, patting her sleek hair. 'Of course, one has to persevere, keep up with the latest looks. I was talking to Lady Connaught on this very subject and she recommended a marvellous corse— er, dressmaker, a Madame Pittier in Exeter and—' Edwin leaned forward and gently placed a finger on her lips.

'I was actually thinking of something else,' he told her.

'Oh yes, the ball,' she replied, sitting back in her seat and sipping daintily at her drink. 'We really do need to make arrangements. Time passes so quickly.'

'Yes, it does,' he agreed, putting down his glass and moving closer. 'Which is why, my darling, I shall be paying you a visit later,' he murmured, giving her a meaningful look. There was a pause and he could almost hear her mind calculating what would be in it for her, before she gazed coyly up at him from under her lashes.

'Goodness, Edwin, what a surprise. It has been so long, I rather thought...' she stopped then murmured breathlessly. 'I rather thought you'd decided you no longer found me desirable.' As she stared at him wide eyed, her cheeks flushed like a ripe cherry, despite everything, Edwin felt his pulses quicken.

Chapter 2

Shielded by the damask drapes at the windows of her Quartz Rose boudoir, Charlotte followed Edwin's progress as he made his way along the path that bordered the walled kitchen garden. His breath spiralled like white plumes in the cold morning air and she wondered that he should be out so early. The roofs of the glasshouses glistened like frosting on a cake, whilst beyond stood the family chapel where his first wife had been laid to rest. The grounds of the estate that housed the workers' cottages lay further to the west, whilst the deer park spread majestically northwards. As Edwin bent to give Ellery a loving pat, she felt a stab of jealousy. That dog roamed the house and grounds as though he owned them, and he obviously came before her in Edwin's affections, she thought, her glance involuntarily going to the interconnecting doors discreetly hidden behind the oak panelling.

Charlotte sighed, recalling the previous evening. Although she had no desire whatsoever to carry another child, she knew how important it was to Edwin that he sire a son to continue the Farringdon line and inherit Nettlecombe. Goodness, he'd told her often enough, along with some gibberish about a gypsy curse. Well, if that was the price she had to pay for being lady of the manor, then so be it. Giving him a son, something his precious first wife hadn't, was appealing. Though, realistically, it was unlikely to happen for pressures of work and a lack of energy now that he was growing older meant Edwin didn't trouble her often. And when he did, it wasn't for long. Long enough to exploit him in a weak moment though, she grinned, already planning her new outfit with appropriately extravagant jewellery. After all, a betrothal necessitated being seen in the very latest mode, did it not? And if the one she chose required a string of the finest akoya pearls with their mirror-like lustre to set it off, then Edwin would have to provide.

As Edwin made his way through the gate and was lost to view, Charlotte shivered and sank onto the velvet button-back chair beside the fire, her mood becoming sombre. She'd tried so hard to be a good wife and stepmother to his daughters. When he'd brought her here as his new bride, the house had held an air of neglect, the staff lackadaisical. She'd taken them in hand and although they'd resented her interference, the household now ran efficiently. Updating the antiquated rooms had taken much thought and time, although Edwin was seemingly unaware of any change. Why, he hadn't even noticed the beautiful new clock she'd designed and had commissioned for the hallway.

Similarly, she'd taken the upbringing of her stepdaughters seriously, although it was no easy task for they showed little regard for their privileged status, ignoring her guidance and carrying on in their own way, even taunting her by saying their mama had always encouraged them to be independent. As if young women of their class had any choice in the matter! It was their duty to marry well and she intended to see that they did. All of them. Still, at least when Sarah and then Maria had arrived, they'd been besotted and couldn't do enough for their little sisters. If only they would afford her at least a modicum of respect. She sighed.

At least Louisa was obeying the rules, unwritten though they might be. Whilst the arrangements for her forthcoming marriage would fall to Charlotte, she was determined to plan a grand society affair that would make Edwin proud. First, she would set a date for the betrothal ball so that invitations could be issued. If it was held at the end of April, she would have time to settle with her sister Emmeline in London before Victoria's debut. She also needed to enrol Beatrice at a prestigious ladies' academy ready for the autumn term. Despite Charlotte trying her best, the girl seemed to take exception to everything she did, and yesterday's accusation that she was trying to get rid of them all rankled. She would be failing in her duty if she didn't ensure her stepdaughter was schooled in how to keep her emotions under control.

As Edwin's wife she had a duty to fulfil, she thought, moving purposefully to her escritoire in the corner of the room. It had been her beloved grandmother's and one of the few items she'd brought with her. Made of walnut with ornate carved legs, it smelled of beeswax which she found comforting, while the slanted front gleamed with the patina of age. Taking four new leather-bound notebooks from the bookcase above, she wrote 'Wedding' inside the first, 'Debut' in the next and 'Academy' in the third. The last she entitled

'Master Plan' in which she devised a brief outline for each occasion. Hopefully, if she involved the girls, they would show more enthusiasm. After all, what woman didn't get excited at the thought of planning a new wardrobe? she thought, taking out a sheet of paper and penning a note to Madame Rosetta Pittier requesting her to visit the following week. A French corsetière was the crème de la crème, and her pending visit would be a *bonne bouche* to drop into the colloquy at her next At Home.

The little clock on her dressing table chimed the half hour bringing her back to the present. Tugging on the bell rope to summon her maid, she couldn't help reflecting that whilst her intentions towards the girls were well meant, their responses made her feel like the wicked stepmother from a fairy tale. Still, at least her own babies, Sarah and Maria, were loving. Deciding to capitalise on the previous evening by sowing the seeds, or indeed the pearls, she asked Shears to lay out the grey silk dress Edwin loved. She would dazzle him over breakfast while memories of their passion the previous night were still uppermost in his mind.

***

However, food was the last thing on Edwin's mind, for returning from his constitutional, he met with Partridge, the gamekeeper, who told him poachers were intent on depleting the deer herd.

'Send Gill to my office,' he instructed, striding back towards the house. If it wasn't one thing it was another, he thought, recalling his meeting at the quarry the previous day. Resisting the urge to sweep the monstrosity of a clock from the hallway table as he passed, he hurried up the staircase that led to the nursery. He loved all his daughters dearly and as he popped his head around the door to see the youngest two, their excited squeals let him know they were delighted to see him.

'Papa,' Sarah cried, her face wreathed in smiles as she looked up from the picture she was painting. At six she considered herself quite proficient although coloured splashes on her pinafore told a different story.

'Puppy,' Maria squealed, using the name she'd adopted before she could manage Papa, and which despite Charlotte's best endeavours, had stuck. 'I've drawn Ellery, come and see.' Edwin stared down at the black smudge with four stick legs and a wiggly tail and grinned.

'I'm sure Ellery will be flattered. I hope they are behaving themselves, Nanny,' he enquired. The old lady who'd been his own nanny and then, in turn, his older daughters', nodded.

'They're little treasures,' she beamed. Edwin nodded, knowing she would say that however they'd been behaving. Being a Saturday, she had let them indulge their artistic talents, as she put it. 'And if it's not too cold later, we're going to see the deer, aren't we?' she said, turning to the girls who bobbed their heads enthusiastically.

'Deer, Puppy,' Maria told him seriously.

'Well, have fun and do as Nanny tells you,' he told them, the clock striking ten reminding him of his meeting with his estate manager.

Feeling brighter, he bid them farewell and retraced his

steps. However, as he passed the Carnelian Room, the sound of agitated voices stopped him in his tracks. Peering round the partially opened door, he saw his older daughters huddled together on the comfortable chesterfield but they were so engrossed in their discussion they didn't notice him.

'It's obvious Step Mama's trying to get rid of us but if she thinks I'm going to any fancy ladies' academy, she can think again,' Bea declared hotly.

'I know that look, Bea, but what are you going to do?' Louisa asked.

'You'll be busy preparing for your wedding, Lou, which is right for you. Anyone can see Henry adores you.'

'And I him,' Louisa admitted, a gentle flush tinging her cheeks as she thought of him.

'But I have no desire to have my life governed by a man. Remember Mama told us we could do anything we put our minds to? Well, I intend to train as a nurse. I shall ask Aunt Emmeline if I can come to London with you in order to make some enquiries,' she told Victoria.

'But Step Mama and Auntie will be busy accompanying me to balls, dances and heaven knows what.'

'You're right about Mama encouraging us to think for ourselves, Bea, but think about it rationally. In order to become a nurse, you'll need to finish your education. Then you'll be better equipped to live your own life and won't have to rely on a man to keep you,' Louisa told her.

'Or spend hours being primped and preened like a peacock,' Victoria added. 'What's the betting Step Mama will appear at any moment flourishing one of her lists?' As they let out a collective groan, Edwin frowned, then mindful of his meeting he continued on his way. Bea wanted to be a nurse? That was news to him and, clearly, she hadn't confided in Charlotte. He obviously needed to have that discussion with each of his daughters before they made their intentions known. Whilst he admired ambition, and had appreciated his late wife's enthusiasm for life, she had always known her duty was to him and Nettlecombe and now he needed to ensure his daughters understood too.

He'd just seated himself at his desk when there was a knock on the door and Ferris announced the arrival of Sam Gill. For the second time that morning, Edwin frowned. Why should his estate manager have sent his son?

'Show him in, Ferris.'

'Good morning, sir,' Sam Gill greeted him, removing his cap as he entered the room. At twenty-two, although he took his job as assistant estate manager seriously, he had a cheerful and jaunty manner. Today, though, his hazel eyes were clouded with worry.

'Good morning, Gill,' Edwin replied. 'Is something wrong?'

'It's Father, he slipped on the ice and Mother fears he has broken his leg.'

'That is grave news. I'll send for Dr Wicken,' Edwin replied but the young man shook his head.

'Thank you, sir, but he'd never agree to seeing a physic. Wise Woman Winnie is with him. She'll see he's all right,' he told him. Then, realising he may have spoken out of turn, he flushed and hurried on. 'Though Father will have to rest until his leg's mended. Of course, I'll carry out his duties until he's fit again. I believe there's been a spot of poaching up at the deer park.'

Edwin raised a brow then wondered why he was surprised. News spread faster than fire around here.

'Indeed, it's a sorry business and one that could cost the estate dearly. I want you to liaise with Partridge, set up a night watch. You'd better let the authorities know. That will be all for now. Give my regards to your father and wish him a speedy recovery. And if things don't improve, let me know. Sometimes medical intervention can be best.'

'Thank you, sir.' Although he replied cordially, his gaze was sceptical.

As the door closed behind him, Edwin lay back in his seat and closed his eyes, memories of Beatrice's terrible accident surfacing. Again, he relived her final days when nothing the doctor prescribed seemed to work. Out of his mind with worry, when Winnie the wise woman of the village had called to offer her services, he'd sent her packing.

'You'll regret it,' she'd warned, her beady eyes burning into him. 'That fever needs the healing of herbs not them draughts the physics prescribe. Her's in such a bad way it wouldn't do no harm to try now, would it?' she'd coaxed.

To his shame, he hadn't listened; instead he'd heard the cackle of another crone from years gone by. Edwin had been only a lad when his father, having discovered stock missing, called for the dogs to be set on gypsies camped on his land. The old woman had vehemently protested their innocence but he'd refused to listen. Pointing her finger at him, she'd decreed the Farringdon dynasty was doomed. The family would never sire another male. Unable to contain his rage, Edwin's father had fired his gun.

'Fool – yer've just sealed yer family's fate,' she'd screeched. 'From here on all yer wives will die young.'

Edwin opened his eyes yet didn't see the comfortable furnishings around him, only the dreadful images of the past. Again, he asked himself the questions that haunted him. Had what he'd witnessed as a boy prejudiced his decision to let local wise woman Winnie help? Could she have saved his beloved Beatrice from an early death? And if his father hadn't driven those travellers from his land would he, Edwin, have sired a son by now? Even realising that the old gypsy crone would long have gone to meet her maker gave him no comfort.

***

Having endured a solitary meal where she'd merely trifled with the grilled kidneys and scramble of eggs, Charlotte pushed her plate aside. After last night, the least Edwin could have done was take breakfast with her, she fumed, as gathering up her books she went in search of her stepdaughters.

'Good morning,' she greeted them, trying not to react to the change in atmosphere or the exchanged looks, as in a rustle of skirts she settled herself on the leather buttoned chair alongside them.

'Good morning, Step Mama,' they dutifully intoned before lapsing into silence.

'As we have so many exciting things to plan, I have begun

preparing one of these for you,' she said, handing them each a book.

'I told you,' Bea muttered, eyeing hers disdainfully. 'More ludicrous lists. Well, I need to put Firecracker through his paces,' she said, jumping to her feet.

'You can exercise that horse of yours later, though to my mind you spend far too much time in the stables as it is,' Charlotte told her firmly. 'We have much to discuss and all your ideas are important. Now,' she said, opening her own book, 'here is the master plan. Firstly, the date of your betrothal ball, Louisa. The last Saturday of April would be perfect, would it not?'

'Yes, Step Mama,' Louisa replied. 'Although, I was wondering if perhaps we might have a small party rather than a ball.'

'Impossible,' Charlotte retorted. 'Think of your papa and his standing in the community.'

'So much for our opinions being important then,' Bea snorted.

'You really must learn to control that tongue of yours, Beatrice,' Charlotte remonstrated. 'Now, as I told your papa, we shall require completely new wardrobes. As it is the underpinning that defines how any gown, however well made, will look, I have sent a letter to the finest corsetière in Devonshire – if not the entire country – requesting she call upon us. She is also renowned for her exquisite dressmaking and can advise on those.' Charlotte looked at them expectantly but instead of delighted smiles, she was met with frowns. 'Don't worry about the cost,' she continued, misunderstanding their concern. 'Your papa will want the best for us.'

'We know that, Step Mama,' Victoria replied. 'However, we usually call upon the services of our local seamstresses.'

'I hardly think locally sewn garments would be appropriate for our prestigious celebrations,' Charlotte told them.

'I'm afraid I disagree, Step Mama,' Louisa murmured. 'Ida Somers and her team have always served us well.'

'Their simple stitching might have sufficed in the past, but not this time,' Charlotte told her brusquely.

'But the villagers rely upon us for their custom and Lily's lacemaking is second to none. Why, she made—'

'Enough.' Charlotte snapped her book shut. 'I said that only the best will do and having been reliably informed that Madame Pittier is the best, my decision stands.'

'And you said our ideas were of value yet you don't even listen to us,' Bea retorted.

'I shall not even dignify that statement with an answer. All I will say is that you girls would do well to elevate your expectations if you wish to succeed in life,' Charlotte told them. Darting them a look of disappointment, she gathered up their unopened books and sailed from the room.

Chapter 3

Jane Haydon placed the silver bowl of bright pink flowers in the centre of the low table then sprayed them lightly with eau de rose. It was Madame Rosetta's signature cologne and the uplifting fragrance subtly wafted throughout every room in the establishment, including the *magasin de corset* at the front of the building where her exquisite merchandise was displayed. In the summer months, when fresh roses were available, she insisted every petal be dried then scattered between the folds of her clients' beautifully beribboned purchases throughout the year.

'Seems stupid to me,' Millie, maid of all, muttered, bending to prod the fire with the poker. As orange flames flared and began warming the cool early morning air, she placed the guard firmly in place. 'I mean, why go to all that bother when everyone knows you don't get roses in January?'

'Madame says it's all about perception, that when our patrons inhale the delicate damask rose, they'll instantly be transported back to Madame Rosetta's. You must admit they do brighten the room and, of course, they are made of the finest silk,' Jane replied.

'What else,' Millie murmured. As the girl bent to retrieve the coal scuttle, Jane noticed she wasn't wearing her corset and knew she'd be in for another telling-off. Madame had exacting standards, and being firmly underpinned was de rigueur. However, at thirteen Millie thought she knew better and would only scoff if Jane, six years her senior, passed comment, so she turned her attention to the preparations for the day ahead.

Being Monday morning, as Madame's apprentice of three years it was Jane's responsibility to ensure everything was ready for the working week before the woman herself appeared. She plumped up the cushions on the two damask chaises longues, checked the cream Persian rug was free from any stray threads, then placed a fresh robe of the finest blush silk on the chair beside the screen in the corner of the room. Not for Madame's clients the indignity of suffering a cold changing room. Her ladies were to be cossetted, benefitting from the warmth of the fire on their skin as they shed their outer garments. Of course, being a shrewd businesswoman, Madame also benefitted, for she knew satisfaction led to repeat custom and recommendation.

'*Bonjour, mesdemoiselles*,' Madame Rosetta trilled, sweeping into the room and glancing around, her sharp eyes missing nothing. Although she wasn't really French, Madame liked to give her clients the impression that she was Parisian, saying it gave her business a certain *je ne sais quoi*. With a little nod of satisfaction, she focused her attention on Jane. Although her look was fleeting, Jane knew it had taken in every detail from the dark hair neatly pinned on top of her head, the crisp white blouse with silk rosebud at her throat, to the long tailored blue skirt and shined black buttoned boots. Then, she turned towards the maid and her expression changed to one of dismay.

'Is there a reason your body is flapping like a helpless bird under your uniform, Millicent?' she asked, her accent slipping.

'Oh, Madame, you're so funny. You know I ain't got no body to speak of. I is straight up and down like the legs on a ragman's cart,' she trilled.

'I do not happen to think that is funny. Haven't I taught you the function of the corset is to refine your non-existent figure, thus giving it definition? You need to support your bust and back in order to move gracefully.'

'But it digs into me bones when I bends to light the fires,' Millie protested.

'That is a small price to pay for having the posture of a lady; an essential requirement if you are to continue in my employ. Of course, if you feel that is too much of an imposition, you are free to return to the poorhouse.' She paused to let her words sink in. As Millie's eyes widened in horror, Jane's heart went out to the girl who'd been dumped by her father when, having moved from London for work, he'd found himself a new wife. Jane knew all about being abandoned, for hadn't her mother, unable to cope with the responsibilities of being a live-in maid with a young child, fled into the night leaving her behind? If Madame hadn't taken pity on her Jane may also have found herself in the poorhouse.

'Of course, if my corset-making does not meet with your requirements, you are quite at liberty to visit a staymaker or even purchase one of those mass-produced, machine-made efforts,' Madame's strident tones continued, breaking into Jane's thoughts. 'At your own expense, of course.'

'No, Madame. Yous corsets is the best. I'll go and put mine on straight away,' Millie said quickly.

'And whilst doing so, I should reflect upon those extra slices of cake you take from the larder or you'll soon find yourself shaped like those,' Madame told her, gesturing to the squat, curved legs of a Regency chair. As Millie swallowed hard, Jane spotted the twinkle in her employer's eye and knew she was enjoying letting the maid know she knew exactly what went on in her establishment.

'Now, the market is open today, is it not?' Madame continued, resuming her professional demeanour.

'Yes, Madame, and I'll go and gets that special cheese you like,' Millie replied, anxious to please. 'Though I hopes them poor people aren't out to make trouble likes they was last week.'

'Unfortunately, there is dissent in the city. The underclass is rebelling against the continuing increase in the price of food, especially the staple of bread.' Madame sighed. 'It is a difficult time and hungry people who can't feed their families are to be pitied. However, should there be any hint of trouble you are to return immediately. Do you understand?'

'Yes, Madame.'

'Now go and prepare my breakfast tray and bring it through to my room. I suggest you then pack up the rest of the cake and take it to the good folk at St Catherine's. I'm sure they need it more than you.'

'Thank you, Madame,' Millie replied, bobbing a curtsy as she left the room. Jane smiled inwardly, for underneath their employer's stern manner lay a heart of gold. She might command a hefty fee from rich clients for her services but she always gave what she could to the poor of the city.

'I take it you have broken your fast this morning?' the woman asked Jane. As ever she was dressed immaculately, her silver hair caught back in a chignon into which she had entwined a damask rosebud that perfectly matched the one beneath the lace collar. She insisted they wear white blouses so that no coloured threads could fall and mark the delicate fabrics they worked on. It was also the perfect foil for accentuating the rich colours of her merchandise.

'Yes, thank you, Madame.'

'In that case, once you have ensured the *magasin* is presentable for clients to enter, please lay out the records diary for me to inspect.'

'Of course, Madame.'

Jane smiled as she made her way into the treasure trove of pink, as she thought of it. When she'd asked why everything was this colour Madame had explained pink was the colour of sweetness and femininity, romance and innocence. Although, of course, corsets and camisoles could always be made up in the colours of the clients' choice.

Madame prided herself on her tasteful displays. Not for her the obvious showing of undergarments like some establishments. Fringed parasols, silk gloves, ornamental hairpins and ribbons were stylishly arranged in the front of the window. Reticules, their colourful beads twinkling in the light, were neatly lined up behind, while to either side stood the mannequins draped in pink silk, the merest hint of lace peeking beneath. Madame was nothing if not imaginative in her use of undergarments, choosing to flout convention with chemises placed over rather than under the corsets. Perhaps she would start a new mode, Jane mused as she unlocked the door.

Outside, the pavement in front of the three-storey building sparkled white with frost and even at this early hour, everyone was hurrying about their business. Jane shivered and quickly began taking down the steel-banded wooden shutters.

The emporium fronted a side street just off Exeter's Cathedral Yard, discreet enough for ladies to arrive in their carriages yet close enough to the city centre for the ordinary woman to pause and peer longingly through the little panes in the bay windows.

'Good morning, Miss Haydon. It's certainly a cold one,' a man's voice called. She looked up to see the assistant manager of the bank, briefcase in hand, raising his top hat in greeting.

'Good morning, Mr Jones,' she acknowledged, her cheeks colouring under his admiring gaze. To hide her confusion, she glanced at the sign above the doorway proclaiming 'Madame Rosetta, Corsetière'. Beneath its flowing script peeked the outline of a corset in blush pink and Jane couldn't help imagining herself as proprietor, the sign displaying her name. Except Jane Haydon didn't sound at all exotic, did it? Even Millie's name had been elevated to Millicent, she thought, letting out a sigh as she hurried back inside.

'Dreaming of the future, were you?' Madame's strident

tones made her jump guiltily. How Jane wished the woman wouldn't creep up on her like that.

'Oh no. I mean…' her voice trailed off as she felt her cheeks going hot.

'Why, Jane, you're quite the colour of my roses, though whether it's from my appearance or that of Mr Jones, I couldn't say,' Madame laughed, then her expression became serious. 'There is nothing wrong with having a dream, you know. You just need to focus on your goal then work hard to make it happen.' Jane stared at her incredulously. There was as much chance of that happening as Millie becoming a lady. 'You might not achieve everything you aspire to, but you'd be surprised where ambition and determination can lead. Now come along, bring *la rose journal* through to the Receiving Room, I have something to discuss with you.'

Snatching up the pink diary, Jane followed the woman back into the room where the fire was now burning brightly. She couldn't think of anything she'd forgotten but Madame was such a perfectionist.

'Have I done something wrong?' she burst out as soon as the woman had taken her seat, crossing her legs neatly at the ankle. Not being born a lady didn't mean you couldn't act like one, was another of her sayings.

'No, Jane. Quite the reverse, in fact. I have been impressed by your diligence these past months. Your stitching is greatly improved and you have a natural empathy with our clients. Even Lady Margarita has passed comment on your courteous manner, and, as you know, she is not easily pleased.' Jane stared at her employer in surprise for that particular client always sailed past with her nose held so high, she could surely only see the ceiling.

'Thank you,' she replied, realising Madame was waiting for a reply.

'It would seem, Jane, that my reputation has gone before me. My services are now in such demand, I can't possibly see to everyone myself. From today, you will move to the final stage of your training, receive any new clients and ascertain their requirements. If they are the crème de la crème, note down their details in here,' she ordered, tapping the pink diary on her lap. 'You can then refer them to me. The rest will be attended by yourself. Of course, should you have any questions, then you must direct them to me,' she added quickly as Jane opened her mouth to speak.

'But how will I know who should be referred to you?' Jane asked, fearful of making a mistake.

'Use your *savoir faire*, Jane,' Madame replied, tapping her head with her silver pencil. 'In order to find out what clients need we ask questions, do we not?'

'Yes, but—'

'You simply ascertain the fabric of their drawers. If, for example, it is chamois, they will be only too pleased to boast, for those are ladies of class. Tell them you will be pleased to make an appointment with Madame Rosetta who, as they must appreciate, is so much in demand there will be a wait, and then you check the diary for my availability.'

'But what about the ladies who don't wear such under-clothing?' Jane frowned. It was a delicate subject, after all.

'This is where you need to become more attuned with

human nature, Jane. These ladies will always confess they aspire to wearing it,' Madame laughed.

'You make it sound so easy,' Jane said.

'Believe you me it is. Just make sure you are polite and respectful at all times, which we both know is not always easy.' She leaned forward, her clear eyes boring into Jane. 'I hope you appreciate the wonderful opportunity I am presenting you. We will trial the new arrangement for one month and see how you get on. Succeed and I will promote you from apprentice to second corsetière with a substantial increase to your wage. Now go and finish Mademoiselle Lillian's corset. Her final fitting is for eleven o'clock, I believe.'

'It is, Madame,' Jane agreed.

'I will take care of things down here so that you are not interrupted. It would never do to keep a client waiting. *Allez-vous en*,' she ordered, tossing her head as she snapped into Parisian mode and waved Jane away.

'Yes, Madame. Thank you,' Jane said, her head buzzing as she made her way upstairs.

Shivering, she entered the workroom, but whether it was from the cold – for fern patterns of frost still rimed the windows – or excitement at the opportunity Madame had presented her, she wasn't sure. Mademoiselle Jane Haydon, Second Corsetière! She smiled, settling herself at the long table where scissors, stiletto, black lead pencils, erasers and pin cushions were set out in the order Madame decreed.

Shaking her head to clear it, she uncovered the corset she'd been working on the previous day. Having already marked out the positions, she took up the stiletto and carefully made a hole in the fabric for the first eyelet to be inserted. Lost in concentration, for one careless slip could result in the whole corset being ruined, it was some moments before she realised the maid had appeared beside her, tears coursing down her cheeks.

'Millie, whatever's the matter?' she cried in alarm.

'I only gone and bust the corset Madame made me. She's goin' to kill me,' she sobbed, holding up the offending garment.

'How on earth...' Jane began, frowning from the frayed fabric around the eyelets to the metal discs in her other hand.

'I was in such a hurry they shot off all over me room,' she wailed.

'You did unlace the corset before you took it off last night, didn't you?' Jane asked, but the flush suffusing the girl's face told its own story.

'Oh, Millie,' she groaned.

'It takes so long. I got this way of loosening the laces to a certain stage then wriggling me body out. When I wriggles back in again it usually works, but I was in a hurry and the corset seemed to have shrunk...' her voice tailed off. Jane stared down at the girl's figure which did appear to have filled out a little. It seemed Madame's prediction was already coming true.

'What am I going to do? I daren't go downstairs without wearing it but Madame will go mad if she sees me corset all torn. After this morning, she'll tell me to go and I don't want to go back to the poorhouse,' Millie wailed.

Jane sighed. The garment could be mended but it would take time. And that was what she didn't have if she was to finish Miss Lillian's corset before she arrived for her fitting.

'Please help me, Jane,' Millie begged. 'You're the only friend I got.'

Jane looked into the little maid's hazel eyes, her heart going out to her.

'Give it here,' she said, sending up a prayer that Madame wouldn't decide to make an impromptu inspection of the workshop. 'Here, put this on,' Jane said, snatching up a dressing robe and thrusting it at the trembling Millie.

'I'm sorry,' the little maid sobbed, quickly wrapping it around her. 'Can I help?'

'Yes, thread a needle with some of that,' Jane told her, gesturing to one of the spools on the work table before turning back to assess the damage. 'Honestly, Millie, you've made a right mess of this corset,' she sighed, glancing worriedly at the clock. 'And Mademoiselle Lillian will be here for her fitting in a couple of hours.'

'Couldn't you just do one of them running repairs to see me through?'

'That would take nearly as long and probably wouldn't hold,' Jane replied, taking the proffered needle and beginning to stitch. Although the cotton twill was harder wearing than the silk taffeta she'd been working on, it was impossible to reinsert the eyelets without hemming the fraying material and making the bodice smaller. It would need reinforcing with another strip of the twill but there was no time to do that now, and with Millie hovering nervously at her side, Jane found herself becoming increasingly exasperated. 'Stand by the door and listen out for Madame,' she told her.

Finally, after a frustrating forty minutes or so, the garment was in a fit state to be worn and Jane handed it to the grateful maid.

'Oh Jane, yous saved me life,' Millie cried.

'You'd better go and dress or Madame will wonder where you are. And for heaven's sake be careful – that corset needs strengthening but we'll have to see to that later,' Jane warned her. 'I know you think Madame's strict, but she has a soft heart really or she wouldn't have made you a corset; one which you have to admit is much finer than anything you could afford on your wages.'

'I knows. I was thinking about that when I was putting the wretched thing on and then…' Millie shrugged.

'Just take better care of it in future, eh?' Jane told her, remembering how many hours it had taken her to make the garment under Madame's critical gaze. Still, it had served as part of her apprenticeship, she thought as the maid scuttled away.

Chapter 4

Reminded of what she should have been doing, Jane picked up the taffeta silk and with another anxious glance at the clock, resumed her work. It was going to be a close-run thing, for the finishing-off stitching was the most exacting of all and any tiny mistake would be glaringly obvious. Finally, she snatched up the lace and began criss-crossing it through the eyelets, smoothing and checking that the boning was lying flat.

As the clock began striking eleven, Jane fled down the stairs, only to bump into Madame who was pacing the hall-way impatiently.

'*Enfin*, Mademoiselle Haydon,' she tutted, her strident tones showing disapproval as she seized the corset. Jane held her breath as the woman held the garment up to the light and inspected every detail.

'Hmm, despite your tardiness, everything appears to be in order,' she finally admitted. 'As ever, Mademoiselle Lillian was punctual to the minute and as I have already shown her through to the dressing room, I will deal with her final fitting myself. Continue with your work then present yourself to me at two o'clock sharp,' she instructed, disappearing in a rustle of skirts.

As the clock began chiming the hour, Jane took a deep breath and knocked on the door of Madame's office which was situated beside the Receiving Room. For once, though, the delicate fragrance of rose failed to calm her nerves. Not having a client's order ready for her arrival was a mortal sin in Madame's eyes and fearful she was about to lose the opportunity she'd only just been granted, Jane hovered nervously as she waited for the woman to respond.

'*Viens.*' Madame's stentorian tones made Jane's stomach turn over making her wish she hadn't eaten her luncheon so quickly. Her employer was reading a letter and didn't look up as she entered. After what was only a couple of minutes but to Jane seemed like ages, the woman carefully folded the notepaper and placed it on the table.

'This is proving to be an eventful day,' she announced, staring at Jane. 'Right, young lady, perhaps you could explain why Mademoiselle Lillian's corset was not in the room prior to her arrival. Having done the measuring yourself, it should have been a straightforward job, so did you encounter any problem?' Scrutinised by those clear blue eyes, Jane stared at the floor and shook her head.

'Yet you know how important it is to have a client's order ready for her to try on?'

'Yes, Madame.'

'I would remind you a client has to be entirely satisfied before she pays her bill and, hopefully, return. Our establishment relies upon its reputation for providing excellent service.

In short, Mademoiselle Haydon, it is the clients that keep us in business, not friends.'

Jane looked up to find the woman giving her a meaningful look. Clearly, she knew exactly why Jane had been delayed.

'Your loyalty is commendable so we'll say no more about it. Although I might be having a word with a certain young maid about taking better care of her clothing. In future, please accede to my golden rule that all garments be ready prior to a client's arrival. Now, have you finished sewing that chemise Madame Seymour ordered to complement her corset?'

'Yes, Madame,' Jane replied, relieved to be back on safe ground.

'*Bon*, Millie can deliver it when she deigns to return.' She turned to the little ormolu clock on the mantel and frowned. 'Even allowing for her late departure, she shouldn't be taking this long. Never mind, I have received some wonderful news. Take a seat, I need to discuss the detail with you.'

Weak with relief that she hadn't lost her job after all, Jane almost sank into the chintz chair but for once Madame was too preoccupied to notice.

'I have received an exciting invitation from Lady Farringdon of Nettlecombe Manor in the east of our county. Lady Connaught herself has recommended my services,' she beamed, patting her immaculate hair. 'Lady Farringdon is to celebrate the forthcoming betrothal of her daughter by holding a ball for the local gentry and she has invited me,' Madame exclaimed, clapping her hands in excitement. Jane stared at the woman in surprise. She knew Madame prided herself on acting like a lady but surely, even she wasn't classed as nobility?

'Did you hear me, Jane?' Madame's impatient voice snapped her back to the present. 'I was saying that I need you to assume responsibility here during my absence.'

'But where are you going?' Jane asked.

'Really, Jane, I do wish you would pay attention,' Madame tutted. 'Having been invited to make the underpinning garments for Lady Farringdon and her daughters is an honour, and who knows, might even lead to further commissions for the nuptials themselves. Naturally, it will take time to ascertain her ladyship's actual requirements, take measurements and run up toiles of the corset patterns to ensure a good fit, before returning here to make the actual garments. With your help, of course,' she conceded graciously.

'I see. That's wonderful, Madame,' Jane added quickly, seeing more enthusiasm was expected. 'When will you be leaving?'

'Next week. I am to catch the Tuesday morning stagecoach and will be away for two, maybe three nights.'

'So long, Madame?' Jane frowned.

'As long as it takes to fulfil her ladyship's requirements.'

'You mean you will be staying at the manor? How exciting,' Jane cried.

'Hmm,' Madame replied, turning quickly away and snatching up her diary. 'You are more than capable of assisting the clients scheduled for those dates and… what on earth?' She stopped as Millie burst into the room. Her bonnet was askew, cheeks red as apples and she was breathing heavily from her exertions.

'Madame, it's worse than last week,' she gasped.

'Steady yourself, Millicent,' the woman replied. 'Jane will get you some water.'

'No time,' Millie muttered. 'Theys coming.'

'Whom is coming?' Madame asked.

'Them crowds. A whole army of them. Theys smashing shop windows then stealing things, bread and food mainly. Theys heading this way. We needs to get the shutters up afore they get here.'

'Oh,' Madame cried, her hand flying to her mouth. But Jane was already running outside, gasping as the bitter easterly wind hit her full in the face. Millie and Madame were right behind her and with the sound of breaking glass, screaming and shouting growing ever louder they hurriedly began lifting the heavy steel-banded wooden shutters. Even when the heavens opened, splattering them with large drops of freezing rain, they didn't dare stop for the nearing crowds were growing angrier and more demanding. They'd just slotted the last one in place when the rioters rounded the corner, bearing down on them at an alarming rate. They were throwing stones and shouting obscenities, their furious faces making them shudder.

'Quick, inside,' Madame ordered before slamming the door and drawing the heavy bolts behind them. Hardly daring to breathe, they cowered in the unnatural darkness as the rioting continued. The sound of breaking glass right outside followed by a sudden banging on the shutters and a violent rattling of the door made them jump with fright. They clung together, terrified the door would give way and they would be at the mercy of the frenzied protesters. But then, by some miracle, they were moving on again, targeting other properties as they marched determinedly on their way. When the din had receded, they stared at each other, letting out sighs of relief.

'I said theys were mad,' Millie muttered, shaking her head.

'Hungry, I think, Millicent,' Madame corrected, staring around her beloved emporium that was miraculously unscathed. 'Although that doesn't excuse their actions, I suspect there can be nothing worse than an empty stomach.'

'I knows that,' Millie replied, nodding solemnly.

'Apart from wet clothes,' Madame added, staring ruefully at the mud and filth spattering her skirts. 'Thank heavens you got home before they reached here.'

'You said home, Madame,' Millie cried happily.

'So I did,' Madame replied, smiling weakly before resuming her brisk self. 'Right, I think we should have a nice cup of tea whilst we dry off and recover from that fright. After all, home is where the tea is, is it not?' Jane smiled; according to Madame, tea was the panacea for all things disagreeable.

'Yes, Madame.' Millie nodded exuberantly.

'And perhaps we could treat ourselves to a slice of that cake I saw on the table in the kitchen.'

'Oh lor, in all that fuss, I forgot to take it to St Catherine's,' Millie gasped, her hand flying to her mouth.

'But I thought the fuss you referred to happened whilst you were out,' Madame replied, her blue eyes twinkling.

'Oh heck. I'll go and make that drink,' the girl muttered, scuttling off to the kitchen.

'Right, Jane, I take it we have no more clients scheduled for this afternoon?'

'No, Madame, although I've sewing to finish for tomorrow.'

'That can wait for now. I'm sure the rioters won't be coming back this way but I'd like us to stay together until we are sure. After that fright and soaking we need to warm up so let's go through to the Receiving Room where the fire's ablaze. Millie can join us when she brings the tray with our refreshment.' Apart from Sundays, her employer never kept her *magasin* closed during the day and Jane stared at her in surprise, but seeing the woman's pallor she just nodded.

What a day, thought Jane as she lay in her little bed under the eaves listening to the noises of the night-time city. It was probably the tiniest room in Madame's establishment, but it was hers. A place to think and dream of the time she would have her own little shop. She pulled the patchwork cover she'd made as one of her apprenticeship pieces tightly round her. Although the rioters hadn't returned, she still felt on edge and the moonlight filtering through the skylight afforded a measure of comfort. Millie had offered to venture out to see what was happening but Madame had forbidden it, suggesting instead they all have an early night ready to begin work at daybreak. Recalling the maid's frightened face when she'd ripped her corset, Jane determined to reinforce the garment before it became ruined beyond repair. She'd have to be discreet because Madame's eagle eyes missed nothing. Still, she was a fair but firm employer and Jane knew the opportunity she'd been given to progress from apprentice to second corsetière would stand her in good stead for the future.

Then, of course, there was the invitation from Lady Farringdon. Jane sat bolt upright in bed. In all the turmoil of the day she'd quite forgotten that Madame had said that she would be in charge whilst the woman was away. Could she really cope in her absence? She began running through the rules of the workroom, the principles of meeting the client, ascertaining her requirements, measuring, fitting and making, but by the time she got to managing the *magasin* her eyelids were too heavy to stay open.

***

'*Mon Dieu*,' Madame exclaimed when Jane entered the Receiving Room the next morning.

'Good morning, Madame,' Jane replied, surprised to see her employer was up, let alone reading the newspaper. She herself had already been sewing for the past two hours and, with her eyes needing a rest she'd intended preparing the *magasin* for the morning's clients.

'They've called that disturbance yesterday the Bread Riots,' Madame read. 'It was even more serious than I feared. The rioters rampaged all around the city, causing untold damage to shops and properties, plundering not only bread but bacon and other foodstuffs. They stole takings from money drawers, broke up furniture to use as weapons for smashing glass, pulled down shutters... Oh my, we've been so lucky.'

'I hope they don't come back again.' Jane shuddered.

'I think that's unlikely,' Madame replied. 'It says here that the mayor called in the military to disperse the crowds and the magistrates of Exeter give notice they shall use vigorous measures to preserve the public peace and punish all who breach the same.' She put down the paper and frowned. 'I can't believe how much bread was stolen. Those poor people must really be starving to go to such lengths. Ah, that reminds me: I am expecting a delivery of fabric this morning, so please ensure there is room for the bales, Jane.'

'Of course,' she replied, shaking her head at the abrupt change of subject. Surely Madame wasn't merely dismissing such a serious issue? But she should have known better.

'Tell Millie she can take the rest of the bread we have to the poor. It's not much but if everyone gave a little, it would surely help.'

'That's very true, Madame,' Jane agreed.

'But she's to bring some fresh back from the bakery with her for we cannot work on empty stomachs. Now, I need to *écrire une réponse* to Lady Farringdon and then we must begin your instruction.'

'My instruction?' Jane frowned.

'Why yes, Jane. If I am to entrust my emporium into your care whilst I'm away, I need to ensure you are completely conversant with all those principles of pleasing clients I've taught you. For one hour each day, I shall be a new client and you will be the corsetière taking me through the experience from arrival to final fitting. After you have broken your fast, we will begin. Oh, and Jane?'

'Yes, Madame?' Jane replied.

'I do not expect to be disappointed at any stage of the modus operandi.'

'No, Madame,' she squeaked, her heart thumping loudly in her chest.

Chapter 5

'Goodness!' Edwin exclaimed, frowning at the article he'd been reading in the *Exeter Flying Post*.

'Is something wrong, dear?' Charlotte asked, smiling at him in what she hoped was a mollifying manner. It had been five days since he'd visited her room but relations between them were still somewhat strained.

'It says here that another disturbance took place in Exeter on Monday afternoon. Apparently, the underclass, women and children included, went on the rampage around the city, smashing windows, looting foodstuff and causing no end of damage.'

'That's appalling, I hope they've locked them all in gaol. The poor should learn to conduct themselves with decorum,' Charlotte tutted.

'I don't think you understand,' Edwin said, staring at her over the top of his reading glasses. 'They're deeming them the Bread Riots because many of them have to subsist on one piece each along with a mug of tea, water or small beer per day. With food prices continually rising these people are desperate.'

'Then why don't they earn more money or eat something else? Wait a moment, did you say Exeter?'

'I did. A bit close to home, isn't it? I wonder what we can do to help. I'll speak to young Gill.'

'But that is where Madame Pittier has her premises,' Charlotte cried. 'I trust this won't affect her visit next week. We have little enough time for our fittings as it is.'

Edwin fought down his irritation. Surely a little compassion wouldn't go amiss? However, knowing better than to comment, he turned back to his papers, another article about the escalating war catching his attention. Things were not looking good and if he wasn't mistaken, Charlotte would soon have something more than balls and outfits to worry about. Should he mention anything to Louisa? He was pondering on this when the footman appeared bearing two letters on a silver tray.

'Thank you, Quick,' he said, checking the envelopes and passing one to Charlotte.

'Ah, the sublime fragrance of rose,' she said, holding it to her nose. 'Would that more people perfumed their notepaper.' Slitting it open with the filigree knife, she hastily scanned the contents.

Meanwhile, Edwin turned his attention to his own letter confirming the details of his meeting with his bank manager and advisors. In order to have time to prepare, he would have to leave the next day. He needed to check the exact state of his finances, for money should never idle in a bank account when it could be invested to make more. In order to put forward a strong case to the bank, he would need to present them with details of all the quarry orders and shipments Tom Wakeley had presented him with. They would also want to see a list of overheads and expenditure so he would also need to visit his accountants. There was a lot to do, but it was vital he present his proposal in the best light, for appearance, or at least perception, was everything in the world of business.

'Oh, thank heavens,' Charlotte exclaimed, propelling him back to the present. 'All is well and Madame Pittier will be arriving on Tuesday as planned.'

'I shall be in London,' Edwin told her.

'Why is that?' she asked, looking at him sharply.

'A financial matter regarding the quarry needs my urgent attention.'

'For heaven's sake, can't you tell someone else to go?' she asked, placing her letter on the table.

'Regrettably no,' he replied.

'Well, I doubt you will be needed here anyway,' she replied. 'By your own admission, you are not an authority on the subject of women's dress.'

'True,' he nodded, remembering his daughters' teasing, then, considering the matter at an end, he returned to his paper.

'Goodness, there is so much to plan for. I shall have to see for myself just how competent this Madame Pittier is before commissioning her to make any other garments. It's a shame I can't come to London with you,' she told him. Edwin looked up sharply.

'Sorry, what did you say?'

'Really, Edwin, I do wish you would pay attention,' she sighed. 'I said it's a shame I can't come with you. It's so deathly quiet around here. How lovely it would be to take in a gallery, visit a couture atelier, browse Harrods and Fortnum's.'

'But you can't?' he checked, fearful his vision of peace and quiet at his house in Grosvenor Square was about to be shattered. The idea of not having to dress for dinner as he enjoyed Mrs Crawford's simple yet delectable cooking beside the fire in his library – still comfortingly known as the library – was appealing after the strain of the past few days.

'Alas, it is out of the question this time,' she replied, shooting him a rueful look. He breathed a sigh of relief, then duly tried to look interested as his wife explained in some length about their attire. 'It gives such a pleasing effect if all the costumes work harmoniously together. I really should begin making a list of requirements.' Pulling her notebook towards her, she began devising what, to Edwin, looked like an alarmingly long one.

'May I ask that you exercise a degree of restraint in your expenditure, at least until I return from the City,' he cautioned, taking out his pocket watch and checking the time. Charlotte stopped and quirked her brow.

'Really, Edwin, the upper echelons will be attending Louisa's betrothal ball and all you can think of is the expenditure,' she exclaimed, her lips forming a moue of disdain. 'We are hosting an event that will be the talk of society for the whole of the season. In fact, I was thinking we should have the Crystal Ballroom redecorated.'

'The Crystal Ballroom? Oh, you mean the Great Hall,' he replied, realisation dawning.

'We could commission some splendid new crystal chandeliers—'

'There is nothing wrong with the chandeliers we have already,' he told her.

'Well, this room definitely needs attention,' she declared, tapping the table for emphasis.

'But you've only recently got it to your liking,' he frowned, staring around the bright green furnishings, which in truth he found far less relaxing than the previous dusky blue.

'I suppose the Emerald Room does have a certain ring to it,' she conceded. 'However, it will still need a bit of sprucing up before we can receive our eminent guests. Although they will be entertained in the major rooms, we must ensure Nettlecombe makes a statement. In fact, we all will, so whilst you are in London, you can pay a visit to your tailor to be measured for a new suit.'

'There is nothing wrong with the one I had made last year,' Edwin protested.

'It was fine for last year but the style is completely wrong for now. Appearance and perception are everything, Edwin, you should know that.'

As she'd echoed his earlier thoughts, Edwin didn't feel he could do anything other than agree.

'How long will you be away?' she asked.

'Two weeks, maybe three,' he replied, knowing he would get little tranquillity or comfort here.

'So long?' she cried, but the relief in her eyes belied her voice.

***

'Poor Papa,' Bea cried, bursting through the door of the Carnelian Room where her sisters were sitting together, their heads bowed.

'Good heavens, you startled me,' Victoria exclaimed, quickly hiding her coveted copy of *Godey's Lady's Magazine* under the cushion.

'Yes, Bea, I do wish you wouldn't charge in like that,' Louisa cried, jumping guiltily. Charlotte had decreed that Thursday mornings be dedicated to practising French conversation. However, the latest fashion plates had proved too tempting and they'd been garnering ideas for their ball gowns.

'Sorry,' Bea muttered. 'But as I was returning from exercising Firecracker, I heard Step Mama telling Papa that not only are we to have entire new wardrobes, she intends having the place redecorated.'

'Not again,' Louisa sighed. 'Honestly, I'm beginning to wish Henry hadn't asked Papa if we could be married. All we want is a small party to celebrate our engagement with family and friends. Not a betrothal ball inviting people we've never met before.'

'Perhaps you could elope,' Bea suggested, blue eyes sparkling wickedly.

'Don't tempt me,' Louisa chuckled.

'That would be so exciting,' Victoria exclaimed, clapping her hands.

'It would, but I know Henry will insist things are done properly. Still, I'll have a word with him at the weekend,' she promised.

'You're so lucky to be getting away,' Bea sighed. 'I don't know what's worse. The icy atmosphere when they're not communicating or the sound of Step Mama's wheedling voice when she's trying to get round Papa. Is it any wonder I have no desire to tie myself to another person? Give me a horse beneath my body anytime.'

'Bea, really. And don't let Step Mama hear you say that. You know it is her ambition to find us all suitable husbands. Besides, you wait until you meet the right man,' Louisa smiled.

'Life was much nicer when Mama was alive,' Victoria murmured. 'She wouldn't be trying to marry us all off at the drop of a hat. Anyway, what is Lady Beauchamp like?'

'She's a darling, actually, and easy to get on with. Whilst she's a stickler for protocol, I've never heard her lay down the law.'

'Not like Step Mama, you mean,' Bea stated. 'She's always throwing her weight around.'

'Because she wasn't born to it, she feels she has to make grand statements and gestures,' Louisa explained.

'Her latest suggestion is that we all wear identical ball gowns,' Bea told them.

'You must be joking,' Louisa exclaimed, throwing up her hands in horror. 'We are all quite different, both in colouring and personality. I mean, I like to wear jewel colours that complement my dark hair and eyes, while your chestnut hair looks stunning against golden or sage tones, Victoria.'

'Well, you know I don't like standing out in a crowd.'

'And I hate being constrained in anything tight,' Bea added.

'Just as well, the way you prance around the place,' Louisa laughed.

'Appearance is all, girls,' Bea giggled, jumping to her feet and giving a fair imitation of the woman as she stuck her nose in the air and sashayed across the room.

Madame Pittier sneezed, then dabbed delicately at her watering eyes with a lace-edged handkerchief. Reclining on the sofa covered by a rose-coloured blanket, she'd valiantly continued testing Jane on the day-to-day procedures of running the *magasin*, checking that she was word perfect and conversant in dealing with clients.

'Please rest, Madame, you are only making yourself worse,' Jane told her. 'After all your training, I am quite capable of running your business for a couple of days.'

'I know you are but…' Seized by a fit of coughing, she was unable to continue. Anxiously, Jane held a glass of water to her lips. The woman took a sip then lay her head back against the cushions. 'It's no good, Jane,' she gasped. 'I can't travel to Nettlecombe like this. Lady Farringdon wouldn't thank me for spreading illness. You will have to go in my place.'

'I couldn't possibly,' Jane protested, her eyes widening in alarm. 'I wouldn't know what to say or do.'

'Fiddlesticks. As you have pointed out yourself, I have trained you well. In fact, from today you can consider your apprenticeship to be complete. You will now officially be known as Second Corsetière.' Jane's heart leapt in delight.

'Really, you mean…' she began, thinking of the promised increase in her wages.

'We will discuss the detail upon your return,' Madame croaked. 'This is a lucrative, not to mention prestigious commission. One I simply can't afford to miss. My reputation depends on it and…' She broke off as coughing overtook her again. 'Leave me to rest now, but return at eight o'clock sharp tomorrow. We will spend the day going through everything you'll need to know.' She closed her eyes and Jane knew she'd been dismissed.

* * *

'Blimey, you mean yous goin' to the manor house?' Millie squeaked, her eyes on stalks.

They were sitting at the kitchen table eating their supper. At least Millie was. Jane was so wound up she couldn't eat any of the chicken soup the girl had cooked especially for their employer.

'If you ain't goin' to eat that, give us it here,' the maid said, reaching over and grabbing Jane's bowl.

'Sorry, Millie, it's delicious but…'

'Yous tum's as knotted as a nun's knickerbockers,' she declared, then tucked into Jane's soup before she could think of a suitable reply. ''Ere, you might meet a charming prince,' Millie cried, waving her spoon in the air excitedly.

'Nettlecombe's a manor house, not a palace. Besides, Lord Farringdon has five daughters.'

'Still, yous never know, yous could meet a handsome man. I reckons yous lucky. With yous gone I'm goin' to be stuck here with her,' Millie groaned, pointing to Madame's room above. 'How long you goin' for?'

'Three days.'

'Three days,' Millie exclaimed, staring at Jane in horror. 'Why so long?'

'Madame says I'm to take down their requirements, list their measurements, make toiles and ensure they fit. Then I must return and make the garments in the workroom under her supervision,' she replied.

'Well, makes sure you come back on time cos she's been a right old tartar since she were taken poorly. I reckons she caught a chill when we was putting up the shutters the day of the riots cos she usually only goes out when it's fine.' As the insistent ringing of Madame's hand bell sounded, Millie rolled her eyes and jumped to her feet. 'Oh blimey, what the heck does she want now?'

Although the next day was Sunday and supposedly a day of rest, it was turning into the most demanding one of Jane's working life. Frustrated at being taken ill, Madame snapped out orders until Jane thought her head would burst. Finally, as the shadows were creeping into the corner of the room, her employer pointed to the smart pink leather bag she always took on her visits to special clients.

'In there you will find all the materials you will need. Use the journal with the pink rose embroidered on it to write down all their requirements, the silver tape for measuring. Appearances are important, Jane. Which reminds me. You'd better wear my best cape with the pink ribbon trim, it will be cold on the coach.' Jane was about to protest that her own would be quite adequate when the woman began to cough.

'Yes, Madame. Will it take me directly to Nettlecombe?'

'Not to the manor itself, no. It will drop you at the Horseshoes coaching inn on the Exeter to Lyme Road which I'm given to understand is a mere couple of miles from there. I have written a letter of introduction and explanation for you to hand to Lady Farringdon upon your arrival. Now I will wish you goodnight and good luck. The stagecoach leaves from the White Hart at first light.'

'I believe you said you were staying at the manor so I presume I shall be shown to my room when I arrive?'

'Ah, well, I might have misread that bit,' the woman admitted, looking unusually shamefaced. 'Your accommodation will be a room in the cottage of the local dressmaker, which I believe is situated in the village itself. You'll find the details in here,' she added, handing Jane a folded sheet of paper. 'But don't worry, you are not expected to present yourself at the manor until eleven o'clock on Tuesday morning so you'll have plenty of time to familiarise yourself with the geography of the place.'

'Oh, that's all right then,' Jane muttered, when she saw an answer was expected.

'Remember, you will be representing me and my business, Jane. Agree to anything and everything Lady Farringdon requests. If in any doubt make notes, take measurements and discuss with me upon your return. If you act confidently and professionally, that is how you will be perceived.'

'Yes, Madame,' Jane replied, thankful her long skirt hid her trembling legs, for in truth she'd never been so nervous in all her life.

Chapter 6

Next morning, with the sky lightening to pearlescent grey, Jane donned the beautiful pink cape, snatched up her bags and let herself out of the *magasin*. Stepping carefully along pavements that glistened like diamonds, Jane didn't know if she felt excited or apprehensive at the adventure that lay ahead. She turned into the road that led to the White Hart where she was to catch the stagecoach and gasped as the chill wind hit her full in the face, threatening to dislodge her bonnet. Even at this hour the city was busy, the pavements crowded with men and women hurrying to work while hawkers shouted the latest news in order to sell their papers. Costers wove their loaded barrows in and out of the traffic, heedless of the horse-drawn buses and hansom cabs or the drivers shaking their fists at them. Boarded-up windows and shops with shutters torn down, or so distorted they were of little use, showed unmistakable evidence of the riots of the previous week.

Reaching the inn, Jane was surprised to see clusters of people, overnight bags and baskets in hand, making their way towards the yard where the stagecoach stood waiting. Its body was painted green and black with matching wheels, and

Jane was pleased to see there were windows for passengers to look out of. Four sturdy horses snorted and stamped their feet impatiently, their breath rising like steam in the cold air. An officious man sporting top hat, long black jacket and green trousers stood stiffly beside the open door as he marshalled passengers onboard. Anxious to get out of the cold, Jane joined the back of the queue, wondering how they would all fit into what appeared to be quite a small vehicle.

'Name?' the man barked, as the person before her clambered inside.

'Jane Haydon,' she replied. He consulted his list then shook his head.

'Nobody by that name here. Next,' he called.

'Oh, the reservation might be under the name of Madame Pittier,' Jane told him. He gave her a strange look, tapped his finger down the page, then nodded. However, instead of ushering her inside the coach, he pointed to the stairs leading up to the roof. 'Is there no room inside?' she asked.

'Yes, for those who've paid the full fare, now are you getting on or not? We've got a schedule to keep to.' With the people behind growing impatient, Jane tightened her grip on her bags and clambered awkwardly up the steps. Perched on one of the hard seats, it became obvious from the dress and odour of unwashed bodies around her that this was the area for the less well-off. Perhaps she'd be glad to be in the open air after all.

'Going far, ducks?' a large lady asked as she flopped down next to Jane, pulling her large basket onto her lap. Although red in the face her kind expression prompted Jane to reply.

'To the Horseshoes.'

'Blimey, you'll be chilled to the marrow in this, though that cape looks nice and snug,' she said, eyeing it enviously. 'Let's hope it don't rain, an all,' she muttered, staring up at the leaden sky. A sudden squawking made Jane jump. 'Don't mind the chook,' the woman chortled, patting the lid. 'She likes a trip out, though this will be her last one before,' she lowered her voice, 'the pot.'

'Oh,' Jane gulped, her stomach lurching as she thought of the broth Millie had made the previous day.

'And we're off,' the woman cried, as a horn sounded. The sudden jolt as they pulled away caused Jane to grab hold of the metal rail which made the woman laugh. 'Yer gets used to it after a while. I uses the time to catch up on me kip,' she said, closing her eyes.

Jane stared at the buildings that seemed to be flashing by at an alarming rate as the wheels clattered over the cobbles. She'd never been out of the city before and couldn't decide if the experience of seeing things from so high up was exciting or terrifying. However, she soon got used to the rhythmic swaying and the chatting passengers who seemed to be enjoying catching up with each other, even if it did necessitate bellowing at the tops of their voices. She even welcomed the gusts of wind that blew the noxious smells away, although she was growing ever more grateful for the warmth Madame's thick cape afforded. Poor Madame, Jane had never known her be ill before and hoped she was feeling better today. She had quite an affection for the woman, who had looked after her since she'd been very young. In fact, these days Jane could hardly remember her mother at all. It was only now, with time to think, that Jane realised just how much she owed her employer who, on seeing how interested she'd been in fabric and stitching, had given her the opportunity to try her hand at sewing. Now, she'd been promoted to the rank of Second Corsetière. Hugging herself in delight, she stared around.

The scenery had changed from tenements and taverns to cottages and countryside. From her lofty position, Jane took in the tall trees and rolling hills, even spotting a shimmer of water in the distance at one stage. Finally, the sleepless night she'd spent trying to memorise everything for her interview with Lady Farringdon at Nettlecombe caught up with her and her eyelids grew heavy.

'Come on, me duck.' Nudging in her side woke Jane. Bleary eyed she stared around and saw the coach had drawn up in the yard of another inn where, heedless of the disembarking passengers, ostlers were hurrying to feed and water the horses.

'This is me.' As the woman began struggling to her feet the chicken squawked loudly. 'Must know she's for the chop. You goin' in for some grub?' she asked, jerking her head towards the inn.

'Er, no, I think I'll stay here,' Jane said quickly.

With a smile the woman disappeared down the steps but her seat was soon taken by a thin-faced older man who gave Jane a leer, looked her up and down then promptly closed his eyes. Suppressing a shudder, Jane focused her attention on the activity below, where the horses were being changed. After about half an hour, the passengers emerged from the inn and regained their seats, but as the coach pulled away Jane felt the man's thigh press against hers. Recoiling in horror, she bumped against the woman on her other side who glared and began muttering about selfish people hogging more than their fair share of the seat. Apologising, Jane turned to stare at the man in dismay but although he gave a snort, his eyes remained closed.

To distract herself from the unwelcome heat, Jane stared at the road ahead but it was straight and seemingly never-ending with horses pulling laden carts and the occasional coach approaching from the opposite direction. As the morning drew on, the vehicles became more resplendent, with private horse-drawn carriages conveying their rich owners, but any pleasure she'd derived from her adventure diminished as the man's leg began moving slowly up and down hers. Hot with embarrassment, Jane raised her boot ready to stamp on his foot, then noticed the woman watching her.

Not wishing to draw attention to herself, she carefully inched away and hunched back in the seat, willing the coach to hurry. But it was no good, the man spread his legs further until once again she felt the unwelcome heat of his body against hers. Jane darted a look at him but still his eyes remained closed. She was debating what to do when an image of Millie brandishing a stiletto flashed into her mind. The girl would never put up with such behaviour and nor would she, Jane thought, quickly fishing in her bag and pulling out a large bodkin.

''Ere, you be careful where you puts that, maid,' the man muttered, suddenly alert.

'I know where I'll put it if you don't move your leg,' she

retorted. Surprised, he stared at her then, muttering under his breath, slowly did as she requested.

A short time later they pulled into the yard of another coaching inn, and to her relief the odious little man got unsteadily to his feet. Pausing, he gave her an outrageous wink.

'Louse,' she muttered, but as she reached into her bag again, he disappeared quickly down the stairs. In order to pass the time, she pulled out Madame's instructions and reread them. Thankfully, as they set off again, it was a quiet mouse of a woman who took the seat next to her.

However, her relief was short-lived for the wind had risen, bending the branches so low she had to duck to avoid being hit. Straightening her bonnet, she shivered, this time with the cold. The sky was growing ever darker and she feared she was in for a soaking as well, but then, just as they hit a bank of mist, the horses slowed. Peering through the swirling grey, Jane could just make out the swinging sign of an inn and relief coursed through her. They'd reached the Horseshoes at last.

'Is it far to Nettlecombe Manor?' she asked the coachman as she clambered numbly down the stairs.

'Three mile or so down that lane opposite,' he replied, before turning his attention to a lady impatiently waiting to board.

Pulling her cape tighter around her, Jane picked up her bags and stepped into the cold, damp mist. Cautiously she made her way along the narrow track, trying to dodge the water-filled ruts. Heedless of her wet clothes and the damp seeping into her boots, she trudged on, barely able to see beyond the hedges that hugged the lane, or the dark branches that loomed out of the mist like menacing monsters. Then she heard the sound of a horse and cart approaching from behind and, heart racing, climbed onto the verge to let it pass. However, to her dismay it pulled up beside her.

'Hop in, it's too dangerous to be walking along here in this murk,' a voice called. Peering through the gloom, she could just make out a young man smiling at her from the cover of the cart. Remembering her experience on the coach, Jane stared around but everywhere was blanketed in swirling grey. Sensing her hesitation, he called again, this time his voice softer. 'It's right to be cautious but I can assure you I'm quite harmless and you are obviously heading for Nettlecombe for this is where the lane leads.' He sounded friendly, and as a sudden gust of wind threatened to send her bonnet flying, Jane knew it would be silly to refuse.

'Thank you,' she cried. Taking her bags, he placed them on the floor behind, while she climbed up beside him.

'It's a bit basic, I'm afraid, but at least you're out of the mizzle.' He grinned. The cart smelled of wood and tar which wasn't unpleasant and the seat, although little more than a wooden plank, was more comfortable than the one on the roof of the stagecoach.

'Whatever are you doing wandering around in weather like this?' he asked after whistling to the pony.

'I have an appointment with Lady Farringdon tomorrow and apparently the nearest stop was the Horseshoes. Do you know Nettlecombe Manor?'

'Sam Gill, Assistant Manager of the Nettlecombe Estate at your service, Miss…?'

'Haydon, Jane Haydon,' she replied, taking an instant liking to the friendly man, as she took in his sandy hair peeping from under a cloth cap and hazel eyes that looked at her in an open manner. 'I have been sent by my employer, Madame Pittier.'

'Do I take it from the bags you were carrying that you are residing there?'

'Oh goodness no. I have the details of where I'm to stay here,' she said fishing in her bag and drawing out the note she'd been given. 'I am to board with Mrs Somers at her cottage in Combe,' she read. He raised a brow but kept his attention focused on the lane ahead. 'I really appreciate you giving me a lift,' she told him.

'Must be both our lucky days then,' he said, his grin broadening. 'Been up at the deer park all morning mending fencing. Poachers after the deer and caused a fair amount of damage in the process. Normally, it would be Father's job but he's broken his leg. And right moody he is too. Glad to be out of the way, to be honest.'

'I know what you mean. Madame Pittier was meant to be seeing Lady Farringdon but she's gone down with a chill and I must admit she's been pretty moody too.' They exchanged sympathetic smiles and their glances locked.

As Jane looked quickly away, she saw the mist was beginning to thin. Then, through the trees she caught a glimpse of a magnificent three-storeyed house of grey stone nestling in the vale of two hills. Surrounded by rolling lawns and clipped hedges, it had tall chimneys and windows made up of lots of panes of leaded glass. She just had time to notice the animal statues on each side of the stone archway before they passed on by. She could hardly believe that a house could be so big or have so much land around it. In Exeter houses were squashed in alongside taverns, shops and other places of employment.

'My word, is that Nettlecombe Manor?' she gasped, staring down at her clothes and wondering how she would have the nerve to knock on the door of such a grand place.

'The very same,' he nodded.

'What is Lady Farringdon like?' she asked.

'Grand, very grand. Likes putting on a show. Whenever she entertains, she calls for the fatted calf to be killed.' Jane looked at him in surprise and saw his lips twitching.

'Madame Pittier is the same. Insists a lamb be roasted when she entertains the Bishop of Exeter, then laughs when he asks which of his flock it is this time.' This was met with a stunned silence followed by a loud guffaw.

'Touché, Miss Haydon,' he said, staring at her in delight. 'A lady with a sense of humour is a rare thing around these parts.' Jane shook her head, wondering at her own wit for she wasn't usually good at repartee, especially with a man she'd only just met. With any man, in fact, for of course most of the people she dealt with were female.

'Don't worry, a smart girl like you will make a good impression on Lady Farringdon, especially wearing that beautiful cape. Places a lot of importance on appearance, does Lady F,' he continued, mistaking her look. Still, she was grateful for his reassurance.

'Oh, look, the mist has completely lifted now,' she cried, staring at the expanse of green to either side.

'Sea fret lifts as soon as it comes around these parts.'

'We're near the sea?' Jane exclaimed, her eyes widening in astonishment as she peered around. 'But it's all countryside around here,' she said, waving at the fields and hills.

'Ah, but we're at the head of the combe here, see?' he replied, laughing at her expression. 'Manor house stands just a couple of hundred yards from the highest point of the parish and the estate cottages lead off round there,' he said, gesturing to a path winding away from the main driveway.

'If you could just point me in the direction of Mrs Somers' cottage, I won't trouble you any further,' Jane said, turning to reach for her bags.

'Ida Somers lives down in the village itself, which is a fair old walk from here. Tell you what, I need to drop off some things with Tom, he's the blacksmith, so I'll drive you there.'

'If you're sure it's not out of your way, then thank you,' Jane replied, relieved not to have another long walk ahead of her. She was already feeling damp and dishevelled and, despite Sam's kind words, hated to think what she looked like. She was roused from her thoughts by the sound of banging and angry shouting.

'Oh my, whatever's going on?' she asked, her eyes widening in alarm.

'That's the quarry down there,' Sam explained, waving his hand to the left. 'The men will be having their stone checked for its quality. There's always bad feeling if someone's block is found to be inferior. When good stone is tapped with a hammer it gives a clear ring so the block will be passed and the man gets his day's pay. If it gives a dull thud that indicates it's cracked then…' He shrugged. 'There's not much money round these parts and a lot of hungry mouths to feed.'

'But surely the men dig more than one in a day,' Jane frowned.

'Believe you me, it takes them all their time to mine the four-ton block that's expected.'

'Gracious. So, who owns the quarry?' Jane asked, horrified to think of some poor men working all day in squalid conditions underground for no pay.

'Lord Farringdon,' he told her. 'And yes, I know what you're thinking, but that's the way of things, isn't it? Anyhow, masons get paid well and the stone from here is favoured for its colour and workability for carving. Some of it was used to build Exeter Cathedral, so Madame Pittier can tell the bishop that when she next invites him for dinner.' Jane smiled and their former easy-going atmosphere was restored. 'Now then, further down the lane you come to the sea and that's where the stone gets loaded on boats and shipped all over the world.'

'I've never seen the sea before,' Jane murmured, peering down the lane as if she could catch a glimpse.

'Well, we'll have to remedy that one day, won't we?' he replied, grinning over at her. Jane's heart flipped at the thought. At least, she was sure it was the thought of seeing the sea and not the way he was looking at her that made her insides flutter.

The noise receded as they descended into the valley with its huddle of cottages that seemed to hug the hillside. They were tiny, like the dolls' houses Jane had seen in one of Madame's books. Further along, a square church tower soared majestically into the sky and she could make out various objects in shop windows on the opposite side of the lane.

'This is the village of Combe where you'll be staying, and that's the forge,' Sam said, pointing to a crooked building with a sloping thatched roof from which smoke was billowing. As they passed the open door, Jane heard the ring of a hammer striking the anvil. 'Tom lives in that end cottage opposite, with his wife Lily and their three children. She runs the dame school as well as making the best lace in the area. Over there's the bakery and just up here you'll find Ida's cottage. She prides herself on being the local seamstress,' he added. 'But then, I guess you already know that.'

'Actually, I didn't.' Jane frowned.

'Well, I'm sure she'll be glad of the extra money, anyhow. Ida's all right once you get used to her ways. Ask her a question and she'll say, oh, I'da done that, if I'da known.'

They were still laughing when Sam pulled up outside the tiniest cottage Jane had ever seen. It stood at right angles to its neighbours and had a chimney running up the end wall.

'It's a bit... cosy, shall we say.' Sam grinned wryly. 'But I'm sure you'll manage for a couple of nights or so.'

As he jumped down, the door swung open and a tiny woman wearing a white mob cap and an apron over her black dress came scurrying out. She stared at Jane through beady eyes that clearly missed nothing.

'Well, Samuel Gill, if I'da known you was coming, I'da had a tea on the brew,' she cried.

'That's all right, Mrs Somers,' he called, handing Jane her bags and giving her such a wicked wink it was all she could do not to burst out laughing. 'This is Miss Jane Haydon who'll be staying with you.' The woman looked her up and down disapprovingly.

'Oh no, she won't. I've been told to expect a Madame Pittier, not some slip of a girl, and an English one at that,' she sniffed and turned to go back indoors.

Chapter 7

Jane stared at the woman in disbelief, but she was tired and hungry, and having travelled all this way was not about to give up.

'I have a letter from Madame Pittier explaining the position along with a small gift for you.'

'Why not read it and if you're still not happy, I'll see if Lily will accommodate Miss Haydon. She'll be glad of the extra money,' Sam added. The woman hesitated, obviously not liking the idea of missing out.

'You've a gift for me?' She turned to Jane, her bird-like eyes burning with curiosity. 'Well, why didn't yer say, I'da let you come in straight away.' She sniffed again and opened the door wider. 'Don't just stand there, boy,' she told Sam. 'Miss Haydon and I have things to discuss.'

'Right you are, Mrs Somers,' he replied, giving her a mock salute before turning to Jane. 'I'll call for you in the morning and drive you up to the manor. Around ten o'clock be all right?'

'I couldn't possibly ask you to do that,' Jane replied, although the thought of seeing a friendly face and not having to walk all the way up the steep hill was appealing.

'You didn't, I volunteered,' he grinned. Jane watched him jump onto his cart and was just thinking what a nice man he was when Mrs Somers caught hold of her arm and pulled her inside.

'Come along, stop flashing those big blue eyes at young Sam, this blow's enough to put out the flames,' she said and before Jane could protest that she was doing no such thing, the woman had firmly pushed the door shut and was pulling a brown heavy curtain across to keep out the draught.

The room was small and dark, even though it was only mid-afternoon, and had beams so low she could reach up and touch them. There was a hearth at one end in which the tiniest of fires was smouldering, while a blackened pot swung on a chain above. A table under the window was strewn with sewing paraphernalia and had a wooden chair set on either side. The shelf running along the back wall was stacked with mismatched crockery and glasses. A prickle ran up Jane's spine and, feeling she was being watched, she swung round to find luminous amber eyes staring intently from a niche set in the wall.

'Right, girl, pull those chairs over by the fire then explain what you're doing here,' Mrs Somers ordered. Jane wanted nothing more than to be shown where she'd be sleeping but, knowing she was representing her employer, she bit back an angry retort and did as she'd been asked.

'Lady Farringdon wrote to Madame Pittier requesting she visit—'

'I know that,' the woman snapped. 'And me the local seamstress too. I've never been so insulted. So where is she then?'

'Unfortunately, Madame caught a chill and sent me in her place. Here is her letter explaining,' Jane said, taking an envelope from her bag along with the little package. Ignoring the letter, the woman tore impatiently at the pink paper.

'Oh my,' she gasped, holding up the length of pink silk ribbon. 'I ain't never had anything like this afore in me life,' she murmured, holding it closer. 'My, it smells of roses in summer. How did she know that's my favourite colour?' Jane was about to say that everything about Madame was pink, then thought better of it. Why spoil the woman's obvious delight?

'I'm glad you like it,' she smiled, her gaze returning to the black cat who was still studying her fixedly. Jane got the feeling it could see inside her soul and with a shudder she turned back to the woman who was now scanning the note. With her bright eyes and hooked nose, she looked just like a crone, Jane thought, jumping as the woman suddenly scrunched the paper into a ball and threw it across the floor.

'So, where's me money for yer board then?' Mrs Somers spat, staring at Jane accusingly.

'Madame said Lady Farringdon would be settling the bill.'

'As if it isn't bad enough her ladyship insulting me by calling in another seamstress when I've served the manor well all these years, now she expects me to wait for me money. What's a poor woman like me to live on, fresh air?' At her high-pitched shriek, the glasses on the shelf began to tinkle, alarming the cat, who sprang down from the shelf and landed with a thud at Jane's feet. As it rubbed against her legs the woman glared.

'Traitor,' she hissed.

'You have a beautiful cat,' Jane said politely, for there was no denying that with its glossy fur and huge paws, it was truly magnificent. Although it was now purring, she was still wary of the way it was staring at her.

'He ain't mine, he belongs to Wise Woman Winnie. When hers out Athame always comes in here for a warm.'

'Oh,' replied Jane, staring at the wisps of smoke that surely would never be hot enough to heat whatever was in the pot. 'That's an unusual name.'

'Summat to do with directing her magical powers, I think. Yer can ask her when yer see her.'

'I'm going to be quite busy so I don't suppose I'll have much time to meet people,' Jane replied, her leg suddenly feeling cold as the cat padded to the door and waited to be let out. What kind of place was this?

'Go on, yer daft bugger,' the woman said, shooing the animal outside then pulling the curtain across the door again. 'When Athame reports back, she'll be round here first thing in the morning, yer'll see.'

'Right.' Jane smiled indulgently.

'Yer'll see,' Mrs Somers repeated. 'And if Athame likes yer, yer must be all right so I'd better show yer where yers sleeping.'

Relief flooding through her, Jane retrieved her bags and followed the woman to the wooden stairs in the corner of the room.

'Privy's in yard outside,' the woman gestured. 'Room's up there on the right. Won't be what a young lady like you is used to, but it's clean. Suppose yer mother dresses you posh like that,' she added, looking Jane up and down.

'My mother left when I was very young, Mrs Somers,' she said quietly.

'Oh, yer poor girl. I hope her rests in peace,' the woman murmured, making the sign of the cross. Even in the darkening room, Jane could see her eyes soften and felt guilty she'd got the wrong end of the stick.

'I live with Madame Pittier and this is her cape,' she added.

'Well, it's very smart. Now yer'd better take this candle upstairs to light yer way, but blow it out when yer've taken off that posh cloak and had a wash. I ain't made of money. When you comes down we'll have summat to eat.'

The room she'd been directed to was half the size of the one downstairs and hardly big enough to house the narrow bed, tiny cupboard and washstand. To Jane's relief the jug was filled with water but the only way she could rinse her face and hands was by sitting on the bed. However, it felt good to wash the dirt of the journey from her skin. Quickly she opened her bag and shook out the clean blouse ready for the morning. It was so cold, she was tempted to put her cape on again, but not wishing to upset Mrs Somers, she hung it carefully on the nail on the back of the door then hurried down the stairs.

To Jane's surprise, the woman had lit another candle and the table, cleared of fabric, was now set with two dishes of stew, a thin slice of bread beside each. Not having eaten since breaking her fast, Jane was starving and didn't need telling twice when the woman invited her to tuck in. The vegetable and bean concoction was different to anything she had eaten before, yet it was surprisingly tasty, warming her insides as she ate.

'That was delicious, thank you,' she said, mopping up the last of the gravy with the crust.

'Glad yer liked it cos it'll be more of the same tomorrow,' the woman said, picking up her dish and licking it clean. Jane turned away, hardly daring to imagine what Madame Pittier's reaction would have been, had she been here.

'This bread is the tastiest I've eaten for ages,' Jane told her, thinking of the lumpy misshapen loaves Millie had been lucky to get of late.

'Well, no one can say I don't look after me guests. And of course, we're lucky to have the mill and a decent baker here in Combe. Though his prices keep going up and up,' she sighed. 'Anyhows, put the chairs back in front of the fire while I get us a drink, then yer can tell me what kind of things yer sew,' she told Jane, taking a bottle and two glasses from the shelf. 'It's me special blackberry cordial. Warms the cockles, it does, and don't think I haven't noticed yer shivering.' She tutted, tossing the scrunched-up letter onto the fire, adding a few twigs then nodding with satisfaction as a flame flared.

'So, what exactly is it yer make?' she asked, sitting back in her seat and stretching out her legs.

'Corsets and underpinnings,' Jane told her, taking a sip of the dark liquid then almost choking as it burnt her throat, making her eyes water.

'Oh, so yer not a dressmaker then?' the woman asked, studying her as closely as the cat had earlier.

'I've recently completed my apprenticeship as a corsetière,'

Jane murmured, thinking it prudent not to admit that she also made camisoles and gowns when requested.

'So, I've been worrying for nothing then,' the woman said, pouring herself another drink. 'I've been that worried, see, cos it's me sewing that pays me rent. It's strange when yer thinks about it. I rents this place from his lordship, then sews for his wife to earn the money to pay him for it.'

'Does he own everything around here?' Jane asked.

'Yep. And her ladyship don't let us forget it, neither. Course it was different when his first wife was alive. Now she were a real lady. Did lots of good work for the village and widows of the quarry workers. It were the curse that killed her.'

'Curse?'

'Yes, put on the Farringdons by them gypsies. Doesn't do to cross them. Then there's the resident ghost.'

'Ghost?' Jane asked, swallowing hard.

'Oh yes, if yer smells lavender up at the manor, beware. 'Tis a warning, see – always happens before a death. Doesn't happen often but when it do manifest itself, well, someone cops it,' she nodded, giving Jane a knowing look.

Gypsies? Wise women? Ghosts? What was this place she was going to? she wondered again.

Whether it was the effect of the food or the cordial, the more the woman talked the more animated she became. Picking up the length of ribbon, she smiled.

'This'll make a fine trimming for me bonnet. Me friends will all be green with envy.'

'I'm sure you'll look splendid, Mrs Somers,' Jane said, trying to stifle a yawn as she got to her feet. 'Thank you so much for a lovely evening. If you'll excuse me, I really must get some sleep, I have a busy day ahead of me tomorrow.'

'Breakfast's at seven. Yer'll not need a timepiece, the church bells ringing for the early service will wake yer. Oh, yer hasn't finished yer drink,' she added, picking up Jane's glass and tipping the contents into her own.

Despite the strange room and scratchy mattress, Jane was so exhausted she fell asleep as soon as she'd pulled the little patchwork cover over her. However, it wasn't the bells that woke her, but the ringing of iron-shod clogs on the cobbles below. Peering through the curtains, she saw what looked like an army of men, in moleskin jackets and trousers, marching through the village and on up the hill as they made their way to the quarry. Some had small bags over their shoulders, others were clutching brew cans, while smoke from their clay pipes curled into the air. As the sound of their footsteps receded, she heard the clock on the church strike five and realising she didn't need to rise yet, she slid back under the cover.

But thoughts of the day ahead crowded her mind and she knew she wouldn't get back to sleep. She began running through everything Madame had taught her. On the one hand she was eager to see inside a manor house, on the other she was afraid of disgracing herself by saying or doing the wrong thing. Finally, when the clock struck six, she rose and washed. Dressing carefully, she placed the rosebud at her throat then brushed her hair until it shone and pinned it on top of her head.

'Porridge,' Mrs Somers greeted her tersely, placing a bowl on the table and nodding for Jane to take her place. Clearly, she was not a morning person, Jane thought, but by now nerves of what lay ahead were knotting her stomach and it took all her willpower to eat anything, so she was glad of the woman's silence.

She settled down to go through Madame's notes and by the time she stepped outside into the cool air of the morning, she feared she might be sick. Clutching Madame's pink bag, she hovered on the step, waiting for sight of Sam's cart.

'Athame said you'd arrived.' Hearing the strange voice, Jane spun round to see an old lady with piercing green eyes and a shock of white hair staring at her knowingly. 'You'll be wasting your time up at the manor, though, for there'll be no wedding there.'

'Oh?' Jane asked, but then the door opened and Mrs Somers appeared.

'I'da told yer Winnie would appear, didn't I?' Before Jane could reply, Sam's cart drew up beside her.

'Morning, ladies,' he called, doffing his cap.

'Morning, Sam, pleased to see your father's leg is healing.'

'That it is, Winnie, thank you. Well, if you'll excuse us, I must ensure Miss Haydon isn't late for her meeting with Lady Farringdon,' he said, holding out his hand to take Jane's bag before helping her into the cart.

'Thank you, Mr Gill.' Jane smiled, settling herself on the wooden seat beside him then holding on to the side, as with a flick of the reins they began to move.

'I hope your evening with Mrs Somers went all right?' he asked, giving her a searching look.

'Yes, her mood seemed to thaw when the cat took a liking

to me. She even told me Winnie would be here first thing. Although Winnie must be an early bird to have visited your father earlier.'

'She didn't, actually. Winnie's a wise woman and when she says she sees things, she "sees" them, if you get my meaning. Don't ask me how. But she's never been wrong.'

'Oh,' Jane murmured, recalling what the woman had just told her. Still, it wasn't her place to say anything, she had a job to do. At the thought of her forthcoming meeting with Lady Farringdon her stomach lurched. As if sensing her nerves, Sam chattered away, pointing out places of interest as they passed and reminding her that she really should see the sea before she left, even getting her to inhale deeply when they reached the brow of the hill.

'Good clean air, that. Salt will clear your lungs, invigorate and set you up for the day,' he told her before regaling her with more stories.

By the time they reached the driveway lined with magnificent lime trees, Jane knew who did what in the village. Instead of passing through the archway topped with the grand stone creatures, Sam veered alongside the boundary wall.

'What were those strange animals?' Jane ventured as they followed the track that sloped down towards the rear of the house.

'Griffins,' he replied. 'Said to guard the property. They combine the best traits of the eagle, which of course is the king of the birds, and the lion, king of the beasts. Regal, eh?' Before Jane could ask any more, he was pulling to a halt beside a beech hedgerow bordering the adjacent field.

'Good gracious, they seem to have everything here,' Jane murmured.

'Certainly do. Even their own well over there,' he replied, waving his hand towards the distance. 'Now, that gate there leads to the staff entrance,' he added pointing to the wooden structure discreetly hidden within the ivy. 'Ferris or Quick will admit you and announce you to her ladyship.'

'Thank you,' she said, jumping down and taking her bag. And she didn't just mean for the lift. Unknowingly, he had saved her from making a fool of herself, for it would never have occurred to her not to approach the front door.

'Don't look so scared. Just remember even her ladyship has to do her daily ablutions the same as the rest of us,' he winked.

That thought made Jane smile as she unlatched the heavy door and hurried up the gravel path. But as she hovered on the step, her nerves returned with a vengeance.

Chapter 8

'Never in my entire life have I been so insulted,' Lady Farringdon cried, glaring at Jane as if she was some form of low-life. 'Madame Pittier promised she would attend personally, not send her young, and doubtless inexperienced, assistant. And to think she was highly recommended by Lady Connaught whom I understand is one of her most prestigious clients.'

Flushing with embarrassment, Jane tried not to feel intimidated as she stared around the grand Amber Room with the gold-painted ceiling that she'd been shown into only minutes before. *Be respectful but resolute.* As Madame's mantra ran through her mind, Jane determined not to be browbeaten. How Lady Connaught, who on her visits to the boutique always treated Jane with kindness and courtesy, came to be friends with this arrogant woman, she had no idea. Judging from the expressions of the three young ladies seated on a sofa covered in the most dreadful orange brocade, they were feeling just as uncomfortable. Jane waited until she'd finished her tirade, then handed over the envelope.

'Regrettably Madame Pittier is too unwell to travel, Lady Farringdon. She sends profuse apologies and asked me to give you this by way of explanation.' The woman took the letter, wrinkling her nose as the fragrance of rose wafted before her. Whilst she was reading, the youngest girl gave Jane a broad wink and her spirits lifted. At least they weren't all hostile.

'Well, this is most unsatisfactory, and you don't even sound French,' Lady Farringdon retorted, placing the letter on the gleaming walnut table beside her. 'Exactly how long have you been with Madame Pittier?'

'Almost nineteen years, Lady Farringdon,' Jane replied, not seeing the need to confess her mother had been Madame's maid. As the woman stared at her in surprise, the sound of laughter rippled around the room.

'This is no laughing matter, girls,' the lady admonished before returning her attention to Jane. 'Well, you obviously make yourself look younger than you are then. Now, in the unlikely event that I should engage your services, perhaps you would enlighten my stepdaughters on what the process of commissioning bespoke corsetry from Madame Pittier would entail. Bearing in mind she isn't actually here to do so herself.'

'Of course, Lady Farringdon,' Jane replied, turning to the three young ladies who nodded enthusiastically. Mentally she ran through Madame's rules on consultation. The first two she discarded, for obviously social class and income were not an issue. 'The choice of undergarments is dictated by many things. First of all, we need to consider age.'

'Goodness, yes, we don't want to be wearing the same as Step Mama who, as you can see, is much older than us.'

'Don't be impertinent, Beatrice, I am really not much older

than you,' Lady Farringdon snapped. 'Remember your manners in front of our visitor.'

'Perhaps you should remember yours, Step Mama,' Beatrice retorted. 'Poor Miss Haydon has been here at least fifteen minutes and despite holding that heavy-looking bag, you have yet to invite her to be seated.'

'Or introduce us. I am Victoria,' the girl with hair gleaming like chestnuts smiled. 'This is my elder sister Louisa whose betrothal ball is what all this performance is for, and as you've probably gathered, this rascal is our youngest sister Beatrice.'

'Known as Bea,' the girl grinned, her blue eyes that perfectly matched the colour of her day dress sparkling with mischief.

'I'm very pleased to meet you,' Jane replied, trying not to chuckle at the look of outrage on Lady Farringdon's face. However, good manners prevailed for she indicated that Jane should take the chair directly opposite her. Thankful to put her bag down at last, Jane perched as daintily as she could, remembering to cross her legs at the ankles as Madame had taught her.

'You may continue,' the woman stated grandly, as if she was bestowing a huge favour.

'Thank you. Next, we need to consider the occasion, which in this case, of course, is your betrothal ball,' she said, smiling at dark-haired Louisa who nodded. 'We should take into account the type of gowns you will be wearing, for naturally changing fashion demands different underpinning.' At this the three young ladies exchanged delighted looks.

'We've been looking at—' Victoria began, only to be cut short by Lady Farringdon.

'You might have found your tongue, Victoria, but I'd be pleased if you wouldn't keep interrupting for I shall, of course, be instrumental in your choice of gown.'

'Heaven help us then,' Bea muttered. 'Besides, I believe Miss Haydon said that magic word "we".'

'If you can't be quiet, Beatrice, then please absent yourself. Do continue, Miss Haydon.'

'Next comes the choice of fabric and quality of source materials, which influence the style of corset.'

'How so?' Lady Farringdon asked.

'Well, with whalebone becoming less plentiful some people are turning to the better-quality steel for their boning.'

'Gracious, I could never countenance such an idea.' The woman shuddered. 'Baleen is the only choice for someone of my standing.'

'What are the advantages of steel?' Victoria asked, only to be quietened with a withering look from Lady Farringdon. In the ensuing awkward silence, Jane asked herself what her employer would do in such circumstances. *Move the situation on, Miss Haydon*, she could almost hear her words.

'If you were to engage our services, Lady Farringdon, the first thing I would need to do is take measurements. Then we would discuss the other things I mentioned so that I can make up toiles to ensure a perfect fit. Madame Pittier insists on perfection. And, of course, client satisfaction is paramount.'

'As it should be,' Lady Farringdon agreed. 'However, if you think you are going to subject me to the indignity of being measured, then you have another think coming,' she retorted, rising to her feet and smoothing her lilac skirts that, although perfectly suited to her colouring, clashed horribly with the furnishings.

'That doesn't mean I have to—' Jane began, but ignoring her, the woman swept from the room. Jane shivered, wishing the butler hadn't taken her cape from her when she'd arrived. Dismayed to think she'd let Madame down, Jane picked up her bag. She must have presented badly, for it was obvious by the fit of her gown that the woman had been measured for her current corsets.

'Please stay,' Victoria begged. 'I was fascinated by all you said. We've never had the procedure explained before.'

'I'm dying to see what's in your lovely pink carrier,' Bea told her.

'Well…' Jane hesitated, turning to Louisa for direction. After all, it was her betrothal ball.

'Don't mind Step Mama, Miss Haydon, she's rather set in her ways. I can't remember when I last spent such an entertaining morning and would love to hear more. Perhaps we could tempt you with some refreshment? You must be thirsty after all that talking.' Louisa tugged the bell pull and almost immediately the butler appeared.

'Could we have a jug of warm cordial please, Ferris,' she said pleasantly.

'And some cake,' Bea added.

'I will bring suitable sustenance, m'lady,' he replied, giving a little bow and departing as silently as he'd arrived.

'Let's go over to the table by the fire and you can show us what's in your bag,' Louisa said, crossing the carpet which, although thick and obviously expensive, was yet another hideous shade of orange, as were the velvet curtains. Perhaps it should be called the Orangery rather than the Amber Room Jane mused as she willingly moved towards the magnificent carved stone fireplace and the warmth from the blazing flames. She thought of Mrs Somers' few sticks that barely smouldered in her minute grate; expense was something they'd never have to worry about here. Then as she stood pondering the inequalities of life, she caught the fragrance of lavender.

'What a heavenly smell,' she murmured. 'Do the flowers come from your garden?'

'What flowers?' Louisa frowned, glancing quickly at her sisters. Sure enough, as she peered around the room, Jane could see no evidence of lavender, or in fact any flowers at all. If the idea hadn't been so absurd, she could have sworn the fragrance was wafting over from the fireplace. Then she remembered what Ida Somers had said and shivered.

'Forgive me, the travelling yesterday must have caught up with me,' she said quickly.

'Or maybe our resident—' Bea began, only to be silenced by a warning glance from Louisa.

'Was it any flower in particular?' Louisa asked, her dark eyes watching carefully as she waited for Jane to answer.

'I thought it was lavender but of course if there are no flowers in here, I was obviously wrong,' Jane admitted reluctantly. Then, anxious they shouldn't dismiss her, she hurried over to the table and began setting out her notebook, pencil and silver measure. Bea, more interested in what Jane had to show them than any discussion about flowers, pounced on the parcel of fabric samples wrapped in pink tissue paper.

'Hmm,' Victoria exclaimed as she pulled back the paper releasing the fragrance of roses. 'Now that does remind me of the garden in summer. It's a pity we can't have flowers in the rooms but Step Mama says that shedding pollen and petals spoil her precious furnishings. I shall have great vases full all around my house one day.'

'Are you sure you don't mind us going through your things?' Louisa asked, as she picked up a material swatch and held it to her nose. 'Is this the fragrance you were referring to, Miss Haydon?' she asked, studying her closely again.

'Er, no. I am well used to the scent of roses for Madame perfumes everything in her boutique with it. Now why don't you all look through the samples to see what you like.' Jane smiled, keen to move the subject back to the reason for her visit. Besides, their hands were soft and clean which were the most important requisites when handling Madame's merchandise.

'Goodness, I never knew we could have corsets in anything other than boring creamy brown. Can we really choose any of these colours?' Bea asked excitedly as Jane set out the patterns alongside the material samples on the table.

'Yes, of course. Madame always recommends one of the pink hues as it is feminine and enhances skin tone. The shape will depend on your choice of gown, though.'

'We've seen some gorgeous ones in Godey's,' Victoria said, hurrying back to the sofa and searching beneath the cushions. 'Here,' she said, triumphantly brandishing the latest edition she'd had sent to her.

As they pored over the illustrations, Jane's eyes widened in surprise. She was so captivated she hardly noticed the butler setting down a tray of drinks on the sideboard, or the maid hovering with a plate of cakes.

'Thank you, Ferris,' Louisa murmured, forgetting her worries as she was caught up in the excitement.

'Oh, I love that one,' Victoria cried, pointing to a full-skirted, tiered gown with an embellished 'v' at the neck, and sleeves ending at the elbow.

'That would suit you perfectly, Lady Victoria,' she said, making the girl smile.

'There is no need for such formality with us,' Louisa chuckled.

'But how should I address you then?' Jane asked.

'By our names, of course,' Bea laughed. 'What is yours? We can hardly call you Miss Haydon all morning.'

'I'm afraid it's just Jane.'

'Just Jane? But your name means a gift from God,' Louisa told her. 'Which is quite splendid, is it not?'

'I had no idea,' she replied, and couldn't help wondering if her mother had known.

'And of course, Jane Austen was a renowned author. Have you read any of her work?' Jane shook her head, worried she might be found wanting, but Bea smiled and continued. 'I was interested in how she explored the dependence of women on marriage in her writings, especially their pursuit of social status and economic security. It's made me want to stay free and single, forge my own way in life.'

'Honestly, Bea, we were discussing names so I'm sure Jane doesn't wish to hear about your intentions for the future,' Louisa told her.

'All right then, I was named after Mother and Beatrice means one who makes people happy, ' Bea declared proudly.

'Which is very apt considering everything she does makes us laugh,' Victoria quipped. 'Victoria means victory, of course, whilst Louisa is a warrior maid.'

'And it does feel as though I'm constantly fighting to get any say in my betrothal arrangements,' she sighed.

'Well, we can soon put that right,' Jane told her. 'What style of gown would you like?'

'For me, it would be that one,' Louisa replied, picking out a full-skirted design, cinched at the waist with a frill running across the chest, leaving the shoulders exposed in a modest fashion.

'That would be perfect for your betrothal ball. Elegant yet grand enough to make a statement, especially if it was in a beautiful green silk that shimmered in the candlelight when you dance.'

'That sounds perfect,' Louisa murmured, holding up the paper to study the picture more closely. 'Henry loves me in green, he says it brings out the flecks in my eyes.' As if suddenly aware she was sharing an intimate secret, she broke off and smiled self-consciously.

'So, you don't think we should be dressed in matching gowns then?' Bea asked, mischief sparking in her eyes.

'Well, no. You all have different colourings and characteristics and...' Jane stuttered to a halt, worried she'd overstepped the mark, but the others were smiling. 'Why?' she ventured.

'Just something someone said,' Bea giggled. 'How old are you, Jane?'

'Bea, really,' Louisa exclaimed.

'I'm nineteen, why do ask?'

'Because unlike Step Mama, your thoughts align with ours, which is not surprising when you consider we are all around the same age. I just knew you weren't pretending to be younger than you really are,' she beamed. 'So is Madame Pittier your mother then?'

'Don't be stupid, Bea, Jane's name is Haydon. And her private life is just that, private.'

'Oh, I don't mind explaining,' she replied, thinking how strange it was to be talking about the subject twice in as many days when it usually remained buried deep inside her. Still, despite their difference in standing, the girls' interest seemed genuine. 'My mother was Madame's maid of all but she disappeared when I was young and Madame brought me up, first as her maid then apprentice.'

'Well, good for her. She sounds kind,' Bea enthused, making Jane smile. Madame was a true professional who liked to keep her soft side well hidden. 'And I would like you to make me a corset in the brightest red you have, with a chemise and dress to match.'

'I'd love to make your corset but Lady Farringdon hasn't given me the commission yet, and I seem to have upset her by mentioning measuring, so...' Jane shrugged.

'Well, I shall insist you make mine,' Louisa declared.

'As will I,' Victoria agreed. 'How Step Mama expects you to carry out your job without measuring, I don't know.'

'Oh, she'll not want to miss out. Any moment now she'll waltz in with a piece of paper bearing the information you require,' Bea said.

At that moment, the door opened and Lady Farringdon sailed into the room. She was brandishing a notebook and had a determined air about her.

'What is this? Cake in the morning?' she sniffed, staring at the refreshments, which in their excitement had been forgotten. 'We will never retain our figures if we indulge,' she tutted. 'Ah, Miss Haydon, still here I see.'

'We have decided to engage Miss Haydon's services and will be happy for her to measure us,' Louisa told her. 'You must forgive us, Miss Haydon, we were so enthralled by your superb suggestions we quite forgot to offer you the refreshment.' As the woman narrowed her eyes and Victoria quickly hid the magazine behind a cushion, Louisa stood and began pouring the liquid in which slices of fruit floated. But as she handed Jane her drink, Lady Farringdon spoke.

'Miss Haydon, despite the impression my stepdaughters may have given, it is I who makes the decisions round here.'

'Of course, Lady Farringdon,' Jane said, looking longingly at the cordial. It had been a long morning and she was parched. Suppressing a sigh, she began collecting together the samples.

'What are you doing? You've yet to show them to me, far less discuss my requirements.'

'But I thought you weren't interested, that you'd decided not to commission me,' Jane murmured, taking a sip of her cordial lest the glass be snatched from her.

'Fiddlesticks. You require measurements and I went to get them. Naturally, Shears has them safely locked away from prying eyes.'

'Shears?' Jane frowned.

'My lady's maid,' Lady Farringdon replied impatiently, handing Jane a sheet of embossed notepaper. Jane glanced at the figures then frowned.

'There's nothing wrong, I trust? Shears is meticulous, as well as discreet.' She tutted at the girls, who were devouring the cakes as though they'd never seen food before. They smelt so delicious and not having had anything since she broke her fast, Jane was tempted to reach out and take one.

'Is there something else, Miss Haydon, or may we move on to discussing fabrics and patterns?'

'Thank you, Lady Farringdon, but in order to ensure a perfect fit, I will also need to know the measurement around your shoulders.'

'Whatever do you mean, girl? It's a corset I require, not a stole. Are you quite sure you know what you're doing?' she asked, fixing Jane with a steely look.

Chapter 9

Louisa prowled restlessly around the room. Whilst Miss Haydon's visit had been beneficial as well as proving a welcome distraction, she couldn't help her thoughts returning to Henry and what he'd told her as she was leaving Woolbrooke House. If only Papa was here so that she could discuss it with him. Desperate for reassurance, she looked across at her stepmother but she was consulting that wretched betrothal book and Louisa knew she would never understand. In her world, a lady kept her emotions well hidden at all times, whatever the circumstances.

'Are you listening, Louisa?' Charlotte asked impatiently, breaking into her thoughts.

'Sorry, Step Mama.'

'For heaven's sake come and sit down, we have so much to plan. It's bad enough your sisters chose to disappear as soon as Miss Haydon left without you moping about the place.' She waited whilst Louisa joined her at the table. 'Now, I asked if you were sure about engaging that women's services?'

'Jane? I liked her and thought her very competent. Besides, you haven't actually commissioned her yet.'

'We do not call tradespeople by their first names, Louisa,'

Charlotte rebuked. 'And you have to admit some of her questions were, well, very peculiar, to say the least.'

'I am sure Miss Haydon knows what she's doing,' Louisa replied, emphasising the words 'Miss Haydon'. 'Besides, you will be able to assess the quality of her work when she brings that toile for you to approve. You'll see then if she got the measuring process right.'

'That's true. It is always better to consider rather than make instant decisions.' Charlotte nodded, giving Louisa a pointed look. 'Now, to the guests.'

As her stepmother began running through the list of people who absolutely must be invited to the ball, many of whom she'd never even heard of, Louisa suppressed a sigh.

'We were hoping to keep the occasion quite small,' she ventured, only to receive a martyred look.

'I am not going to all this trouble for myself, you know,' Charlotte snapped. 'With your father's standing in society, to host anything less than a grand affair would be seen as insulting. Did you ask Lady Beauchamp whom she wishes to invite?'

'I did and she thanks you for your thoughtfulness. Henry will bring her guest list when he next visits.'

'Which will be when?'

'Very soon, I hope. He has an important meeting to attend first,' she replied, trying not to recall his grave expression when they'd parted or the news he might have when next she saw him. 'In the meantime, what's next on your list, Step Mama?' she asked quickly, not wishing to discuss Henry any further.

'We need to hire a musical band for the dancing and I've had the most marvellous idea. I'm going to have a bandstand built in the grounds. The weather should be clement come the end of April,' Charlotte cried, her grey eyes sparkling with excitement. It wouldn't dare be anything but, Louisa thought. 'I shall have arrangements made immediately.'

'Don't you think we should wait until Papa returns?' she ventured, staring at the woman in alarm. A bandstand sounded expensive and should the event have to be deferred or even cancelled it would be money ill spent. Besides, Papa loved his gardens and was particular about how they were laid out. 'He might not like the idea.'

'Rubbish, Edwin will agree to anything that makes me— us happy,' Charlotte amended quickly. 'Besides, if it is already under way, it will be a fait accompli. You know, Louisa, you'd do well to learn from me the methods by which a woman achieves her own way. It makes one's life so much easier, not to mention enjoyable,' she said, writing more in the precious book which she'd allegedly given to Louisa and yet had never let her see inside.

Louisa stared out of the window wishing she too had made her escape when Jane had left. The room was stifling hot as Charlotte insisted every fire in the house be banked up at all times. Reluctantly, she turned back to listen to the next item on this seemingly interminable list. The sooner they got through it, the sooner she could disappear.

'The banquet. We'll need to devise a menu with Mrs Spick but I already have ideas for that.' Naturally, Louisa thought, feeling sorry for the housekeeper who, despite her best endeavours, hardly ever got a word in about anything. 'As for drink, your papa can get Ferris to check the cellar is adequately stocked with champagne, claret, cognac and port, etc. Cookson can make her special summer punch and perhaps an elderflower cordial.' As Charlotte's voice droned on, it was evident to Louisa that, whilst it might be her betrothal ball, she was not going to have much, if any, say in the arrangements.

Still, her attire would be her own decision. Listening to Jane earlier, she'd decided that a corset and chemise in blush taffeta would complement her colouring and sit well under the green silk dress she intended having made up to the design in Godey's. Louisa wanted to look sophisticated and enticing so that Henry would remember her that way. She was just imagining herself dancing in the moonlight, Henry's arms tightly around her, when Charlotte's strident tones cut through her daydream.

'For heaven's sake, Louisa, do stop fidgeting.'

'I'm sorry, Step Mama, I need some fresh air so perhaps we could finish this later,' she said, rising to her feet. 'I really must call upon Mr and Mrs Gill and find out how Wilfred's leg is. Ellery can accompany me; with Papa away the poor boy will probably be glad of a walk.'

'Well, if you consider that more important than planning your betrothal ball, then go ahead. I'm sure I can manage.' As Charlotte gave a long-suffering sigh then turned back to her book, Louisa stifled a grin. For all her protestations, the woman was never happier than when she was left alone to make the plans she wanted.

Carrying a small basket of provisions and with Ellery

padding at her side, Louisa hardly noticed the brisk wind as she made her way towards the cottages where the estate workers lived. As she waved to Reed, the head gardener, who was happily potting up some plants in the hothouse, she was reminded of Jane Haydon thinking she'd smelled lavender.

She couldn't have known that Nettlecombe had a resident ghost, purported to be that of Charles II who, according to the records, sought shelter back in 1651. His infrequent manifestations were detected only by the waft of lavender-scented water, although she herself had never experienced it. The worrying thing was that it was said he only paid a visit prior to tragedy befalling the family, and only those of an incredibly sensitive nature smelled it. Obviously, Jane had picked up on something although Louisa was certain she hadn't actually seen anything.

She'd really taken to the woman who'd not only been helpful but had a sense of purpose about her. The trouble was it had made Louisa realise that apart from preparing for her betrothal ball and ensuing wedding, she had no real purpose of her own. Now she felt restless, questioning what she was to do with her life.

Samuel Gill was also restless. Over the past few months, he'd seen how the running of the estate could be improved, and now he was keen to implement some of his ideas. Sitting by the fire in the living room of their cosy cottage, which although one of the largest on the estate was modest, he'd tried to explain this to his father.

'Just cos you're keeping things ticking over while I'm out

of action, doesn't mean you can go round changing things, Samuel,' Wilfred grunted, glaring at his bandaged leg that was propped up on a stool.

'Keeping things ticking over?' he cried. 'I'll have you know everything's been running efficiently, and without me having to bother you.'

'I keep telling yer, I'm incapacitated not ill, boy,' his father snapped, lighting his pipe and jamming it into his mouth. Fighting down his exasperation, Sam tried appealing to his better nature.

'Things are moving on, Father. You wouldn't want Nettlecombe to be stuck in the past.' His father continued puffing his pipe and staring into the fire for some moments. Finally, he turned to Sam.

'I've been running things the same way for the past twenty years and—'

'That's it precisely, everything has stayed the same.'

'Now come along, you two, no falling out,' Edith chuckled, coming in from the scullery with a basket of clean laundry.

'And you can stay out of it,' Wilfred retorted.

'It don't do no harm to listen, Wilf,' she cajoled, bending down to retrieve the flat iron that was heating on the hearth. Spitting on it and giving a nod of satisfaction when it sizzled, she took it over to the table by the window on which an old sheet had been spread. 'Why, I remember you was just the same when your father was manager here. You came up with all those "new fangly" ideas as he called them, and got just as cross as young Sam is now, when he wouldn't listen.' Knowing not to push her luck, she turned her attention to smoothing the creases from his shirt.

'Well, thanks for the tea, Ma, but I've work to do,' Sam said, getting to his feet. 'Work that I could get done in half the time given the chance.' The older man snorted.

'There'll be a nice bit of rabbit stew for your tea,' she told him.

Sam forced a smile and strode from the room. Why did his father have to be so obstinate? Hoping the biting wind would help cool his temper, he stamped his way past the neighbouring cottages and on across the field that abutted the manor. Lost in his thoughts, he didn't notice the dog until he was almost upon him.

'Hello, old boy,' he said, bending to stroke Ellery's head.

'Good afternoon, Sam,' Louisa called, making her way towards him. Despite her stepmother's insistence that staff be addressed by their surname, having played with Sam and his sister Mary as a child, she refused to stop calling them by their first names.

'Good afternoon to you too,' he said, his face relaxing into a grin.

'That's better, you looked like you wanted to kill someone,' she teased. 'How is your father?'

'Moody and stubborn,' Sam replied. 'But Winnie assures us his leg is healing. He's talking about returning to work again next week, but in truth he can barely hobble about.'

'Poor Wilfred. I've brought a few provisions to help tide your mother over. There's one of Mrs Cookson's meat and potato pies.' She smiled, knowing they were his weakness.

'That's kind of you. Ma will be most obliged, and so will I come supper. Do you want me to take that?' he asked, nodding to her basket.

'Actually, I was hoping she might have the kettle on the boil. It's cosy chatting over one of her mugs of tea and you like lying beside the fire without being hassled, don't you, Ellery?' As if he understood every word, the dog barked, making them laugh.

'Who'd have thought Lady Louisa would prefer to sit in our humble home rather than take afternoon tea at the grand manor,' he teased.

'That's it though, Sam, yours is a home. Somewhere to relax. Besides, your ma is easy to talk to.' Knowing things had been difficult since Lady Farringdon with her grand ideas had moved into the manor, Sam nodded sympathetically.

'Ma thinks of you as another daughter and she'll be pleased of the company, especially now Mary's married and got her own place. How is the handsome Henry Beauchamp? Did you enjoy your weekend at Woolbrooke?'

'Henry's well, thank you,' Louisa said, refusing to rise to his ribbing. 'And I had such a lovely time I extended my visit. In fact, I only returned yesterday evening because Step Mama had arranged for us to be fitted for some new clothes.'

'And all went well?' he asked.

'Yes,' she replied, giving him a strange look. 'Although why you would be interested in such things, I really don't know. Goodness, this wind is keen,' she shivered. 'I'd better get moving.'

Feeling somewhat brighter at the prospect of a slice of Mrs Cookson's pie, Sam continued making his way towards the barn where the cart was waiting. It wasn't really his job to take tools for sharpening but it gave him an excuse to visit his friend Tom in the village. Of course, it had nothing to do with the pretty girl whose big blue eyes had beguiled him, he told himself. Then, almost as if he'd conjured her up, he spotted her, or rather he saw her bonnet and pink cape bobbing above the hedge as she made her way round the path from the servants' entrance.

Breaking into a run, he harnessed the pony and caught up with her just as she turned into the lane leading to the village.

'Can I offer you a lift?' he asked, heart thumping as she smiled up at him. Her cheeks were flushed but whether from the wind or something else, he wasn't sure. To his surprise she didn't even demur when he took her bag as she climbed up beside him.

'Your visit must have gone well if you're only just leaving,' he said.

'Mrs Cookson insisted that I eat luncheon with her in the staff dining room. I never realised the manor had so many servants,' she cried, shaking her head in astonishment.

'That woman's a treasure,' he agreed. 'So, how did you find the indomitable Lady Farringdon?'

'Precisely that, indomitable,' she said, sighing. 'She made me feel as if I didn't know my job.'

'Which you do,' he told her.

'Of course I do. Madame Pittier would never have let me come here otherwise. I just hope I haven't let her down.' Slowing the cart to take the bend, he glanced at her from under his cap. She looked so despondent, he wanted to reach out and take her hand but knew, even if he found the courage, it would be inappropriate. Then, like a dam bursting,

Jane's anger came flooding out. 'Nothing I did pleased Lady Farringdon. She even questioned my methods, saying she was reserving judgement until I proved my competence.'

'Ouch, that's a bit much even for her,' he replied. 'Still, I dare say you are going to show her.'

'I most certainly am,' she retorted, and Sam had to stifle a smile as he saw her chin jut out determinedly. 'Her stepdaughters were lovely though.'

'Yes, they've had quite a lot to put up with recently. Oh, bad timing,' he muttered as, once again, the sound of angry voices carried from the quarry below. 'It sounds as if you're not the only one who's had a bad day.'

'Is it always like this?' She frowned.

'I've heard the Touchstone is getting even stricter.'

'The what?'

'He's the man who measures then assesses the value of the stone once it's been passed as sound by the Tapstone.'

'I was woken by the workers marching by the window at some unearthly hour.'

'They have to start early to get in their fourteen-hour shift.'

'Are you saying they work beneath ground all that time then have to queue to have their work passed and valued before they get paid?' she asked, her eyes widening in horror.

'That's about it. It's a hard life and if they don't suffer an accident, they'll die of the drink.'

'They have money for liquor?'

'No, they don't, but it's the only way they know how to relax. Of course, it means there's no money for their wives to feed the children or pay the rent.'

'But that's terrible,' Jane cried. 'It certainly puts my troubles into perspective. Beatrice was saying earlier that she didn't intend to marry and I'm beginning to think she's right.'

As Sam turned to look at her, he was seized by a sudden urge to make her change her mind.

Chapter 10

Much as she felt for the quarrymen, Jane had little time to ponder on their plight, or wonder why Sam Gill always appeared with his cart when she needed a lift, for in order to secure the commission she had to present herself to Lady Farringdon with the finished toile at ten thirty sharp the next morning.

'Blimey, maid, yer'll be sewing all night,' Ida declared looking out of the window, as Jane explained. 'It's getting dimpsy already. Yer'd better sit here and I'll light me flash.'

'Your what?' Jane asked. 'And if I start now, you'll soon be wanting to clear the table for supper.'

'This is me flash,' she said, taking a glass globe from the shelf. It was filled with water and as the candle was lit, Jane saw that it intensified the light from the flame. 'All us lacemakers and dressmakers use these else we'd never be able to finish our work this time of year. As for supper, well, it won't hurt to eat on our laps for once.'

'Thank you, Mrs Somers,' Jane replied, staring at the woman in surprise.

'Not at all, now I knows what yer makes, I'da no reason to worry. It's poor Jeanie the staymaker who needs to watch out,' the woman sighed.

'Surely you're not in competition?'

'Course we is, it's our livelihoods. Like I says last night, no work, no money, no food. Poor Jeanie's already suffering now the clothier's started bringing them ready-mades when he visits. Has to do a spot of cleaning up at the vicarage to get by, and with her bad back as well.' She shook her head. 'Now let's make a start, eh?' She sank into the chair on the other side of the table and stared at Jane expectantly.

'It's very kind of you, but I've so much to do,' Jane said, opening her bag.

'All the more reason for me to help then.' Seeing the gleam in the woman's eye as she began setting out her things on the table, Jane's heart sank. Clearly she couldn't tell Mrs Somers what to do in her own home, she thought, surreptitiously checking the tablecloth for any crumbs.

'As I'm sure you know this is very exacting work, so if you could thread a needle that would be really helpful,' she said passing Madame's little silver case and bobbin across the table. Then while she was occupied, Jane took out the bundle of calico, spread it out then consulted her notebook.

'I'da done it,' the woman cried, holding the needle up some minutes later. 'What can I do now?'

'Would you mind counting me out fifteen pins?' Jane asked, indicating the little wooden box. 'I know it doesn't seem much to a skilled seamstress like yourself, but it would save me time.'

'Don't mind what I do, girl. Unlike a dog, Ida's never too old to learn new tricks,' she chortled. 'Can't wait to see people's faces when I tell them I've helped make her ladyship's underpinnings.'

'I think we should be discreet,' Jane said, quickly.

'Ooh, a secret job, even better,' the woman crowed delightedly. 'I remember when…' Jane let Mrs Somers' reminiscences go over her head and focused on the toile. Luckily, after a while, her interest waned. 'Me stomach thinks me throat's been cut,' she said, getting up and stirring the pot hanging above the paltry fire. 'Good, almost warm enough. Seeing as how I ain't got no fresh bread, I'll toast the old crusts.'

'That will be very nice,' Jane said, feeling guilty she hadn't been given any money to pay for her board. 'I'm sure you'll soon be reimbursed for my stay.'

'Yeah, and Athame might fly,' the woman snorted. 'Though with that cat, you never know. Now bring them chairs over and we'll eat. Then you can tell me how you found her ladyship.'

Although she would have preferred to press on with her cutting out, Jane moved over towards the fire, surprised to find she was hungry despite having enjoyed Mrs Cookson's pie earlier. She couldn't help comparing this damp little cottage, its few twigs smouldering in the tiny grate, to the more salubrious manor and flames burning brightly in the huge marble fireplace.

'Course, like I said, Lord Farringdon's first wife were a real lady. Always did what she could to help the villagers in the combe. So how did you find this one?'

'Gracious,' Jane replied, trying to be tactful.

'Very polite, I'm sure,' she chuckled. 'I'da bet she put yer through yer paces.'

'She certainly will if I don't finish that toile,' Jane smiled ruefully. 'Thank you for supper but if you'll excuse me, I really must get on.'

'Here, give us yer dish,' the woman said, stifling a yawn. 'I'll clean up in the morning. Now, if I can't be of any further help, I'll make me way up the wooden hill. Don't forget to blow the candle out afore yer go to bed, if there's any left, that is,' she added, frowning at the dwindling stump.

It was gone two in the morning by the time Jane had measured, cut and sewn up the toile to her satisfaction. Freezing cold, for the fire had long gone out, she rose and stretched her aching limbs. With a final glance at her work, she left it on the table to check in the daylight, blew out the candle and guided by the moonlight, made her way to bed. It was just as cold upstairs with frost already patterning the windows but Jane was so exhausted, she hardly noticed.

Vaguely Jane heard the ring of boots on the cobbles outside, but it was only when the clock chimed seven o'clock that she forced herself to get up and dressed. Making her way down to the living room she was met by a howling gale.

'Ah, yer up then,' Ida Somers said, coming through the open doors. 'I've spent yer board money in advance,' she said, gleefully brandishing a fresh loaf of bread. 'Thought we'd have a decent bite of breakfast, what with you working half the night. Oh, Athame, what yer doing up there?' she cried. Following her glance, Jane's hand flew to her mouth when she saw the cat perched on the table, its enormous paws kneading her toile. Rushing across the room, she lifted the protesting animal down, then heedless of its hissing and spitting, held up the material to the light.

'Oh no,' she cried in dismay. 'It's covered in black hair and muddy marks.'

'What's wrong with yer, Athame, it's not like yer to behave like this.' But the animal gave a baleful glare, padded across the floor and disappeared through the open door.

'It's ruined. I can't possibly take it to Lady Farringdon like this,' Jane wailed.

'I'll see what I can do,' the woman said briskly. 'We can't have all our hard work going to waste,' she added, seizing the toile. 'Don't take on so, it's nothing a little gin won't solve.'

'Gin?' she shrieked. 'I can't be drinking gin at this time of the morning. I'm meant to be seeing Lady Farringdon in less than three hours.'

'Not to drink, yer nink – though by the looks of yer it would probably do yer good. Look, put that iron to heat in front of the fire,' she told her. Then snatching a bottle from the shelf, she disappeared into the tiny scullery.

Jane did as she'd been asked, then paced round the tiny room. How could she face Lady Farringdon? She could hardly tell her the toile for her corset had been ruined by a cat. Perhaps she should go home straight away. But whatever would Madame say? She'd trusted her and, despite her best efforts, Jane had let her down.

'Here yer go,' Mrs Somers said, hurrying back into the room. 'Just needs a run over with the flat iron and it'll be good as new.'

'Really?' Jane asked, hardly daring to believe it.

'I'da said so, didn't I? Now come and have some bread then the iron should be hot enough to use,' the woman said, taking a sharp knife from the drawer and hacking into the loaf. 'Young Sam picking you up again?'

'Yes, he has some tools to collect.'

'Does he now?' she said, giving Jane a knowing look.

***

Jane held her breath as Lady Farringdon inspected the toile. By the time Mrs Somers had pressed the material, even Jane struggled to see where it had been marked. Although there was a slight mordant smell to it.

'It looks all right but of course we shall have to see if it fits,' she said, tugging on the bell. 'Although I must say I don't really approve of this rough material.'

'I used the best quality calico, Lady Farringdon. But of course, the choice and colour of fabric will be yours.'

'If I choose to place my order. Ah, Shears,' she said, turning to the thin woman dressed in a fitted dark blue dress with lace collar, who was waiting in the doorway. 'We will take this to the anteroom of the Quartz Rose Chamber to see how it fits. Well, come along,' she urged, as Jane hesitated, not sure whether she was meant to follow. 'And bring those fabric samples, Miss Haydon.'

To her surprise Lady Farringdon's dressing room was almost as pink as Madame's rooms, although this was more lavishly furnished.

'Has this been washed?' the maid asked, frowning at the toile as Lady Farringdon disappeared behind a screen. She held it to her nose and frowned. 'Never known calico to smell like this.'

'I thought it only right to ensure it was scrupulously clean,' Jane replied, her heart beating faster under the woman's scrutiny. Then, to her relief, Shears was summoned to assist her ladyship.

It was some moments before Jane was called, and after a brief inspection and adjustment, she let out the breath she hadn't realised she was holding. The fit was perfect.

'It's a different shape to the ones I usually wear,' the woman frowned.

'You wanted one that sits well under a ball gown and as you are aware, Lady Farringdon, skirts are now becoming fuller. This cut is absolutely perfect for your slender form, if you don't mind me saying.'

'I suppose it does do my youthful figure justice,' the lady grudgingly admitted, turning this way and that in front of the long mirror. 'Now let me see those samples.' There was a pause while she studied them. 'Tell Madame Pittier I'll have my corset made up in cream silk. It is always my colour of choice.'

'Of course, Lady Farringdon.' Jane began writing in her notebook then stopped, wondering if she dared to put forward an opinion, yet hadn't Madame taught her to always offer the client the best advice?

'Well, what is it?' the woman snapped. 'I don't have all day, girl.'

'I was wondering if you had considered pink. The rose blush would sit so well against your skin tone and enhance your youthful bloom. It is quite the choice this season, which, as I can see from this wonderful room, you already know.'

'I don't listen to sales script, Miss Haydon,' Lady Farringdon replied, grey eyes narrowed. 'My choice has always been accepted without question, has it not, Shears?'

'Yes, m'lady. You have impeccable taste and I cannot believe anyone would dare to suggest otherwise,' the maid said, giving Jane a patronising look.

'But I didn't mean—' she began, but Lady Farringdon held up her hand to silence her.

'The girls have been summoned to the Amber Room and Vanstone will assist with their measuring. Then you can go away and make up a toile for each of them for me to inspect.'

'Yes, Lady Farringdon,' Jane replied, hurrying from the room. How could she have been so stupid as to try and advise a woman who clearly knew what she wanted? And supposing she now changed her mind about placing her order?

The girls' maid, whom they called Vanny, proved to be friendly and helpful, providing their measurements and assisting with the extra ones Jane required. Bea laughed when Jane meticulously recorded them in Madame's notebook.

'Goodness, you're as bad as Step Mama and her books.'

'What was that you said, Beatrice?' Lady Farringdon asked, sailing into the room.

'Erm, just that what Miss Haydon has learned about corsets from her books was fascinating,' the girl stuttered, staring pleadingly at Jane.

'Then perhaps you could enlighten me on these fascinating facts, Miss Haydon.'

'Of course, Lady Farringdon,' Jane replied, thanking her lucky stars Madame had insisted she learn the history of underpinning. 'The corset had its origin in Italy. It was later introduced into France by Catherine de Medici where the women of court embraced it.'

'There, girls, did I not tell you to embrace your corsets?' Lady Farringdon purred.

'Must have missed that,' Bea muttered.

'In fact, it is time to have Sarah and Maria fitted. One is never too young to learn about posture,' the woman declared, ignoring their incredulous looks. 'Now, Miss Haydon, time is getting on so I will see you tomorrow to examine the toiles.'

'Very well, Lady Farringdon. I can have them ready by early afternoon,' Jane replied, knowing there would be no time to lose as she had to catch the four o'clock stagecoach back to Exeter.

'I am at home tomorrow afternoon,' Lady Farringdon said.

'Well, that's good then,' Jane smiled.

'I don't think you understand, Miss Haydon. I said I shall be *At Home* then.'

'That means she's entertaining,' Victoria whispered.

'How many times must I tell you it's rude to whisper, Victoria,' she admonished. 'I shall expect you at ten thirty tomorrow, Miss Haydon. Good morning.'

Gathering up her things, Jane quickly left the room. How could she possibly make three toiles by tomorrow morning? It was nearly noon now, she thought, panicking when she caught sight of the clock in the hallway as she headed down the stairs to retrieve her cape.

'Hello, dearie, have you come for more of my pie?'

'I'm afraid I don't have time for luncheon today, Mrs Cookson. Even though your pie was absolutely delicious.'

'Nonsense, everyone needs to eat. Are you quite well? You're looking a bit peaky,' she asked, taking a closer look at Jane.

'Not really. I've to make three toiles by first thing tomorrow but—'

'Calm down, dearie,' Mrs Cookson said, taking Jane by the arm and leading her into a room next to the kitchen. 'Bring through two mugs of tea with sugar in both, please, Dottie.'

'Yes, Mrs Cookson,' a young voice called.

'Now sit yourself down and tell me exactly what the problem is,' the woman said, settling her ample body onto the wooden chair.

'By the time I get back to the village it will already be growing dark and although Mrs Somers was kind enough to let me use her table and flash, it was still hard to see and it took me all my time to make one toile, and now I've three to make up for her ladyship. I daren't fail, Madame Pittier is depending upon me. And I fear I've already upset Lady Farringdon.'

'Well that's not hard to do. Steady, Dottie,' the woman said, as the little maid, clearly anxious to please, hurried in with a laden tray. 'More haste, more waste,' she tutted as the girl set the mugs down clumsily, causing liquid to spill over onto the table. 'That girl is well named.' The woman shook her head. 'Now drink up and we'll ponder this problem.'

Grateful for the woman's kindness, yet not sure how she could possibly help, Jane sipped her drink. As a sudden crash sounded from the kitchen, followed by an angry shout, she looked up and noticed for the first time that the room, although clean, was basically furnished. Clearly the opulence of upstairs didn't extend to the basement rooms.

'I'm pleased to see you have time to entertain, Mrs Cookson.' The strident voice preceded the appearance of a reed-thin woman whose stern expression perfectly matched the severe black of her hat and coat. 'And who, may I ask, are you?' she asked, glaring at Jane with eyes as dark as coal.

Chapter 11

'Miss Haydon,' Jane replied, getting to her feet and holding out her hand politely. Ignoring it, the woman turned to the cook.

'Lady Farringdon asked me to see she was given refreshment before she leaves,' Mrs Cookson said, clearly not in the least put out by the woman's manner. 'This is Mrs Spick, housekeeper here at Nettlecombe,' she told Jane.

'And she said you were to join her, did she?' Mrs Spick replied, her attention still focused on the cook.

'She asked me to see she was well looked after, yes. Anyway, don't let me detain you on your afternoon off, Mrs Spick.'

'Well, I do have an important meeting to attend, otherwise I might have investigated this further. Get Quick to pick me up outside St Winifred's at four thirty. And tell him not to be late. He kept me waiting in the cold for three minutes last week,' the woman sniffed.

'Right you are, Mrs Spick,' the cook replied. She waited until the housekeeper had left then turned to Jane. 'Don't mind her, she gets puffed up on her afternoon off, thinks this place can't run without her. Anyhow, I've had a thought. You can use the sewing room. It's next to the laundry and has a good-sized window. Come on, I'll show you where it is and then send Dottie along with some bread and cheese. You can't work on an empty stomach.'

'This is perfect,' Jane cried, looking around the airy room with its large table that looked as if it had been scrubbed within an inch of its life.

'So, you're staying with Ida Somers then?'

'Yes, that's right, for three nights. She's been very kind,' Jane replied, omitting to mention the woman's unfriendly reception when she'd first arrived.

'Well that's a surprise, I must say. Only Winnie and that cat of hers have been allowed over her doorstep since her husband was killed at the quarry. Nasty business, that were.' She shook her head. 'Still, happen some company will do her good. Anyhow, her cot is only a spit from the church so, if you come down to the kitchen just before four o'clock you can cadge a lift into Combe with Quick.'

'I can't thank you enough for your kindness, Mrs Cookson,' Jane replied.

'We all helps each other here, well, downstairs, anyhow. Now, I'd best go and see what other chaos Dottie has managed to create. That girl, it's like having a whirlwind in my kitchen.'

Opening Madame's capacious bag, Jane carefully set out her tools before spreading the calico along the length of the table. Then she began the painstaking process of pinning, measuring and checking ready for cutting and was so absorbed in her work that the appearance of the young girl made her jump.

'Mrs Cookson said she'd be obliged if you'd bring the empties back when you comes,' she muttered, almost stumbling into the room. Her hands were shaking as she set down the tray and Jane could only watch in horror as the beaker toppled over, spilling its contents over the calico.

'Oh no,' the maid cried, dabbing frantically at the cloth with her apron. 'Mrs Spick said if I spilt anything else, I'd have to go.'

'Don't worry, Dottie,' Jane assured her, seeing the girl was about to burst into tears. 'It's only water, isn't it?'

'Yes, but it's special cos it comes from the well in the garden and Mrs Cookson said it was pure and would refresh you,' Dottie gabbled, as she continued wiping furiously. 'It's only wet on this one end. I can run and get one of the flat irons to dry it off,' she offered, looking at Jane hopefully.

'If you would,' Jane smiled. 'Don't look so worried, Dottie, there's no harm done.'

'Yous not cross?' Dottie asked, staring at Jane incredulously.

'It was an accident. Look, go and bring that iron while I eat my luncheon,' she smiled reassuringly. As the maid scuttled away, Jane didn't know whether to laugh at the irony or cry in frustration. What were the chances of virtually the same thing happening twice in one day? Perhaps the job was jinxed, she thought, picking at the tempting array of bread, cheese, ham and pickles that were set out on the tray. Unbelievably, after all that had happened, she found she was hungry and the food was so delicious she savoured every morsel. She was just wiping her hands on her handkerchief when the door opened.

'I's sorry I bin so long but Mrs Cookson needed me to set the table. I was trying to be as quick as possible but I dropped the napkins and she told me off again. Then Ferris called her into the dining room, so I snatched up the iron and ran. It's nice and hot cos it was by the range,' she grinned, holding it over the material.

'Thank you, Dottie, but I'll do that,' Jane said quickly taking it from her then running it over a spare piece of cloth to test both the heat and cleanliness of the plate. Satisfied, she then gently pressed the iron over the calico while the girl watched in silence. 'There, all dry. You'd never know now, would you?'

'Will you tell Mrs Cookson?' Dottie asked tremulously. 'Only it's me first week and I already bin in so much trouble. It's not as if I don't try and hurry to do everything.'

'Don't worry, Dottie, my lips are sealed. And I know how difficult it is learning to be a good maid.'

'You do?' she gasped.

'I was a maid of all to Madame Pittier before being trained as a corsetière.'

'But yous all posh,' Dottie cried, staring at her incredulously.

'I'm not really. But I have worked hard to get where I am. Like you, I was so anxious to please I'd try and do everything at once. Then I found the thing to do was take my time over each job, and do you know what?'

'What?'

'Everything got done without any mishaps. Why don't you try that and see if it works for you? First though, you'd better put that iron back before anyone notices it's missing.'

Poor Dottie, Jane thought as she resumed her task of checking everything was accurately measured before making the first cut. How well she remembered trying to please Madame by rushing through each job, only to spill and drop things just as Dottie had. Satisfied everything was correct, Jane picked up the scissors and was soon so focused on cutting the material, there was no room for any further reminiscence.

When the first toile was finished to her satisfaction, she immediately began on the next, but the shadows were already creeping into the corners of the room and the hands on the clock seemed to be racing around the dial at an alarming rate. Knowing it would be prudent to cut everything out whilst she had access to the large, clean table then finish the stitching back at the cottage, she took up the scissors once more. Then, with the light fading fast, she packed everything into the bag and carrying the tray in her other hand, made her way to the kitchen.

'How did you get on, dear?' Mrs Cookson asked, looking up from the large pan she was stirring.

'I've made good progress, thank you. And thank you so much for the delicious food. I had no idea I was so hungry until I began eating.' The woman smiled knowingly.

'Knew you'd need some sustenance. What did you think of our reviving water?'

'It certainly made me move quickly,' Jane replied, winking at Dottie. 'It was very kind of Dottie to bring that tray to me, I'm sure she is going to make a very good maid.'

'Well, in that case you can go and fetch Miss Haydon's cape, Dottie. I can hear Quick pulling up outside.'

As the cart clattered along the path that skirted the front of the manor, Jane had time to really notice the detail of the building for the first time. With its tall chimneys and feature stone quoins, it was certainly imposing, yet even with the lights from the oil lamps glowing through the many mullioned windows, it managed to exude an air of sadness. Whereas

Sam had taken the side path, Quick headed down the main driveway and Jane's eyes widened when she saw the bronze cannons placed along the tree-lined avenue. Surely they didn't still have battles round these parts?

As Quick called to the horse and their pace increased, Jane leaned wearily back against the seat. It had been very kind of Mrs Cookson to arrange this lift for her, yet she couldn't help wishing it was the man with the mischievous hazel eyes driving the cart.

'Oh,' she squealed, as something large and dark flew towards her out of the darkness, almost brushing her cheeks. She waved it away only to be attacked by another thing with great wings. 'What are they?' she gasped, as it emitted a high-pitched squeak.

'Them be the flitter-mice,' Quick laughed. 'Or bats to the uninitiated,' he added, seeing her puzzled expression. 'Live in the quarry, hundreds of them. Biggest in the land they be, but then there's plenty of dead bodies for them to feast on down in them caves.' As Jane shuddered, he gave a guffaw that echoed loudly in the darkness and she wished even more that it was the friendly assistant estate manager driving the cart. She wondered if she dared hope that he would appear to give her a lift in the morning and crossed her fingers that he might.

***

Sam, meanwhile, was toying with his supper. Despite finding jobs to do close to the manor, he'd missed seeing Jane leave and it had left him feeling empty and frustrated. He'd really fallen for the girl whose keen sense of humour belied her gentle manner. With dark hair sleek as a raven's wing and eyes blue as a summer sky, she was unlike any other girl he'd ever met. Tomorrow she would be returning to Exeter and the need to see her before she left was burning away inside him. He'd run out of tools to take for sharpening and was trying to think of another excuse to drive into Combe first thing in the morning, when he was brought back to the present by his father banging his fist on the table.

'Are yer listening to me, Samuel Gill?' Wilfred asked, pushing his plate away and taking up his pipe.

'Yes, Father,' he nodded, quickly finishing the last of his pie, which for once he'd hardly tasted.

'Good. So yer'll know tomorrow's task is to make a start on the coppicing. Take the cart up to Blackbury Wood and meet up with the woodsmen at first light.' Sam stared at his father in dismay.

'Could it wait until Friday, Father? I've something else planned…'

'No, it flippin' can't wait until Friday. Trees don't stop growing just cos you might have something else planned, and you of all people should know that this cold weather's the best time to coppice,' Wilfred grunted, tapping tobacco into the bulb and looking at the fire in frustration. 'Bloomin' leg. Get me a light, son.' Glad of the distraction, Sam jumped up, lit a spill and handed it to his father. Then, while his father lit his pipe, he frantically tried to think of a good reason to go into Combe first thing. His mother, clearing the table, gave him a puzzled look but he shrugged and sat back down.

'With me out of action, the men will be looking to yer for

the final say in which of the wands to cut for wattle work and what thicker timbers will be suitable for rafters. The villagers rely on us to get their roofs repaired this time of year and won't thank yer if they has to wait.'

'Surely one day won't make any difference?' Sam asked.

'And yer have more important things to do than help me follow Lord Farringdon's orders, do yer?'

'Well no, but…'

'There's no argument, son. His lordship returns in a couple of weeks and will be expecting me to tell him what work needs doing on which cottage. And he'll be trusting me to have the materials ready. I've never let him down yet and don't intend to now. Remember to take the bow-saw, bill and hedging hooks.'

'I know what I need to take, Father. I've been helping you for long enough, haven't I?' he snapped.

'Yer have, so I really don't see the point of this conversation. And after all yer said t'other day about making changes around here an' all,' he snorted. 'If yer wants to take over from me, and it won't be till I'm cold in me coffin, yer'd do well to prove yer knows what goes on. The cycle of the seasons and rhythm of the land always stays the same,' he huffed, clamping his lips tighter round his pipe.

'I'll pack you extra food, in case you're late back for supper,' his mother said, looking at Sam knowingly.

He nodded gratefully, although his mind was already working out how far the wood was from the Horseshoes Inn where Jane would be catching the stagecoach.

Chapter 12

Jane followed Ferris up the stairs from the servants' wing to the more opulent hallway with its deep red carpet and walls lined with pictures of the Farringdon family from years gone by. She would have loved to have stopped and studied some of the stylish attire of the day, but the straight-backed butler was already marching towards the Amber Room.

In order to finish the three toiles, she'd been up all night, sewing by the light of the flash, and she just hoped her work would pass the eagle eye of her ladyship and she could return to Madame Pittier with the commission. Much to Mrs Somers' indignation, there'd been no sign of Sam this morning and Jane had had to trek the two miles over frosty ground lugging her bags to reach the manor. She shouldn't have been disappointed he hadn't shown up for they'd made no arrangements, yet she was.

'Miss Haydon, m'lady,' he announced solemnly, and Jane had to suppress a smile as the clock behind them chimed the half hour.

'Good morning, Lady Farringdon,' she said, smiling. She stared around, surprised to find there was no sign of the girls. The woman nodded and gestured to the small table in front of her chair.

'Perhaps you would lay out your work so I can inspect it.'

'Of course, Lady Farringdon,' Jane replied, taking the toiles from her bag then standing back while the woman picked up each one and examined it with the same thoroughness Madame would have done.

'Well, they look all right but, of course, the proof will come when we see if they fit. You have the fabric samples?'

'Of course,' Jane began but the woman was already sweeping from the room, leaving her to gather up everything and follow.

'I have requested everyone assemble in the Moonstone Chamber,' Lady Farringdon announced, after they'd climbed the sweeping staircase hung with the largest chandelier Jane had ever seen. Even in the harsh light of a winter's morning it sparkled like the frost outside and she couldn't help wondering who had the job of cleaning it. For everyone's sake she hoped it wasn't Dottie. The woman paused before throwing open the door to a room furnished in a blend of silver and white-blue tones where the three girls were sitting on a velvet day bed. They were wearing silk robes that echoed these tones and Jane thought they looked like dainty little fairies. Behind them stood Vanny who smiled in welcome.

'Hello, Jane,' they chorused. Then ignoring the look of disapproval from their stepmother, they clamoured round her demanding to see their toiles.

'Oh, they're white,' Bea murmured.

'Of course, they are, dummy,' Victoria laughed. 'Jane has to make sure they fit us before she makes the real thing. Weren't you listening?'

'That's quite enough. Please go behind the screens and try them on. Vanstone, call me when they are ready to be inspected.'

'We're not in the army, Step Mama,' Bea protested, as she took the calico garment and disappeared behind one of the screens. The others did the same and, before long, squeals of laughter filled the room.

'Bet you're glad Henry can't see you looking like that,' Bea called.

'Beatrice,' Lady Farringdon reproved, her lips tightening into a line, 'I will not tolerate such unseemly talk.' A muttered retort was followed by more giggling until, with Vanny's calm intervention, order was restored.

'They all fit like gloves, m'lady,' the maid pronounced, appearing some minutes later.

'I think that is for me to decide,' Lady Farringdon replied. 'Come, Miss Haydon.'

With a little adjusting and final appraisal, Jane was happy the toiles fitted and turned to tell Lady Farringdon.

'Clearly, I can see that,' the woman tutted. 'Change back into your gowns and we will see about colour,' she told the girls. 'Miss Haydon, you must have the samples and your notebook to hand.'

'I've already decided I shall have red,' Bea announced, emerging from behind the screen.

'You most will certainly not,' Lady Farringdon retorted. 'You will choose something suitable for a girl of seventeen, otherwise it will be the usual.'

'How about this one?' Jane suggested, surreptitiously indicating the brightest pink.

'What colour is that? I can't see from here.'

'It's called blush, Lady Farringdon, and I think, being the next step up from the usual creamy colour, that would be most appropriate for a young lady of seventeen.'

'Very well. One corset and chemise in blush for Beatrice.' As the girl gave her a triumphant look, Jane began writing in her notebook in order to hide her smile.

'It's the charcoal with matching chemise for me,' Victoria said.

'Very well. Louisa?'

'The gold, I think,' she replied, holding the swatch against her skin and looking at Jane who nodded.

'Right, Miss Haydon, you may tell Madame Pittier I will grant her the commission.' Jane's heart leapt but Lady Farringdon hadn't finished speaking. 'However, that is on the understanding that she makes the garments herself then delivers them in person, shall we say in one month's time. If the garments meet with my satisfaction, I will then discuss my requirements for Sarah and Maria.'

'Oh,' Jane murmured.

'Now, if there is nothing else, I need to prepare myself for this afternoon.'

'Well actually, Lady Farringdon, I have been staying with Mrs Somers in the village and I understand she has yet to be paid—' The woman held up her hand to stop Jane from speaking, then with a look of disdain she swept from the room.

'Well,' Jane cried.

'Step Mama will never discuss anything so vulgar as money,' Louisa explained, but her sympathetic look told Jane she understood. 'It is always better to address matters involving finance to Papa… I mean, Lord Farringdon, of course.'

'Don't worry about Step Mama, Jane. I think you're a real friend getting her to approve my blush colour like that. At least I'll look grown up even if the perishing corset hurts like hell when I ride Firecracker.'

'Actually, there is a pattern designed to allow for extra movement of the body when riding a horse,' Jane told her.

'Really? That would make life much more comfortable,' she cried, eyes shining.

'I'll have to ask Madame Pittier to bring her book of patterns when she delivers your finished garments,' Jane said, making a note in her book.

'I wish it was you coming back,' Victoria sighed. 'You understand what we want.'

'I agree. You even took the time to explain that the corset we need depends on the style of gown we intend wearing.'

'And I took that into account. Now that waistlines are rising again you won't even have to be so tightly laced,' Jane confirmed. 'Did you not notice the difference between your toiles?'

'No,' they chorused, looking at one another in astonishment.

'And Step Mama didn't spot any either.' Bea smiled, clapping her hands in glee. 'Oh Jane, I do hope we will see you again.'

'I hope so too,' she replied, quickly packing everything back into her bag. 'Now I'd better leave you to get dressed.'

Bubbling with excitement that she'd won the commission,

yet sad she wouldn't be the one delivering the finished garments, Jane descended the sweeping staircase then made her way along the wide hallway and down the back steps leading to the basement.

'How did it go, dear?' Mrs Cookson asked, peering through the open door. As usual, there was a delicious aroma wafting from the kitchen.

'I did it,' she cried excitedly. 'I can't thank you enough for letting me use that room. I never would have finished everything otherwise.' The woman grinned.

'Like I said, we all help each other down here. Now, this cottage pie's ready to be served, so I hope you'll have a bite to eat before you go. It'll have to be in here though, cos old Spick's on the prowl.'

'I'll keep me eyes open,' Dottie offered, looking up from the pan she was stirring. 'I is getting better, I haven't dropped anything today, have I, Mrs Cookson?'

'Apart from that gravy you're dripping all over the stove,' the cook sighed, shaking her head.

'Oh 'eck,' she groaned.

Half an hour later, feeling warm and replete, Jane retrieved her cape and was making her way down the path when she heard a shout. Looking up, she saw two young children hurtling towards her.

'Stop right this moment,' the woman chasing after them called. Giggling with glee the girls ignored her.

'Whoa,' Jane said, holding out her bag.

'We're not horses,' the older one said, indignantly.

'More like minxes,' their chaperone puffed, catching up

with them. 'Sarah, Maria, apologise to the lady for nearly knocking her over.' Bravado gone, the girls looked down at the ground.

'Sorry,' the taller one murmured.

'You could at least sound as though you mean it. I'm Nanny by the way,' she told Jane. 'We were going to see the deer, but these two are running me a merry dance whilst their father is away so perhaps we'll go and do some sums instead,' she said, winking at Jane when the girls groaned.

'Jane Haydon. I'm just making my way towards the lane,' she told the woman.

'Well in that case, I'd use the main driveway, it's much quicker. If anyone questions, just say Nanny gave you permission. Nobody will argue with me – apart from these scallywags. A pleasure meeting you.' She smiled and, catching hold of her charges' hands, she began frogmarching them back towards the manor.

Poor little things, fancy constraining them in corsets at their ages. Perhaps Madame Pittier could suggest a light one for them to wear at night, Jane thought, as she headed towards the wide drive. She had a long walk ahead of her so she might as well take the shortest route, she mused, putting her head down as a sudden gust of wind tugged at her bonnet.

Lost in thought, it took her a moment to realise the noise she heard was a carriage approaching. Obviously, Lady Farringdon's guests were already arriving, so she stepped onto the grass out of the way. But instead of passing by it stopped and, to her surprise, Lady Connaught's head appeared through the open window.

'Good afternoon, Miss Haydon. I trust you found Lady Farringdon agreeable to do business with,' she asked, her green eyes twinkling.

'I have had a most successful visit, thank you, Lady Connaught.'

'Well, that's the main thing. I'm sure Madame Pittier will be delighted. In fact, I must make an appointment to call and see her. These changing fashions play havoc with one's wardrobe. It's such a shame you don't have such an establishment in Salthaven – it would be so much more convenient than having to trail into the city. Goodness, this wind is biting so I mustn't keep you. Such a pity you are going in the other direction or we could have shared the journey. Good day to you, Miss Haydon.'

'Good day to you too, Lady Connaught,' Jane replied. What a shame Lady Farringdon couldn't have been as polite, she thought as the carriage moved away. She'd just reached the end of the driveway when she saw another two coaches turning in. Clearly the lady of the manor entertained in style.

Trudging along the rutted lane, her feet keeping time to the ringing of hammers rising from the quarry below, Jane thought back over the past few days. In the main, the people she'd met had been very kind and she'd certainly learned a lot about how people lived. Thinking of Mrs Somers, Jane couldn't believe how callous Lady Farringdon had been when she'd tried to explain how the woman hadn't been paid. She would speak to Madame Pittier as soon as she arrived home. Still, overall, she'd refused to let herself be intimidated, and had succeeded in winning the commission. In fact, her visit could be deemed a success, so why did the image of a sandy-haired, hazel-eyed young man keep popping into her mind? And why, when he hadn't mentioned seeing her again, did it matter that she hadn't?

Finally, just when she thought her legs would give way, she reached the junction and saw the Horseshoes Inn looming ahead. The coach was drawn up outside and people were already boarding. Not wishing to miss it, Jane hefted her heavy bags and hurried across the road. Fearful of her last experience, she peered around, relief flooding through her when she spotted a space between two women. She'd just squeezed onto the hard bench when the larger one nudged her in the side.

'I think that chap's trying to get yer attention. He looks a bit of all right an' all,' she chortled. Looking down, Jane's heart jumped when she saw Sam standing on the seat of his cart, waving frantically. Although he was calling up to her, she couldn't hear what he was saying. She shook her head in frustration, but then the horn sounded and, with a jolt, the coach was pulling away.

'Ah, shame,' the woman next to her sighed. 'Yer follower, is he?'

'No, nothing like that,' Jane replied, wishing her pulse would stop racing. After all, Sam had only come to wave her off, hadn't he?

The rolling of the coach combined with her sleepless night and ordeal of wondering if she would win the commission soon caught up with her, and the next thing she knew, the woman was nudging her in her side again.

'Wake up, sleepy 'ead. Yer dozed all the way, didn't even open yer eyes when we stopped at the inns. Could 'ave nabbed anything from yer smart carrier, I could.' Jane sat bolt upright and stared at her bag in horror. The woman laughed. 'Lucky for you I'm honest, but there's plenty who ain't. Come on, time we got off.'

Bleary eyed, Jane followed the woman down the stairs and out into the street. She was frozen stiff and could hardly feel her feet although the biting wind ensured she was soon wide awake. Hurrying along the shadowy streets, where lamps cast ghostly pools of light over the pavement, she thought how eerily quiet it was, then realised she never usually ventured out at this time.

Turning into the street just off Cathedral Yard, Jane's pulses started racing as she thought of the good news she had to tell Madame. To her consternation, when she reached the *magasin* it was in darkness. There was just a glimmer of candlelight shining through the gaps in the shutters. A prickle of apprehension ran down her spine as she turned the handle, only to find it didn't turn. Suddenly the door was thrown open and Millie stood there, tears coursing down her cheeks.

'Thank heavens you've come back.'

'What's the matter, Millie? Whatever's happened?' Jane asked, setting her bags on the floor and pulling the sobbing girl into her arms.

'It's Madame, she was taken real bad, coughing and gasping for breath like anything. Then it all went quiet. Oh God, Jane, I think she's croaked it.'

Horrified, Jane stared at the maid for a long moment before

gathering her senses and hurrying through to Madame's chamber. Stumbling in the darkness, Jane almost retched at the foul smell that permeated the room. Throwing herself down beside the bed, she reached for her hand, alarmed to find it cold to the touch.

'Oh Madame,' she cried.

'Jane,' a weak voice wavered. It was so faint, Jane had to bend closer. The woman's eyes fluttered open. 'I… couldn't… go… till…' Her voice petered out and she closed her eyes in defeat.

'Don't try and speak,' Jane murmured, pushing back a wisp of white hair that had strayed from Madame's nightcap then reaching for the beaker of water on the bedside table.

'No… time.' There was a sigh and wheeze and the woman shook her head helplessly before turning her penetrating gaze on Jane. 'Lady Far…'

'Hush, Madame. Lady Farringdon was very pleased with your designs and has placed her order along with one for her younger daughters.' Madame's lips twitched slightly.

'Wouldn't… have… expected…' she fought to gain breath, 'any… less. You have—' She broke off, fighting desperately for more breath. Then she continued and Jane had to lean even closer to hear. '…been…' she gasped, determined to continue, 'like… a… daughter… made… provis…' Then before she could finish, she gave one last shudder and was still.

'No, Madame,' Jane sobbed. 'You can't leave us.' But the room was quiet and Jane knew she had gone. 'Rest in peace,' she whispered, tears coursing down her cheeks as she reached up and touched the woman's cheek for one last time then got up and opened the window to let her soul fly free.

***

Jane and Millie huddled closer to the meagre fire, blankets round their shoulders, in an effort to get warm. But it was no good, shock had set in and neither of them could stop shivering. Knowing she had to do something, Jane got up and poured two measures of Madame's special nectar.

'Drink this then tell me exactly what happened,' Jane coaxed, handing Millie a glass.

'That nasty chill did for her, it did. One minute she were calling for me to bring her rose water, the next she had another fit of the coughing. Then all went quiet and I thought she were a goner, just like that,' the little maid said, snapping her fingers to emphasise the point. 'But she got to say goodbye to you?'

'Yes, Millie, she rallied briefly and for that I'll be eternally grateful,' Jane replied. 'Although I can't help wishing I could have returned earlier.' She sighed, her elation of the day turning to dismay as she thought of the wonderful woman who'd taken them both under her wing. And now she was dead, what did the future hold for them?

Chapter 13

The funeral was held at St Martin's just five days later. To Jane's surprise, the church was packed with people wishing to pay their respects, many of whom Jane recognised as being Madame's clients, along with the sisters of St Catherine's and mourners from other organisations she had helped over the years.

Blinking back her tears, Jane focused on the pink pall covering the coffin which Madame had commissioned. It had a single embroidered damask rose in the centre and, as the woman had stipulated that no money should be wasted on flowers, it was the only splash of colour amongst the sea of black. The air was scented with eau de rose and Jane shook her head. Even in death, Madame had perfectly orchestrated her swan song.

'Blimey, I didn't know Madame knew so many people. Perhaps she should have booked the cathedral itself,' Millie whispered as they made their way down the aisle after the short but poignant service. At her request there was to be no burial or wake. 'What will they do with her body?'

'Mr Farquharson said she insisted it be put to good use rather than buried beneath the earth, so I can only think she's donated it to the hospital.'

'Creepy.' Millie shivered. 'She were like one of her corsets, weren't she, all stiff and upright yet with a soft lining.' Jane couldn't help smiling at the girl's analogy for it really did sum up their former employer.

'I was so sorry to hear about Madame Pittier.' Jane turned to find the assistant manager from the bank staring solemnly at her. 'If I can be of any assistance, do let me know,' he added quietly.

'Thank you, Mr Jones, that is very kind of you.' Jane nodded before turning away to speak to others who were waiting to pay their condolences. Although tears weren't far away she knew how much Madame had loathed shows of emotion and was determined not to break down in public. Finally, everyone drifted away and there was nothing else for them to do but head back to the *magasin*.

Although the day was cold, the sun was shining from a clear, cobalt sky as they walked briskly along the street.

'I reckon she's having a laugh up there. Probably got all the angels measured for their underpinnings already.' Although Millie was trying to keep their spirits up, her trembling voice and watery eyes belied her words and Jane had to bite her lip to stop herself from howling.

'Do you think we'll be out on our ear?' the girl asked for the umpteenth time as they let themselves into the shop and locked the door behind them. They'd pulled down the blinds out of respect and the colourful interior was shrouded in black.

'I don't know, Millie,' Jane sighed, although in truth she feared that was exactly what was going to happen. 'Mr

Farquharson said he would let us know how things stand after the funeral so we'll just have to wait. In the meantime, let's go through to the Receiving Room and pay our respects to Madame with a glass of her special nectar.'

'Good thinking, me insides is all froze up,' the maid muttered, shrugging off her coat.

Having toasted their former employer, an air of gloom and uncertainty had descended and neither Jane nor Millie had the energy or inclination to get on with their work. Instead, they sat in front of the fire reminiscing how they'd both come to be living with Madame and fretting about their future.

'I nearly jumped off the pew when the vicar referred to her as Rose,' Millie said, breaking the silence. 'I mean it's a nice name but a bit plain when we've thought of her as Rosetta all these years.'

'It was the French image she liked to portray to her clients,' Jane replied.

'And a right tartar she were when she were doing that posh French act. Still, her heart were in the right place. Like a mother to us really, weren't she, which means you could say we're sisters,' Millie said, staring at Jane over her glass.

'Goodness, I'd never thought of it like that but yes, I suppose we are in a way.' Jane smiled for she really was fond of the little maid. Now, of course, both their futures hung in the balance.

'So, you didn't meet your prince in Nettlecombe then?' Millie asked.

'No, I didn't,' she replied, blinking away the image of the man with the hazel eyes and sense of humour. Even if he had turned up to wave her goodbye, he'd probably just been passing by the Horseshoes. 'I told you, Nettlecombe's a manor house not a castle.'

'Well, I reckons that Mr Jones from the bank's got his eye on you.'

'Really, Millie, you do have some ridiculous notions.'

'He always goes red when he speaks to you, and that's a good way of telling. Got a good job, though, so you could do worse than wed him.'

'I'm not marrying for years yet, if ever,' Jane declared hotly.

'Well, don't be hasty if he does ask you to step out. You got to think of your future now Madame's gone. We both have,' she sighed and took another sip of her drink. Jane was just marvelling at the young girl's perception, and reflecting on what she was going to do when there was a sudden knocking at the door.

'Who's that?' Millie asked, panic making her voice shrill.

'Only one way to find out,' Jane said, springing to her feet and hurrying through, the little maid following at her heel like a puppy.

'Miss Haydon?' the gentleman asked.

'Yes, and you are?' Jane asked, eyeing him and his ill-fitting suit with suspicion.

'Mr Jarvis, assistant to Mr Farquharson,' he said, perfecting a little bow. 'Please accept my sincere condolences. Madame Pittier was a wonderful woman.'

'You knew her?'

'Well no, but Mr Farquharson said she was. He regrets he is unable to come here in person but obviously I can deal with the matter. What I have to say is confidential,' he said, looking up and down the busy street. 'Perhaps I could come in?' Jane eyed his shiny Gladstone bag warily then stepped back to let him enter. 'I'm surprised you are not open for business,' he commented.

'We are closed out of respect to Madame Pittier.'

'Well, perhaps that is best under the circumstances,' the man said smoothly.

'And we needs to know what is happening. Is that what you're here for?' Millie asked.

'Perhaps Mr Jarvis would like some refreshment,' Jane said quickly when she saw the solicitor frowning over his spectacles.

'Thank you,' he replied.

'Please bring a tray through to the Receiving Room, Millie,' she said. 'I'll show you through, Mr Jarvis,' she added, wishing it was the softly spoken Mr Farquharson and not this oily-looking man.

Although Jane's insides were churning, she sat hands clasped in her lap whilst the man opened his bag. After making a great show of arranging papers on the table beside him, he removed his spectacles then methodically began to wipe the lenses on a cloth. Just as she thought she would scream, Millie appeared with their tea.

'I'll pour, thank you,' she said, grateful for something to do, for by now the tension was unbearable. She didn't even have the heart to chastise Millie for hovering in the doorway.

'Well, Miss Haydon, Madame Pittier was the proprietor of this establishment called,' he paused to refer to his papers.

'Madame Rosetta, Corsetière,' he said quickly. 'And you are Jane Haydon, employee?'

'Yes,' she confirmed, wondering why he needed to state the obvious.

'As I'm sure you are aware, Madame Pittier was meticulous in all her dealings. She, shall we say, knew her own mind.' Jane nodded, then bit her tongue in frustration as he paused to add sugar to his cup and proceeded to stir. She watched the liquid swirling round and round and was seized with the urge to snatch the clattering spoon from him. Finally, having taken a sip of his drink, he turned back to the papers.

'Now, where was I? Ah yes, Madame Pittier has made some strange bequests.' He paused and stared at Jane over the top of his spectacles then continued. 'She had a brother, I believe.'

'So I understand, although I've never met him. I believe he lives abroad.'

'And that is why Mr Farquharson is unable to be here today.'

'I'm not sure I understand.' Jane frowned.

'I don't think any of us quite do.' He sighed loudly. 'And the legalities of the law are a minefield.'

'Mr Jarvis, would you mind getting to the point?' Jane asked, her nerves fraying.

'Which is exactly what I'm trying to do. You'll be pleased to know the rent on this, er, shop is paid up to the next quarter day, Miss Haydon. Which is Lady Day, the twenty-fifth of March,' he said, packing his papers away then rising quickly to his feet. 'Mr Farquharson will be in touch when the legalities have been finalised.'

'Is that it?' Jane asked, her head spinning with what would happen after that time. As ever, though, Millie wasn't backward in coming forward.

'Yes, what happens after that? Will we be out on our ear?' Millie was staring at the man in dismay.

'I really cannot say. All I know is that Mr Farquharson sent me here so you know you can stay on the premises until Lady Day. And as I said earlier, he will be in touch when everything has been sorted.'

'Thank you, Mr Jarvis, I'll show you out,' Jane told him, determined not to lose her composure.

'I'm sorry I cannot be of more help,' he said, doffing his hat. Jane watched him disappearing down the street. She wanted to scream after him, but knew he was only doing his job. Closing the door behind him, she stood for a moment looking around the little shop she so loved. March was less than two months away.

'Blimey, what are we going to do now?' Millie asked, her eyes on stalks.

'Carry on as normal,' Jane said with a confidence she didn't feel. 'We can't look for any new trade, obviously, but I checked the workroom yesterday and there is enough fabric to make up the outstanding orders, including Lady Farringdon's. We owe it to Madame to ensure her reputation is kept intact.'

'Then what?'

'I don't know, Millie. I really don't know,' Jane sighed. 'But sure as silk is silk, we will not give in. We'll do our best not to let you down, Madame,' she added, her resolve hardening.

She'd just convinced herself that they could manage the impossible when the postman arrived.

'Letter for you, Miss Haydon,' he chirped, handing her an envelope then hoisting his sack higher on his shoulder, the little bell tinkling as he left.

Jane stared at the official-looking missive before ripping it open.

'What is it?' Millie asked, hopping up and down as Jane read the contents.

'A notice from the landlord informing us that if we can't pay the next quarter's rent come Lady Day, he will be letting the premises to someone else.' Jane and Millie looked at each other in alarm. As panic flared in the little maid's eyes, Jane reached out and put her arm around her. 'Don't worry, Millie, whatever happens we'll stick together,' she murmured. Yet as she sought to reassure the young girl, her own feelings were in torment. How on earth were they going to find a whole quarter's rent?

***

As Sam Gill took his pent-up frustration out on cutting down the trees, the woodsmen working alongside him at Blackbury Wood stared at him in astonishment. Usually their boss was unruffled and mild mannered so they could only guess at what was wrong.

'Got to be woman trouble,' one speculated, pushing back his cap and scratching his head, then jumping back deftly as the ash came toppling down.

'Here, steady on, young Gill,' he shouted, but Sam was already picking up his bow saw again. Physical exertion was the only way he could keep his exasperation at bay.

Having been delayed yesterday, he'd ridden like the wind in order to speak with Jane, only to see her already taking her seat on the box of the coach. He'd wanted to ask if he could see her again, but clearly she had other ideas, for when he'd called up to her, she'd shaken her head. He could have sworn she'd felt the spark between them, but not being experienced in the ways of women, he must have got it wrong. If only he'd had time to speak with her properly.

Finally, when the branches were lopped, he began dragging them over to the cart. Although the day was cold, he'd worked himself into a lather.

'You all right?' another man asked, running over to help him lift the boughs up.

'Been better,' Sam admitted ruefully, knowing his manner had been surly. But the man wasn't one to bear a grudge.

'Want us to separate these wands for the wattle and roofing rafters?' he asked, gesturing over to the hazel he'd graded earlier.

'Yes please, Giffy,' Sam replied, taking the kerchief from his neck and wiping the sweat from his brow. 'I'll take this lot back to the workshop.'

'Right yer are.' He nodded, wandering off to join the others.

Carefully steering the cart over the rutted ground so that he didn't lose any of the timbers gave Sam time to think. As the vision of the sleek-haired, blue-eyed laughing woman came into his mind, he slapped the side of the cart in annoyance. She was the only girl to have affected him this way and he couldn't just give up on her. He wouldn't. The question was how was he going to contact her? More importantly, bearing in mind the way she'd shaken her head at him, should he even try? He was so confused. He wasn't one to give up on something he wanted, and yet he wasn't one to make a nuisance of himself. If she didn't want to see him again, well, that was that, wasn't it?

By the time he reached the workshop, he was no further forward in his deliberations. He could tell by the sun being overhead that it was time for nuncheon and although he wasn't hungry, he had to report back to his father on the progress being made with the coppicing.

'Jed, look lively, these timbers need unloading. Get young Paul to give you a hand, then see to the horse,' he shouted to the lad leaning against the barn, before striding out across the field. Despite racking his brains, he could not find an answer to his dilemma, and the thought of being cooped up in the cottage while his father compiled his report didn't fill him with joy.

'Lost your smile as well as your manners, Samuel Gill?' a voice called. Looking up, he saw Louisa walking towards him.

'Sorry, Louisa, didn't see you there,' he murmured.

'I've just been talking to your ma. She's having a right time with your father being grumpy, so don't you go adding to her misery.'

'Father's frustrated at not being able to help on the estate at the moment.'

'And what about you, Sam? What's your problem?' she asked. She was staring candidly at him as only a good friend could and he knew there was no point in fabricating. When he'd finished relaying his tale, she shook her head in dismay.

'Samuel Gill, you are hopeless. Fancy shouting to her like that. And in front of others too. I'd have been mortified. And with all the noise from the horses and people chatting, you don't really know if she heard what you said or not, do you?'

'But she shook her head,' he sighed.

'Well, why don't you write to her? That would give her the option to reply or not. At least it would put you out of your misery.'

'That's true.' He nodded, then shook his head. 'But I don't know her address.'

'Honestly, Sam, you mustn't be defeatist. Faint heart and all that. Look, I've had an idea. Step Mama wants us to go through yet more plans for this wretched ball this afternoon. I'll make up some excuse about needing to know the address of Madame Pittier.'

'Louisa, you're a genius,' he cried, his mood lifting.

'I know, but keep it a secret or everyone will be picking my brains,' she laughed.

'When do we have the pleasure of seeing the dashing Henry again?'

'Soon, hopefully. I can't wait, and Papa had better return soon too or he'll have no garden or money left. Step Mama only wants to have a bandstand built for the ball.'

'That's a bit extravagant, even by her standards.' Sam whistled. 'Well, better not be late for nuncheon or I'll be in even more trouble. You won't forget about that address, will you?'

'I'll bring it up to the cottage later,' she promised.

Sam grinned – suddenly the day seemed a whole lot brighter.

Chapter 14

Edwin Farringdon was feeling more optimistic and relaxed than he'd been for some time. His business meetings in London had been successful and whilst he wouldn't be able to meet all the quarrymen's demands, he was confident the modest raise in their wage he could now offer would appease them. Of course, it would come at great expense to the estate but, as he'd explained to the bank, the last thing he needed at this time of resurgence was for them to down tools. First thing tomorrow, he would arrange a meeting with Tom Wakeley to discuss the detail. He also needed to call on Wilfred Gill to see how his leg was progressing and to check all was well with the estate. While poaching was always a problem, the number of deer now being taken was higher than ever.

As the carriage turned into the driveway arched with lime trees leading to the manor, his thoughts turned to family. He hoped Charlotte would be in a good mood and also that she'd heeded his advice on curbing her expenditure.

He'd enjoyed his time in Grosvenor Square, reading his newspaper beside the fire without interruption, whilst enjoying Mrs Crawford's simple fare, but now needed to concentrate on his life in the family home. Banished also were thoughts of his gentle mistress, her hands caressing and teasing, making him feel loved and appreciated again. He was no fool and knew Charlotte only tolerated his attentions, her lust being for the material things of life. However, she knew how desperate he was to sire an heir and he couldn't help hoping it wouldn't be long before she gave him the news he was longing to hear.

Squeals of laughter brought him back to the here and now. Looking out of the window, he smiled when he saw Sarah and Maria hurtling across the grass towards him, with poor Nanny chasing after them. Tapping on the roof for the driver to stop, he opened the door and climbed down.

'Puppy,' Maria cried, running into his open arms.

'Papa, you've been away for ages,' Sarah grumbled.

'Well, I'm home now,' he said, smiling. 'After I've seen your mama, I shall come and read you both a story. If that's all right with Nanny,' he said, turning to the woman as she caught up with them.

'Whew, that was some run, girls,' she gasped, clearly out of breath, and it struck Edwin forcibly just how much she had aged.

'I hope they haven't been misbehaving, Nanny?' he asked.

'They've been little treasures,' the woman replied, as she always did. 'Good to see you home again, Edwin.' She paused as if she wanted to say something else.

'Is something wrong?' he prompted.

'I just hope you'll find things all right,' she murmured awkwardly.

'Well, I'm just off to find out,' he replied, tugging at the lock of Maria's fair hair that had escaped her bonnet.

'I four now, Puppy. Big girls don't have their hair messed.'

'Mama says we will be grand ladies one day,' Sarah told him, her expression serious.

'Let's hope you aren't too grand to see what I've got in my bag for you.' Laughing at their squeals of delight, he tipped his hat at Nanny and climbed back into the waiting carriage. Despite Charlotte's protestation that, as Lord of Nettlecombe, he should treat her like the other servants, he had a deep affection for the woman. She'd seemed uneasy though. Perhaps, despite her protestations, the girls were getting too much for her and it was time to consider getting someone else to assist. Or perhaps Charlotte had a surprise for him, he thought, his heart leaping at the thought.

As the carriage continued on its way, he stared around the grounds, noticing with satisfaction that Reed and his team of gardeners had pruned the topiary bushes into perfect balls, for he still delighted in their lollipop shapes. The borders, a riot of white, yellow and mauve even this early in the year, reminded him that he needed to visit the hothouse and check on his surprise. In another life he might have been a gardener, he mused, for there was nothing that pleased him more than the sight of plants and flowers thriving in immaculate grounds.

Rounding the side of the house, his daydreaming was rudely interrupted by a cacophony of banging and shouting. To his horror, he saw the carefully landscaped grounds had been excavated and some monstrosity was in the process of being erected. Swearing under his breath, he leapt from the carriage.

'Stop this minute,' he roared to the man directing the operation. 'What the hell are you doing?' he asked.

'Just following orders, guv.' The man, wearing a thick jacket, frowned, pushing the flat cap to the back of his head. 'Summat wrong?'

'Yes, there is,' he snapped. 'Stop work right this minute.'

'I'm sorry, sir. The lady—'

'I am the lord; this is my estate and I am telling you to dismantle this atrocity and remove every stone immediately.'

'Ah, right you are, my lord. I was just following orders, you understand?' the man asked, looking distinctly worried now.

'Only too well,' Edwin snapped, turning on his heel and marching into the manor. Charlotte had gone too far this time, he thought, his former contentment and good intent gone in an instant. Even poor Ellery who padded over to greet him only got a cursory pat.

'Where is she?' he asked the butler, who stood ready to take Edwin's hat and coat.

'I believe you'll find her ladyship in the Ruby Room, my lord,' Ferris replied. With a curt nod, Edwin marched down the hallway, tempted again to knock the gaudy clock from its pedestal.

'What is the meaning of this?' he demanded, storming into the Ruby Room.

'Why, Edwin, must you burst through the door like that? You quite upset my equilibrium,' Charlotte cried. 'And you've mud all over your shoes.'

'Is that surprising when I've just been confronted by the sight of that appalling eyesore being erected outside?'

'Oh, you mean my little surprise, the bandstand?' she asked, sitting up straighter in her chair. 'I was seized with the inspiration whilst Louisa and I were discussing plans for her betrothal ball. You see— What do you mean *was* being erected?'

'Just that,' he snapped, clenching his fists to quash the urge to seize her. Walking over to the fireplace, he took a few deep breaths to steady himself. 'I will get Reed to see the land is restored to its former pleasing vista. I am extremely disappointed, Charlotte. My express instruction before I left was that you were mindful of expenditure.'

'You mean you'd begrudge your eldest daughter the opportunity to shine on her big day?'

'I never wanted a bandstand, Step Mama,' Louisa said, coming into the room. 'Hello, Papa, welcome home.' She walked over and kissed his cheek. 'In fact, as I keep saying, Henry and I would prefer a small gathering with just our closest family and friends.'

'And as I keep saying, you are being utterly selfish, Louisa. Lady Beauchamp will be expecting us to host a grand event to honour the uniting of our two families. I do not intend being accused of scrimping—'

'Louisa should have the celebration she wishes,' Edwin interrupted, catching sight of his daughter's anxious face. 'In fact, the planning may be a little presumptuous anyway. There will be no further spending until I say so.'

'Are you overruling me, Edwin?' Charlotte asked, her voice dangerously quiet.

'I prefer to call it taking a pragmatic approach,' he replied. 'When are you expecting Henry to visit?' he asked, turning to Louisa.

'Any day now, Papa. He is awaiting—'

'Are you telling me we are to receive guests without prior notice?' Charlotte interrupted. 'Appearances dictate—'

'You order a monstrosity be built then have the audacity to talk about appearances?' Edwin exclaimed. 'I give up. Louisa, please go and change for dinner. I wish to speak with your stepmother. And our discussion is long overdue. Perhaps you'd join me in the library tomorrow afternoon.'

'You mean the Carnelian Room,' Charlotte murmured.

'Yes, Papa,' Louisa replied, ignoring the woman. Edwin waited until she'd gone, then went over to the sideboard and poured himself a stiff drink, downing it in one. As the heat spread through his insides, he replenished his glass. 'Can I get anything for you?' he asked, breaking the ominous silence that filled the room.

'No, thank you,' Charlotte replied stiffly, fixing him with her glacial stare. 'I have spent an inordinate time trying to ensure your daughter has a ball that will be the talk of society, and then you come home from doing I know not what, and overrule me.'

Edwin sighed and walked over to stand in front of the fire again. He knew there was little point him explaining again about his responsibility of ensuring wages were paid, that the income from his estate was not limitless, for she'd simply ignore him as usual. Or worse, wave his words away like a bothersome fly. Although the upkeep of Nettlecombe was growing ever more expensive, with judicious planning, he had enough to provide for them well enough. However, his funds were not the bottomless pit she seemed to think. He decided to try the reasonable approach.

'I don't want you to think I don't appreciate all you do for us. However, the girls are growing up and I feel it is important their wishes are taken into account. Louisa is twenty and will come of age at the end of the year. Surely, she should be able to have the betrothal celebration she wishes? Besides, there is something—'

'But Edwin, it is our duty to host a grand social event. You don't want people to turn their noses up at us,' Charlotte interjected.

'True friends will be pleased to wish Louisa and Henry well however they choose to celebrate. And anyone who cares more about appearances and extravagant gestures isn't worth worrying about. Talking of appearances, I saw Nanny earlier. Do you think she is looking old?'

'I can't say I take notice of how the staff look,' Charlotte replied, her lips forming a moue.

'Maybe you should,' Edwin said mildly. 'Sarah and Maria are very lively these days, as they should be,' he added quickly when she shot him a look. 'I was thinking it might be time to get someone to assist Nanny.'

'First of all you dared question my spending, now it's the running of the house. That is my responsibility so I'd be obliged if you'd concentrate on your own business affairs, of which you appear to have plenty,' Charlotte said, rising to her feet and sweeping from the room.

So much for his resolve to restore harmony in their relationship, Edwin thought, replenishing his glass then sinking into the chair beside the fire.

***

Despite his best endeavours, relations with Charlotte had been strained over supper and Edwin was pleased to be out in the early morning air before she emerged from her chamber. Even the mist that rolled in from the sea, swirling and drifting around him, was warmer than the atmosphere in the house. Ellery padded at his side, having quite forgiven his master's abrupt greeting the previous day.

Striding down the lane, he revelled in the peace and quiet. The contrast between here and the bustle of City life never ceased to amaze him. If only his wife didn't have such grandiose ideas and could appreciate the great outdoors, he thought, taking in the lowing of cattle coming from the shed as they waited their turn to be milked, the tiny violets sprinkled with pearls of frost, the cry of the pheasant as it shot out of a nearby hedge in front of him, its bright plumage straight as the feathers on a dart. He grinned wryly, knowing the only pearls she'd appreciate would be of the jewelled variety, the pheasant covered in a rich madeira sauce.

He walked on, the vista becoming dirtier and noisier the nearer he got to the quarry. Men called out to each other as the heavy blocks were lifted by hand cranes and guided to where they could be split. Further on, the masons waited impatiently, eager to shape the creamy grey stone to the correct measurements. These men were highly skilled and Edwin never ceased to be amazed at the lengths they would go to guard their trade secrets, working behind rigged up shelters or hiding in the crevices of the quarry.

Sensing the men eyeing him, Edwin strode purposefully on, acknowledging their greetings but not stopping. His business was with Wakeley, and as quarry manager it was up to him to tell them if they would be getting an increase in wage. There was nothing Edwin would have liked better than to impart the news himself, but he knew from past experience that they all had to be told together, or a fight could break out, causing disruption to the works.

Further along, the horse-drawn wagons were waiting to transport their freight down to the beach at Beer or Seaton harbour, depending on the tide. From there it would be shipped out on barges to Exeter, London, or wherever the order was for. At eight horses for each two blocks of stone moved, it was an expensive business and one his accountant had questioned, but there could be no short cuts. As another group of workers touched their hands to their caps, Edwin raised his cane in acknowledgement.

'Morning, Wakeley,' he called, striding into the large hut that served as the works' office. A fire burning in the corner to keep out the damp was the only concession to comfort in the place and, weary after his walk, Ellery settled himself down in front of it. The quarry manager nodded in greeting and hurried to pull out a chair for his employer.

'Hope everything went well in London?' the man asked, cutting to the reason for his visit. At forty-two he'd been working with Lord Farringdon for so many years, that whilst respectful, there was no need to waste time on small talk.

'Not too badly, thank you,' Edwin replied, circumspect as ever. 'But before I elaborate, tell me how things have been here and what new orders have come in.'

They spent the next hour going through the books,

discussing the amount of stone that had been quarried and shipped out on the barges, and the future workload.

'And what about the invoices? As I have explained, we really need to ensure the bills are paid on time.'

'Getting paid is one thing, on time quite another,' the man snorted. 'The richer the customer the tighter the purse, begging your pardon, sir. Don't suppose it matters a jot to them that these men risk their lives so they can have their fancy features.' He paused and looked at Edwin expectantly.

'The men can have an increase in payment for each four ton block the Tapstone passes but currently we're not making enough to pay for their candles. However, should output increase, then we can reconsider.'

'The men work hard enough as it is,' Tom Wakeley pointed out. 'But any increase will be welcomed, the way the cost of living is shooting up.'

'I understand. Now here is a summary of the increases I propose for the workers – you will see your name is at the top. I hope this serves to show my appreciation for all you do here.'

'Thank you, sir,' he said, taking the list and studying it.

'I only wish I could pay more, but I have to be guided by my advisors,' Edwin replied, getting stiffly to his feet.

'And the men working underground have to be guided by their candles,' the man reminded him.

Chapter 15

Louisa looked out of her bedroom window and through the swirling mist rolling in from the sea, could see the men already hard at work restoring her papa's beloved garden. Thank heavens he'd vetoed the idea of the bandstand. While she had nothing against them, for she loved music and dancing, the design her stepmother had chosen was so large and ostentatious it bordered on the vulgar.

Turning back to the mirror, she checked her appearance for the second time in as many minutes. Having woken that morning with the fizzy feeling she always got whenever she saw Henry, Louisa just knew he would be visiting today. Wanting to look her best, she'd asked Vanny to set out her prettiest day gown, knowing the apricot suited her colouring, reflecting the golden flecks in her dark eyes.

Satisfied she was suitably attired, Louisa took herself downstairs for breakfast only to find her stepmother glaring into her teacup while her sisters sat studiously scrutinising their plates. The atmosphere was as icy as the frost still covering the lawn and not wishing anything to spoil her feelings of anticipation, Louisa snatched a bread roll from the basket on the sideboard and made her escape.

She took it through to the sun room, recently renamed the Citrine Room, from where she had a good view of the driveway, especially now the veil of grey was lifting. Excited at the thought of seeing Henry again, yet anxious at what he might have to tell her, she couldn't sit still, far less eat. Abandoning the partly devoured roll, she prowled around picking things up then putting them down again. Then, less than an hour later, she saw his coach making its way towards the house and her heart flipped. Tempted though she was to run out to meet him, Ferris had seen her come in here and would conduct Henry to her. As this was the last room her stepmother would think of entering, she decided to stay hidden away. Despite the woman's insistence that she be chaperoned at all times, Louisa wanted to receive Henry alone.

'Captain Beauchamp,' Ferris announced quietly. As he discreetly withdrew, Louisa looked up and smiled. With chiselled cheekbones, piercing blue eyes and fair hair that stubbornly curled at the ends despite the regulation cut, his handsome features never failed to take her breath away. Her gaze travelled lower and as she took in the close-fitting red jacket with stiff gold collar and tasselled epaulettes, his tight black trousers, she knew and her stomach turned over.

'Hello, dearest Louisa,' he said, taking her hand and raising it to his lips.

'You've to go then?' she replied, the breath catching in her throat as she fought to keep her composure.

'I'm afraid so. I've instructions to join my regiment in two days' time.'

'So soon?' she asked, her stomach knotting with fear at what lay ahead for him.

'We have to embark from Southampton on a steamer complete with necessary equipment and horses.'

'Do you know when you will return?' He shook his head.

'Destination secret, mission secret, return unknown. But you must not worry, Louisa dearest, as soon as I get back, we will celebrate like never before.'

'But I've never celebrated my betrothal before,' she quipped, determined to keep things light and not spoil their last few hours together. Tears could come later, after he'd gone.

'I should hope not,' he exclaimed, pretending mock horror. 'I will write whenever I can and hope you will write back?'

'Of course. Oh, Henry,' she cried.

'I know. I was hoping we might enjoy a few carefree hours together before telling you, but as ever you are too perceptive.'

'The uniform betrayed it,' she laughed. 'However, I would love for us to spend time by ourselves before you leave. Is it too cold for a walk?'

'Although the mist has disappeared, there are still pockets of frost and I wouldn't want you to catch a chill. However, I asked Droves to park the carriage round the west side of the building, out of the way, so perhaps we could take a ride?'

'Yes, let's go to the deer park,' Louisa cried. 'We'll need to be discreet though. If Step Mama sees you, she'll pounce and we'll never get away. I'll get my wrap then slip out through the servants' entrance and join you in your carriage.'

'Mama's the word – or should that be Step Mama?' He grinned, before proceeding to make an exaggerated show of tiptoeing out. With her hand over her mouth to stop laughter bubbling over, Louisa also stole from the room and headed in the opposite direction, only to stop abruptly when she heard Charlotte's strident tones emanating from the Breakfast Room or Sapphire Room as it was now known.

'You spend far too much time riding that horse, Beatrice. Come with me and we'll discuss the prospectus I have received from the ladies' academy.' Clearly, they had finished breakfast and were making their way towards the door. As a furious Bea emerged, Louisa put a finger to her lips. Quick on the uptake, her sister winked and turned around.

'I appear to have dropped my handkerchief, Step Mama,' she said, all but pushing the woman back into the room. Breathing a sigh of relief, Louisa ran up to her bedchamber. Snuggled in her fur-trimmed cape, she crept down the stairs, through the door that led down to the lower floor and outside.

Henry handed her into the carriage then, as they began to move, proceeded to cover them both with a soft woollen blanket. As ever, they were easy in each other's company, discussing their plans and joking about Charlotte's grand ideas, but by the time they reached the park, the realisation that they were going to be parted for the foreseeable future began to sink in. Mindful their time together was short, they sat side by side, heads bent close, hands clasped tightly. In an effort to lift the sombre atmosphere, Louisa turned to face him.

'I must say, Henry, I do think it's a bit drastic going to such lengths to get away from me,' she quipped, biting her lip as tears threatened. She would not embarrass him by crying.

'I know, but what's a man to do?' Henry sighed, waving his hands in the air theatrically. 'That the lady in question is beautiful goes without saying, but she has this peculiar sense of humour.' However, the gravity of the situation was too dire for mirth and his eyes clouded. 'I'm going to miss you dreadfully,' he murmured. 'You will be in my thoughts constantly but…' He turned to face her, his expression grave as he once more grasped her hands tightly. 'Forgive me, Louisa, but I really do have to say this. If I am…' he paused, swallowed and then continued, 'Should I not return then please know I would want you to make a new life for yourself—'

'No,' she gasped. 'Never. You are my love, my life, Henry Beauchamp. I will wait for you to come home, for I am certain you will,' she told him, praying desperately that he would.

'Oh, Louisa, my love,' he murmured. He broke away, leaving a cold space where before she'd felt bathed in his warmth. She stared at him in alarm but he was reaching for the cord on the blinds.

Cocooned in their own cosy world of whispered endearments and passionate embrace they didn't notice the carriage circling the park again and again, or the snowflakes that fluttered from the leaden sky. As their emotions heightened, threatening to get the better of them, Louisa knew she should pull away. Yet somehow couldn't.

'I cannot ask this of you, Louisa, I have too much respect,' Henry groaned. Fighting to control his ardour, he fumbled in his pocket, drew out his fob watch and grimaced. 'Much as I would love to spend the rest of the day like this, regrettably, like an obedient soldier, time is marching on and I cannot leave without speaking to your father.'

'Papa should be back from the quarry by now,' Louisa

sighed, nestling into the warmth of his chest. 'But surely another few minutes won't make any difference?'

However, it was some time before they could tear themselves away and even on the return journey, they couldn't bear to let go of each other. It was only when the driver tactfully tapped on the roof to let them know they were approaching the manor that Henry remembered to raise the blinds.

'Oh goodness, it's snowing,' Louisa exclaimed as the carriage drew to a halt, frowning at the thought of the long journey he had ahead.

'Well, it is winter,' he replied. 'Still, it's only a few flakes, not nearly enough for a snowball fight.' He grinned before jumping down then turning to assist her.

Hands entwined they walked up the steps but no sooner had the door opened than Charlotte, her expression glacial, advanced.

'Louisa, wherever have you been? Surely you haven't been out alone with Captain Beauchamp. Sir, I would have expected better of you.' Charlotte's querulous voice echoed around the hallway.

'Henry has to join his regiment, Step Mama.'

'Where? When?' she demanded.

'I leave straight away, Lady Farringdon,' Henry told her.

'Well, how inconvenient. I trust you will return in time for your betrothal ball?'

'Depending on when that is to be, I will do my best, Lady Farringdon, but—'

'There can be no buts, Captain Beauchamp. You simply must be back, I insist.'

'I hardly think Henry is in a position to make any promises, Charlotte,' Edwin declared, appearing behind them and proffering his hand to Henry. 'Do you have time for a drink to wish you God speed?'

'I thank you, sir, but regret I am already later leaving than I intended. The morning seems to have run away with me,' Henry replied, staring meaningfully at Louisa.

'Well, good luck, my boy. Keep safe. Come along, my dear, we must permit these young things to say their farewells in private,' he said, turning to Charlotte and ushering her towards the Ruby Room.

'But Edwin, it is improper…' Louisa waited until Charlotte's petulant voice had receded then turned to Henry.

'If only she knew,' she murmured, endeavouring to keep her voice light, although her chest was tightening by the minute.

'God and all his angels willing, my dearest Louisa, when I return, we shall spend the rest of our lives being improper,' he replied, his eyes full of promise. Then his arms were enfolding her and she leaned into him, silently willing him to stay. Instead she felt his lips kissing the top of her head, heard his voice whispering. 'Be assured it is those improper thoughts that will keep me going through the weeks ahead. You will wait for me?' he asked, tearing himself away and staring at her as if fixing the image of her in his mind.

'For ever,' she promised, and wishing him to remember her smiling, she blinked back her tears. Yet as she forced herself to turn away, she recalled Miss Haydon smelling the scent of lavender and shivered. The portent had never been wrong before but she couldn't, no, *wouldn't* dwell on that.

Yet, unable to contain her emotions any longer, she fled to her room and sobbed her heart out.

* * *

Edwin looked at Charlotte's mutinous expression and knew he was in for another tirade. However, he felt so strongly that Louisa and Henry should make the most of the little time they had left together, he decided to pre-empt her.

'Henry is going to be away for some time, Charlotte. The war in Crimea is escalating again.'

'Well, nobody told me about this. Anyway, Edwin, I do not think that excuses impropriety,' she retorted, sinking into the chair nearest the fire.

'I hardly think saying farewell to her betrothed can be classed as that.'

'Nearly betrothed,' his wife corrected. 'And until Louisa is safely wed, she is my responsibility.'

'I appreciate that you care so deeply, my dear. However, she's young and in love, but then you probably don't remember what that feels like,' he murmured, looking at her closely.

'Oh, but I do,' Charlotte assured him. She spoke so quietly he wondered if he'd misheard until he saw the faintest blush colour her cheeks.

'Then perhaps tonight we could—' he began.

'Please, Edwin, it's daylight,' she spluttered, looking around in case someone else had entered the room. 'Now, about Louisa,' she continued briskly.

'I will give her an hour or so to come to terms with the

situation then speak with her,' he replied. 'Now, unless there is any other household matter you wish to discuss, I have work to catch up on.'

'But Edwin, there's Victoria's debut to arrange and as for Beatrice, she refuses point-blank to even look at the prospectus for the ladies' academy.'

'Please don't concern yourself, Charlotte. I intend having a discussion with both of them as well. Now, if you'll excuse me, I really must get on. I'll see you in time for a drink before supper.'

Without waiting for a reply, he strode from the room. The peace and tranquillity of his office, with its smell of wood and leather, wrapped around him as he sank into his button-backed chair. As ever the paperwork had mounted up in his absence and, hating to have correspondence outstanding, he pulled the pile towards him. Forcing domestic issues from his mind, he began working his way methodically through each item and was just signing the final letter when there was a knock and Louisa put her head around the door. She was again dressed in her fur-lined cape but now with matching hat.

'Are you busy, Papa?'

'Never too busy for one of my beloved daughters. Are you going out?' he asked, staring at her in surprise.

'I have something for Sam so I thought I'd walk over to his cottage and get some fresh air at the same time. First, though, I would like to speak with you if you can spare a few moments?'

'Of course, come in.' He smiled, gesturing for her to be

seated beside the fire. Carefully sealing the envelope with his private stamp, he placed it on the plate with the others for Ferris to collect, then settled himself on the opposite side of the hearth. 'I won't be trite and ask if you are all right, my dear, for clearly it is a difficult time for you, as indeed the months ahead will be.'

'Thank you, Papa. And that is why I particularly wanted to speak with you. Although, naturally, Henry will be constantly in my thoughts, I don't wish to spend my days merely planning for my betrothal. Especially when I don't even know when it will take place. Nor indeed do I wish to while away the hours with mindless embroidery or tapestry as Step Mama suggests. I want to have a purpose; do something worthwhile with my time.' As Edwin stared at his daughter, he found his heart swelling with pride. Not for her the tears and tantrums many in her situation would have resorted to.

'You are so like your dear mother; not just in appearance, you also have her strength of character. You have clearly been doing some serious thinking whilst I've been away, so do you have any idea of what you wish to do?'

'Mother used to do charitable works for the poor folk of Combe and I would also like to help them in some way.'

'That is admirable, Louisa. I will call for some tea and we can discuss the matter.'

'Thank you, Papa, I knew you'd understand. You see—'

'Louisa? Edwin, is she in there with you?' As Charlotte's querulous tones came closer, Louisa looked at her father in dismay.

'Come on,' he whispered, jumping up and snatching his

woollen coat from the closet in the corner. 'I need to speak with Wilfred, see how his leg is and check on estate matters. We can talk while we walk.'

'Louisa? Edwin, will you please answer me,' Charlotte cried. As the knob on his office door rattled, Edwin beckoned for Louisa to follow him. Pulling aside a heavy tapestry, he led the way through a studded oak door that opened out into the courtyard.

Chapter 16

Edwin and Louisa fled along the path that would take them to the estate workers' cottages. The wind was biting, the ground beneath their feet still frozen. She shivered, glad of her thick cape and hat.

'I didn't know you had a secret door in your office, Papa,' Louisa said, when they were safely hidden from the house by a screen of trees and had slowed to a walk. 'Poor Step Mama, I suppose we shouldn't have run off like that, but... she really has no idea about life, has she?'

'She did when I first met her. I can't help feeling it's the life in a country manor house that isn't what she expected,' he sighed.

'Especially with three wicked stepdaughters to chaperone,' Louisa added, tucking her arm through the crook of his elbow. 'If only she wasn't so domineering.'

'I know she's a little overbearing. Perhaps she'll relax now she's no longer under pressure to throw the grandest ball in living memory,' Edwin said.

'I think you're being optimistic, Papa,' she replied, squeezing his arm. 'Anyway, as I was saying earlier, I wish to spend my days doing something more worthwhile than stitching a picture with silks.'

'What brought all this on?'

'Apart from the threads getting in a complete tangle? Actually, it was Miss Haydon.'

'Miss Haydon?'

'The corsetière. Madame Pittier was taken ill and Jane Haydon came in her place. She had such a sense of purpose and you could tell she loved what she was doing. When she mentioned Mrs Somers hadn't been paid for her board and really needed the money, it made me think about the widows in the community.'

'You mean Ida Somers, the dressmaker?' he asked.

'Yes, Papa, she's lived in near poverty since her husband was killed. Anyway, when Step Mama decided to engage the services of Madame Pittier, she arranged for her to stay with Mrs Somers and—'

'The woman hasn't been paid? I will see that is rectified immediately. How many nights did this Miss Haydon stay?'

'Three, I believe, Papa. Anyway, I've made enquiries and found there are many poor women living hand to mouth in Combe. Some have ten children or more and work at whatever menial jobs they can find in order to buy food.'

'I understand your concern, and of course your mama was also active in the community so I'm sure we can find a way to help.'

'Thank you, Papa. Poor old Ellery, you realise we've done him out of a walk.'

'He came with me to the quarry earlier so I'm sure that's enough exercise for the old boy. Right, well, here we are,' he said, knocking on the door, which was opened almost immediately. 'Good afternoon, Sam, I hope this is a convenient time to speak with your father?' Edwin asked, his breath spiralling in the cold air as he smiled at the sandy-haired youth.

'Of course it is, Lord Farringdon,' he answered politely. Edwin took off his hat and ducked beneath the low beam as Sam stood back to let them enter.

'There's only the two of us so you needn't stand on ceremony,' Louisa laughed. 'I do love it in here,' she murmured, inhaling the fragrant smell of woodsmoke that wafted from the fire in the corner of the room. Although the furniture was old and mis-matched the bright cherry-red curtains and chair covers gave the room a cosy feel and for the first time since Henry had left, she felt herself relax.

'Honestly, Louisa, anyone would think you'd never been in here before,' Sam teased.

'I know, but it always feels so welcoming. Oh, hello, Wilf, how's your leg?' she asked, going over to the table where the man was almost hidden behind a stack of papers.

'I can hobble around now, thank yer for asking,' he replied.

'Goodness, Wilfred, that pile looks worse than the one on my desk,' Edwin said, pulling out a chair and sitting down beside him. 'How are things?'

'On the improve, thanks. Winnie brought me one of her concoctions. Tastes vile but it's perked me up no end.'

'Which is just as well seeing as how he were that crotchety I were going to make a poppet of him,' Edith laughed, bustling in with the teapot. 'Saw you coming across the fields so I made a brew,' she said, setting it down on the dresser where mugs were laid out ready.

'Hello, Edith,' Louisa said, going over to assist. 'What's a poppet?' she asked.

'It's a doll you fashion to look like the person you want to put a spell on,' she said, giving Wilfred a pointed look. 'Winnie was telling me about them.'

'I think I could use one of those,' Louisa murmured, giving Sam a rueful look as she handed him his tea.

'Right, young'uns, we have work to do so yer'll have to amuse yerselves,' Wilfred declared, as though they were children.

'Come on, Louisa, we might as well warm ourselves beside the blaze. I'm sure Father will shout if he needs me to interpret any of my scribblings,' he said, raising his brow. 'These are apple thinnings from last year,' he said, picking up a handful of sticks from the basket and tossing them onto the flames.

'I wondered what was smelling so nice,' Louisa replied, settling herself into the sagging yet comfortable armchair.

As Edwin and Wilfred began going through the estate's papers and Edith returned to the scullery, Sam turned to Louisa.

'Do I gather her ladyship's playing up?'

'You could say that. Do you know she told Henry he had to be back in time for our ball?' She shook her head.

'I saw him leaving earlier, and as he was dressed in his uniform, I guessed he'd been called back to his regiment.'

'Yes,' she sighed, her stomach knotting again at the thought. 'He doesn't know exactly where he's going or when he'll be back, but that's the nature of his job, isn't it?' She forced a smile.

'I'm sure he'll come home safe and well as soon as he can,' he replied, patting her hand reassuringly. 'In the meantime, I'm here if you need a friendly ear.'

'Which one are you offering?' she quipped, determined not to let her dark thoughts take over.

'Well, they both have excellent hearing so you can choose. I'm generous like that. Do you want me to take your coat?'

'No thank you. However, I will take this off,' she said, placing her hat beside her feet.

'Looks like a dead cat,' Sam joked.

'Behave yourself, Samuel Gill, or I won't let you have a certain young lady's address,' she said, reaching into her pocket and pulling out a slip of paper. 'At least, the one for where she works,' she amended, handing it to him.

'Thanks for that. Do you think she'd mind me writing to her?' he asked, looking worried.

'For heaven's sake, what are you, man or mouse?' Louisa asked, keeping her voice low so the others didn't hear. 'Just pen a letter saying you've been thinking of her and would she mind if you could call and see her. Explain you were hoping to speak to her before she left, but unfortunately you got detained and arrived too late. Tell her she's the most beautiful lady you've ever met and that you lie awake at night dreaming of her.'

'I can't do that,' he cried, flushing as his father shot him a look.

'You should see your face,' she laughed. 'I've been reading

The Lady of the Lake so you can blame that. Although, all we ladies dream of being swept off our feet.'

'Really?' he asked, staring at her in surprise. 'Very well then, I will write. And if she doesn't answer, at least I'll have tried.'

'Of course she'll answer, Sam. You're not that bad-looking really, especially in the light of the fire,' she grinned, then looked serious. 'You should have more confidence in your dealings with the fairer sex. Now tell me, what's been happening in Combe?'

They were so caught up in their discussion that before Louisa knew it, Edwin was rising to his feet.

'You've done a good job compiling all this, Wilfred,' he said, tapping the folder in his hand. 'I'll see the necessary repairs are put in hand. As for you, Sam, I'm impressed with how you've kept things running while your father's been out of action. You'll make a good manager when the time comes.'

'Which isn't yet being as how my leg's almost good as new. I'll be back out there in a day or two,' Wilfred said quickly.

As they made their farewells, Louisa noticed her father slip something into Sam's hand and guessed he was giving him a bonus for taking charge of the running of the estate.

***

Charlotte threw open the door to Edwin's office only to find the room empty. Where had the man disappeared to? Her plans for a bandstand might have been thwarted, but she'd had another, even better idea which she urgently wanted to discuss with him. Really, the man was exasperating.

And where had Louisa got to? Honestly, that girl had no idea how much preparation a wedding took, she thought, retracing her steps. The pictures she'd asked her sister, Emmeline, to send illustrating what society brides were wearing in London had arrived that very morning and she was eager to show them to her. After all, the bridal gown was the pièce de résistance and it was never too soon to start planning. She'd thought that if they'd chosen the style by the time Madame Pittier arrived, she could advise on appropriate corsetry. Of course, that Miss Haydon had done a reasonable job but Madame with her wealth of experience would know exactly what was required. And she was French.

There was so much to organise and although it was inconvenient that Captain Beauchamp had to go away, at least it meant Louisa could devote her attention to preparing for both her ball and the wedding ceremony itself. As well as wishing to show Edwin what a competent wife he had, Charlotte was desperate for Louisa to recognise her as the wonderful stepmother she tried so hard to be. Charlotte could visualise them both sitting beside the fire embroidering items for the marital home as they discussed her future. After all, every girl needed a woman's guidance before her wedding night, didn't she? And who better than she to advise Louisa on how to use the opportunities when men are at their most vulnerable to get her own way?

Passing the stairs, Charlotte decided to pay a visit to the schoolroom. After what Edwin had said, she should check that the governess, or Nanny as he insisted she be called, was attending to her duties. However, on entering the room, she saw the three of them, backs towards her, gathered around the large globe. The woman was pointing out the various countries of the British Empire while Sarah and Maria looked on, enthralled.

'I shall buy a big ship and visit them all when I'm grown up,' Sarah exclaimed, clapping her hands excitedly.

'And me,' Maria cried, determined not to be left out.

Smiling at their enthusiasm, yet making a note to instruct them on the responsibilities required of young ladies, Charlotte decided not to interrupt their lesson. It was only just over an hour before the girls were brought to her anyway so she'd use the time to peruse the pictures in peace. At least then she'd be in a position to advise Louisa which was the best gown to choose.

How typical it was of Edwin to make a fuss about nothing when he returned from a business trip, she thought, gliding back down the staircase. As if she wasn't capable of overseeing the running of the household in his absence. It really was time he appreciated all she did. Picking up the cherub clock in the hallway, she smiled at its beauty and wondered if she should commission another to be made for Louisa and Henry's betrothal present.

She'd just settled onto her favourite chaise and begun studying the images when there was a loud and persistent knocking on the front door. How uncouth some people were, she thought. Thank heavens she wasn't hosting an At Home this afternoon.

'Excuse me, Lady Farringdon.'

'What is it, Ferris?' she frowned.

'There's been an accident at the quarry and—'

'Thank you, Ferris. I'll deal with this,' Edwin said, striding into the room and taking charge. 'Ask Quick to bring the cart, it can manage the narrow lanes and will be quicker than walking.'

'Edwin, where on earth have you been? I've been searching everywhere for you—' Charlotte began.

'I've just called in to let you know Sam has taken Louisa to collect Victoria and Beatrice from Neavesham Hall. The recital was due to finish at four o'clock,' he cut in. 'Now I really must go. I'll be back as soon as I can.'

'Well really, Edwin. Why can't that quarry manager of yours deal with it?' But she was talking to an empty room.

***

As the cart rattled its way down the driveway in the dimpsy light, Edwin's thoughts were running amok and he hoped it was only a minor mishap. However, as soon as they turned into the lane leading to the quarry, they could hear the commotion and see pinpricks of light from the swinging lamps.

'Looks like a rum do, guv,' Quick muttered as the sound of shouting and cries of distress reached them. 'I'd better pull in here, out of the way.'

As soon as they jolted to a halt, Edwin jumped out and hurried over to where Wakeley was directing a group of men to move the frenzied horses out of the way. The remains of an upturned wagon were slewed across the entrance to the cave, part of its broken load pinioned beneath the wreckage.

Further along, Edwin could see a group of men standing over a body that had obviously been dragged away from it. The low muttering and shaking of heads told Edwin there was nothing that could be done for him.

'What happened?' Edwin asked.

'A team of men were hoisting a stone the Touchstone had valued as usual, but the idiots rested the block on the edge of the wagon and the whole thing toppled over, trapping them beneath. We've managed to pull them all out but four were already dead and the two others are badly crushed, so...' He shrugged.

'Has the physician been called?'

'He's seeing to young Cal now but his legs got left behind under the wreckage. Luckily for him, he passed out with the pain and shock but God knows if he'll make it. As for the other one, his head were badly smashed.' Wakeley shook his head and even in the dwindling light, Edwin could see how shaken he was.

'You seem to have things in hand – does anything else need doing?' Edwin asked, anxious to help.

'Yes, you can drum some common sense into their thick heads,' Wakeley roared. 'They know full well it's against the rules to load the wagons themselves, but they do it to save time. Sorry,' the man muttered, wiping the sweat from his brow with the back of his hand.

'I understand. What about the next of kin?'

'Fletcher and Doolie have gone to tell them. I'll see everything is cleared up here so it won't affect the next shift. I'll make a full investigation, gather further details then make my report,' he said briskly. 'There's no need for you to stay, my lord,' he added as the mutterings from the men assembled nearby grew louder.

'I'll be sure to visit the women and pay my condolences in the morning,' Edwin murmured.

'Best leave it a few days, emotions will be running high,' Wakeley advised. Then someone called out and touching his hand to his cap he turned away.

'I'll see you tomorrow,' Edwin called after him.

Knowing there was nothing he could do to help and that if he stayed, he'd only be in the way, or worse inflame the situation, Edwin made his way back to the cart. At every step, he could feel the eyes of the men following him and knew they'd be worrying that the stupidity of those workers would impact on all of them. Despite the indifferent attitude of other quarry owners for whom maximum output was the only thing they worried about, Edwin had put in place strict rules so that preventable accidents like this didn't happen. Angry his instructions had been flouted and sad at the futile loss of life, he nodded curtly in their direction then climbed up beside Quick.

Chapter 17

The past few days, during which the accident at the quarry was investigated and a report compiled, had taken their toll on her father and knowing that, Louisa insisted on accompanying him on his visit to Combe. Now he sat rigid and tense whilst the carriage wended its way down the steep hill towards the village.

'It wasn't your fault, Papa,' she told him, patting his arm.

'That's as maybe, but the unnecessary loss of life was brought about by impatience fuelled by greed and it sickens me. I have insisted Wakeley put stricter measures in place to ensure that only the crane driver loads the wagons and the foreman checks the lewis is hammered in properly. Then, please God, nothing like this will ever happen again.'

Louisa sat back in her seat and stared out of the window. She knew that accidents were an occupational hazard at the quarry, with those working underground at greater risk, but for some reason this particular incident had affected everyone more than usual. Or perhaps, now she was older, she understood things better. Which is more than her stepmother did, demanding Edwin behave in the manner befitting the lord of the manor whilst the quarry manager assumed the responsibility he was paid for. And she had declined to join them today, insisting her social diary was full with engagements too important to be deferred.

'We must find out how we can best help these families, Papa,' Louisa said, as the carriage pulled up outside the row of tiny cots huddled into the side of the hill.

'I agree. If only those men had thought about the misery their impetuous actions could cause, this wouldn't be necessary.' He sighed as he climbed down the steps and turned to help his daughter. 'Perhaps, whilst I'm talking, you could take note of any particular hardship you think should be addressed. Being a woman, you might pick up on something I wouldn't.'

However, as they went from home to home, it was evident these women already lived in poverty and the lack of future wages would inevitably lead to the children going hungry.

'What do yer know of hardship, coming here in yer posh carriage wearing them fancy clothes and jewels?' one woman spat, eyeing them up and down contemptuously.

'I'm so sorry for your loss, you must have loved your husband very much,' Louisa replied, her heart lurching as she thought of how bereft she'd be if anything happened to Henry.

'Love?' the woman cackled. 'He brought in the money; I saw to his needs. That's the way it is for the likes of us.'

'But we want to help,' Louisa said quickly when she saw the tic in her father's cheek, a sure sign his anger was about to boil over.

'Then when we can't pays our rent yer can move us into yer fine manor 'ouse. Get off with yer, fine words don't butter no parsnips here.' And with that she slammed the door.

However, the woman in the next cottage, who couldn't have been much older than Louisa, was more respectful as she explained their plight. Whilst talking, she was trying to feed her baby under the cover of her tatty shawl, her other children clutching at her skirts as they stared at Edwin suspiciously.

''Tis all right for thems as got boys eight or over for they can earn a few pence taking candles to the men at the workface or feed the horses while they're underground, but the likes of me with four children under five ain't got no hope.'

'But there must be something we can do?' Louisa cried.

'Look, you're very kind, but it'll be the workhouse or walking the streets for us now. Ain't that right, Flo?' she called to the girl standing at the adjoining door.

'Yeah, the only way me and Rosa could afford even the cheapest coffin was to put my Cal and her Nobby in one together. Even then, what remains they found only half filled it,' the woman told her, lines of worry already etched into her young skin. 'We was only wed two year and gawd knows what I'll do now,' she sobbed, cradling her baby close while her swollen stomach was a testament to the new life soon to be born.

'I will see that supplies are sent for the children—' Edwin began.

'We don't take charity,' Rosa said quietly. 'We has our pride if nothin' else.'

'This is terrible,' Louisa told Edwin, feeling the tears welling as they turned away.

'I know,' he murmured, his eyes bleak. 'I must speak with Parson Preetcher, see what the parish is doing to help.'

'I'll take a walk around while you do,' Louisa told him, for the seemingly hopeless lives these poor women had ahead of them, not to mention their hungry children, had left her feeling despondent.

'For heaven's sake, Louisa, you can't wander around by yourself,' he muttered, staring at the filthy urchins playing in the muddy lane. Louisa sighed at the sight of their ill-fitting, threadbare clothes that were wholly inadequate for the inclement February weather. They'd stopped their game and were watching with the same suspicion their mothers had, before going back to kicking up the detritus.

'You sound just like Step Mama,' Louisa snapped, frustrated at not being able to help. 'Look, there's Sam Gill over there. I'll see you at the carriage,' she told Edwin and before he could say anything, she hurried towards the man who was coming out of the forge.

'Hello, Louisa, it's not often we see you in Combe. Are you quite well?' he asked, studying her closely.

'Oh, Sam, I've just been with Papa to see the quarry workers' widows. Those poor souls. Some of them are really young and have large families to feed yet, unbelievably, they've refused Papa's offer of food. I must do something but I don't know how to go about it,' she cried. He thought for a moment then smiled gently.

'Look, I've just dropped off the tools we used for coppicing with Tom to sharpen. He's asked me to give a message to his wife Lily, so why not come with me? She runs the dame school and if anyone knows how you can best help, she will.'

He led the way across the road to the cottage opposite,

which was thatched in the same material as the forge and surrounded by a neat garden. His knock was answered by a tall, dark-haired woman in her early thirties.

'Hello, stranger,' she greeted Sam enthusiastically, then turned to Louisa.

'Lily, this is Lady Louisa Farringdon from Nettlecombe Manor.'

'Delighted to make your acquaintance, Lady Louisa,' she replied, dipping a curtsy. 'Won't you come in?' Her glance took in Louisa's cape and matching hat but in an interested way and not contemptuously like the widows had earlier.

'If you're sure it's not inconvenient, and please, it's Louisa,' she replied, taking an immediate liking to her.

The front door led straight into the living room which had bright yellow curtains at the windows and matching cushions on the chairs. The table was set for luncheon and a delicious savoury aroma was wafting from a pot swinging over the fire. A little girl was playing with a rag doll on the colourful pegged mat whilst a baby burbled in a wicker cradle in the corner.

'Goodness, is it noon already?' Sam asked, sniffing the air appreciatively.

'Not yet, but I have a class this afternoon so I like to get forward. Johnny and Michael are over at the forge with Tom, but you're both welcome to join us for a bowl of barley soup when they come back.'

'That's very kind of you, Lily, but I have to meet with Papa when he's finished with the parson. He's gone to find out what is being done for the families of those men who died in the accident at the quarry.'

'Precious little, probably,' Lily retorted. 'It was different when old Parson Peddicombe was here. He was a good man.' The way she stressed the last few words left Louisa in no doubt as to what she thought of the current incumbent.

'Well, I'd be more than happy to stay,' said Sam, grinning. 'Oh, and Tom said to tell you he'll be a bit late because the baker's horse has shed one of its shoes and he's promised to fit a new one straight away.'

'Well, we mustn't turn our noses up at business and the poor man won't be able to finish his rounds otherwise. Now, apart from cadging some food, Samuel Gill, I'm thinking there must another reason for your visit.'

'Guilty as charged,' Sam admitted. 'We've come to pick your brains. Louisa went with his lordship to visit the new quarry widows. She's keen to help the families, but doesn't really know how best to go about things. I said what with you running the dame school you'd have some idea.'

'Why don't you sit down and we can discuss it,' she said, gesturing to the cosy chairs beside the fire. The little girl looked up and gave a toothy grin.

'Hello, Beth, how's baby today?' Sam asked, squatting down beside her.

'Naughty baby cry,' the little girl told him.

'Oh dear, do you think a tiny piece of fudge might help?' He took a bag from his pocket and solemnly handed her a piece of the creamy confection.

'Her mama eat it.' Beth grinned, popping it into her own mouth.

'You'll go far, little one.' Sam smiled as he got to his feet, then he pulled one of the wooden chairs from beside the table and placed it beside Louisa.

'What had you in mind?' Lily asked, perching delicately on the other armchair.

'Well, Papa offered to have supplies sent but they refused.' Louisa frowned, still unable to understand why they should turn his offer down.

'They would.' Lily nodded. 'Pride aplenty, that lot. Though it doesn't make much sense when their nippers need food.'

'Perhaps I can help in some other way? You see, for a while I've been wanting to do something for the people of the village. Now, after the accident, helping the widows and their families seems an opportune time to start. They don't have much, and with all those children to provide for I thought they'd appreciate some assistance.' There was a moment's silence while Lily mulled things over.

'I can see you are sincere, Louisa, and it's admirable you should want to help. But, as I said, these women are incredibly proud and it would need to be done in a way that wouldn't offend. A donation of food or money wouldn't be accepted.'

'Which is why I want to start up a charitable institution of some sort. An ongoing project I can oversee.'

'Louisa's betrothed has been called up and she will have plenty of time at her disposal,' Sam pointed out. 'Running the school, you obviously know these families.'

'Yes, I do, and I know that at the first opportunity to earn money the children are sent off to work rather than attend their lessons. One day ten or so children turn up, the next I'm lucky if there are any pupils. It's understandable, but a precarious way for me to try and add a few coppers to the family finances. Which means late nights making lace,' she added, nodding towards the shelf where her pillow was covered in a white cloth.

'Lily's work is exquisite,' Sam said.

'And I have the bags under the eyes to prove it,' she laughed. 'However, back to your proposal, Louisa. I've thought for a long time that the best way to help any widows and their families would be to help them earn their own living.'

'What, you mean have them making things?' Louisa asked, thinking of Jane Haydon.

'That could be one way, yes. If they were to be paid for producing something, that would help their self-worth as well as the bills. And if they had somewhere to work near here, they could send their children to school knowing they were being taken care of. But they would need to be paid cash rather than in kind at the hucksters' shops.'

'I thought the Trucking System had been abolished long ago.' Louisa frowned.

'It was, but for many employers around these parts it's still standard practice.' Lily smiled wryly.

'Then why do people put up with it?' Louisa asked, smiling down at the little girl as she toddled over and held out her doll.

'Now then, Beth, mind the lady's nice clothes with your sticky fingers,' Lily said, picking her up and placing her on her lap. 'They put up with it because they are desperate for work. The politicians talk about change but the reality is that everything stays the same for the likes of us.'

'But that is so wrong,' Louisa retorted.

'Which is why I was moved to run the dame school. I'm hoping to educate the adults as well as the children, but it's an uphill struggle. Now, young lady, go and rinse your hands ready for luncheon.' With a grin, the girl jumped down and ran out to the yard.

'I mustn't take up any more of your time,' Louisa said, getting to her feet. 'Thank you so much for speaking with me. I shall go and ponder on all you've said and then talk things over with Papa. Good day, Sam, enjoy your broth, it smells delicious.'

'Oh, I will, especially if Lily's baked her delicious bread to go with it.'

'Honestly, Sam, you're as bad as Tom,' Lily chuckled, jumping up and showing Louisa to the door. 'Feel free to call again,' she invited. 'It will be wonderful if you can do something to help before those women are either driven to prostitution or end up in the workhouse.'

Horrified by those thoughts, Louisa was impatient to discuss the matter with her father. However, when his carriage drew up alongside, she could tell from the set of his face that he was more enraged than he'd been when they'd set out. Clearly, his meeting with the parson had not gone well. Knowing from experience it was better to wait until he was ready to speak, she settled back in her seat and watched as they climbed the hill, where the cottages were larger and more spaced out as they left the village behind.

A horse overtook them at a gallop and for some reason it made Louisa think of Henry. She wondered if he'd arrived in Southampton yet and how soon it would be before he sailed.

So much had happened, it was incredible to think he'd only been gone a few days. Yet war was such a terrible thing and she knew the danger he was in. Closing her eyes, she prayed he would return safely.

'Are you all right, my dear?' Hearing her father's voice, she nodded. 'I know this morning was harrowing, but I was proud of the way you spoke to the widows.'

'Those poor women, Papa. I had no idea life was so difficult for them. And now…' She shook her head, hardly daring to voice the terrible futures they faced.

'I'm afraid Parson Preetcher was less than helpful. He kept going on about immorality, dens of iniquity, fallen women and how they would burn in hell. I tried pointing out that if they were given assistance now it could save them from having to compromise themselves in order to feed their children, but he wouldn't listen.'

'Lily, she's the mistress at the dame school, said he wouldn't. However, I've decided I'm going to help. With your permission, Papa, I would like to use some of the trust fund Mama left me to set up a place for these women to work.' As Edwin stared at her in surprise, Louisa took his hand. 'Do you think Mama would mind me using her money in this way?'

'I think… no, I *know*, she would be very proud of you.' Edwin sighed. 'It is just the kind of thing she would have done herself.'

'You still miss her?' Louisa asked softly.

'I do,' he said, nodding. 'Yet, as for those poor widows, life must go on. I've been making allowances for Charlotte's behaviour, telling myself she's still a young woman, but you are even younger and have far more compassion and under-standing.'

'Thank you, Papa. I must confess to knowing little about the hardships people suffer until this week, but now I intend putting what I've learned to good use.'

Chapter 18

As Jane travelled along the main Exeter to Lyme Road, her thoughts were spinning faster than the wheels on the little trap. The envelope Mr Farquharson had given her lay unopened on her lap but she was still too stunned by his revelation to read any paperwork. And to think she'd tried to defer their meeting until later in the week. But he'd been insistent, saying what he had to tell her couldn't wait. It meant that now she had to rush to keep the appointment with Lady Farringdon, for it would never do to keep her waiting. Yet her thoughts were far from the new corsets in her bag. They kept returning to the solicitor outlining the details of Madame's will. When Jane voiced her disbelief and the ensuing doubts that flooded her mind, he'd waved them away, saying he was sure she could rise to such a challenge. This had been Madame's express wish and he was sure Jane wouldn't want to let her down.

Luckily, knowing there was a full day ahead, she'd already hired the little vehicle and driver. Jane had wondered about writing to let the woman know it would be herself and not Madame Pittier visiting, but not wishing to risk rebuttal, had decided it would be better to make it a fait accompli. Despite the turmoil of the past few weeks, she'd managed to fulfil the order and couldn't afford all her hard work to be wasted.

What a time it had been. Amongst the letters of condolences had been two personal ones. The first had been from Lady Connaught requesting Jane visit her in Salthaven to discuss additions for her spring wardrobe. With Lady Day and the termination of their lease fast approaching, Jane needed to secure any commission possible in order for them both to survive. Millie had been right when she'd said they were like sisters, and Jane was determined to find a way for them to stay together.

Taking the other letter from her bag, she reread the simple words from Sam asking if he could call upon her on his next day off. Of course, he didn't know of her visit to Nettlecombe today, but she couldn't help hoping they might bump into each other. Her pulse racing at the thought, she hoped Lady Farringdon wouldn't detain her for too long.

Looking around, Jane was surprised to see they were already travelling along the tree-lined driveway leading to the manor. How beautiful everywhere looked in the bright winter sunshine, with the hint of buds on the limes heralding the dawn of a brand-new season. A bit like her life, she thought, tingling with excitement at the opportunities that were now opening up to her. She stared at the violets and snowdrops peeping from verdant borders as if, like her, they too were emerging into a new world. As the manor rose majestically ahead, she couldn't help wondering how anyone living in such splendid surroundings could be anything other than contented.

'Miss Jane Haydon, my lady,' the butler announced solemnly.

'This is outrageous,' the woman exclaimed, staring disapprovingly at Jane as she was shown into the Amber Room. Of course, today she was wearing her own clothes, thinking it disrespectful to wear her deceased employer's cape. 'I was expecting Madame Pittier.'

'Hello, Jane,' Bea cried, smiling delightedly.

'What a lovely surprise,' Louisa said, and Victoria nodded in agreement.

'Girls,' their stepmother reproved. 'May I ask what is the meaning of this, Miss Haydon? I was expecting the proprietor not her puppet.'

'And it is she who stands before you,' Jane replied, clutching her bag tighter.

'Really, girl, I do not have the time to play games,' Lady Farringdon retorted, the look in her eyes hardening.

'I'm afraid Madame Pittier passed away last month.'

'Well, it's a shame nobody thought to inform me,' Lady Farringdon tutted.

'A notice was placed in the obituary column of the *Exeter Flying Post*,' she told her.

'I do not read provincial newspapers such as the *Post*, Miss Haydon. Although his lordship casts his eye over them from time to time, he has been away on business.'

'We are very sorry to hear your news, Jane,' Victoria said quickly.

'Please accept our condolences. Things can't have been easy for you,' Louisa added.

'Thank you. It came as a dreadful shock,' she murmured. 'However, you'll be pleased to hear there was sufficient fabric in the workshop to make up all your corsets and chemises,' she told them, then turned back to Lady Farringdon. 'I deemed it good manners to honour the appointment we made, but if you don't wish to deal with me, then of course, I will leave.'

'What did you mean when you said the proprietor was standing before me?' the woman demanded.

'Exactly that, Lady Farringdon. Remarkable as it may seem, Madame Pittier endowed me with her business.'

'That is truly wonderful, is it not?' Louisa smiled at Lady Farringdon, who seemed momentarily lost for words.

'It was most generous of Madame and totally unexpected. I will need to secure alternative premises but it is my intention to carry on her business as she desired.'

'Good for you,' Bea declared.

'Beatrice,' Lady Farringdon chided. 'Well, Miss Haydon, now you are here you may as well show me the unmentionables.'

As Jane walked over to the table, she started, again catching the slight fragrance of lavender but, eager to please her ladyship, rather than comment she began setting out the garments on the highly polished surface. While the girls eagerly clustered around, Lady Farringdon picked up the cream chemise, her critical inspection reminding Jane of Madame Pittier.

'This stitching is nigh on invisible so was obviously done by Madame herself before she died, which is something, I suppose.' Jane opened her mouth to say it was her own work then closed it again. If it pleased Lady Farringdon to think that, why should she disillusion her and risk not being paid?

'Oh, this pink is absolutely gorgeous,' Bea declared, holding the chemise against her.

'It is somewhat brighter than the blush I was led to believe it would be,' her stepmother said tersely. 'And why anyone would want to wear grey, I do not know.'

'It's charcoal, and I love it,' Victoria retorted, holding up the garment to the light. 'Come on, Jane, you can help us try them on,' she added, snatching up the matching corset and heading towards the door.

'At least yours has the subtlety befitting a lady, Louisa,' Lady Farringdon acknowledged. 'We shall adjourn to the Rose Quartz anteroom where Shears and Vanstone are waiting.'

For the next hour or more, Jane was kept busy checking that the garments were all fitted to Lady Farringdon's satisfaction.

'I suppose that will do,' she grudgingly pronounced.

'Why, Step Mama, these are exquisitely made and fit like a second skin,' Louisa replied.

'And you're right, Jane, this colour makes my skin glow,' Bea cried, shooting her stepmother a triumphant look.

Relieved her work had gained approval, Jane glanced at the clock on the mantel, pleased to see she would have time to take a ride around the grounds in the hope of spotting Sam. However, it seemed Lady Farringdon had other ideas.

'Miss Haydon, I have asked Vanstone to furnish me with the necessary requirements for Sarah and Maria's underpinnings so we will return to the Amber Room and discuss suitable fabric.'

'Really, Step Mama, they are far too young for such restrictions, surely?' Louisa frowned.

'Are you suggesting I don't know what is best for my own daughters?'

'Of course not, but they are only six and four years of age.'

'And their bodies need to be moulded into shape, isn't that right, Miss Haydon?'

'It is admirable you should want the best for them, your ladyship. Perhaps a lightly corded bodice for night-time would suit the requirement?' Jane suggested. Although privately she agreed with Louisa, she was hardly in a position to argue with Lady Farringdon.

'Well, come along, we are wasting time and I have to prepare myself for this afternoon. You too, girls,' she added when they didn't move. 'We still have Louisa's wedding dress to discuss and undoubtedly new underpinnings will be required for that.'

Trying to curb her impatience, for this was business after all, Jane followed the little group back down the stairs and into the room that seemed more garish every time she entered it. Although she knew Madame had made corsets for girls as young as eight, Sarah and Maria had hardly outgrown infancy. However, Lady Farringdon had already seated herself on the chaise and was waiting for Jane to provide suitable samples.

'Perhaps a bodice in this cotton would be suitable. It is lovely and soft and the addition of a little piping would help train their bodies,' Jane suggested, hoping for the young girls' sakes the woman wouldn't insist on having boning inserted.

'Very well, but make sure you use pure white. They are children, after all.' As Jane bit back a retort, the woman continued. 'Now to Louisa's wedding gown.'

'Oh, can't that wait?' Louisa sighed. 'I've so much to do.'

'Fiddlesticks, nothing can be more important than that.'

'Take a seat, Miss Haydon, and give me your considered opinion of these illustrations,' Lady Farringdon said, handing Jane a file.

'The only gown I like is that one,' Louisa said, pointing to the elegant silhouette of a fitted white lace bodice with a band of embroidered flowers at the waist, from which silk skirts gently flowed. Its simplicity was stunning and Jane could see the shape would enhance Louisa's delicate frame.

'You can't possibly have one like that,' Lady Farringdon declared, looking aghast. 'The skirts aren't nearly wide enough. People would think we'd skimped on material. This is the one I favour.' She pointed to a dress with skirts a froth of fabric as wide as they were long.

'You'd look like you were covered in bunches of cow parsley, Lou,' Bea chortled.

'If you must make such a facetious remark, Beatrice, at least refer to it by its correct name, *anthriscus sylvestris*,' Lady Farringdon rebuked.

'Louisa wouldn't be able to sit down in that gown,' Victoria pointed out.

'It is the appearance that matters,' the woman retorted.

'I agree, Lady Farringdon, and it is important to look appealing from every angle, is it not? Although you are absolutely correct, skirts are becoming fuller. However, might it not look as if Louisa hadn't exercised self-control over her eating wearing something that immense?' Jane replied, winking surreptitiously at Louisa.

'Quelle horror!' Victoria mocked, covering her face with her hand. 'The peers of the realm might consider Louisa a Devonshire Dumpling.'

'Or worse, that she'd been presumptuous with Henry...'

'Beatrice Farringdon, I will not tolerate such wicked or ridiculous ruminations. Louisa's virtue is indubitable and you'd do well to follow her example,' Lady Farringdon advised.

'Did you hear that, Louisa, Step Mama actually paid you a compliment?' an unrepentant Bea smirked.

'Perhaps we could return to discussing the actual design,' Louisa said, flushing as she looked down at the illustration.

'I suppose Miss Haydon does have a point. It's just that this dress seems so plain.' Charlotte sighed, tapping the picture with her finger.

'A flowing train would add grandeur and sophistication,' Jane suggested.

'That's a marvellous idea,' Louisa cried. 'We could ask Lily to make one.'

'Surely you don't mean the woman who runs the dame school in the village?' Lady Farringdon grimaced.

'Why not? After all, she did help make the lace for Queen Victoria's wedding dress.'

'Well, why didn't you say so?' the woman exclaimed. 'Miss Haydon, perhaps you could call and discuss arrangements with her immediately.'

'I would, your ladyship, however, I am expected at Lady Connaught's this afternoon.' The ensuing silence was deafening.

'Indeed?' the woman finally replied. 'Well in that case, do not let me detain you any longer.' Jane frowned, perplexed by the woman's abrupt change in demeanour. How could she present her invoice now?

'I'll see you out,' Louisa said, jumping to her feet as Jane hurriedly returned the samples to her bag. They were halfway along the hallway before Jane realised they were heading towards the front door.

'But I can't—' she began.

'It's all right, there's another exit over there,' the girl said, opening a door hidden in the wooden panelling. Jane found herself in a bright room with tall windows and a grand piano in the centre but before she had time to take everything in, Louisa was speaking. 'This will save you having to go down to the staff quarters, and actually I wanted a chance to talk with you. First, though, give me the statement for your fee and I'll see Papa settles it straight away.'

'Oh, thank you,' Jane cried, relief flooding through her, for without payment she couldn't purchase new fabric. 'I didn't like to mention it just now for somehow I seem to have upset her ladyship.'

'I know and it's really amusing,' Louisa said, chuckling. 'Without realising it you have put her nose well and truly out of joint for Step Mama is holding an At Home this afternoon and Lady Connaught declined her invitation, claiming a prior engagement.'

'Oh,' Jane murmured. 'I didn't know.'

'Of course you didn't. Anyway, more importantly, did you receive the letter from Sam?'

'Yes, I did,' Jane replied, staring at her in surprise. 'But how did you know about that?'

'Sam and I have been friends for, well, ever. Oh, do put me out of my misery and say whether you agreed to him calling upon you?' Louisa asked, eyes bright with curiosity.

'I was rather hoping I might see him today but...'

'Come on then, he usually breaks for his luncheon about now. If we hurry, we might catch him.'

'But...' Jane began.

'At least let's try. Not having heard from you, the poor man is convinced you aren't interested,' Louisa said, urging Jane outside and along the path that skirted the manor. 'Actually, I wanted to thank you, Jane.'

'Me? Whatever for?'

'While my betrothed is away fighting in the Crimea, I want to do something worthwhile with my time. I'm not one for embroidery or needlework, you see, and can you imagine anything worse than spending endless hours bent over a hoop opposite Step Mama?' she asked, raising an immaculately arched brow. 'It was your sense of purpose and positivity that got me thinking.'

'I'm not sure I understand,' Jane told her.

'The widows in the village need some way of providing for their families and I thought I might set up a sort of sewing room where they can earn their own money. The only trouble is I have no idea what they could make, for I doubt they have much experience. It would need to be something simple – oh, and cheap to produce.' Jane thought for a moment then remembered the workers she'd seen marching to work at the quarry.

'Could they produce something for the quarry workers, like work shirts? The material wouldn't be that expensive and they could be made to a simple pattern.'

'That's a thought. Thank you, Jane. I knew you'd come up with something. Oh, here we are.'

Louisa stopped outside a stone cottage and pushed open the wicket gate, marching purposefully up the path. As she knocked on the door, Jane's heart began beating a tattoo. Suppose Sam thought her forward coming here unannounced? A pleasant-looking woman appeared in the doorway, wiping her hands on her apron.

'Sam's not due back until supper,' she told them, glancing at Jane curiously. Although her heart had flopped in disappointment, she managed to smile at the woman. 'Can I give him a message?'

'No, that's all right, Edith, I'll see him later. How is Wilfred managing?'

'Stubborn old fool thinks he can carry on where he left off. Still, at least he's out of my hair for most of the day now. I'll tell him you called by, Louisa, with your friend…?' she said, looking pointedly at Jane.

'Miss Haydon, Jane Haydon.'

'Well, nice to have met you. Now if you'll excuse me, by the smell of it, I think my pie's ready.' As the woman scuttled back inside, Louisa turned to Jane and shrugged.

'Oh well, it was worth a try. Shall I tell him he can call on you?'

'Please, if you would.' Jane nodded, forcing another smile. How ridiculous to feel so dejected when the man hadn't even known she was coming, she thought as they made their way back to the manor.

After thanking Louisa for her help, Jane located the trap by the stables and directed the driver to head for Combe. She'd been advised there was a lane leading from there to Salthaven and she needed to pay a visit to Mrs Somers en route.

Passing the lane to the quarry, she remembered Sam telling her it led right down to the sea and that he'd promised to show her one day. She had a sudden urge to ask the driver to turn left but realised she didn't have time to take a detour now. However, she would remind Sam when next they met, she thought as they made their way down the steep path towards the village. Then, as if thinking about him had conjured him up, she saw his cart coming towards her. Talk of the devil, she thought, her heart soaring as she gave a wave. However, to her dismay he frowned in her direction then carried on his way.

Chapter 19

Hoping Sam might have pulled in further along, Jane peered over her shoulder, but all she could see was a rising cloud of dust as his cart continued climbing the hill. She couldn't believe it. Having written asking to see her, why had he ignored her like that? How naive she'd been, hoping to surprise him, for clearly he'd changed his mind. Thank heavens he hadn't been at home; at least she'd been spared the embarrassment of him having to explain. Well, she had more important things to worry about, she thought, trying to blot out the image of his twinkling hazel eyes and cheeky grin as they shared a joke.

The sudden jolting of the trap as it turned into Combe brought her sharply back to the present. They'd already passed the forge and the school house where the children would be learning their lessons, and were heading along the meandering lane where the colourful spring flowers peeped bravely from the hedgerows. The row of thatched cottages spread out before them, beyond which the church of St Winifred's with its Norman square tower soared. Despite everything, she couldn't help admiring the magnificent stone building which had been set on a terrace so that it couldn't be seen by Viking raiders sailing along the coast all those years ago. Finally, they pulled to a halt outside Ida Somers' tiny dwelling, a wispy plume of smoke drifting up from the crooked chimney.

'I'll only be a few moments,' Jane told the driver as she climbed down. He nodded uninterestedly, but before she'd even reached the door, it burst open and the woman stood staring from her to the pony and trap beyond. Below her bonnet, which was trimmed with the pink ribbon Jane had given her, beady eyes burned bright with curiosity.

'Well, yer a sight for sore eyes,' she muttered. 'Come into money, have yer?'

'Hello, Mrs Somers, and no, not exactly,' Jane laughed. 'Although I have called to pay you for my board last month.' She drew out a purse from her pocket and counted out some coins.

'I'da can't deny that'd come in useful,' Mrs Somers said, gazing greedily at the money.

'Then you must take it—' Jane began, only for the woman to interrupt.

'But I'da be a truthful soul so that would be wrong when Lady Louisa did call by and pay me herself.'

'Oh, I didn't know,' Jane replied, amazed at the woman's honesty when she had so little.

'Being poor don't make me a thief,' the woman declared, as if she'd read Jane's mind.

'No, of course not,' Jane replied hastily. 'I'm glad you're not out of pocket. I've brought you a little gift to thank you for having me,' she added, handing over a small packet. The woman took it and tore eagerly at the wrapping.

'Oh my,' she gasped, holding up the square of satin fabric

in the same colour as the ribbon. 'Here, yer didn't steal it from your employer, did yer?' Her bird-like eyes bored into Jane.

'No, it was mine to give to whomever I please.'

'Well, that's all right then cos I'da really enjoyed working with yer on them toiles so if yer need any more help yer knows where I am. Oh look, Winnie's sent her familiar to find out what's goin' on.' She grinned as Athame suddenly appeared and began rubbing herself against Jane's legs. Wondering again at the strange ways of these people, she bent to stroke the cat only to find herself fixed with that luminous amber gaze that seemed to see right inside her.

'It'll be all round the village that yer've called by,' said Ida.

'I'd love to stay longer, but I'm afraid I have another appointment,' Jane replied, unnerved by the animal. She'd heard of witches' cats, of course, but always dismissed them as being the subject of old wives' stories. There again, this one did seem to like her. 'It's been nice seeing you again, Mrs Somers.'

'Don't forget to call by if yer needs any more stitching done,' the woman called after her.

Dear Mrs Somers, she really did think she'd helped make those toiles, Jane thought. Involuntarily, she glanced back along the lane but it was empty, and hardening her heart, she climbed back into the vehicle. She could have sworn Sam was genuine, but knowing little about the ways of men, she'd have to put this down to experience and be more wary in the future.

As instructed, the driver steered them past the rest of the cottages and out through the village on the other side. Seeing lanes leading off both to the left and right, Jane realised that

Combe was bigger than she'd originally thought and that it was well protected by the bank of rolling fields and hills that screened the cottages from the sea. They began the slow climb up yet another steep gradient and it seemed to Jane that all the hamlets around these parts nestled in valleys with cots clinging precariously to the sheer slopes. Then, in an instant the temperature dropped and they were cloaked in a grey mist that swirled around the stunted tree trunks making them look like grinning ghosts as they passed by.

'Always happens round here. Don't 'e worry, sea fret will be gone soon as it came,' the driver muttered as Jane shivered. Pulling her shawl tighter around her, Jane wished she had the benefit of Madame Pittier's thick cape to keep her warm, but deeming it unseemly to wear the deceased woman's things, she'd asked Millie to take them to St Catherine's. Now, with the chill air almost freezing her to the bone, she couldn't help thinking she'd been too rash.

However, just as the driver had said, no sooner had they gained the crest than the sky cleared and she caught the tang of salt on the breeze. Far below, bright blue waters topped with white foam shimmered in the fickle early spring sun. Despite her mood, she couldn't help a flutter of excitement at her first glimpse of the sea and craned her neck for a better view.

'Goin' as quick as I can, miss,' he grunted, mistaking her expression before turning his attention back to the lane ahead.

Realising she still had a way to go and needing to calm herself before her appointment, she decided to open the envelope Mr Farquharson had given her earlier that morning. Setting aside the official documentation listing the financial affairs of the business, she pulled out the letter left by Madame Pittier. Seeing the familiar neat script caused Jane's breath to catch in her throat and it was with shaking hands that she unfolded the notepaper, yet she couldn't help smiling when she caught a drift of rose fragrance.

Dearest Jane,

If you are reading this, then my time on earth has come to an end. As you will by now have come to realise, I am not one to show my personal feelings. However, I want you to know that I have always looked upon you as the daughter I never had. You have probably thought my behaviour towards you exacting over the years, but that is because you are a talented young woman and I wanted to help you to reach your potential. Having surpassed even my expectations, I can think of no one better to leave my business to. Yes Jane, you are now free to have that new sign written declaring Jane Haydon, Corsetière.

Be happy, my dear, and should you ever think of me, I hope it is with the same affection I feel for you.

Sincerely yours,

Rosetta Pittier

PS: As you well know, it is my view that rose pink best symbolises femininity, tenderness and romance.

However, you are, of course, at liberty to choose which colour best defines the ethos of your own establishment. Choose wisely, for it is this that your business will become known for.

So, what Mr Farquharson had told her was true. Dear Madame, Jane thought, dashing away a tear. An exacting employer she may have been, but there was no denying her kindness and generosity in taking Jane under her wing when her mother had abandoned both her job as maid and her young child, fleeing into the night, never to be seen again.

Sitting back on the hard seat, she stared down over the heather-clad cliffs, not seeing the fishing boats bobbing on the waves or the seagulls wheeling noisily above. In her mind's eye she saw a young girl running from room to room as she searched for her mother, Madame's calm voice telling her everything would come right, she could stay to help clean and cook. Which Jane had. Yet how longingly she'd stared at the well-dressed ladies who called at the *magasin* to choose fabulous fabrics for their unmentionables. How she'd watched, fascinated, as the lengths of fabrics were turned into the most beautiful corsets and chemises. The day Madame had caught her in the workshop, a pattern set out on the silk as she pretended to cut out a corset. Fearing dismissal, Jane had stared at Madame aghast. Instead the woman had encouraged and trained her until finally, after years of practice, she'd deemed Jane proficient to conduct consultations, determine clients' requirements and make up the garments. Of course, each one had to pass her employer's stringent test and at the beginning, many times, she'd been sent back to unpick and perfect.

Now, not only had Jane completed her apprenticeship, she was the proprietor of her own business. She shook her head in wonderment, warmth flooding through her as she began making plans. Then she started, remembering Mr Farquharson had also warned her that, regrettably, after other bequests and expenses, there was no money left in the will to renew the lease on Lady Day. Well, having been given such a wonderful opportunity, she wasn't about to fail at the first fence. What she needed was a strategy. Heedless of the passing scenery, she sat pondering. Would it be acceptable to ask Lady Connaught to pay in advance for her order, or at least furnish a deposit? Madame would be appalled at such an idea but did Jane have any choice if she wanted to continue trading?

'Here we are, miss.' As the driver's voice penetrated her thoughts, Jane looked up to see they were in a tree-lined driveway leading towards a handsome brick house with bow windows and pillared porches. The grounds surrounded it like a huge patchwork cushion and Jane wondered how many men it took to keep everything looking so immaculate. They came to a halt by a flight of steps that led up to the main entrance and climbing down, Jane marvelled at the vista over the town and on towards the sea.

'I'll probably be about an hour,' she told the driver as he handed her bag down.

'That's all right, miss, I'll park the trap around the back, see to the pony and cadge a cuppa off Jim, the groom. Don't worry, I'll be waiting right here when you come out,' he smiled, tipping his hand to his cloth cap.

As Jane climbed the steps, she saw the windows had stained glass and was reminded of the ones in Exeter Cathedral. It seemed presumptuous to be using the front door, yet Lady Connaught had said in her letter to come to the main entrance. Butterflies skittered in her stomach and she clutched her bag tighter, but she needn't have worried for she was ushered into a bright hallway by an immaculately dressed butler who seemed to have been expecting her.

'Lady Connaught is waiting in the Green Room, Miss Haydon,' he said, leading the way across the beautiful black and white tiles before rapping discreetly on an elegant pan-elled door.

'Miss Haydon, your ladyship,' he said, showing Jane into an airy room with high ceilings and tall windows. The walls were painted in a subtle hue of green with emerald velvet drapes at the casement windows.

'Thank you, Baines. We will take tea in half an hour,' she told him. 'Miss Haydon,' Lady Connaught greeted her warmly. She was wearing a pink dress with pearl buttons from collar to gently flaring waist, which whilst a nod to the changing mode, was elegant and flattered her fair colouring. 'I hate being formal so may I call you Jane?'

'Of course, Lady Connaught. What a delightful room,' she enthused, taking in the carved walnut armchairs uphol-stered in fabric that matched the drapes. They were arranged around the decorative hearth where a welcome fire was gently burning.

'I was so sorry to read of Madame Pittier's demise in the *Post*,' the woman said softly. 'She was a very accomplished lady and will be sorely missed.'

'Yes.' Jane nodded, feeling a lump rising in her throat. Still, at least Lady Connaught hadn't made her feel as though she'd placed the obituary in some obscure newspaper.

'Come, sit down and tell me how you have been, for I'm sure this must have come as a dreadful shock,' she said, gesturing to the seat beside her. 'I know Madame held you in great esteem.'

'Thank you. It has been a difficult time,' Jane admitted.

'It is I who must thank you for coming to visit, especially when you must have much to do. Having returned from Bath and found myself invited to some rather important social engagements, I am urgently in need of new attire. As you well know, Madame always said that good grooming begins with good underpinning.' The twinkle in her eye showed her affection for the woman as she repeated her maxim. 'And as time is of the essence, I am hoping you can advise me today then give my commission precedence.'

'Of course, Lady Connaught,' Jane agreed, mentally running through the limited stock of fabric she had left in the workroom after completing the orders Madame had taken before her demise.

'That is, I am assuming you intend carrying on running Madame's establishment?' Lady Connaught frowned as if the thought had just occurred to her.

'To be honest, Lady Connaught, I am feeling more than a little shocked. You see, I learned only this morning that Madame has kindly and most generously endowed her emporium to me.'

'Well, goodness. That is indeed most generous of her. Although, as I said before, I know she held you in great esteem.'

'And I her. I shall, of course, endeavour to continue working as she taught me. Although, I can't help but feel anxious. It is such a responsibility…' She broke off, worried she shouldn't be voicing her doubts to Lady Connaught.

'It is indeed admirable that you wish to continue Madame's emporium. It was her life's work, after all. However, you are certainly talented with the needle and Madame would never have endowed her precious business to you if she had any doubts about your capabilities.'

'Thank you. Madame taught me well,' Jane replied, wondering if she dared mention that her new terms of trading would require a deposit being paid in advance.

'This a marvellous opportunity for you, Jane, and I shall certainly be pleased to recommend your services,' the woman enthused. 'As you know, it was I who pointed Lady Farringdon in your direction and, of course, I have a wealth of society contacts.'

Jane stared at Lady Connaught in surprise. Although she'd always got on well with her when she'd visited the shop, that she was prepared to go to so much trouble to help her was astonishing. It was then she realised she couldn't mislead this lovely woman, or anyone else for that matter. How stupid she'd been to think she could blithely carry on trading when, currently, the only money she had coming in was from Lady Farringdon and a few outstanding invoices. And that would only be sufficient to purchase a limited supply of fabric. There would still be nothing left to pay the rent.

As Jane opened her mouth to reply, there was a tap on the

door and the butler appeared with a tray followed by a maid who was concentrating carefully on the tiered stand she was carrying.

'Ah, afternoon tea.' Lady Connaught smiled. 'Yes, please do,' she told the butler in answer to his unspoken question. Jane waited impatiently whilst he poured their refreshment and the little maid proffered tiny sandwiches then withdrew. Although the food looked delicious, her stomach was so knotted she couldn't even think of eating and knew what she had to do.

'I'm sorry, Lady Connaught, I'm afraid I cannot accept your commission,' she murmured.

For a moment, Lady Connaught didn't respond. Instead she gazed at Jane thoughtfully, took a sip of her tea then placed her cup and saucer on the low walnut table in front of them.

'Having told me you intend carrying on Madame's business I can only assume you do not wish me to continue as a client. May I ask why, Miss Haydon?'

Jane stared at Lady Connaught in dismay. Not only had she refused her commission, she'd insulted the woman as well. Madame Pittier would have been mortified. Picking up her bag, she rose to her feet.

'Please don't leave before answering my question. Have I offended you in some way?'

'Oh no, quite the reverse. You've been so kind and I...' Emotion getting the better of her, Jane blinked back her tears. 'I want to carry on Madame's business, it's like a dream come true, only I can't until I have sorted out the finances.'

Chapter 20

Oh heavens, now she'd committed the ultimate sin and mentioned the dreaded money word, Jane thought, waiting for Lady Connaught to recoil in disgust. Instead, the woman gave her a searching look then smiled gently.

'I'm sure there is a solution to whatever is troubling you, so do please stay and have a cup of tea at least. If you don't mind my saying you look as if you could do with something to eat and I promise you will regret not trying those sandwiches. Cook makes the best smoked salmon and cucumber you'll ever have savoured. Now sit down and relax. I find things gain a better perspective when one has had some refreshment.'

Not wishing to offend the woman further, Jane sat back down and picked up her cup. If she hadn't been so upset, she might have laughed at the woman's assumption she'd never tasted better smoked salmon, for she'd never even seen that delicacy before.

'This is my favourite meal of the day,' Lady Connaught confided, smiling as though nothing was wrong. 'Sandwiches and cake are far more appealing than the sauce-laden dishes one is expected to partake of at dinner. Why not try a little something? I don't suppose you were given any luncheon at Nettlecombe,' she added, quirking a brow conspiratorially.

To please the woman, Jane took a tiny sandwich, and despite the awkwardness of the situation, couldn't help savouring the salty taste of the fish layered between soft bread and butter. However, the black tea with a slice of lemon floating on the top tasted fragrant and she wasn't sure she liked it. Aware Lady Connaught was surreptitiously watching her, she gingerly sipped the liquid and tried not to grimace. In order to rid her throat of the cloying taste, she accepted a tiny scone and found that, after all, she was quite hungry.

Finally, when the tea things had been removed, the woman leaned forward in her seat.

'There, that's better, you've regained some colour and I no longer need worry that you will collapse at my feet.'

'I'm sorry, Lady Connaught, I didn't mean to cause offence,' Jane murmured.

'None taken, my dear. Now, please tell me why you feel unable to carry on with Madame's Pittier's business when by your own admission it has always been your life's ambition?'

'Oh, it has, and I really am grateful. However, the solicitor has told me that when her estate is settled there will be nothing left to renew the lease, so unless I can find a solution, I will have to vacate the premises.' She stuttered to a halt, realising that once again she was discussing affairs Lady Connaught wouldn't have the slightest interest in. However, she'd under-estimated the woman.

'Oh, my dear, how simply terrible. Surely someone as astute as Madame would have set aside money from her takings for the rent?'

'Yes, which was fine whilst she was alive, but Mr

Farquharson explained that her brother, who lives abroad, relied on Madame to fund her nephew's education in this country. Apparently, she'd set up some kind of fund which she paid into each month, but a lump sum for him to finish his schooling was bequeathed to her brother on her death. As I said earlier, I only saw Mr Farquharson this morning and my mind is still reeling from everything he told me.'

'Goodness yes, it must be.' Lady Connaught nodded thoughtfully. 'Madame must have been very fond of you. Now you can call me a nosy old woman, but would it be awfully rude of me to enquire why she should leave you, an employee, the establishment of which she was inordinately proud?'

Briefly Jane explained about her mother disappearing and Madame training her, yet Lady Connaught still didn't look convinced.

'I have the message she left me,' she added, scrabbling in her bag and handing the envelope to Lady Connaught. 'I hate the thought of letting her down when she's been so good to me.' As the woman read, Jane sat back, overcome with fatigue. The day had been so eventful, her emotions having gone from surprise to elation, despair and now exhaustion all in the space of a few hours. All this talk of her former employer made her realise just how much she missed the woman too.

'I see,' Lady Connaught said, passing back the letter. 'But surely you are not going to give up such an opportunity lightly?'

'Goodness me, no. Mr Farquharson suggested I take a copy of the accounts to the bank and secure a loan but that seems such a daunting task.'

'But one that is borne out of necessity perhaps?' Lady Connaught said, eyeing her shrewdly. She let her words hang in the air for a moment before becoming brisk and businesslike. 'Time is getting on, so perhaps we should turn our discussion to my requirements. The fashions change so quickly, already I find last season's corsets inappropriate.'

It was another hour before Jane left with details of Lady Connaught's commission safely in her bag and the promise to return in ten days' time to fit the new undergarments. She should be feeling happy and confident but the thought of having to find funds to pay the rent sat like a stone in her stomach. Did she really have the nerve to approach the manager at the bank?

***

'Good morning, Miss Haydon.' Jane looked up from lifting down the heavy wooden shutters of the shop to see Mr Jones, raising his top hat in greeting.

'Good morning, Mr Jones,' she replied, her breath spiralling in the early morning air.

'It is a cold one again but thankfully dry,' he said, pausing instead of hurrying by as usual. He lowered his voice as a group of men dressed in business attire passed by. 'I was just wondering how you were managing after the sad demise of your employer?'

'Well enough, thank you, although...' Jane stuttered to a halt, wondering if she dare voice her concern.

'Although?' he repeated, sending her an encouraging look.

'I wondered how one went about seeing the manager of your bank?' she said quickly before her nerve deserted her.

'One makes an appointment. May I be of assistance? Perhaps if you could tell me who wishes to see him?'

'The appointment would be for myself, Mr Jones,' Jane replied, trying not to quail under his incredulous stare.

'Gracious. Still, why not, eh? I happen to know Mr Swindley has a space in his diary between noon and one o'clock today. Would you like me to put your name in for then?'

'Oh yes, please, Mr Jones,' Jane cried. Having spent the previous evening reading through the documentation Mr Farquharson had given her, along with trying to fathom out the accounts, she was keen to get the meeting over whilst the facts were still in her mind.

'I'll look forward to seeing you later then, Miss Haydon.' He smiled and politely doffing his hat, continued on his way.

She could do this, *would* do this, for Madame, Millie and herself, she thought, glancing up at the sign above the door and imagining it declaring Jane Haydon, Corsetière. Then she stopped in her tracks. How could she even think of changing the name? Having generously endowed the business she's so painstakingly built up to Jane, the least she could do was continue trading as Madame Rosetta Pittier. Knowing it was the right decision, she went inside and set about tidying the merchandise that was displayed in the window, delighting at the exotic smell of silks and satins mixed with the eau de rose she'd sprayed around earlier.

Of course, she could always put her own stamp on the

business by changing the fragrance and house colour, but Madame had known her profession inside out and Jane couldn't think of anything that better portrayed the quintessence of femininity than rose pink. Nevertheless, she could extend her range, she thought, recalling the way the Farringdon ladies had delighted in choosing the sheen of gold, the sophistication of charcoal and the brightness of blush. She would purchase fabrics that would appeal to a younger clientele and lavish trimmings for those wishing to tempt and tease their gentlemen. With her thoughts positively bubbling, she set about her morning tasks.

However, her excitement was overtaken by nerves as she sat before the bank manager. Having studied the documents she presented him with, Mr Swindley leaned back in his leather chair and frowned at Jane over his half-moon glasses.

'Exactly how old are you, Miss Haydon?'

'I shall be twenty in November, sir,' she told him sitting up straighter in her chair.

'As you have yet to reach your majority, not to mention being female, I assume you have someone to act as guarantor?' he asked.

'Guarantor? I'm sorry, I don't…' Jane faltered to a halt, not wishing to admit she had no idea what he meant.

'A father or some other male relative, perhaps, who will guarantee to repay the loan if you were to default.'

'I don't have a father, sir. But I can assure you I would never miss a payment. I'm honest and reliable,' she declared, clutching her bag tighter.

'I am sure you are. However, it is not your integrity that's in question, rather the fact that trade can be fickle. Predictions of profit and loss can change with the wind or stock market,' he told her, smiling at his little joke. 'How about collateral, then? Equity or surety that would equal the value of the loan, to safeguard the bank and ensure it will have some way of getting its money back,' he explained, seeing her bemusement. 'Obviously, a businesswoman like yourself understands about minimising risk.'

'Of course.' She nodded, wishing the room wasn't so stuffy. 'I don't think I have anything that would meet your requirement, although with fashions constantly changing, many ladies will be flocking to the boutique for new clothes.'

'I don't see a list of future orders here,' he said, stabbing at the book with his pudgy finger.

'At the moment I have firm commissions from two clients, but I also intend to create a new range and—' Jane began, only for the man to let out a whistle between his teeth.

'That would cost money. I'm sorry, Miss Haydon,' he said, gathering up the documentation and handing it back to her. 'I'm afraid you don't fulfil the bank's criteria and therefore regret I cannot sanction a loan. Good afternoon.' He rose to his feet and showed her the door. Trying not to scream with frustration, Jane nodded politely, then, head held high, walked from his office.

Although the bank was busy, as if he'd been waiting for Jane to reappear, Mr Jones looked up from his work and quirked a brow enquiringly. Feeling humiliated and not wishing to discuss her futile visit, she forced a smile and pushed her way through the queue. Hurrying down the street, she could feel her spirits sinking lower and lower. In the space of twenty minutes, all her hopes and dreams for the future had been crushed. Now, despite her best endeavours, come Lady Day she and Millie would have to vacate after all. She could no longer waste time dreaming of colour or fragrance, she urgently needed to find somewhere else to live and sew, or they would find themselves on the streets.

'Here, yer got a visitor,' Millie cried, her face flushed with excitement as she swooped on Jane the moment she let herself in the door. 'I put him in the Receiving Room as the fire's lit in there.'

'Thank you, Millie,' Jane replied, forcing a smile as she shrugged off her shawl and placed it carefully on the peg. She hoped it was Mr Farquharson and not that upstart assistant of his.

'Oh,' she gasped, coming to a halt in the doorway when she saw who her visitor was. Ignoring the fluttering of her heart, she forced herself to be cool and gave him a professional smile. 'Mr Gill, I wasn't expecting to see you again.'

'Miss Haydon, I have come to apologise,' Sam began, flushing uncomfortably. 'I'm afraid I didn't recognise you when we passed in the lane yesterday. I wasn't expecting to see you, far less riding in a pony and trap, and it was only when Louisa mentioned you'd called by...' He paused, turning his cap round and round in his hands.

'Do go on, Mr Gill,' Jane said, her voice sounding icy even to her own ears.

'Sorry, I always gabble when I'm nervous. Ma says I should take a deep breath... Sorry, you don't need to know that.

Anyway, it was only when Louisa told me about your visit and that you were on your way to see Mrs Somers, that I realised it was you I'd passed in the lane. I turned straight round and made my way to Combe as fast as I could, but Ida told me you'd already left for another appointment.' Jane waited until he finally stuttered to a halt.

'Do you really expect me to believe you didn't recognise me?'

'Well, that's the thing. Had you been wearing that lovely bright pink cape I probably would have.'

'Are you telling me, Mr Gill, that you judge a person by what they wear?' Jane cried. 'Really, I hardly think—'

'Please let me explain,' he interrupted. 'The measles disease I had as a child left me with a sight impairment and I should have been wearing these.' He held out something for her to see. Jane looked from his grave expression to the wire-rimmed glasses in his hand.

'Having never seen you in spectacles, I presume you are too vain to wear them?' she asked, trying to keep a straight face as he fidgeted uncomfortably.

'It's not that, although I admit they're hardly flattering. The arms hurt the back of my ears and get caught up in my cap. It can be distracting when I'm working and driving the cart so I find it safer to leave them off.'

'You'd rather shun people you know?' she persisted, not yet ready to forgive the hurt he'd inflicted on her the previous day, albeit unintentionally. But it was no good, she couldn't keep up her stern manner and, whether from relief that he hadn't intentionally ignored her, or release of her earlier pent-up frustration, she burst out laughing.

'It's no laughing matter. You wouldn't believe the lengths I've gone to in order to see you today. Lady Louisa even invented a spurious errand for me to do in Exeter,' he cried indignantly, then his lips twitched and he began chuckling too. 'Oh, Miss Haydon, or Jane if I may still call you that, can you forgive me?'

'Well, in all fairness you weren't expecting to see me yesterday, so yes on both counts, Sam.' She smiled, relieved the mystery had been cleared up.

'Can I brings the tea in now?' Millie squeaked. 'Only it sounded like we was having another one of them riots.' She placed the tray on the table then tutted. 'It's a good job we had no clients in the shop.'

Jane and Sam exchanged sheepish looks but the atmosphere fizzed between them and neither could look away.

'Don't mind me, I'm sure,' Millie huffed, but neither of them heard her and with a shake of her head, she left them to it.

Sam took a step closer then hesitated just as Jane realised she was staring and tore her gaze away. There was a moment's silence and then they both spoke at the same time.

'May I offer you some refreshment?'

'Would you let me take you out for luncheon by way of apology?' Sam asked.

They laughed again, the tension replaced by one of awareness.

'Millie will kill me if I let her tea go to waste, so why don't we make ourselves comfortable here,' Jane said, gesturing to the chair nearest the fire.

'If it means I can sit here and look at you for longer, then yes please.' Sam grinned, folding his frame into the elegant seat and almost swamping the pink cushions.

'Don't be ridiculous,' she replied, trying to sound serious as she poured their drinks. 'After all, by your own admission, you can't see much without your spectacles.'

'Touché, Miss Haydon,' he grinned, taking the cup from her. He placed it carefully on the table then turned to her, his expression solemn. 'I do have an important question to ask, though, one that doesn't require me to wear them.'

'Go on.' Jane frowned, wondering what was coming.

'I spent all last night thinking of you, dreaming of you even, and wonder, would you do me the honour of walking out with me?'

Chapter 21

Edwin glanced at his wife and thought how lovely she looked with the rays of sunshine glinting her hair like spun gold. Satisfied the new systems he had put in place at the quarry would help ensure the men's safety, he decided to spend the next few days focusing on his family.

'It's a beautiful morning, shall we take a walk around the garden, my dear?' There was a stunned silence as Charlotte looked up from the list she was compiling and stared at him in astonishment.

'May I ask what has prompted this?' she asked.

'I thought it would be nice for us to spend time together and I'd also like to discuss our daughters' futures. But of course, if you're too busy,' he said, gesturing to her notebook.

'I was just checking the details for Louisa's ball. The invitations should arrive this week,' she told him. 'And before you say anything, Louisa received a communication from Henry earlier. Of course, I don't know what it said but her cheeks flushed with delight as she read it.'

'Well, that's good. However...' Edwin hesitated, not sure whether to go on. Having read reports of the accelerating war in the papers, he could only guess what would be awaiting

Henry when he arrived in Gallipoli, yet would it be fair to voice his concern? 'You don't think you're being a bit presumptuous under the circumstances?' he finally ventured.

'Edwin, I'm well aware of the situation in the Crimea. However, as Louisa's stepmother it is my duty to support her and if that means planning a ball Henry might not be here to attend, then so be it. It will help take her mind off things. In the event that Henry's return is delayed, the ball will still go ahead.'

'You surely don't mean hosting two balls?' Edwin stared at his wife, aghast.

'Why not? It will be a good opportunity to introduce the Beauchamps to our friends. We can always reschedule the official occasion for later in the year when Victoria and I return after the season. We don't have to go overboard and I really am trying to do the best for your daughters.'

'Thank you, Charlotte,' he murmured, knowing he couldn't argue, for hadn't he wanted them all to get on? 'Although, I understand Louisa intends setting up a sewing establishment for the widows in Combe, so I think she will have enough to keep her busy.'

'What, a sewing school?' Charlotte grimaced. 'Really, Edwin, I do wish you wouldn't encourage her. Quite apart from the fact you have a position to uphold, as the future wife of a captain in the Guards, Louisa really shouldn't be seen associating with that kind of women.'

'I'm sorry but I disagree,' Edwin said, firmly. 'We have always encouraged the girls to be respectful of their privileged standing in the community whilst being sympathetic to the plight of the villagers. I'm proud that she plans to help these poor widows earn their own money so they can help pay their way in life. Just putting bread on the table to feed their children is a challenge at the moment. What's more, as all this has come about as a result of the accident at the quarry, I intend financing some of the venture myself.' Charlotte gave him a glacial stare then shrugged.

'Obviously, you and Louisa have made up your minds and my opinion is of little value.'

'That is not true. In fact, I'd be delighted if you would take an interest in the people of Combe as well. We have to remember that it is fate that determines which class we are born into, and the lifestyle that affords – or not, as the case may be.'

'If that was a dig at me, Edwin, it was a low one. Now, I agree that it's a beautiful morning for a stroll around the estate so I'll go and get my wrap,' she said hastily, getting to her feet.

Edwin watched her go, cursing his clumsiness. Charlotte was so accomplished at acting as lady of the manor, he sometimes forgot she hadn't been born to it.

As soon as he felt the fresh air on his face, Edwin began to relax again. The sky was brilliant azure, and the stiff breeze sent the few fluffy clouds scudding above the trees along with the cobwebs from his head. Edwin took his wife's gloved hand and placed it through the crook of his arm. The trill of a blackbird and the fragrance wafting from early flowering hyacinths and snowdrops made him feel content. Soon the lime trees bordering the estate would be bursting into bud, a sight which never failed to fill him with hope.

'It's been a long time since we've done this,' Charlotte told him. 'I cannot understand why you employ a manager yet still insist on going to that wretched quarry each day.' Hearing the accusation in her voice, Edwin patted her hand.

'As I said earlier, the Farringdons have always prided themselves on working closely with the villagers and I have a duty to the men I employ. Accidents leave a nasty taste and I feel it my responsibility to ensure safety measures are in place. Now they are, and it is up to Wakeley to see they are observed. Anyway, that is quite enough talk of work,' he said, leading her along one of the gravel paths that divided the lawn bordering the walled kitchen garden, and on towards the glasshouses. Opening the door of the nearest one, he gestured for her to enter.

'Why have we come in here?' she cried, wrinkling her nose at the pungent smell of damp earth and fertiliser.

'I have something special to show you,' Edwin told her, firmly shutting the draught out behind him. 'I have been coming in here most mornings before going to the quarry.'

'You have?' she asked, stopping to stare at him. 'You mean you haven't been visiting the chapel graveyard each day?'

'No, of course I haven't. I admit I do visit Beatrice's grave from time to time, but certainly not every day,' he told her, shaking his head when he saw her look of relief. 'I wouldn't expect you to tolerate that, my dear. Now come and see what I have been doing.' As his wife looked around in bewilderment he smiled.

'With Reed's help, I'm cultivating a new type of rose. Look,' he said, pointing proudly to a pot on the bench where a row of tiny plants flourished.

'But these are weeds,' Charlotte murmured, frowning at the straggly green shoots.

'Believe you me, it has taken a lot of work, both from the bees and Reed's expertise at hybridisation to get this far. However, he assures me that come late spring these will be handsome little rose bushes which, when they flower, will be apricot in colour.'

'My favourite colour. Oh, Edwin, you are a darling,' she cried, her eyes lighting up in delight.

'Well yes, and I thought they'd be perfect for the wedding, which is why I'm going to name the rose—'

'Charlotte,' she cried, cutting in before he'd finished.

'Actually, my dear—' he began.

'You marvellous man. I do love you so.' She was staring at him with such adulation, there was only one thing he could do. Swallowing down his disappointment he nodded. 'Of course, what else?' For months now he'd been working on his own wedding gift for Louisa. Was it too late to cultivate another rose? he wondered, vowing to speak to Reed as soon as he could.

'Come along,' he said, gently leading her outside and back along the path, Charlotte chattering at his side.

'Why, Edwin, that is the most marvellous present you could have given me. I shall be the envy of all our guests at the betrothal ball.'

Dismayed at the way his surprise had backfired, Edwin could only nod. They wandered on past the circular flower beds which in summer would be a riot of roses, until they came to the land that had been reinstated after the bandstand episode.

'At least the ground is beginning to look presentable again,' he observed, stopping to study the area. He would ask Reed to see that some of the more mature shrubs were transplanted here to cover the empty expanse of earth.

'I admit that was a mistake, Edwin,' Charlotte said softly. 'However, I have had another, much better idea. Don't you think this site would be perfect for a folly?'

'A what?' he gasped, turning to face her.

'A folly, Edwin,' she repeated. 'It's a decorative building or tower.'

'I know what one is, but what purpose would it serve here?'

'With windows on each side we could sit and take in the splendid views of both the coast and the rolling countryside. Lady Connaught was telling me about a friend of hers who has one. It's called Lawrence Castle and is so tall you can see the tors of Dartmoor and Exmoor as well as over the Exe Valley right to the estuary and sea beyond. Can't you visualise one like that here?' she exclaimed, making an elaborate sweeping gesture. The trouble was, Edwin could.

'It's a lovely idea but regrettably there's not enough room for such a large building here…'

'I've already thought of that. If we moved the estate cottages, we could—'

'For heaven's sake, that's an appalling suggestion and absolutely out of the question,' he exclaimed, horrified at the thought. 'These are the homes of our workers and their families.'

'Which I understand they have at a peppercorn rent.'

'That constitutes a major part of their wages. Just imagine how upset they'd be if they had to move. Besides, the cost would be astronomical and Nettlecombe doesn't have that kind of money available, I'm afraid. Come on, let's continue our walk,' he added quickly when he saw her lips form a moue. 'Oh look, the primroses are coming out and that always heralds a sign of spring.'

'That's true,' she agreed, much to his relief. 'Talking of the new season reminds me, I really must see about appropriate attire for there will be concerts and recitals to attend. And of course, you have made my choice of colour for me, you clever man. Apricot will be perfect and will match my roses perfectly.'

As Charlotte chattered on, Edwin hardly heard for his attention had been caught by the sounds of laughter as Sarah and Maria tore across the grass followed by Nanny. Even from this distance he could see the woman was struggling to keep up.

'Poor Nanny,' he muttered. 'I really do think we should hire a governess to assist.'

'Now, Edwin, I've told you before, that is my department,' Charlotte told him. 'Although I do think the woman should ensure they act with decorum rather than run round like rapscallions. Leave it to me – after all, it is I who oversees the smooth running of your household whilst you are playing quarries and attending to business in London.'

'And very well you do it all too, my dear,' he replied, peering up at the dark clouds which had gathered and were now looming ominously over the nearby hills. 'I think we should be getting back before it rains. It wouldn't do for you to get chilled, now, would it?'

'Oh Edwin, you really do care for me, don't you?' she murmured, a delicate flush staining her cheeks.

'Yes, Charlotte, I do, and I would like it very much if you would permit me to prove it to you tonight.'

'Very well, Edwin,' she agreed, looking up at him coyly as she squeezed his arm.

Feeling happy and hopeful after his exchange with his wife, Edwin let himself into his study. He just had time to look at the latest figures Wakeley had provided before the meeting with his eldest daughter.

***

Louisa took her letter through to the Citrine Room where it was quiet and she was unlikely to be disturbed. Since Henry's last visit, she felt closest to him in here and carefully picking up the letter opener, she slit the envelope, puzzled when a shiny gold button fell into her skirts.

My Dearest Louisa,

I trust this letter finds you in good health. Sincere apologies for not having written before, but as I am sure you can imagine, things have been hectic since arriving in Southampton. We are now in the process of embarking ready to leave for foreign shores, exactly where I am unable to divulge, although I'm sure your papa will have a good idea.

Anyway, my dearest, as we decided we would keep the betrothal ring until our party, I realise I have not given you anything to remember me by. Please accept this button from my military jacket. It is the one worn nearest my heart, so I hope you will see this as the romantic gesture it is intended to be. Please keep it safe and I look forward to receiving it back when next we meet.

I think of you often, dearest, and dream about that wonderful morning we spent riding around the deer park. My darling Louisa, no man could have better memories to sustain him in the difficult times ahead.

With all my love and affection until next we meet.

Henry

xxxxxx

It was only when tears fell onto the notepaper that Louisa realised she was crying. How many times had she, too, recalled that special, intimate time they'd spent alone in his carriage? Picking up the button, she kissed it then placed it into the pocket closest to her own heart. Was it her imagination, or did her skin suddenly feel warmer?

'God speed, my love, and come safely home,' she whispered. Getting to her feet, she walked over to the window, shivering as a dark black cloud appeared and hovered ominously overhead.

As promised, she would visit Henry's parents then keep herself busy until he returned, whenever that would be. Setting up a business for the widows to earn their own living was important to her and she wanted to ensure she had all the facts ready before discussing it with her papa. Picking up the folder with her notes inside, she made her way to his office.

'Am I too early, Papa?' she asked, popping her head around the door.

'Of course not, come in and take a seat. You are looking well,' he said, noting the sparkle in her eyes as she set the folder down on the desk before him.

'I received a letter from Henry this morning. He enclosed one of his dress buttons.' She smiled happily.

'An honour indeed,' Edwin replied, recognising the significance. 'I will pray for his safe return.'

'Thank you, Papa.' She fell silent, wondering if she should voice the fear that had plagued her since Jane's visit.

'What is it, my dear?' Edwin asked, looking at her shrewdly.

'Papa, do you believe we really have a ghost here? Only Miss Haydon smelled lavender when there were no flowers in the room, and you know it's said to foretell a death at Nettlecombe. With Henry away…' She broke off, blinking back the tears that welled. Edwin jumped to his feet and took his daughter's hands in his.

'You have enough to worry about without listening to something that may or may not be true. I can't deny Henry and his troops are facing danger, but they are well trained and, God willing, the fighting will be short-lived. Besides, it is my understanding that this portent, should it be true, foretells accidents that happen on the estate, and Henry is far away, is he not?'

'Yes, he is,' Louisa replied, for the first time grateful her beloved wasn't here. 'Thank you, Papa. Only after Mama's accident and that gypsy's curse…'

'Which is an entirely different thing altogether,' he said, not wishing to revisit his first wife's untimely death. 'Now, I take it from this that you have something else you wish to discuss,' he said, tapping the folder.

'Yes, I've put together my ideas for the Quarry Crafters,' she said.

'An intriguing name,' Edwin replied, resuming his seat and scanning through her notes.

'As you saw when we paid them a visit, these women are very proud so I thought it best to steer clear of anything that hinted at charity. The idea is for them to make money from the proceeds of what they sell.' Edwin smiled encouragingly at her enthusiasm.

'And I am sure that is what will happen ultimately. In the meantime, we have to find suitable premises, then purchase materials for whatever they are going to make.'

'Miss Haydon suggested work shirts for the quarry workers to start with, Papa. She said they would be simple to make and the fabric would be cheap.'

'That's a good idea, Louisa. If you intend producing goods for the quarrymen then I shall be able to assist with the funding with profits from the stone.'

'That would be splendid, Papa,' she enthused. 'I've worked out that initially there would be eight widows to help with the sewing.'

'And they can all sew, can they?' he asked.

'Oh,' Louisa murmured, looking at him in dismay. 'I never thought to enquire.' Surely, she wasn't going to fall at the first hurdle?

Chapter 22

Edwin leaned back in his chair and studied his eldest daughter whose earnest expression was so reminiscent of her mother.

'Whilst I applaud your enthusiasm, Louisa, the first thing you need to understand about business is that, in order to succeed, every detail of your project needs to be explored and any snags ironed out before you start. It is all too easy to waste time and money otherwise. Of course, as far as your step mama is concerned this will be a charitable institution and the word "business" will never be referred to in her hearing, although the principles are the same,' he said, grinning wryly.

'Of course, Papa.' Louisa smiled, understanding completely. 'You do think this is a good idea though?'

'Most certainly, and I'll do anything I can to help you get the Quarry Crafters up and running. Have you given any thought to premises?'

'There are two buildings that could be appropriate. The first is the empty barn just along from the forge. The location would be perfect for the children to attend the dame school, which would leave the women free to work. However, as you know, that is virtually derelict and would require a lot of work to make it habitable. The other is the old workshop the lacemakers used before Heathcote set up his factory in Tiverton and demand for pillow lace waned. It's been empty for some years now but would only take some maintenance and a thorough clean to make it habitable. The disadvantage is that it's located outside Combe, which would mean the women having to travel.'

'So, the old barn it is then. I'll get Wilfred or Sam to find out exactly what is required to make it serviceable.'

'I suppose it will be horribly expensive?' Louisa mused.

'It certainly won't be cheap, but we are looking at the long term here. Women gainfully employed and providing for their children will boost morale and save parish funds. It would give me great delight to prove the parson wrong in his assumption that the widows will resort to earning money immorally. Always supposing we can get the women to agree.'

'Oh, I had assumed they'd be pleased,' Louisa replied, looking dismayed.

'It never does to assume, my dear. Whilst we wait for the costings, might I suggest you call upon these widows and find out who can actually sew and, more importantly, if they are willing to do so.'

'Yes, Papa. I shall visit them this very afternoon,' she said, rising to her feet.

'I should wait until tomorrow morning, my dear. And I insist you get Quick to accompany you whenever you pay a visit to Combe, just to be on the safe side. Do I have your word?' he asked, when Louisa opened her mouth to protest.

'Yes, Papa,' she agreed.

'Now, afternoon tea will be brought at three o'clock and

I've asked your sisters to join us. It's been far too long since we had a tête-à-tête and with Charlotte visiting some of her cronies, this is the ideal opportunity,' he said candidly and Louisa gave him a knowing smile.

'I don't know about you, but I think the temperature's falling already,' he added, getting up to add more fuel to the fire.

'Let me call one of the maids to do that,' Louisa said.

'No need to trouble them. To tell the truth, I think of this as my sanctuary and enjoy being totally in charge.' He grinned mischievously, and Louisa caught a glimpse of the boy he must have once been. 'There that's better,' he said as the flames flared. 'Why don't we make ourselves comfortable,' he added, gesturing to the leather arm chairs either side of the hearth.

'Oh, this is lovely,' Louisa sighed, sinking into the comfy chair and smoothing down her silk skirts.

'Now tell me to mind my own business, but have you thought of asking Victoria to help you establish your institution? I only ask because I can't help feeling she's at a loose end now lessons have finished.'

'Apart from our Thursday mornings of conversational French,' Louisa reminded him.

'Well, you never know when that might come in useful,' Edwin told her, holding his hands to the fire.

'That's true, Papa. I would love to visit Paris one day. Perhaps Henry and I could honeymoon there. That would be so romantic.' Edwin smiled indulgently. 'Although from the reports in the paper, it sounds as if it might be some time before I see him again.'

'Keeping busy is the answer,' her father said softly. Truth

to tell he was proud of his daughter whose gentle manner hid a fortitude he feared she might need in the months ahead. 'And just think how much good you can be doing for those widows of Combe and their families.'

They were interrupted by a tapping on the door.

'Come in, Victoria,' Edwin called. 'We were just talking about you,' he smiled as she looked askance. 'All good things I assure you. Draw up another chair and tell me how you are passing these days of liberty now you are free from Master Forder's lessons.'

'Apart from balancing a book on my head and practising my curtsy in order to ensure my deportment and manners won't let Step Mama down in London, nothing important,' she sighed, sitting down and putting her feet up on the fender.

'Victoria,' Edwin chided.

'Sorry, Papa, but you must agree Step Mama's all posing and prickles. Oh, can I get you some water?' she cried as Edwin tried to choke back his laughter at the accurate portrayal of Charlotte.

'You do realise being presented at Court will offer wonderful opportunities for your future prospects,' Edwin said, when he'd recovered his composure.

'But I hate meeting new people, Papa. I never know what to say.'

'Then it will be an ideal opportunity to learn how it is done. Confidence comes with practice, you know. And you get on well with your cousin Hester, don't you?'

'Yes, she's great fun,' Victoria admitted.

'And you'll get to wear all the latest fashions,' Louisa pointed out.

'As I've said before, I can think of better ways of spending my time than being primped and preened.'

'Such as?' Edwin probed, quirking a brow.

'Anything, actually,' Victoria admitted. 'No, something constructive, like growing and arranging flowers. I have been studying their many properties; it's fascinating what they can be used for. Oh, I do wish we could have lovely blooms around the house like we used to when Mama was alive. When I marry, I shall have huge vases of them everywhere.'

'So, you do intend marrying then?'

'Of course, Papa. One day. Although, like Louisa, I shall marry for love rather than money.'

'Bravo,' Louisa said, clapping her hands.

'I agree with your sentiment, Victoria. However, Henry comes from a respected family and Louisa will have the luxury of living the life she is used to. A fact worth remembering when you are being courted in London perhaps?'

'Why, Papa,' she cried, quickly turning to look at the fire.

A sharp rap on the door heralded the arrival of Bea in a whirl of black bombazine bringing with her the faint smell of horse and tang of salt.

'Goodness, I'm famished,' she cried, throwing herself down on the red and cream Aubusson rug before the fire.

'And good afternoon to you too, Beatrice,' Edwin said mildly.

'Oh yes, sorry. Good afternoon, Papa, Louisa, Victoria,' she said, looking anything but contrite.

'Honestly, Bea, you could have changed before joining us – the bottom of your skirts are all muddied and your cheeks are flushed,' Louisa chided.

'I went for a ride along the beach and forgot the time. The bracing air has given me the most enormous appetite and I couldn't risk missing tea,' she said, grinning at their incredulous expressions. They'd be even more shocked if they knew that in the privacy of her own company, she'd shunned the more sedate side-saddle in favour of sitting astride her horse like a man. If only the tightness of her corsets hadn't restricted her movements, she thought, vowing to speak with Miss Haydon on her next visit.

As the clock on the mantel began chiming the hour, there was another knock on the door.

'I hope you ordered crumpets,' Bea said, making Edwin smile. For all her exuberance, to his knowledge she had never missed a meal.

'Yes, I did, and here they are,' he said, as the young maid all but stumbled into the room.

'Sorry,' she mumbled, setting down the tray with a thud that sent the cups rattling in their saucers. 'Agnes has got the afternoon off so Cook sent me.'

'That's all right, Dottie, I'll pour.' Bea smiled. 'Oh goodo, you've brought extra butter, well done.' As the young girl flushed with pleasure and scurried away, Bea picked up the silver teapot. Then when they were served, she slathered more of the golden spread onto her crumpet and bit into it with relish, heedless of the drips running down her chin.

Edwin swallowed down the lump that had risen in his throat as he remembered her mother doing the same. As the fire crackled in the grate, he sipped his drink whilst studying his daughters. How quickly the years had sped by and now, here they were, beautiful young ladies about to embark on adventures of their own. Of course, Sarah and Maria were growing up too and it wouldn't be long before they were old enough to join him here in his office for afternoon tea.

'This is my favourite room in the house,' Victoria murmured, unconsciously echoing his thoughts as she carefully placed her empty plate on the table. 'It's ages since we've had afternoon tea in here.'

'One simply must not sprawl in the Ruby Room,' Bea intoned in a fair imitation of her stepmother.

'You shouldn't sprawl anywhere,' Edwin reminded her. 'Although I agree it is nice spending time together.'

'Perhaps we can do it again soon, for Step Mama is always out visiting,' Louisa suggested.

'I'm sure we can,' Edwin agreed. 'Although perhaps we should ask her to join us occasionally,' he added loyally. 'Now if you've all finished your refreshment, there is something I would like to discuss with you. Louisa is intending to set up a charitable institution to help the widows of Combe and I wondered if you would assist her to get it up and running?'

'Oh yes, there is so much to do, please say you'll both help?' she asked her sisters, eyes alight with enthusiasm. 'With your permission, Papa, I was thinking we might look through those old pieces of furniture Step Mama discarded when she had the rooms redecorated. We will need tables and chairs and there are some very serviceable ones in the storeroom.'

'Don't I know it,' Edwin sighed, thinking of the perfectly good items that Charlotte had discarded without a care. 'It would probably be best to use the less fancy ones though.'

'I'll make sure they're protected with thick cloths and covers,' Louisa told him.

'Come on then, it sounds like fun so let's go and make a start,' Victoria cried, jumping to her feet.

'Beatrice will join you later,' Edwin told them. 'We need to have a little chat first.'

'That sounds ominous,' Bea groaned, slumping into the chair Louisa had just vacated.

As the door shut behind them, Edwin turned to Beatrice.

'Firecracker is on good form then?' he asked.

'Very, he flew like the wind earlier,' she told him proudly. 'But we were careful, of course,' she added quickly, mindful of her mama's accident. 'You didn't ask me to stay behind just to talk about him though, did you?' She stared at her father candidly.

'You know me too well,' he laughed. 'Actually, I wanted to talk about your future.'

'I absolutely refuse to go to some posh ladies' academy, Papa. I'd be bored out of my tree. I mean, I know perfectly well how to behave in company and simply cannot abide the thought of wasting my days learning the best ways of sucking up to pompous males and making them feel important. Who says men know more than we do anyway? Well, apart from you, Papa, of course.'

'Thank you,' he said, smothering another smile. 'However, despite your protestations, the fact remains it is men who rule. And before you start lecturing me on the unfairness of life,' he said, holding up his hand as Bea opened her mouth to speak, 'it is the way of the world.'

'Oh, you're not planning to marry me off, are you?' she cried. 'I know Step Mama wants to be shot of us as soon as she can but I'm only seventeen.'

'You misjudge your stepmother, Bea. She only wants the best for you,' he told her, ignoring the cynical look she shot him.

'I have no desire to become a married man's possession. I wish to train to become a nurse, Papa,' she told him. Having heard her discussing this with her sisters, Edwin had done his homework and was prepared.

'That is a very noble ambition, my dear, although I'm sure in due course you will meet a handsome man you deem a suitable match.'

'Gosh, Papa, now you sound like Step Mama.' Bea grimaced.

'Sorry, Bea, but you are very young and our aspirations can change over time. However,' he added quickly, seeing her mutinous expression, 'back to nursing. You do realise it is poorly paid with long hours and terrible working conditions?'

'I do, Papa, but I feel a burning need here,' she thumped her chest, 'to be doing something worthwhile with my life. Whatever you may think, marriage or being presented in court is not for me,' she declared. Edwin studied his daughter's face, noting the passion that deepened her eyes to navy, the stubborn set of her chin.

'You realise you would have to leave Firecracker behind?'

'Of course,' she replied, her eyes clouding. 'However, even nurses get to come home sometimes, so I'll see him then.'

'Very well, I will do all I can to support you. As it

happens, I know of a hospital for gentlewomen in Harley Street. It has twenty wards and the lady superintendent, a Miss Florence Nightingale, is not only well respected, she has been tasked with setting up a training school for nurses.'

'Papa,' Bea cried, staring at him in delight. 'How do I go about applying?'

'I will make enquiries. Before that, I will have to discuss the matter with Charlotte and have every faith she will support your decision.'

'Really? Well, I'd be very surprised if she'll be agreeable to having a working nurse in the family. Although you can at least assure her I'll be leaving home.'

'Leave that to me. In the meantime, you can fulfil your desire to do something worthwhile by helping Louisa set up the Quarry Crafters. The sooner we get it up and running the better it will be for all those concerned.'

'I'll be happy to. Do you think Step Mama will help too?'

Edwin gave a rueful smile. Not for the first time, he wished Charlotte would take an interest in the villagers rather than spending her time dreaming up fanciful ideas. Perhaps he should point out that working with the people of the village rather than lording it over them would help her be accepted, as she purported to want.

'I will ask Charlotte when I see her,' Edwin replied.

'Exactly what are you going to ask me?' Edwin and Bea both jumped as the woman in question materialised before them.

'Oh, hello, my dear, I didn't hear you come in.' Edwin smiled, getting to his feet. 'You're back early.'

'I got fed up with hearing everyone boasting of their latest acquisitions, although it was rewarding to see their faces when I told them about the special rose you have grown for me,' she said, frowning as she looked at their used tea things on the table. 'I can see you've been having a tea party of your own in my absence.' Recognising the imperious tones, Edwin smiled placatingly.

'I've been catching up with the girls.'

'We've been planning our futures,' Bea said excitedly. 'And we all want to do something worthwhile, starting with setting up the Quarry Crafters for the widows of Combe. Papa was going to ask if you would care to assist.'

There was a horrified silence as Charlotte shot him a look of disbelief, and Edwin knew that once again he was in trouble.

Chapter 23

'Goodness, I thought Step Mama would never let us go,' Victoria grumbled, clutching the side of the cart as it clattered its way towards Combe. 'Her face was a study when she saw us wearing these old capes.'

'I know,' Louisa chuckled. 'And she'd be appalled if she knew we were travelling in one of the estate's wagons, but I want the widows to take my proposition seriously and dare not risk more sarcastic remarks about fancy clothes and posh carriages. It was a good job Papa intervened or we'd still be trying to reason with the woman.'

'I'm sorry we left him to her wrath. It will take him ages to calm her down. Strange, really, he's always so confident and in command with everything else and yet seems unable to deal with her tantrums.' Victoria was silent for a moment, grimacing as Quick tried to avoid the ruts in the lane as he navigated the steep descent into the village. 'They've got a strange relationship. I can't think why Papa married her.'

'I agree,' Louisa sighed, for she often wondered herself why he'd married again. Admittedly, when she wasn't scowling, Charlotte was quite pretty and, of course, style personified.

If only she wasn't so acquisitive and intent on proving she was lady of the manor.

'I reckon it was she who chased him?'

'Really, Victoria, you sound like Bea now.'

'It makes sense though, doesn't it. I mean, much as I love Papa, he's much older than her but he is Lord of Nettlecombe. He gives her everything she asks for but she's never content, always nagging him for more.'

'Perhaps she's looking for a sign that he loves her,' she said, automatically reaching under her cape for the button that brought her comfort.

'Goodness, when did you become so philosophical?' Victoria asked. 'Ah, I know, it's since Henry's last visit. What exactly happened on that carriage ride, elder sister? You've been all dreamy since then,' she added, raising a brow questioningly.

'We drove around the park observing nature at its best,' Louisa replied, looking quickly away as she felt her cheeks growing hot. 'Oh look, we're here already,' she added thankfully, as they shuddered to a halt outside the row of tiny cots huddled into the side of the hill.

'But what about nature inside the carriage?' Victoria persisted, giving her sister a shrewd look as they clambered down. Louisa pretended not to hear as she squared her shoulders, ready to do battle with the widows who were eyeing them suspiciously. Then she thought of Henry sailing dangerous seas as he prepared for the fighting ahead, and realised her task was trivial by comparison.

'Are yer sure I shouldn't come with yer?' Quick asked,

frowning at the group of shawl-clad women who had stopped their chattering and were agog to see what they wanted.

'Please wait here. We'll call if we need anything,' Louisa replied. 'Come on, Victoria.

'Good morning, ladies,' she called, lifting her skirts as she picked her way over the mud and litter.

'Yer talking to us, love?' the brassy woman who'd sneered at her before hollered.

'We're not used to being referred to as ladies, well, only at night, eh, Edna?' another tittered, nudging her blowsy companion with her elbow.

'Honestly,' Victoria muttered under her breath, trying not to grimace at the little lad relieving himself in the road.

'Courage, sister,' Louisa murmured. 'Hello, everyone.'

'We ain't about to listen to no preaching. We has enough of that from the parson.'

'Oh, is he assisting you?' Louisa asked, staring in surprise as she recalled her papa saying the man had been less than helpful. The women exchanged glances but didn't answer.

'I think we should listen to what the ladies have to say,' Rosa finally said, jiggling the baby on her hip whilst the unkempt children made patterns in the mud with sticks.

'Please tell us why you have come here today,' her friend Flo asked, patting the toddler who was sleeping peacefully on her swollen bump. The little group gathered around Louisa and Victoria, anxious not to miss anything.

'I'm thinking of setting up a crafting room, where anyone seeking employment can stitch shirts for the quarry workers.'

'Us? Sew?' Edna snorted. 'Why would us want to do that?'

'Yer, and what about us kids?' another asked, narrowing her eyes.

'And where would us do this stitching?'

'Papa— Lord Farringdon is having the barn near the forge restored,' Louisa told them.

'Why'd he do that? Feeling guilty about the accident that took our men, is he?' snapped Edna, who was obviously the leader of the group.

'Why should he when it was their own greed that caused the accident?' Victoria retorted, stepping quickly backwards when the woman advanced menacingly.

'It's all right for you,' she hissed. 'Bet yer've never gone hungry in yer life.'

'Look, ladies. If you could just listen to what I have to say, I'd be obliged,' Louisa said, shooting Victoria a warning look when she saw Quick jump from the cart and walk towards them. Summoning a smile, she waved to let him know everything was all right.

'Come over here, me handsome, I'll show yer a good time,' Edna cackled, giving the footman a salacious wink then hooting when he blushed.

'Please, Edna, we want to hear what the ladies have to say,' Flo pleaded and Rosa nodded in agreement.

'Well, of course yous would want to, the parson ain't got no use for yer in that condition,' the brassy woman sniffed, gesturing to their swollen bellies. 'Means extra business and more money for us, though. Now listen here, Missy Do-Gooder,' she said, staring fiercely at Louisa. 'Old Preetcher finds us work when the kids are abed and feeds us good too, don't he, Leah?'

'Yeah, deer meat casserole we had last night before the, er, guests arrived,' she boasted.

'Shut up, you two, the parson said we weren't to say nowt,' a curly-haired woman hissed.

Louisa and Victoria exchanged glances for their papa had told them more deer had been poached from the park so the gamekeepers' patrols were increasing. Misunderstanding their looks, Rosa sighed.

'I realise it's not worth your while discussing things further…' she began.

'Oh, but it is,' Louisa assured her, determination rising as she saw the girl's dejected expression. 'May I suggest that those who want to hear my proposition stay, and the rest can go about their business.' She waited but to her surprise nobody moved.

'Might as well hear what yer up to,' said Edna, shrugging.

'Yer, don't want to miss nuffin',' another woman murmured, edging closer. Her long nose and thin downturned lips reminded Louisa of a shrew, but it was the ripe smell of unwashed body that turned her stomach. As the women stared at her expectantly, Louisa briefly outlined her proposal.

'…and whilst you're working and earning, your children can be learning at the dame school. They will only be a stone's throw away should they need you.'

'It sounds like a dream to be able to earn summat towards food and rent,' Rosa murmured. 'And the babies being able to be with us will help. I'm not that good at stitching but I'm willing to learn.'

'Me and all, cos I can't even thread a needle,' Flo sighed.

'Can anyone here sew?' Victoria asked, looking around the huddle of women who were clearly weighing up what Louisa had said.

'I can sew on a button,' Leah ventured.

'Yer needs to, girl, what with the number gets ripped off yer blouse each night,' Edna chortled. 'What about food? Like I says, the vicar sees we're well fed, and ginned too.'

'I'm sure something can be arranged for the food, but liquor will not be allowed on the premises. But then, of course, you will be working during the day so that won't be an issue, will it?'

'Oh no, we only ever drinks at night, don't we?' Edna grinned at her cronies.

'So hands up who would like to join the Quarry Crafters?' Louisa asked.

'Coo, hear that, girls, the Quarry Crafters. That'd be a step up from the fallen floozies Preetcher calls us. It'd almost be worth it just to see his face,' she sniggered. 'But this stitching lark sounds too much like hard work so yer can count me out.' Giving Louisa and Victoria a hard stare, she turned and began walking away. Others hurried after her, calling their barefoot urchins to follow, until finally only three women remained.

'Well, that's that then,' Rosa sighed.

'Not at all. We'll start small and who knows, there may be other women who'll want to earn some money too.'

'Yer mean we can still do it?' Flo asked.

'All I need to do is find someone to show us how to sew the shirts and we'll be in business,' Louisa told her.

'How long do you think it will be before we can start?' Rosa asked, staring anxiously at her children who looked sorely in need of a good meal.

'Truth is, we need to find work as soon as possible,' Flo added. 'As you've gathered, we don't have the luxury of being able to provide the services the parson requires, even if we wanted to. And Lizzie here wouldn't stoop so low, would you, dear?' The thin woman shook her head as she stared down at the ground.

'Well, that's no bad thing,' Victoria said quickly. 'I thought they were joking to begin with. I mean the parson providing… Who'd have thought it?'

'He knows people in high places, and I don't just mean up there,' Rosa said, pointing to the sky.

'I shall need help getting everything ready. Can you cut fabric?' Louisa asked. They nodded enthusiastically. 'I shall find a supplier then,' she promised them. 'In the meantime…' She opened her purse.

'Oh no, we never takes charity,' Flo told her.

'And I admire that. Actually, I was about to ask if you could purchase some victuals and make a stew or something similar to try out on your families. If we are to offer a hot meal at noon, I shall need your help with the cooking and I'd feel easier knowing the food has been sampled. From the little I know about children, they soon let you know if things don't taste right.'

'They gets what they're given and think themselves lucky,' Flo muttered.

'And mine wolf their food down too quick to taste anything.

But we'll be happy to help with the cooking and the cutting out, won't we?' Rosa asked the others.

'I'll say. Me ma taught me to make a mean mutton stew with beans and barley,' Lizzie ventured shyly.

'That sounds perfect,' Louisa cried. 'If you could make that, Victoria and I will call by tomorrow and sample some.'

'My cottage is on the end,' Lizzie told them. 'And you'll be most welcome, although you'll probably find things a bit shabby, still it's clean though.'

'I'm sure it is.' Louisa smiled. 'Now, the sea fret's rolling in so we really must be going.'

Luckily, Quick had pulled up the cover on the wagon which afforded Louisa and Victoria some shelter from the cold damp mist which was now swirling around.

'At least we have three willing workers,' Louisa said, sitting back against the hard bench.

'And I'm sure more will follow when word gets round. Do you think we should tell Papa about the parson?' Victoria asked, giving a shudder.

'Definitely. He'll soon put a stop to these nefarious activities, as well as alert Wilf and Partridge about the venison. Now we just need to find someone who can teach the women to sew. I don't think our tapestry stitches will be appropriate somehow.'

***

Incensed, Charlotte flounced off to the Amber Room. Her stepdaughters seemed determined to ignore the plans she had made for their futures. What's more, Edwin seemed to endorse them. She'd just settled herself onto the chaise when the door opened and Ellery lumbered into the room.

'And you can get out,' she snarled. The dog gave a long-suffering look, plonked himself in front of the fire and put his paws over his head. 'Even the stupid animal ignores me,' she muttered, returning to her grievances about Edwin's daughters.

Louisa should be spending her time making things for her new home instead of setting up a charitable establishment stitching with women whose morals were questionable to say the least. And Victoria was assisting her when she should have been preparing for her coming-out debut. Thank heavens none of her friends had seen them going out dressed like common peasants.

As for Beatrice, Edwin must see that her wild nature needed the genteel guidance of a ladies' academy if she were ever to become marriageable material. Instead, she'd persuaded him to write to some physician in London about training to become a nurse. No wonder relations with him were frosty again.

It was such a shame when he'd grown that beautiful new rose in her honour. She'd had high hopes that this signalled the start of a new phase in their marriage, that he'd finally come to understand her need to be surrounded by beautiful things. Then she'd returned home early from visiting friends to find they'd been plotting and scheming behind her back. Well, blow them, she'd keep her brilliant idea of hosting a Charlotte Rose Ball to introduce Louisa's future in-laws into their social circle to herself. The arrangements would be made and it would be a fait accompli. And to think she'd toyed with the idea of mentioning it to Louisa, for if the reports coming out of Crimea were to be believed, things were going to get a lot worse before they improved and it could be some time before Henry returned. At least the girl had chosen to marry a presentable young man from a respectable family. She stared around the room, wondering again if it needed updating before then. Apricot to complement her rose would be perfect. The colour would sit well against the wooden panelling and if there was one thing that she'd learned from her new society friends it was that appearances mattered.

'Miss Haydon, my lady,' the butler announced, his quiet appearance rousing her from her thoughts.

'Thank you, Ferris. Ask Nanny to bring Sarah and Maria down from the schoolroom.' As the butler bowed and left, she turned to the woman who'd entered. 'Miss Haydon?'

'Good morning, Lady Farringdon.' She frowned uncertainly. 'You did request that I bring the girl's night foundations today.'

Lady Farringdon shook her head. Honestly, these women in trade had no idea how to conduct themselves. Did she not know it was always advantageous to gain the upper hand?

'You'll have to forgive me, Miss Haydon. I have many important things on my mind. Perhaps you would set the garments out for me to examine,' she said, gesturing to the table by the French doors. She watched as the woman began crossing the room, only to stop and inhale deeply when she reached the fireplace.

'Is something wrong, Miss Haydon?'

'Not at all, Lady Farringdon. I was just appreciating the beautiful fragrance of lavender that seems particularly intense today.'

'I can't smell anything,' she said, bemused. 'Perhaps you'd get on with the matter in hand.'

'Of course,' Jane replied, taking the corselets from her bag.

The door clattered open and two pretty little girls, fair haired like their mother, burst into the room. They were followed by an elderly woman who was looking flushed from her exertions.

'Please conduct yourselves like young ladies,' she chided, but ignoring her they ran over to inspect the things on the table.

'You may go now but we will speak about this later,' Lady Farringdon told the nanny, fixing her with a gimlet stare.

'What are these funny-looking things?' the girls asked, picking up the bodices.

'They are for you to wear at night,' Lady Farringdon told them.

'Instead of our nightgowns?' Sarah asked, her eyes wide. 'But this won't even cover my—'

'Miss Haydon will ensure they are a good fit and explain their purpose,' Lady Farringdon interjected, turning to Jane. 'And then I wish to talk to you about another, more, er, feminine underpinning.'

Chapter 24

As Jane hurried out of the staff entrance, her mind was whirring like one of those new sewing machines that were coming into vogue. Fancy Lady Farringdon asking her to make a corset and chemise in apricot silk, and both trimmed with lace. Whilst it was good to have secured another commission, how she would deliver it would pose a problem, for after today, there'd be no money left for hiring another pony and trap. And, of course, Louisa hadn't been there to receive the invoice for the bodices.

As the sound of Sarah and Maria's laughter filtered down from an upstairs window, her heart went out to the dear little souls. Although she'd made the corselets in the softest fabric available, their tiny little bodies would still be unnecessarily constrained each night. As for the poor nanny, there was no doubt she was going to be reprimanded, yet surely the woman was too elderly to have care of such lively charges? Still, she was in good time for her next appointment, and she felt her heart flip at the prospect.

Since she'd agreed to walk out with Sam, they'd had no time to snatch any meetings as their jobs had not permitted. Having heard she was visiting Nettlecombe today, he'd written to suggest she meet him by the barn he was working on in Combe. She was about to climb into the trap when she heard the thunder of hoofs galloping towards her.

'Jane.' The rider waved. 'I'm so glad I caught you,' she said breathlessly.

'Hello, Beatrice, how are you?' Jane asked, thinking how full of life she looked with her flushed cheeks and sparkling eyes.

'I've just put Firecracker through his paces again,' she replied, sliding from the back of the beautiful bay and landing beside the trap. Before Jane could comment on the magnificent animal, Bea gently pulled her to one side. 'You said there were corsets suitable for riding and I wondered if you could make one for me. This thing nearly cuts me in two when I sit astride.' She grimaced, lowering her voice. 'I only revert to side-saddle when I arrive back here, except, as you can see, I don't bother with the saddle. Step Mama would have a fit if she saw me.'

'I could certainly make one to accommodate the extra movement.'

'Would you need any different measurements?'

'No, I can easily modify the cut and shape. Just tell me the colour you want.'

'The pink blush or something even brighter.' Bea grinned. 'Will it take long?'

'I'm making some things for your stepmother and have promised to have them ready by the middle of March. I'm sure I can make your corset by then too.'

'Step Mama mustn't know about this,' Bea said, her expression serious. 'She already thinks I'm a lost cause so perhaps I could call at your shop and collect it?'

'Of course,' Jane nodded, 'you're welcome anytime.'

'Excellent, I'd love to see all your wonderful silks. Now I'd better go and change, Step Mama is entertaining this afternoon.' With a raise of her brows, she turned and led Firecracker away.

'The old barn in Combe village, please,' Jane said, clambering up beside the driver. She'd never actually made a corset suitable for riding before, but Madame Pittier had carefully cut a pattern for one from her periodical and stored it in the cupboard in the workroom. To have secured yet another order was fantastic. Maybe the gods were smiling down on her today? If only she had enough money to secure the lease on new premises, Jane thought, as they pulled to a halt outside the dilapidated building which was now in the process of being renovated.

'Miss Haydon, how lovely to see you,' Sam said, proffering his hand to help her down. Ignoring the way her heart was hammering at the sight of him, she smiled demurely.

'Thank you, Mr Gill,' she replied, then turned to the driver. 'I shall be about half an hour, so feel free to go and find yourself something to eat.'

'Ta, the missus filled one of her splits with cheese and pickled onion so I'll sit right here and enjoy it,' he replied, patting his stomach in anticipation.

'And I've set out some things for us to eat in the lean-to at the back,' Sam said, leading her into the dim interior of the barn. 'I've also sent the men off for their noon break so we shouldn't be disturbed. I hope that's to your liking?' he asked, frowning. 'Unless you feel it would be inappropriate to be alone.'

'Indeed, I do, Mr Gill,' she teased. 'However, I'm sure should I feel the need to scream the driver will run to my aid.'

'Quite right too, although I can assure you my intentions are honourable. Now please take a seat, m'lady, and allow me to get you a drink.' Sam gave a mock bow then gestured to the blanket spread over a wooden bench. He busied himself pouring cold tea from a flagon then handed her a mug.

'That's most welcome,' she said, sighing appreciatively. 'It's been a long morning.'

'Ma baked cheese scones,' he said, beaming and holding out a bag.

'Mm, delicious,' Jane sighed, biting into the savoury bake. 'I'm sorry I haven't brought anything to contribute to the party,' she told him, not wishing to admit there hadn't been anything left in the larder when she'd looked.

'If a man can't wine and dine his lady in salubrious surroundings, then it's a rum do,' he replied, poker faced as he gestured around the dusty room that was littered with planks of wood and buckets filled with suspicious-looking pink liquid.

'I would imagine Queen Victoria herself has never feasted in such a setting,' Jane replied, her expression equally deadpan. 'What exactly are you doing here?'

'Lady Louisa is setting up a charitable institution for the quarry widows and his lordship wants this place made habitable as soon as possible. As Father is still slow on his pins, I've been tasked with overseeing everything. We're working flat out to get it finished. Then we've to cart a load of furniture down from the manor, so it will be some time before I get a day off. Still, I expect you're busy too?' he asked, studying her seriously.

'I am, although I've no idea what will happen when we have to vacate the *magasin* on Lady Day. Premises are so expensive Millie and I might have to rent a room and work from there. The trouble is it won't give the professional image the business requires to attract the right calibre of client. Still, something will turn up, I'm sure.'

'That's what I love about you, Jane, you always manage to sound positive.'

'Well, I should be, for Lady Farringdon has commissioned me to make some more garments,' she told him.

'That's good. How did you find her today?'

'I'm getting used to her forthright manner, although her sense of smell is lacking. She didn't even notice the fragrance of lavender which was really overpowering today.' There was silence whilst Sam stared at her in dismay.

'Are you sure it was lavender?' he asked.

'Of course, it is a most distinctive scent. Why?'

'Oh, just some family myth about it being a portent.' He shrugged. She gave him a sharp look.

'Goodness, yes, I remember Ida Somers telling me. Still, I noticed it last time I visited and nothing bad has happened, has it?'

'Not yet. Although I understand it's never been wrong before. Well, come on, eat up. Ma will be miffed if I take any home.'

Determined not to let anything encroach on their precious time together, Jane returned to her food. However, she was acutely conscious of him sitting beside her, could even feel the heat emanating from his body. When she could no longer resist glancing at him from under her lashes, it was to find him staring at her.

'I've missed you,' he said quietly, his gaze holding hers. Jane opened her mouth to tell him she'd missed him too but before she could speak, they heard the sound of voices and the ring of boots on the cobbles outside. 'The men are back,' he groaned.

'I should be leaving anyway,' Jane said, jumping to her feet. 'Thank you so much for the picnic. Please tell your ma she makes delicious scones.'

'Like I said, I'm going to be working all hours but as soon as this job is finished can I visit you?' he asked. His hazel eyes bored into her, making her pulse race, but the spell was broken by a piercing whistle followed by raucous shouts.

'Hey, Sam, you dark horse,' one man called.

'I must leave,' Jane said quickly, rushing outside.

'But I can call upon you?' Sam persisted as he followed.

'Yes,' she replied, then conscious they were being watched, she clambered into the trap and told the driver to make haste to Salthaven.

'Ha, this old nag don't do more than plod up them hills,' he replied. 'Still, it'll give yer time to calm down,' he added, darting her a shrewd look.

By the time they descended into the town and crossed the two-arched bridge over the river, dark clouds were lowering over the nearby hills and as she clambered from the cart, fat drops of rain began to fall.

'I shall take the nag round to the stables for a drink and snatch one meself,' the driver told her.

As before, Jane was shown into the elegant Green Room where Lady Connaught was waiting.

'Do come in, Jane, and take a seat,' she invited, gesturing to the armchair beside her. 'Now, let me see the delights you have made for me.'

Jane opened her bag and carefully set out the rose-pink garments on the table before her.

'Oh, my dear, these are exquisite,' Lady Connaught said admiringly, holding each garment up before her. 'You are truly talented. Now tell me what plans you have made. I seem to recall that last time we met you were hoping to secure funding from the bank.'

'I'm afraid my request was rejected,' she sighed.

'Hmm,' the woman said. 'May I ask what you intend doing now? You have secured the backing of a philanthropist, perhaps? A patron or sponsor?' she added.

'Regrettably not. I don't have any contacts, you see,' Jane admitted.

'Well, you could well be wrong there.' Lady Connaught leaned forward in her seat. 'Having been a client of Madame Pittier for a number of years and greatly admired the way through sheer hard work and determination she built up her emporium, I would be sad if her legacy were not to continue.'

'Oh, but I intend to carry on. I know working from a room won't be the same but—'

'No, Miss Haydon, it would not,' she interjected. Jane

swallowed as the woman continued staring at her with her no-nonsense look. 'Let's talk business.'

'I beg your pardon?' Jane murmured, sure her ears must be deceiving her.

'Oh, I might be an old woman but I'm also a rich old woman. A rich, bored old woman,' she corrected. 'If you recall, I have always said that Salthaven would benefit from having a corsetière in its midst. Well, Miss Haydon, what do you say? Would you be willing to move to Salthaven and open such an establishment? The clientele would be more elite here, and nobility arriving to take the air would swell the numbers, and profits. It is my belief that you could offer them a valuable service.'

'Goodness, that sounds so exciting,' Jane cried. Already she could visualise ladies out for their promenade stopping to admire the merchandise in her own shop window. Then reality hit. 'But I don't have…' she began.

'Yet you could. As I said before, I am rich and have far too much time on my hands. My husband's dead, my son and his family live in Mayfair and are far too busy to visit often. At Homes bore me rigid, for these days they comprise bragging about one's latest acquisitions which I find distasteful. No, Miss Haydon, I need something to get my teeth into and have taken the liberty of optioning the lease on premises between the High Street and the promenade. If you would be interested in seeing them, Mr Armitage who acts on my behalf can take you there.'

'Oh yes, I'd love to,' Jane cried, staring at the woman in surprise as she tugged on the bell pull. Immediately, the butler appeared.

'Please escort Miss Haydon to Mr Armitage's carriage. Should you approve, Miss Haydon, we will discuss matters further when you return.'

Bemused, Jane followed the butler outside and as the driver let down the steps, a man of middle years, silver hair curling from under his top hat, smiled pleasantly.

'Good afternoon, James Armitage at your service, although I think this rain makes the "good" rather superfluous. Tell me, Miss Haydon, how well do you know Salthaven?'

'Not very well at all, I'm afraid,' she murmured, wondering how he knew her name.

'Then permit me to be your guide,' he offered. As they set off, he proceeded to point out the places of interest so that by the time they'd travelled along the seafront where grey waves merged with grey sky, and pulled to a halt outside a three-storeyed Regency building, her head was buzzing.

Mr Armitage alighted then unfurled a gamp which he solicitously held over Jane's head for the three steps it took to reach the ornate front door with fan-shaped window above. Whilst he unlocked it Jane couldn't help admiring the large bow window. The little panes would ensure clients would have to peer through to see the merchandise and Jane knew full well there was nothing like a little mystery to stir imagination and create hunger to buy.

The shop was empty of stock, enabling Jane to visualise bolts of exotic silks on the shelves, ribbons, lace and trimmings displayed to best effect in the little drawers beneath the glass-fronted counter.

'Oh, it's perfect,' she cried.

'Good. Now come and see the rest of the premises.' The man smiled, leading the way through double doors. With its ornate fireplace, Jane knew this would be perfect for a Receiving Room. The hallway outside led to a scullery with privy and coal bunker in the yard. The flight of stairs led up to areas suitable for a living room and workshop behind, whilst on the top floor there were two good sized bedrooms.

Surely, this must all be a dream, Jane thought as they climbed back into the carriage. If it was, then it was one she was going to do her best to make come true, for as she stared out of the window at the front door, she could visualise the sign saying, 'Madame Rosetta, Corsetière, Proprietor: Jane Haydon.'

Chapter 25

'What did you think of the premises?' Lady Connaught asked, as soon as Jane was shown back into the Green Room.

'Absolutely perfect,' she replied. 'There is so much potential, and I can just visualise how it could look. Why, there's even room for Millie...'

'Millie? You mean you intend bringing the maid?' Lady Connaught asked, quirking an immaculate brow.

'Yes, Lady Connaught. We vowed we'd stay together and I shall keep my promise,' Jane explained, her heart sinking when the woman shook her head.

'I'm impressed by your loyalty but surprised you can afford her services. However, as proprietor you will of course have factored in that expense.'

'Of course,' Jane replied, determined she would make it work somehow.

'Now we need to discuss terms. Although I am happy to help, I expect a healthy return on my investment. Don't look so surprised, Miss Haydon. Regardless of what your bigoted bank manager said, there is no reason on God's earth why women cannot make a success of business. In fact, they do, and that is why I direct my philanthropic activities towards what males will insist on referring to as the weaker sex. Basically, Miss Haydon, I will give you the wherewithal to set up your emporium in Salthaven and when you are making sufficient profit you begin repaying me so that I can give another woman the opportunity to set up her business and so it goes on. Do you understand?'

'You mean you're loaning me the money?' Jane asked, to check she'd got things right.

'Does that disappoint you?'

'Oh no. Far from it. I think that's the most wonderful thing I've heard.' And it was. The prospect of becoming a business-woman in her own right was something Jane had dreamed of as she'd painstakingly learned her trade.

'Good, because you will have a lot of work ahead of you. As I have previously mentioned, I shall be happy to recommend your services but then it is up to you to establish your reputation. I shall, of course, expect preferential treatment.' She smiled benevolently.

'But of course,' Jane agreed enthusiastically.

'I will have the lease signed over to you for a trial period of six months, ensure you have sufficient working capital to purchase stock, and then we will see how things go from there. My lawyer will draw up a contract and once you have signed that, you may move into the premises.'

'Thank you so much, Lady Connaught. I promise I won't let you down,' Jane cried, still unable to believe she was being granted such a marvellous opportunity.

'I know you won't, my dear. And when you need to take on an apprentice, I know the very person. A young girl from the orphanage of which I am patron. She does the most beautiful stitching and is eager to make her way in life. Does that sound acceptable?'

'Why, yes, Lady Connaught.'

'Good. As you see, we can all play our part in assisting women to make something of themselves. Now, I wish you good luck and will call in to see you once you have the business up and running.'

***

'Yous what!' Millie exclaimed. 'Why would a toff like Lady Connaught help us? They usually sticks with their own class.'

'I pondered that on the way home and came to the conclusion that it must be because Lady Connaught really respected Madame. That and the fact that she's keen to have a corsetière in Salthaven. Anyway, whatever the reason, I intend to take on this venture and work hard to make it a success. So, Millie, are you coming with me?'

They were in the scullery eating a meagre supper of tatties fried in dripping. Although the fire had gone out and there was no money for fuel, Jane was burning with excitement, her head buzzing with plans.

'Course I'm coming with yous. Gawd knows what yous get up to else.'

Jane smiled, for all the young maid's brash manner she couldn't hide the relief in her eyes. 'Then you'll have to be suitably attired, Millie. It won't do to have your body flapping like a helpless bird in the new *magasin*,' she said, gesturing to the maid's corsetless figure beneath her uniform.

'Blimey, Jane, yous sound just like Madame,' the maid sighed. Then, not one to be down for long, she grinned. 'Anyhow, did yous see the handsome Sam today?'

'Goodness, after all that's happened, I'd almost forgotten,' Jane exclaimed, warmth flooding through her as she recalled the tender way he'd looked at her.

'Wonder what he'll think of walking out with yous now?'

'Whatever do you mean?' Jane frowned, her fork halfway to her mouth.

'Well, yous going to be the proprietor of a fancy shop in snooty Salthaven while he be a farm hand.'

'Don't be silly, Millie, Sam is Assistant Estate Manager at Nettlecombe Manor. He's doing a very important job.'

'That's as may be but he's still a labourer and yous'll be dealing with them higher-ups. It's a good chance for yous to better youself. Think of all them rich dandies yous'll meet when they bring their darling mamas to you for a fitting.' She grinned, waggling her eyebrows outrageously.

'Really, Millie, you know most men wouldn't be seen in a corsetière's,' she said, pushing her plate away.

'Don't stop some of them taking a sneaky peek through the windows though. Men is men after all's said and done. And if yous not goin' to eat them tatties, I'll have them.' Jane shook her head as the maid stabbed the vegetables with her fork then stuffed them into her mouth in one fell swoop.

'You'll need better manners than that in Salthaven. As for

that vivid imagination of yours, you can put it to good use by thinking how we're going to transport all our things.'

'Well, that's simple, ain't it. Get Sam to bring his cart.'

'He's really busy at the moment doing up a dilapidated barn for Lord Farringdon.'

'Not too busy to help the love of his life, I'll be bound.'

'Millie,' Jane gasped.

'Well, all men love the chance to show off their muscles,' she chortled. 'Bet yous the rest of Madame's special nectar he'll do it.' Millie greedily eyed the half-empty bottle on the shelf.

'You're on,' Jane laughed. 'I shall write to Sam, let him know our new address and that we will be moving on Lady Day. Then leave it up to him. In the meantime, Millie, we are both going to be very busy ourselves. The hire of the trap today took the last of our funds but, luckily, I have another commission from Lady Farringdon as well as one from her daughter Beatrice which will need to be finished before we move. Whilst I'm in the workroom, you can begin packing up our things then give this place a good clean. The landlord will be sending somebody to check everything is in order before we vacate.'

'Don't worry, Jane, yous'll be able to eat your supper off the floor by the time I've finished,' Millie told her.

In order to concentrate on her sewing, Jane closed the shop. As instructed, Millie carefully boxed up the little remaining stock and gave the place a thorough dusting. Meanwhile, Jane shut herself away in the workroom and sorted through the depleted bales of fabric to make the apricot chemise with matching underpinning for Lady Farringdon. It was paler than she remembered but by steeping some lace in a mixture of onion skins and walnut shells, she was sure it would produce a brighter hue for the edging.

It took nearly a week before Jane was satisfied with the finished result. Then, before she could make a start on the riding corset for Beatrice, two letters arrived. One was from Mr Farquharson requesting her to call upon him that afternoon. The other was from Sam, apologising for being too busy to help her with packing up, but offering to bring his cart on Lady Day to transport her things to Salthaven.

'See, I told yous,' Millie cried, eagerly eyeing the bottle on the shelf again. 'And yer knows what? I think you're moving at a good time.'

'Oh, why's that?' Jane frowned.

'Old Paynter put a notice in his window saying he'd got a whole new stock of them ready-made corsets at bargain prices. When I went to the market first thing this morning there was women queuing all down the street. Like a line of ducks eagerly waiting for scraps they was. Anyhows, theys much cheaper than yous bespokes, so stands to reason only the toffs'll be buying yous soon. Specially as the price of food is still goin' up faster than wages. And that's for those lucky enough to have a job.'

Jane stared at her in astonishment. A maid she might be, but there was no denying she was shrewd when it came to business.

'No needs to gawp at me like that.' Millie sniffed. 'I might only be a skivvy but I know how many beans make five. Which reminds me, yous better put that Mr Jones out of his misery. He's taken to stopping outside and peering through the door. Jumped a mile when I opened it this morning,' she giggled.

'I see,' Jane sighed. Since her humiliating experience with the bank manager, she'd avoided taking down the shutters until she knew Mr Jones had passed by. In fact, if it wasn't that they blocked out the light, she wouldn't remove them at all.

'You may have the rest of Madame's nectar,' she said, jumping to her feet and thrusting the bottle at the maid. 'Just don't drink it all in one go.'

'Blimey, I doesn't want to get squiffy. I thought I'd take it to St Catherine's and share a goodbye nip.'

'Oh,' Jane replied, chastened.

'But don't worry,' Millie continued, mistaking her look. 'I'll save us a drop to toast our new home. Now, though, I'll make us a bite before yous goes to see that soliciting chap.'

Mr Farquharson greeted her warmly as she was shown into his office. It had a comforting smell of old books, paper and beeswax and as she took the chair he indicated Jane felt herself relaxing.

'Well, Miss Haydon, is this not a marvellous turn of events?' He smiled, holding up a sheaf of papers. 'Lady Connaught's lawyer has set everything out quite clearly, but I'd feel happier if you would permit me to go through the detail.'

'Please, I'd be grateful if you would,' Jane replied. Although it was straightforward, it took some time as he went through the lease, schedule of repayments and amount advanced for working capital.

'Obviously the latter, whilst a reasonable sum, does not allow for luxuries like holidays in Scotland or fancy meals in fine hotels,' he cautioned.

'No, of course, not,' she protested, affronted that he should think that of her.

'I'm just ensuring you understand how important it will be to make the repayments on time. The terms are set out quite clearly and the only other stipulation appears to be that any hired help will be on Lady Connaught's recommendation.' He looked at Jane questioningly.

'I understand. It's all about women who have been helped helping others, you see.'

'Lady Connaught is, of course, renowned for her philanthropic works. A wonderful woman with a generous heart,' he murmured. 'Now, Miss Haydon, if you are happy, perhaps you could sign the lease and acceptance of terms.'

'Oh yes,' Jane replied and, with hands shaking from excitement rather than nerves, she penned her name in the places indicated.

'Wonderful. I will return these to Mr Palmerston for registration and you will be sent a copy in due course. May I wish you every success in your new venture, Miss Haydon,' he said, rising to his feet and proffering his hand.

What a charming man, Jane thought, making her way back to the *magasin*. How different to that pompous bank manager. What a lot she would have to tell Sam when she next saw him. As an image of his hazel eyes and cheeky grin popped into her head, she was surprised to find how much she missed him.

The next few days went by in a whirl as Jane located the pattern for the riding corset, then realised that with the extra allowance required for reinforcement, she only just had sufficient fabric. Knowing Beatrice's penchant for galloping along the coast, she dare not skimp on strengthening, for the garment would need to withstand the rigours of strenuous exercise. Luckily Madame had shown her how to lay a pattern in the most efficient way and after checking the measurements again, she began cutting.

As she worked, Jane couldn't help thinking once again how advantageous it would be to purchase one of those sewing machines. Offering a special line in underpinnings for horse riders would surely be popular with the ladies of Salthaven. While she had no desire to offer the mass-produced garments the industrialised factories were churning out, it would definitely be beneficial using a machine for strengthening seams. Although it would be subject to the cost, for despite Lady Connaught's generous provision for purchasing stock, Jane would have to proceed with caution. Everything would need to be repaid. Still, it would do no harm to make enquiries and in order to be successful, she needed to move with the times. As a bubble of excitement tingled her spine, she knew she was on to something.

'Oh, Madame, if only you could see me now,' she whispered. Then her eyes widened as she caught a glimpse of the woman smiling and nodding her approval. Dropping her work in astonishment Jane stared around the room, but all she could see were the shadows creeping into the corners. 'Goodness, I must be working too hard,' she murmured. And yet the fragrance of damask rose was overpowering, and although it was only March, Jane felt as warm as a summer's day.

Whether it had been an apparition or her imagination, she felt herself filled with a new confidence as she made plans for the future of her boutique.

***

When Lady Day dawned, she and Millie dragged their furniture into the shop ready for Sam to load on his cart. However, despite his promise to arrive early, there was no sign of him when the shop bell tinkled.

'Sprockett,' a man dressed in an ill-fitting coat, tufts of greasy grey hair sprouting from under his bowler hat, announced in a brusque voice.

'Miss Haydon,' Jane replied, trying to keep her voice pleasant.

'I'm here to do the inventory and collect the two keys to the premises,' he growled, tapping his notepad with a stub of pencil then holding out his hand.

'Well, here are the keys,' Jane told him, swallowing down her revulsion at the man's filthy hands as she handed them over. 'And please start on the inventory. We were hoping to have all the furniture loaded onto the cart by now,' Jane sighed, peering through the open door in the hope that Sam had arrived.

'Oh, yer were, were yer?' the man sneered. 'Well, see here, miss, thieving's a crime.'

'But we're only taking what's ours,' Jane protested.

'Except that ain't yours.'

'Of course it is. Well, it was Madame Pittier's so we're entitled to—'

'According to the inventory here the furniture was offset against the rent when the lady couldn't pay on time,' he cut in, waving the notebook in front of her face. 'All the furnishings belong to the landlord and it's my job to make sure they stay here for the next tenant. So, yer only entitled to take the boxes here and yer personal stuff. Yer got five minutes to get them outside then I'm locking the door.'

As Jane opened her mouth to protest, he took a step closer. The menacing expression on his face sent a shiver down her spine and she knew it would serve no purpose.

Chapter 26

Jane and Millie stared at each other in dismay then, ignoring the incredulous looks of the people passing by, they placed the mannequins carefully onto the pavement.

'Like yer friends,' one man called, nudging his companion.

'Wouldn't mind a cuddle with the one in pink,' the other agreed, grinning.

'On yer way, perverts.' Millie scowled, turning to glare fiercely at Sprockett who stood sniggering at their discomfort.

'Ignore them, Millie,' Jane murmured, as they continued piling up the boxes and bags. 'I wish Sam would hurry up, the weather's looking ominous,' she added, staring up at the dark clouds that were gathering. Where was he? Surely he hadn't forgotten?

'Hurry up, I ain't got all day,' the man snarled.

'Yous could always help if yous in that much of a hurry,' Millie cried, then ducked quickly when the final box just missed her head as it came flying through the air, its contents spilling onto the mud and muck. As it landed beside them the door slammed and they heard the lock being clicked into place.

Jane stared down the street but there was still no sign of

any cart. What on earth could have happened to him? He should have been here by now. Surely he wasn't going to let her down? She knew the amount in her purse wouldn't cover the cost of hiring a trap and was just wondering what to do when someone stopped behind her.

'Are you all right, Miss Haydon?' She turned to find Mr Jones staring anxiously at them.

'Goodness, is it that time already?' she stuttered, embarrassed at having been caught in such a predicament.

'Whatever has happened, ladies?' Mr Jones asked, frowning down at their belongings.

'Just a misunderstanding, Mr Jones,' Jane told him.

'I have a few minutes to spare if I can be of assistance?' he told her.

'Thank you but we really are…' she began. Then remembering how humiliated that bigoted bank manager had made her feel, she seized the opportunity to make him aware of her change of fortune. 'Actually, I'm just waiting for our transport to arrive. I'm setting up a new *magasin* in Salthaven.'

'Oh, I see. I didn't realise,' he replied, looking crestfallen.

'Ah, I believe I can hear the cart now,' she added, relieved to hear the clip-clop of hooves approaching.

'Whatever's happened?' Sam asked, frowning at their things as he hurriedly climbed down. 'You should have waited until I arrived before hefting those boxes.'

'But yous is late,' Millie declared, looking him up and down. 'And a right state yous in an' all,' she added, taking in the tear in his jacket and mud on his trousers.

'I'm sorry, things took longer in Combe than anticipated,'

he shrugged, staring enquiringly at the assistant bank manager who was hovering uncertainly.

'It was nice of you to stop, Mr Jones, but we mustn't make you late for work,' Jane told him.

'Oh, right. Good luck in Salthaven,' he said, raising his hat politely before striding towards the bank.

'Well, that's spoilt his day, he'll have to carry his candle for someone else now,' Millie muttered.

'Still littering the street? Yer got two minutes to get gone or I'm calling the constable,' the coarse voice from inside bellowed.

'I still don't understand what's happened,' Sam said as Jane hastily began gathering up their things. 'And where's your furniture?'

'There isn't any. It's a long story which I'll tell you when we're on our way. Perhaps you could begin by loading those mannequins while Millie and I take the bags.' It was only as Sam, dummy under his arm, made his way back to the cart that Jane noticed he was limping.

'What's wrong with your foot?' she asked.

'Had an argument with a table,' he replied, grinning ruefully.

'I am sorry—' she began then jumped as Sprockett rapped angrily on the window.

'He looks a nasty piece,' said Sam, frowning.

'Been shouting his gob off since he turned up,' Millie said, shaking her fists at the man who was glaring at them through the glass.

'Ignore him, Millie. Let's just leave as quickly as possible,' Jane urged.

With their things safely stowed under the cover, Jane and Millie climbed up beside Sam and they began their journey out of the city. Being Saturday and the biggest market day of the week, the traffic was busy, their going slow as horse-drawn vehicles jostled for position. When they'd finally left the buildings behind and were on the road to Lyme, Sam turned to Jane.

'I'm so sorry you had to deal with that insufferable man by yourselves. If I hadn't been late, I would have taken him to task. Shouting at you like that, I've never heard the like,' he said indignantly.

'Why was yous late?' the maid asked. 'I'd have betted me last drop of Madame's nectar you'd be raring to help Jane, what with yous being her follower and keen like.'

'Millie…' Jane exclaimed.

'Just sayin'. Coo, look at them cows. Theys huge. Wouldn't want to get too close to them,' she said, pointing to the black and white animals grazing in the fields.

'They're quite harmless unless they've got a calf with them,' Sam laughed, slowing by a coaching house to let a carriage go past before turning up the hill that led to Salthaven. 'You're right though, Millie, I had planned to arrive earlier but Lord Farringdon wanted some furniture transporting to the barn today and agreed I could have use of the cart when that was done.'

'Don't worry, Sam. It's good of you to help at all. But what happened to your foot?'

'Jim and I were lifting a heavy table when the thing slipped and landed on yours truly,' he grimaced.

'Sounds painful,' said Jane sympathetically.

'It was, but I'll live.' He grinned as she looked concerned.

'Wouldn't have made yous that late,' Millie scoffed. 'I reckons yous slept in.'

'I'll have you know I was up at first light,' he protested. 'But you're right, Millie, it wasn't just that incident that delayed me. There was another spate of poaching and Partridge, the gamekeeper, needed assistance. Still, we caught the blighters red-handed, though as you can see, one of them turned nasty,' he told them, grimacing at his torn jacket. 'It was when he knocked off my glasses that I had to retaliate.'

'Yous need them that bad then?' Millie frowned.

'Helps when I'm holding a shotgun, yes.'

'Blimey, didn't have yous down as a heavy,' Millie said, staring at him with a grudging respect.

'Goodness, Sam, you have had an eventful morning,' Jane cried.

'Goes like that sometimes,' he shrugged, clearly eager to play things down. 'Anyhow, what was all that about with Mr Charming back there, and where's your furniture?'

'It appears we don't have any. Apparently, Madame couldn't pay her rent at one stage and the landlord agreed to offset her furniture against it so she could stay. Still, at least we've got our clothes and the rest of the stock.'

'And some pots and plates,' Millie announced gleefully. 'I hid some in me things when that oaf was shouting his mouth off.'

Jane stared at her in astonishment. The maid's quick thinking never ceased to amaze her.

'Well done, Millie. We might have to sleep on the floor but at least we'll have something to eat and drink from,' she chuckled. With the tension of the morning broken, they sat back and enjoyed the rest of the journey. By the time they began the descent into Salthaven the sun had broken through the clouds.

'The shops will be busy here as well today so it'll be quicker to go the long way round rather than travel through the main thoroughfare,' Sam told them. They plodded on, until they passed a neatly kept green that flanked an elegant terrace of three- and four-storeyed houses, then saw a great brightness ahead.

'Coo, would yous look at all that water,' Millie cried excitedly as the sea spread out before them. 'And it smells fresh, an' all.'

'It is certainly a welcome change from the city odours,' Jane agreed, tying the ribbons on her bonnet tighter as a gust of wind tugged at it. 'It looks different close up, somehow.'

'I didn't think you'd seen the sea before,' Sam replied, staring at her in surprise.

'I glimpsed it from the cliffs on my way to Salthaven. It was the day you chose to ignore me on your way out of Combe,' she teased.

'Ah,' he murmured, his hands automatically going to his spectacles. 'Well, perhaps we could take a walk along the front one day when you've settled in.'

'Just look at all them toffs in their finery,' Millie gasped, gesturing to people wearing luxurious furs and fine woollen coats who were strolling along the esplanade.

'Salthaven is popular for those wishing to take the air, not to mention those hardy souls who brave the waters,' Sam told them.

While Millie gazed around in wonderment, Jane began to feel a prickle of unease. Although she knew Salthaven was a fashionable resort, she'd never realised just how smartly attired everyone would be. She stared down at her own clothes in dismay. While the mud on her skirts could be sponged, they were still outmoded. If she was to be a successful proprietor of a *magasin* that dealt with wealthy, fashionable ladies, she needed to look stylish herself. As if picking up on her thoughts, Sam reached out and patted her hand.

'You look just fine to me,' he whispered. Although Jane smiled at his kind words, she knew that before she could open for business, she must make herself a new outfit. She was mentally going through the meagre stock of fabric she had left when Millie jolted her back to the present.

'So, where's this shop then?'

'Oh, you need to turn left here,' Jane told Sam as she recognised the lane she'd driven along with Mr Armitage. 'There, that's the one in the middle,' she added and despite her misgivings, her spirits soared when Sam pulled to a halt outside the three-storey Regency building with the large bow window.

'Just look at that,' Millie squealed, pointing to the fan light at the top of the door. 'What do the other shops sell?' she asked.

'Do you know, in all the excitement, I never thought to enquire,' Jane replied.

'The one on the right with all the bottles displayed is an apothecary, the other is a gentleman's outfitters,' Sam told them.

'Ooh, I likes the sound of that,' Millie cried. 'Well, come on, I can't wait to have a look inside.' As she jumped down onto the pavement and reached behind for one of the bags, Sam and Jane smiled at each other.

'I've really missed you, Jane,' he murmured, the tender look in his hazel eyes making her tingle. 'And now I can get a word in, I'd like to apologise properly for being late this morning. I really do feel dreadful for not being there to deal with—'

'Sam,' Jane interrupted. 'Let's leave that behind, eh? I'm truly grateful that you've been able to remove us. Now, I was told the key would be in the door, but I think Millie's beaten us to it,' she grinned, gesturing as the girl disappeared inside. 'Come on, I can't wait to get settled.'

'This is lovely,' Millie cried as Jane and Sam followed her into the shop area and set down the boxes they were carrying. 'It's so airy and bright and that big window with all them panes will be perfect to make a show to tempt in all them toffs.'

Jane looked around, pleased to see that the shelves were clean and the floor had been swept. It wouldn't take long to set out her merchandise for she'd spent her evenings planning how she wanted everything to look. Of course, she needed to order in new stock but had thought it best to wait until she'd seen what would be popular. What a wise decision that had been, for already she knew they would need to be more sumptuous than before. Even with Lady Connaught's generous allowance, she would need to budget carefully. Still, at least she'd already ordered her new sign.

'You go and see if the other rooms are to your liking, Millie, whilst I finish helping Sam unpack the cart.'

'Coo, can I pick me own bedroom?' the maid cried, clattering up the stairs to investigate.

'I'll unload the rest of your things while you begin sorting everything,' said Sam. 'And then perhaps Millie can find the wherewithal to make us a hot drink while I buy pies for luncheon.'

Luckily Jane had thought to label the boxes and bags and it wasn't long before they were all in the right rooms. She was just wondering whether to begin with the window display or start setting out the fabric on the shelves, when the bell tinkled and a woman wearing a smart black dress, her greying hair in a tight knot on top of her head, strode into the shop.

'Good morning, or should that be afternoon,' said Jane, smiling in greeting.

'Nothing good about either when my customers can't get through the door for that old cart parked outside,' the woman grumbled.

'Goodness, I do apologise, I'll get Sam— Mr Gill to move it when he returns. I'm Miss Haydon, Jane, and am the new proprietor here,' Jane told her, proffering her hand.

'Well, Miss Haydon. We are a respectable neighbourhood, not used to having our pathways cluttered with old vehicles or strange women,' she replied, ignoring Jane's hand as she stared around. 'What services exactly are you going to be offering? Someone said they saw scantily clad females leaping around in here like mad things,' she whispered.

'Scantily clad… Oh, you must mean…' Jane began, realisation dawning just as Millie burst into the room.

'I just bin talking to the maid of all from the men's shop on the left. The facilities in our yards back on to each other. Anyhow, she says to warn yous that the woman next door on the other side is a nosy old so-and-so… Oh, sorry,' she paused. 'I didn't realise you had a customer.'

'Well, really,' the woman exclaimed. 'Get that cart moved immediately, Miss Haydon. And be warned, if I find a hint of any goings-on in this place, you can be sure the authorities will be notified. This has always been a respectable area and I intend to see it stays that way.' With a final glare at Millie, she stalked from the shop just as Sam returned with their pies.

'Oops,' he said, trying not to drop them as the woman barged past, frowning at his crumpled clothes. 'Did I say something wrong?'

'No,' Jane laughed, tears of mirth rolling down her cheeks. 'Our new neighbour saw you bringing in our mannequins and thinks we're about to lower the tone of the neighbourhood. Still, we'd better not antagonise her further, so before we eat these can you move your cart?'

Later, perched on boxes in what was to be the Receiving Room they ravenously tucked into their meal.

'Coo, we might have to sleep on the floor but with pies like this, I'm goin' to like living here,' Millie sighed, licking the gravy from her fingers. 'Are yous goin' to put them dummies in the window?'

'No, Millie, we don't want to antagonise our neighbours any further. I shall dress the mannequins discreetly and place them at the back of the shop. Sorry, Sam, I don't suppose you are used to such conversations,' Jane said, turning to face him.

'I have to say it has been a most unusual day so far,' he joked. 'But I agree, it would be better if you can get on with the other shopkeepers. Gossip spreads like wildfire and you don't want to risk getting a bad reputation before you even open.'

'Crikey, we're busy already,' Millie said, getting to her feet as the little bell tinkled again.

'It were the postman,' she said, returning moments later with an envelope. 'Blimey, it smells even posher than Madame's used to,' she added, holding it to her nose before handing it to Jane.

'It's from Lady Connaught,' Jane said, scanning the page. 'She hopes we will find everyone friendly in Salthaven and looks forward to paying us a visit next Thursday,' she cried, staring at Sam in dismay. 'I'll never be ready to receive her by then. Why, I can't even offer her a chair to sit on.'

Chapter 27

As Lord Farringdon led his family down the aisle of St Winifred's church, there was muttering amongst the congregation.

'For heaven's sake, why couldn't we attend morning service in the cathedral or our own temple as usual?' Charlotte hissed, as he nodded to the estate and quarry workers who were all dressed in their Sunday best.

'Because it's good for us to worship in our own parish sometimes,' Edwin told her. 'However, it might make you feel better to know this church was once owned by the monks of the cathedral. And it is a chapel, not a temple, on our estate, my dear,' he added, smiling to Parson Preetcher who was watching them keenly as they took their seats in the family pew at the front.

'I'm not sure the parson thinks it's good to see us,' said Beatrice happily. 'His expression would turn the milk, as Cook says.'

'I do hope you haven't been associating with the hired help again,' Lady Farringdon admonished, turning her attention to Sarah and Maria who were debating why the parson was wearing a dress.

'He doesn't look anything like an angel,' Maria whispered.

'Perhaps he's the devil in disguise,' Sarah replied. As Nanny told her charges to be quiet, Edwin hid a smile. Out of the mouths, he thought, for the more he heard of the parson's activities, the more determined he was to bring the man to justice.

The service was long, the sermon decrying the sins of the flesh protracted, with Parson Preetcher living up to his name as he railed incessantly against immorality and fallen women.

'Blinkin' hypocrite. And him creaming off their earnings and all,' a woman behind muttered.

'Don't know how he's got the gall to look us in the eye when we knows he's abusing them poor widows. It's down-right sinful,' her companion murmured in agreement.

Louisa gave her father a meaningful look which he acknowledged with a slight nod. As Lord of Nettlecombe, he wouldn't stand by knowing the parson was corrupt, but before he could take action, he needed proof. As they knelt on the hassocks, he noticed Louisa clutching Henry's button tightly in her hand and guessed she was praying for his safe return. Closing his eyes, he added his plea that the young man he'd begun to admire would come safely through the conflict.

The service finally drew to a close and as the organist crashed chords that threatened to raise the roof, everybody rose hurriedly to their feet. Etiquette decreed that they couldn't leave before the Farringdon family, so they hovered impatiently in their pews, anxious to escape the awful racket and be on their way home for luncheon. Head high, with her lips in a moue, Charlotte took Edwin's arm and sailed down the aisle, looking neither left nor right. As they passed the fifteenth-century font, carved from the Beer stone excavated from his quarry, Edwin felt a surge of pride, and was glad to be instrumental in carrying on a tradition that went back hundreds of years.

'Good of you to grace our humble church, your lordship,' Parson Preetcher gushed as they reached the door.

'It is, of course, our family seat,' Edwin reminded him. 'A most interesting choice of topic for your sermon, Parson.'

'One has to do what one can to keep those widows on the straight and narrow,' he said with an ingratiating smile.

'Well, I must admit I'm surprised at your change of heart, for when I visited you after the accident, you were adamant you were unable to help,' Edwin persisted, ignoring his wife's obvious exasperation.

'Ah yes. I'm afraid parish obligations are extensive and you caught me at a particularly busy moment, my lord,' the parson murmured, letting out a long sigh. 'After you left, I realised it was my duty to assist in any way I could and prayed for guidance. After which a way to make provision for those unfortunate women presented itself. God works in a mysterious way but you can rest assured they are serving, I mean being served, well. Now, allow me to escort you and your good family to your carriage,' he added, clearly anxious for them to leave.

'Thank you, but I shall take this opportunity to converse with some of your parishioners. I like to keep abreast of what is currently going on.' There was an uncomfortable silence which Edwin didn't fill.

'Well, if you'll excuse me, my flock awaits. As I said, a parson's lot is a busy one,' the man said eventually, and with a little bow, he turned to greet the villagers waiting impatiently in the doorway.

'Come along, do,' Charlotte said, tugging at Edwin's arm. 'This wind is quite bitter and I wish to get home before another storm blows up. Nanny, please,' she exclaimed, gesturing to Sarah and Maria who were chasing each other in and out of the graves, then frowning as Beatrice ran over to gather them up. 'Honestly, Edwin…'

'You go ahead, my dear, I can see Wakeley is waiting to have a word,' he said quickly, anxious to avoid being drawn into any dispute. 'I'll join you in the carriage shortly,' he added, striding over to join the man.

'Good morning, sir,' the manager greeted Edwin in his usual brusque way. 'Wouldn't bother you on the Sabbath but one of the ships coming in to collect stone caught up on the rocks when they attempted to sail in after sunset last night. We've sent out a lugger and the men are working to free it on the flood tide. Luckily there doesn't seem to be much damage done.'

Edwin frowned; mishaps like this happened all too frequently in bad weather and it wasn't like the man to bother him unnecessarily. Sure enough, after staring around the graveyard to check they were out of earshot, he continued.

'It appears the ship has a consignment of brandy and wine casks in the hold, which reduced their draught more than expected. When they thought they were clear of the headland a back eddy at the foot of the cliffs put them aground on Point Ledge.'

'But we don't import liquor, or anything else for that matter. It takes all the men's time to get the stone loaded before the tide turns,' said Edwin, frowning.

'Quite. Word has it, these men are also in the parson's pay. They're offered a bonus by way of, er… their needs being met, if you get my meaning?' Wakeley said, coughing with embarrassment. Edwin was silent, his mind trying to fit the pieces together. 'That Preetcher's a nasty bit of work but the difficulty will be proving it.'

'How the hell did those men expect to unload their haul and get it to him without being detected?' Edwin asked.

'Ah well, it appears they store it in the caves of the old workings and move it through the tunnel to the parsonage between the workers' shifts.'

'You mean this has happened before?' Edwin cried, then aware he was attracting attention, he lowered his voice. 'Keep this to yourself, but I'm already looking into the parson's nefarious ways. He's bad for the village and I certainly don't want my daughter to be married by a man like that. I am preparing a case to present to the bishop and would appreciate any help you can give. My gamekeeper and assistant estate manager caught a couple of poachers red-handed a few days back and turned them over to the constabulary. The men squealed, saying it was Preetcher who'd put them up to it.'

'Doesn't surprise me. Apparently, he promised those widows a lucrative living, even rich husbands in exchange for, well, you know. Of course, wealthy men never want to be seen with that type of woman, never mind marry them, and as he never pays them enough to settle their bills, they're trapped in his net, as it were.'

'Something needs to be done, and quickly. Louisa is opening a workshop to offer the widows employment whilst their children attend the dame school. A few have already put their names down so perhaps these will agree to join as well.'

'Hmm,' the man said, eyeing Edwin sceptically. 'I gather these particular women aren't too fond of work, but who knows. Getting back to the liquor. The authorities are trying to put an end to this type of smuggling so I could have a word with them if you wish?'

'Please do, Wakeley. Report your findings back to me and when this despicable parson is sent packing, I will see you rewarded for your efforts. And let me know when that last consignment of stone is safely on its way.'

Seeing Charlotte gesturing impatiently, he hurried towards the carriage, his mind a whirl as he tried to process everything his quarry manager had told him. He needed to speak with Partridge and check that no further deer had been taken. If there were more men visiting the parson, then it stood to reason he would be entertaining them, and Edwin was determined it wouldn't be with meat provided from his estate.

'Really, Edwin, is it too much to ask that you do not devote the whole of the Sabbath to business matters?' Charlotte asked, as the driver called to the horses and they began the short journey home. 'Even your daughters felt the need to spend time talking to those quarry women and the schoolmistress rather than sit with their sisters. Sarah and Maria became so restless, I had to send them home in the other carriage with

Nanny. Beatrice seemed to think the woman was looking tired and insisted on going with them. I don't know what things are coming to – Nanny goes home to a decent meal then has the rest of the day off,' she tutted.

'I'd be tired looking after those young scallywags,' Victoria laughed. 'Their energy is boundless.'

'They are somewhat enthusiastic,' Edwin agreed. 'And for all Beatrice's antics, she has a caring nature which will stand her in good stead for the nurse's training she wishes to undertake.' As Charlotte looked even more displeased, Louisa turned to her father.

'We were discussing details for the workshop tomorrow, Papa, and trying to coordinate them with the hours the children attend lessons. Did you see the barn? It looks splendid now it's finished,' she enthused. 'Sam and his men have certainly done a fine job.'

'I've told you before, Louisa, it is not dignified to refer to estate workers by their Christian names.'

'Not even on the Sabbath, Step Mama?' she asked, trying to look innocent.

'Don't be impertinent, Louisa,' Lady Farringdon remonstrated.

'I don't recall seeing young Gill in church,' Edwin pondered. 'Unusual for him not to be worshipping with his family.'

'I understand there was some problem with Jane Haydon's new premises and he has returned to help,' Louisa told him.

'She has removed?' Charlotte asked, taking a sudden interest in the conversation.

'Yes, she has secured shop premises in Salthaven.'

'Well really, nobody told me. How has this come about? I should have thought premises in a prestigious town like Salthaven would be beyond her means,' Charlotte retorted.

'I understand Lady Connaught has taken her under her wing,' Louisa replied, watching as her stepmother's frown grew deeper.

'Really? How extraordinary. I'm surprised she hasn't shared that information with me. But why would Mr Gill, a worker on our estate, assist Miss Haydon?'

'He is walking out with her, Step Mama.' Victoria smiled, delighting in imparting this news.

'Honestly, does no one have the courtesy to tell me anything? I suppose you knew all this,' Charlotte asked, turning her glacial stare on Edwin.

'He did ask permission to borrow the cart,' Edwin confirmed. 'And before you say anything, he has been working seven days a week to get that barn finished so it was the least I could do.'

'Oh Edwin, you do let people take advantage of your good nature.' Charlotte smiled, her mood changing in an instant. 'And you are looking weary yourself, my dear. Those lines around your eyes are getting ever deeper.'

'Forgive me, I have much on my mind at the moment,' he replied. Whilst never able to understand her sudden change of mood, but wishing to enjoy a pleasant luncheon, he was happy to go along with it.

'Not too much to spend some time with your family, I hope.'

'Of course not,' Edwin replied.

'Good. It seems ages since we were all together. After we

have enjoyed our meal, I suggest we gather in the Ruby Room to discuss future plans. Remember to bring your books,' she said, turning her gaze on Louisa and Victoria.

'Actually, Step Mama, I think you still have them. And with Henry still on his way to the Crimea, I don't think there is any point in going through our betrothal arrangements,' Louisa told her. 'Besides, with the Quarry Crafters opening tomorrow, I need to spend the time ensuring everything is ready.'

'And I must help Louisa,' Victoria said quickly.

Before Charlotte could protest, as the carriage drew to a halt outside the manor they threw open the door and jumped down without waiting for the steps to be lowered.

'Honestly.' Charlotte let out a long-suffering sigh as she watched them hurry indoors. 'How am I supposed to turn them into ladies?' Making a supreme effort to put his worries from his mind, Edwin reached out and patted her hand.

'You are doing a splendid job, my dear. Why don't we make the most of the opportunity to spend the afternoon by ourselves? The wind seems to have died down, so perhaps we could take a stroll around the gardens, check on your rose.' As he'd hoped, she perked up at the prospect.

'Oh yes, I have given much thought to garments that would match that sublime apricot colour and I think you will be pleased when you see what I have chosen. At least I hope you will be,' she said, gazing at him from under her lashes.

As Edwin handed her from the carriage, she smiled coyly up at him and he felt the stirrings of desire. Surely if he paid her the attention she now appeared to want, she would reciprocate. Time was passing by quickly and he was conscious he had yet to fulfil his duty to provide a son and heir so that Nettlecombe Manor remained in the family.

'Come along, my dear,' he urged, tenderly leading her indoors. Determinedly, he pushed his troubles to the back of his mind. He had every faith in Wakeley and would pay the quarry a visit first thing in the morning.

—

Chapter 28

'Didn't you think Papa looked happier this morning?' Louisa asked Victoria, as the cart rocked its way into Combe.

'Yes, and the way Step Mama was gazing at him over breakfast, well, you'd think they were young lovers. You don't suppose they…?' she wondered, giggling.

'Well, they are married, as we've said before. Although it's more likely she's got Papa to agree to something, she simply must have. The trouble is, Step Mama's so volatile you never know how long her good mood will last.'

'Or what she is after,' Victoria sighed. 'She really should be more tolerant of Papa's involvement with the quarry though; after all, that's what keeps her in the latest fashions she's forever having made.'

'I still chuckle when I imagine her expression if she were to see us in our working attire,' Louisa grinned, pulling the old black cape tighter around her.

'Or caught us travelling in the oldest cart on the estate. I must say that these hoods come in jolly handy for keeping one's hair in place,' Victoria said, pulling hers further forward. 'I'm quite tempted to have one made in a lighter, floaty fabric for the Season. A rich burgundy maybe, or even emerald.

If I must suffer being primped and preened, it can jolly well be on my terms.'

'At least it sounds as though you are getting used to the idea, and you never know who you're going to meet,' Louisa grinned, as they bumped to a stop outside the barn. 'Now remember Papa wants us to glean anything we can about the parson's movements. Although he emphasised that we mustn't put ourselves in any danger.'

'I don't like the man, but can he really be that bad?' Victoria murmured.

'Well, Papa insists Quick is to stay in Combe all day,' she replied as the man in question came round to hand them down.

'It would be nice to have everything ready for when the workers arrive so you can begin unloading the equipment,' Louisa told him just as a figure came scurrying towards them.

'The schoolmistress said you wished to see me,' Ida Somers said, her beady eyes drilling in to them.

'Hello, Mrs Somers, it's lovely to see you again,' said Louisa, smiling.

'Could have been sooner if the new Lady Farringdon hadn't seen fit to engage someone else. Yer Mama always found my services good enough and by the look of them worn cloaks, I'da said yer can do with them an' all,' she sniffed.

'Which is why we have a proposition for you. Won't you step inside so we can discuss the matter?' Knowing the seamstress would be unable to resist finding out more, Louisa led the way, leaving Victoria to oversee their things were put in the places they'd already agreed.

'So, what's this all about then?' Ida asked, taking in the

newly limewashed walls and the fire laid ready to be lit in the newly installed fireplace. Two large tables had been pushed together taking up almost the length of the long room, chairs placed neatly beneath. Although not matching, the quality of craftsmanship was evident.

'I've heard that yer setting up some kind of work place for them quarry widows,' she said, eager to let them know she wasn't completely in the dark. 'Mind yer, old Preetcher got his hands on some of them first.'

'Our idea is for the women to earn some money sewing shirts for the workers while their children are at school.'

'Yer mean the men can afford to buy new ones?' she gasped, eyes widening in astonishment.

'With Papa's, I mean Lord Farringdon's help, we shall be able to sell them at very competitive prices. We were wondering if you'd be willing to help us.'

'Me?' she scoffed. 'I'da have yer know my stitching is much more skilled than that.'

'Exactly, Mrs Somers, which is why you would be the perfect person to teach us all. If you're not too busy, of course,' Louisa added as the woman's eyes bulged even more.

'What, I'da be in charge, you mean?'

'Victoria and I will have overall responsibility, although once everything's up and running, we won't be here every day. Let me explain,' Louisa said quickly, not wishing the woman to get the wrong idea. 'The widows are keen to work but admit their knowledge of sewing is limited. I have secured fabric but need someone who can show them how to make it up into shirts.'

'Well, that's easy enough,' Ida said, puffing out her skinny little chest. 'How many will I be in charge of?'

'We have three ladies starting this morning and hope that once word spreads, more will join.'

'How much will they get?'

'Their pay will be based on how many shirts they turn out, but of course, as supervisor, you would get an enhanced rate.'

'Well, I'da be,' the woman cried, her eyes shining. 'Right then,' she said, shrugging off her coat and pulling up her sleeves. 'Where's this fabric?' she asked, just as Quick placed a bale of thick green material on the table before them.

'And the tools are in here,' Victoria added, setting down a couple of wooden sewing boxes. 'So, you're going to help us then, Mrs Somers?'

'Never let it be said Ida Somers don't do her duty by the parish,' the woman sniffed. Yet as she ran her hand over the fabric, Louisa could see she was pleased to have been asked. Relieved to have someone to instruct them, Louisa left her sorting through the needles and threads and hurried over to the three young widows hovering uncertainly in the doorway.

'Come in, ladies, and welcome. You'll be pleased to know that Mrs Somers, whom you already know, has agreed to show us all how to make the shirts.'

'Well, that's a relief. We've dropped the older kids off at the school and this one's out for the count, so we can get started,' Rosa said, taking a seat at the table and putting the basket with her new-born baby in on the floor beside her. 'Yer'll hardly know she's there, until I has to feed her,' she laughed.

'The schoolmistress said my Freddie could stay and play with her Rosie,' Flo added, easing her swollen body onto a chair beside her friend. 'At least it'll give me a chance to learn stitching.'

'I've prepared our luncheon,' Lizzie said, holding up a large pot.

'Thank you, Lizzie. If it's anything like that delicious mutton stew you made for us before, we shall eat very well indeed,' Louisa said and the woman flushed in delight. 'Perhaps you can light the fire, Quick, then it can be heating up while we work,' she said, turning to the man who bowed as he took the dish, causing Lizzie's cheeks to redden even more.

'Yer'll be getting ideas above yer station, our Lizzie,' Flo told her. 'He yer bodyguard, is he?' she asked Louisa.

'Quick offered to help us set up this morning and then he has his own tasks to carry out,' Louisa said swiftly. 'Let's get things under way, shall we? Perhaps, Mrs Somers, you can show us what to do.'

The woman nodded solemnly and they watched as she quickly sketched out a pattern on some paper from the work-box then deftly pinned it onto the fabric.

'Won't the men need to be measured?' Victoria ventured.

'This ain't blinkin' Savile Row, yer know,' Ida sniffed. 'Yer could always make two sizes, one for the men, the other for the boys, but they usually gets handed down anyhow.'

'My Nobby always said it was so bitter down the quarry, he needed summat long to keep his backside warm,' Flo muttered and Rosa sighed in agreement.

'We'll leave it to your expertise, Mrs Somers.' Louisa smiled, not wishing the widows to dwell on sad memories.

'Right, now yers has to cut round the pattern pieces, careful like,' Ida continued, taking up the large scissors and snapping them in the air for effect before snipping the material. 'Next yer has to sew the front to the back and put in the sleeves.' She held up each piece in turn. 'Someone thread me up a needle.'

Although Rosa tried, her hands were shaking too much and she passed it to Lizzie, who shook her head.

'That pinprick of a hole ain't big enough for me to see.'

'Suffering saints, am I goin' to have to do everything meself?' Ida muttered, snatching it from her. 'Look, this is how yer does it,' she said, sucking the end of the thread then pinching it. As it passed easily through the eye, she gave a smug smile.

'Wouldn't have hurt yer to explain,' Flo muttered.

'Didn't realise I was dealing with dimwits,' Ida sighed.

'Came here to learn, didn't we? Ain't my fault you can't teach properly,' Flo protested, rubbing her hands over her bump.

'Well, if that's the way yer feel, I ain't staying here to be insulted,' Ida cried, jumping to her feet.

'Please, Mrs Somers, I'm sure Flo meant no offence,' Louisa said quickly, fearful the woman would leave. 'As you can see, we are all novices and need every stage explained.'

'Yer well, it does take a time to become skilled,' Ida admitted.

But it seemed even the simplest task was beyond Lizzie as when the little group progressed to sewing, she let out a scream.

'Ouch, I've pricked meself.'

'Yer got blood all over the material, yer silly cow,' said Ida, exasperated.

'It's only a tiny drop,' she wailed, dabbing at it with her thumb.

'Well, put yer hankie round it so it don't happen again. Bloomin' Nora, how come you're sewing one of them sleeves to the back of that shirt?' Ida asked Flo.

'Wondered why it was a different size. Oh, this sewing lark's plain daft,' the woman cried. 'And me flipping bump's stuck under the table an' all. Me poor baby'll be like a flippin' sausage at this rate.' Even Rosa, who'd managed to sew one of the seams together, looked relieved when her baby began crying to be fed. Louisa and Victoria stared at each other in dismay. Was this mission doomed to fail before they'd even given it a chance?

Just then the church bells began ringing out their noontime message.

'Time for luncheon,' Louisa told them.

'Thank God for that,' Flo muttered.

'Make sure to put your sewing things down one end of the table. We don't want no stew on the fabric,' Ida commanded, now seemingly happy in her new role.

Just then the door burst open and the widows' children rushed in, clamouring for their food.

'Perhaps you could get them in a line then dish up, Lizzie,' Victoria suggested, anxious to distract the woman who looked as if she was about to burst into tears.

After much pushing and shoving they all had their luncheon and the only sound was the eager scraping of spoons on dishes.

'Can't claim this morning's been a roaring success, can we?' Victoria said to Louisa. 'This is the first time they've looked happy since they arrived.'

'I know, but I refuse to give up,' Louisa replied. 'They just need a bit more time to get used to dealing with the fabric. Mind you, I was surprised at how rough it felt and that thread is certainly different to our embroidery silks.'

'Don't suppose the quarrymen would thank us if we produced clothes with brightly coloured stitching,' Victoria pointed out. 'Ida Somers is looking very pensive. You don't think she's about to give up, do you?' she whispered as the woman rose to her feet and headed towards them.

'Eh, that were a good drop of stew,' Ida exclaimed. 'Seems yer cookin's better than yer stitching,' she told Lizzie.

'Well, I has a recipe to follow for that,' she sighed.

'Sewing all them bits together is too complicated,' Flo grumbled. 'Right, kids, back to school or you'll be late,' she called, shaking her head as they clattered noisily away, yelling at the top of their voices. 'Don't know what's worse, them bawling cos they're hungry or bellowing after they've been fed.'

'I'da don't want to interfere but I'da bin thinking.'

'Yes, Mrs Somers?' Louisa smiled brightly at the woman, although her heart was sinking.

'How abouts we starts with vests instead?' she suggested. 'They only takes a front and back and has no sleeves to worry about so it would make things easier.'

'That's a splendid idea,' Louisa cried. 'What do you think, ladies? Shall we give vests a try?'

'Can't be any worse,' Flo muttered. ''Ere, we will still get paid for this morning, even though we made a pig's ear of things, won't we?'

'Of course, we'll call it a trial run,' Louisa said quickly.

'Long as we ain't on trial proper for messing up material,' she retorted. And for all her bravado, Louisa could see she was really worried.

'Goodness no. Now let's see if we can learn how to make vests.'

The afternoon proved more successful, although Lizzie was still struggling.

'Right, school's out so you can finish for today,' Louisa called as the church bell chimed sometime later. 'I'm off to see Lily,' she told Victoria, the agreement being that she would pay the schoolmistress at the end of each day.

'I'll come with you. I could do with some fresh air after breathing in all those fibres. See you tomorrow, Mrs Somers,' she called as they let themselves out into the afternoon.

'I'm going to speak to Lily about my veil,' Louisa told her as they sauntered down the lane.

'But I thought you said there was no point in making any more arrangements until you know when Henry will be home.'

'That's what I told Step Mama because, quite frankly, I'd had enough of hearing about plans that would be nothing more than a farce. Henry and I will hold a party for our betrothal when he returns. However, when Jane Haydon pointed out a lace veil would perfectly set off the style of wedding dress I intend wearing, I could see what she meant.

Lily's lacemaking is exquisite, as you know, but as she's always so busy, I thought I'd better give her enough time to make it. Although, it seems I shall have plenty of that before Henry returns,' she sighed. 'Apparently the ship hasn't even arrived in Gallipoli yet.'

'Chin up, he'll be back under your feet before you know it,' Victoria said, linking arms with her sister.

Lily was delighted both to receive the fees for her pupils and the commission to make the veil. She gave Louisa samples of her patterned sprigs for her to compose her own design and the two girls chattered excitedly as they made their way back to the barn to collect their things. To their surprise Ida and Lizzie were still sitting at the table and they could hear the woman explaining once again how a vest should be made.

'Oh,' Lizzie cried, staring like a startled rabbit when she saw them in the doorway. 'I was just going. Thank you, Mrs Somers,' she muttered, gathering up paper and pencil and scuttling out of the barn.

'Is everything all right?' Louisa asked.

'That Lizzie's goin' to be the best of them. She just needed everything writing down in big letters so she can refer to her notes as she goes along. That's how she does her cooking.'

'Goodness, how clever of you to realise that, Mrs Somers. So, you think we will make a go of this then?' Louisa asked.

'Course, I'da said else. We don't have a privileged life likes yer. We has to make things work else we starve. By the way, Lizzie seems to think a couple of the others would like to join yer workshop. Seems the option they've chosen is, er, cutting up rough. Want me to tell them it's all right for them to come along?'

'Of course, Mrs Somers.' Louisa frowned, then saw Quick glance in their direction and realised he was taking everything in.

Chapter 29

Edwin whistled happily as, with a spring in his step and Ellery by his side, he made his way towards the quarry. It had been a good weekend and he was confident Charlotte would soon be telling him the news he was desperate to hear. Although, no doubt, some new ornament or trinket she simply couldn't resist would make its appearance.

Turning his attention to the report he was preparing, he pondered on what Quick had told him yesterday. Louisa and Victoria might have protested at him escorting them to Combe, but until the parson and his despicable activities had been eradicated, it was his fatherly duty to protect them. He hoped Wakeley would have more news about the smuggled liquor so that he could inform the bishop that Preetcher needed to be defrocked. Of course, as Lord of Nettlecombe, he had the authority to insist the man was removed immediately, but then there was the likelihood he would simply move to another parish and continue his activities and Edwin didn't want that on his conscience.

The banging and shouting told him he was nearing the quarry, and as workers tipped their caps when he passed, he was pleased to see they were correctly using the crane to lift the stone that had been excavated. He certainly didn't want any more accidents.

'Good morning, Wakeley,' he called, entering the man's office. 'Good to see the men are heeding the safety instructions.'

'Know they'll be out on their ear if they don't. Turnover's good. Heard that consignment's arrived in London and they want another next month.'

'Good, good.' Edwin nodded, sinking gratefully into a chair. 'That walk seems to get longer.'

'Don't know why you don't let me come to you, sir. It would take…' The man stopped and shrugged.

'Half the time,' Edwin finished for him. 'Well, the exercise is good for both of us,' he added as Ellery settled himself in his customary position in front of the stove. 'And I like to see what's going on here, although I know you run a tight ship. Talking of which, what's the news on that smuggled liquor?'

'Happen it's disappeared.'

'Don't be silly, man, it can't just have vanished.'

'Somehow the men got word the authorities were sniffing around, for not a whiff of either them or the casks was to be had,' he said wryly.

'You mean some of the workers tipped them off? Even though I've just given them a pay rise?' Edwin growled.

'Yer can't blame them. Any extra is welcome, what with the way the price of everything is going up. Some are really struggling, specially with the rent having been collected.'

'And others are plain avaricious,' Edwin retorted, refusing to feel guilty. After all, it was he who provided them with a roof over their heads. 'So, the parson gets away scot-free?'

'This time,' the man nodded, 'but they'll try again and next time we'll be ready. That parson's a greedy sod, and if he were to hear someone was needing liquor, say, for a party or special occasion...' He shrugged and looked pointedly at Edwin.

'You're a wily one, Wakeley. And what better occasion than a wedding. I'll leave it to you to sow the seeds,' he told him, getting to his feet.

All he needed to do was be vigilant and bide his time, he thought, making his way home.

**

As the coach turned out of the driveway, Charlotte settled back against the velvet cushions and breathed a sigh of relief. The past week had seemed endless with Edwin being overly attentive, showering her with compliments and scarcely leaving her side. Usually, when she complained he spent too much time on his work, he just nodded and carried on. But yesterday, when normally he'd be ensconced in his office with Gill or down at the quarry with Wakeley, he'd stayed at home. With the two elder girls busy at the workshop in Combe, Beatrice attending some medical talk in Exeter, and Sarah and Maria at their lessons, she'd found herself alone with him for nearly another whole day.

Of course, it had been enjoyable strolling around the garden and checking on her namesake rose in the hothouse, and she never needed persuading to share a bottle of champagne with caviar on toast beside the fire. However, Edwin had become increasingly affectionate and she was starting to worry she would become pregnant again after all. Despite her earlier thoughts, that was something she did not want. Life in the country had become tedious and dull, return invitations to At Homes almost non-existent, and she needed to find some other source of amusement. She should be having fun, visiting top ateliers, then dressing up in her finery to attend parties and prestigious social gatherings. With Louisa declaring there would be no betrothal ball before Henry returned, whenever that would be, there was no reason for Charlotte to delay her departure to London. It would be better for Victoria to familiarise herself with city life before the season started, rather than associating with those common quarry widows. Really, she didn't understand how Edwin could condone it. Of course, she'd done her part by allowing them to furnish the barn with her tables and chairs. Not that they realised she knew, however – there was little that went on at the manor she was unaware of. She'd done her best for Edwin's daughters, but none of them saw fit to listen to her womanly counsel. And despite his qualms about Nanny, as Edwin would insist on calling the woman, Sarah and Maria would be quite safe in her care whilst Charlotte was away.

Could anyone blame her if she yearned for a little excitement, dancing and fun? Then she would be content to settle back as lady of the manor. All she had to do was bide her time until the right moment to broach the subject with Edwin presented itself.

Feeling the coach jolt to a halt, Charlotte stared out of the window at the quaint little Regency building, its sign announcing the name of the proprietor and her business picked out in gilt lettering above the bay window. It was stylish, she'd say that for the woman. And portraying the French name Madame Rosetta above Miss Haydon gave it a degree of class.

***

Hearing the tinkle of the bell, Jane finished tidying the ribbons the previous client had been sorting through and smoothed down her skirt. Although she'd already received many visitors curious to meet the new owner and see what exactly she was selling, Jane fixed a smile of welcome on her face.

'Goodness, Lady Farringdon,' she gasped, as the woman stepped regally into the *magasin*. As always, she was stylishly dressed in the latest mode and Jane was pleased she was wearing the new skirt and pink satin blouse which contrasted well with the blush rose she wore at her throat.

'And good afternoon to you too, Miss Haydon. Although, as you have kept the name of Madame Rosetta, I am surprised not to have been addressed in French,' she replied.

'I have kept Madame's name out of respect. However, I do not believe in pretending to be something I am not, Lady Farringdon,' Jane replied.

'Indeed? Yet appearances are everything, are they not?' the woman enquired, quirking an immaculate brow as she caught sight of the mannequins, now dressed in their blush silk camisoles, a hint of lace corset peeking beneath. Unabashed, she stood gazing around at the bright pink flowers arranged in Madame's silver bowl, the array of brightly coloured fabrics, the fringed trimmed parasols and reticules on the shelves, the silk gloves and ornamental hairpins neatly arranged beneath the glass-fronted counter. Then she inhaled deeply. 'Ah, I recognise that fragrance.'

'It's eau de rose, Lady Farringdon. We always dry some of the petals and enclose them when wrapping clients' purchases. Now, I expect you have called for your apricot corset and chemise so if you'd like to take a seat, I will get them for you,' Jane said, gesturing to the pink chair beside the counter. It had been a lucky find that Sam had purchased very reasonably from the local dealer, then painted. She'd covered the cushion in pink velvet and was pleased at how elegant it looked.

'Oh, I was rather expecting you to want to ensure they are a perfect fit,' the woman replied, clearly eager to see more of the premises.

'Of course, Lady Farringdon. If you'd like to come through to the Receiving Room, I'll just call someone to mind the *magasin*.'

'Have no fear, I is here,' Millie cried, appearing in the doorway.

'Goodness, and whom, may I ask, are you?' Lady Farringdon enquired, her lips forming a moue as she looked her up and down.

'I'm Millie the maid. Who are you?' she chirped.

'The maid?' Lady Farringdon gasped, sinking into the chair. 'Good heavens, whatever next?'

'This is Millicent, Lady Farringdon. She has been of great assistance since I removed. Now if you'd like to come this way,' Jane said, trying to hide a smile.

'But really, a maid in public view,' the woman muttered,

shaking her head as she was shown into the room behind the shop. Luckily, the fire had been lit in preparation for Lady Connaught's visit and the warmth intensified the fragrance of rose, giving the Receiving Room a welcoming ambience.

'Do feel free to take a seat, or you might like to get yourself ready behind the screen, whilst I retrieve your order, Lady Farringdon,' Jane said, indicating the pink embroidered divider, another wondrous find by Sam, which Millie had carefully sponged back to pristine condition.

'I must say I am surprised how organised everything is considering you only removed last Saturday.' How had she known that? Jane wondered, staring at the woman in surprise. 'Have you had many clients visit?' the woman continued.

'Quite a few.'

'And are you expecting anyone in particular this afternoon?'

'It's always good to be prepared so if you'll excuse me, I'll return in a moment.' Jane retreated, tripping up to the workroom, which, unlike the downstairs rooms merely contained her workbox and equipment. She could just imagine the woman's face if she saw the upstairs, for they were sleeping on the floor, using spare bedding for mattresses. Knowing time was of the essence, for Lady Connaught was due in less than an hour, and Jane wasn't sure they had enough china to entertain them both at the same time, she snatched up the items she'd wrapped in tissue paper for protection. Beatrice's corset was also complete but knowing the girl wouldn't appreciate Jane giving it to her stepmother, she left it there and hurried back down the stairs. She would have to make alternative arrangements to see Beatrice, for being the first riding one she'd made, Jane really needed to ensure it fitted correctly. Luckily, Lady Farringdon was already behind the screen and Jane carefully draped the corset and chemise over the top and waited. However, the woman wasn't to be hurried.

'I'm not sure this corset fits correctly,' she declared.

'Allow me to check for you, Lady Farringdon,' Jane said, hurrying round to help. 'Ah, the back isn't lying flat,' she said, tugging it gently into place. 'That's better. Oh, that colour suits you wonderfully.'

'Yes, I can see that. Did I tell you my husband has cultivated a rose that exact hue and named it for me?'

'I believe you did, and what a wonderful thing for him to do,' Jane replied. 'Now, I can see the chemise is a perfect fit, so I'll leave you to change. I'll have your garments ready for you to take home so do come through when you are ready, Lady Farringdon.'

'Blimey, what's she doin' in there?' Millie whispered, ten minutes later. 'We can't have her here when Lady Connaught arrives. We ain't got enough cake.'

'Perhaps you could go and prepare everything,' Jane told her, seizing the opportunity to send the maid upstairs out of the way. She didn't want to risk upsetting Lady Farringdon or delaying her departure.

The church clock had just chimed a quarter to three when the woman finally emerged from the Receiving Room, and even then she seemed in no hurry to leave. It was almost as if she knew Lady Connaught was due, Jane thought. Then an idea popped into her head.

'Will I give you the invoice now or send it to Nettlecombe Manor, Lady Farringdon?'

'Good gracious, I never deal with such matters,' the woman snapped, as with a look of disdain, she gestured towards the parcel. 'I'll have my driver collect this.'

Jane sighed with relief as she swanned towards the door but before she could open it, the bell tinkled and an elegant figure appeared.

'Lady Connaught, what a lovely surprise,' Lady Farringdon gushed, her hand going to her face in such an exaggerated show of amazement, it was obvious she'd known the woman's arrival was imminent.

'Indeed, Lady Farringdon. I saw your carriage waiting outside so please don't let me detain you,' she said, as Charlotte stepped back towards the counter. 'I'm sure you are very busy.'

'Not too busy to spend a few moments catching up with a dear friend. Why, I haven't had the pleasure of your company at one of my At Homes for some time now.'

'No, my time has been taken up elsewhere with more, shall we say, *important* matters.'

'Yes, I did hear you had been engaged in your philanthropic interests,' Charlotte replied, gesturing to Jane.

'Then obviously those scuttlebutts who do attend your functions haven't been idle. However, I'm afraid I find such pastimes futile these days and will not be attending any more of them.'

Lady Farringdon's mouth opened then snapped shut again and a heavy silence fell over the shop.

'Well, Charlotte, it has been a remarkable coincidence

bumping into you like this but if you have finished your business with Miss Haydon, I have matters to discuss with her.'

'Well, never let it be said I stay where I'm not welcome,' Lady Farringdon retorted. 'And you'd do well to tell your prodigy that having her maid taking care of the place is infra dig,' she added, stalking from the shop and slamming the door behind her.

When the bell had finally finished clanging its protest at such violent treatment, Lady Connaught shook her head and turned to Jane.

'Now, tell me, my dear. How are you settling in?'

Chapter 30

'We have settled in very well, thank you,' Jane told Lady Connaught.

'I see you have kept the name of dear Madame Rosetta and I must say that is both a wonderful tribute to your former employer as well as being a shrewd business move. Most ladies around here have heard of her wonderful creations and will no doubt be curious to see yours,' she said, smiling graciously.

'Why thank you, Lady Connaught. Won't you come through to the Receiving Room and take some refreshment?'

'That would be lovely, but please may I look around in here first?' she asked, studying the bales of bright fabric before moving on to the ornamental pins. 'These are simply exquisite. Why, this is a veritable treasure trove and I simply cannot see myself leaving without purchasing something.'

'Please, take as long as you'd like,' Jane replied, feeling a rush of pride as she stared around the shop that had always been her dream.

'Everything is so artistically displayed, it's hard to believe you only moved in, what, five days ago? I expect you have received many visitors wanting to see what you have to sell?'

'Yes, it's been busier than I anticipated.' Jane smiled happily. 'Although most purchases have been quite small.'

'Ah, from little acorns,' Lady Connaught smiled.

'Or knickerbocker elastic,' Millie chirped.

'Indeed,' she agreed, nodding. 'Have you met the proprietors of the other shops yet?'

'That one next door is as sour as an unripe plum,' the maid cried, raising her brows.

'Thank you, Millicent, perhaps you would bring our refreshments down to the Receiving Room,' Jane said quickly.

'I was only sayin'',' she mumbled, shrugging. 'Hims all right the other side though,' she added for good measure.

'I'd forgotten what a character Millie was.' Lady Connaught smiled. 'I must say I'm glad you kept the fragrance of eau de rose, I do think it epitomises the very essence of femininity.' Jane nodded, for although she'd thought about changing it, she realised that if she could entice Madame Pittier's clients to travel to Salthaven they would surely want to find things the same. There was a fine balance between fresh and familiar and she would see how things went. 'Now, perhaps you would like to show me the rest of the premises.'

'Of course, do come through.' Jane hoped the woman wouldn't ask to see upstairs, with its bare windows and floors.

'Oh, Jane,' the woman cried. 'I hope you don't mind me calling you that, this is absolutely delightful.'

'Of course not. And I'm so glad you approve of the room. Please do take a seat,' she offered, gesturing to the chaise at the side of the hearth where a small fire was burning in the grate. Although it was nearly the end of March the air was still nippy, especially when the wind blew in from the sea.

'It lends a nice ambience and I must say this seat could have been made for the room.'

Jane nodded. It was another inexpensive purchase from the dealer which really needed doing up, but luckily the cherry shawl artfully draped over the back hid the worst of the wear. She planned to re-cover it in a fabric to match the screen as soon as she had time.

'And I must say your new outfit is very stylish. I can see you fitting in well here.'

Jane smiled. If Lady Connaught thought she looked modish then it had been worth burning down the candle as she sewed late into the night.

'Well, 'ere we is,' Millie chirped, placing a tray carefully on the stool which served as a table. ''Fraid the cups don't match the saucers and one of the plates got chipped in the move, but it was all I could rescue before old Sprockett threw us out.'

'I'm sure Lady Connaught doesn't wish to hear about that, Millicent. Won't you have some cake?' she asked, shooting the maid a look as she proffered the plate.

'It does look tempting,' the woman said, taking a slice. 'My, this sponge is light as a feather. You surely didn't make it yourself?' Lady Connaught asked a few moments later.

'With me own fair hands,' Millie nodded.

'Goodness, you'll have to give my cook a few lessons, young lady.'

'Coo, ta very much.'

'So, tell me, Millie, is your room satisfactory?'

'Well, the floor's a bit hard on the old backside,' Millie sighed, then laughed at the woman's look of astonishment. 'We got no beds, see, or any furniture upstairs, come to that, well apart from a table in the workroom that Sam found, although it looks good down here which is the main thing,' she added quickly, as Jane shot her another warning look. 'Yous could say we're all fur coat and no knickerbockers here.'

'Indeed? Well, I'm sure you are very busy so I won't keep you any longer,' Lady Connaught replied, smiling graciously.

'Eh? Oh, I get it, yous wants to have a private chat. Never let it be said Millie can't take a hint,' she grinned, clattering from the room.

'She's got a good heart,' Jane murmured.

'I can see that. And maids like that are worth their weight. However, you must remember that is what she is, a maid. From what Lady Farringdon said earlier, I gather Millie has been helping in the shop itself.'

'She has. I need someone to attend to any clients whilst I'm undertaking a fitting in here or sewing in the workshop.'

'That makes sense. However, for once I have to agree with Lady Farringdon that appearances are everything, especially to the clientele you will be dealing with in Salthaven. Ladies will expect to be attended to on a level they understand and, of course, it is important you get on with your neighbours. What I'm saying, is that Millie's place really is behind the scenes.'

'But she has been such a help, especially since Madame died.'

'I'm sure she has, but things are different here. Please don't misunderstand me, you might think I'm just a rich old lady but, believe me, I know how business works. You have so much enthusiasm and ambition, I want to see you succeed.' She looked so earnest, there was no doubting her sincerity.

'I know I have much to learn,' Jane admitted. 'And I have noticed the clientele are very different here.'

'They are, and you will soon learn that there is nothing people round here like better than to be seen patronising establishments visited by those more eminent. Now, I have a suggestion to make. You might remember my mentioning a young orphan girl who does the most beautiful stitching?'

'The one you said would make a good apprentice in the future?'

'That's the one. It appears the housemaster has started paying her unwanted attention.'

'Oh, the poor thing.' Jane grimaced.

'It's something that often happens when girls start, how shall we say, blossoming,' Lady Connaught sighed. 'Naturally, the man denies it, insisting the girl is delusional but, despite her unfortunate start in life, she is the sweetest little thing and I have no doubt she is telling the truth. My conscience will not permit me to ignore the situation. So, what do you think? You need someone to assist in the *magasin*, she needs someone to help improve her skills.'

'Well, I'd like to help but...' Jane stuttered to a halt, not sure how to voice the fact she hadn't budgeted for such an expense.

'Obviously, I shall be happy to sponsor her until she is earning her keep,' Lady Connaught said, rising to her feet. 'Mouse really would benefit from some motherly influence.'

'Mouse?'

'That's what she is known as. On account of her being timid, I suppose. Although, under your caring tutelage that might change, of course. Well, now that's agreed, I really must bid you a good afternoon and set the wheels in motion.'

Still reeling from the woman's visit Jane set about tidying the already immaculate shop. Was she ready to take on an apprentice? And where would this Mouse sleep? Then she remembered how bewildered and lost she'd felt when her own mother had abandoned her. How Madame, without a murmur, had taken Jane under her wing and taught her all she knew without once making her feel she was a nuisance, even though she must have been. Could she in all conscience deny a young orphan the same care and opportunity?

The tinkling of the bell roused her from her thoughts and she looked up to see two well-attired ladies in their late twenties step grandly inside, their soft calfskin boots gliding silently over the floor.

'Good afternoon. How may I be of service?'

'We've just arrived on vacation from Bath and having seen the ladies' carriages pulling up outside, realise this must be *the* place to be fitted for new underpinnings,' the taller one announced. She was sporting an emerald velvet bonnet in the new open form worn towards the back of her head so that it set off her auburn tresses to perfection. Removing a soft white hand from the matching muff, she gently ran an elegant finger over the silk satin on the mannequin. 'I rather like this,' she declared.

Her fair-haired companion was wearing a similar hat in rich claret, its feather bobbing up and down as she nodded in agreement.

'Oh yes, Clarissa, I can just see you in that.'

'Do you think so, darling? We have many soirees and concerts to attend whilst we are here but, alas, find our outfits quite outmoded,' she said, turning back to Jane. 'We shall require suitable underpinnings before we can even think about new gowns. Styles are changing so quickly with skirts becoming wider, waists more defined, it is imperative to get the basics right, is it not?'

'Indeed, it is,' Jane agreed. 'May I make an appointment for you to be fitted individually or would you prefer to come along together? And when would be convenient?' She turned away and waited discreetly whilst they conferred.

'Tomorrow morning at eleven thirty,' Clarissa announced.

'I'll just check my availability,' Jane replied, consulting her appointments book. 'Ladies, you are in luck. I have just enough time to fit you both before her ladyship the duchess arrives for her appointment.'

'Splendid,' they chorused, nonchalant expressions changing to such wonderment, Jane almost laughed aloud. Thank heavens they didn't ask exactly which duchess, she thought, as she showed them out.

Just wait until she told Sam, she chuckled, amusement bubbling up inside. Her heart flipped as she recalled the tenderness in his eyes when he'd asked if she would take a stroll along the esplanade with him on Sunday afternoon. He'd even promised to treat her to afternoon tea at the little tea rooms there and although she still had much to do to get everything the way she wanted, nothing was going to keep her from seeing him. Jane might have only known him a short while but, unlike anybody she'd ever met before, he had reached right to her heart and she knew he was the man for her. Not that she'd let him know that yet, of course.

'Just nipping out,' Millie called, rousing Jane from her musing and reminding her of what Lady Connaught had said earlier.

Although it pained her to admit it, she could see it was inappropriate for Millie to attend to her new clientele. The question was, how could she tell the girl without hurting her feelings? For all her brash ways, she really was quite sensitive underneath. Still pondering the subject, she went outside to put up the grilles over the window. The smell of the sea was invigorating after being cooped up inside and she was enjoying its salty tang when the woman from the apothecary next door bustled out. Bracing herself for another outburst, Jane was surprised when she smiled.

'I'm pleased to see a better class of vehicle drawing up outside your premises these days, Miss Haydon. I was quite worried when I saw you unloading that battered old cart, but as Mr Findle said, you wouldn't use a fine carriage to transport those dummy things.'

'Quite, Mrs Findle,' she replied.

'You've had a busy afternoon, then, what with Lady Farringdon calling by and then Lady Connaught. Comes in here sometimes, does Lady Connaught, always asks how I am, such a lovely lady. Know them both well, do you?'

'They are both clients,' Jane confirmed.

'Lucky them being able to afford such luxury. I've seen your fabrics through the window when I was passing, not that I was being nosy, you understand. Beautiful they are,' she sighed wistfully.

'Well, talking of window displays, I just love yours, Mrs Findle. All those coloured bottles are so pretty, especially the way they reflect the sunlight in the morning.'

'Why thank you, Miss Haydon. It's good to see a fellow proprietor appreciating my hard work. I must get on. Good afternoon to you.'

'Good afternoon, Mrs Findle,' she replied, pleased that bridges had been built. It would be far preferable to be on good terms with her neighbours. Lesson number one learned and dealt with. This evening, she would have to deal with lesson two, Millie. Being a proprietor was far more compli-cated than she'd anticipated.

She was just about to resume shutting up for the night when she saw a figure emerge from the shadows.

'Goodness, you made me jump,' Jane cried.

'Excuse me, but I'm looking for Miss Haydon.' Her dark eyes looked luminous against her pale skin as she stood there staring fearfully up at Jane, clutching a bundle protectively in front of her.

'I am Miss Haydon, and are you Mouse, by any chance?'

'How did you guess?' the girl squeaked.

'Just a hunch,' Jane replied, thinking that she was going

to have to spend another night burning the candle as she sewed a new outfit.

'Lady Connaught said that if you liked me and I worked very hard, you might take me on. My stitching is very good,' she mumbled, her eyes lighting up as she caught sight of the merchandise in the window. Then she looked down at her ragged clothes and her face resumed its haunted look. 'Of course, I won't stay if you don't want me here.'

Chapter 31

Edwin sat hunched over his desk compiling the report he was to present to the bishop. The evidence against Parson Preetcher was stacking up, but he still didn't have enough to warrant him being defrocked. A sudden banging disturbed his concentration. It was followed by a curse, then the slamming of another door signalled the abrupt departure of his wife. The walls of Nettlecombe might have been built to withstand invaders in days gone by, but they weren't thick enough to protect its inhabitants from Charlotte's tantrums.

He really didn't know what had become of the woman. Ever since her return from Salthaven the previous week, she'd been insufferable. His gentle enquiry as to what had upset her had been met with mutterings about conspiracy, humiliation and revenge. She'd then taken to her room, only emerging to disappear in her carriage each morning.

He was about to resume writing when a knock on the door signalled the arrival of Beatrice. She was brandishing a letter and he put down his pen knowing he wouldn't be getting any more work done for a while.

'Are you busy, Papa?' she asked. Then without waiting for

an answer she perched on the corner of the desk and handed him the envelope postmarked London.

'Not doing Ferris out of his job, I hope,' he said, quirking his brow as he picked up the silver letter opener.

'Of course not,' she laughed. 'Anyway, he's soft as butter underneath, as you know. Well?' she asked impatiently, as he scanned the contents.

'It seems Professor Todd would be interested in meeting you, Beatrice, to discuss your training with the sisters in Westminster. If you are serious about nursing, it will be a good start as I understand they have introduced new standards and established a fine reputation. You do realise it will mean long hours and poor pay?'

'You've already asked me that, Papa. As I told you, it is just something I feel the need to do,' she declared, placing her hand on her heart.

'Then we must try and make it happen,' he assured her, returning to the letter. 'He suggests we meet him on his return to London in May.'

'That's wonderful,' she cried, clapping her hands in delight. 'Although I don't think I'll mention it to Step Mama at present. I know she has her moods but she's positively evil at the moment. Do you know what is troubling her?'

'If only I were privy to her innermost thoughts,' Edwin sighed. 'Still, I dare say she will recover from whatever ails her soon.'

'She is very volatile though, isn't she, Papa?'

'Highly strung, perhaps,' he agreed, loyalty preventing him

from saying any more. 'Now tell me, how are the Quarry Crafters getting on?'

'Well, to be honest, Papa, I haven't had time to actually help there yet,' she admitted, biting her lip in the way he recognised meant she was hiding something.

'Looking after that horse of yours, eh?' he grinned.

'No,' she protested. 'Well, I mean, yes, of course I have taken him out. He does need regular exercise, as you know. I wasn't going to mention this, but I've been helping Nanny with Sarah and Maria. Not with their lessons, you understand,' she said quickly. 'Just taking them out and about, mainly in the afternoons.'

'I see.' Edwin frowned, steepling his fingers. 'I don't wish to go against Charlotte but it is time Nanny took things easier. As soon as I have finished compiling this report, I will advertise for a governess. In the meantime, I would be very grateful if you could continue helping out when you can.'

'Of course, Papa.'

'And when you do go into Combe, keep your ears and eyes open. Oh, and like Louisa and Victoria, you must promise me you'll have Quick with you at all times.'

***

As the rasp of her shears cut through the layers of coarse fabric, seven pairs of eyes followed Ida's every movement. Two of the widows who'd been working for the parson had declared they'd had enough of his unreasonable expectations and had joined the Quarry Crafters along with a young mother whose boys attended the dame school. With Flo having gone into labour that morning, and an order from the quarry for twenty vests having been received, the additional help was welcome.

'Right now, you new ladies watch me, the rest of you can start yer sewing. So, this is how we place the pieces together,' Ida demonstrated. 'Then yer takes up yer needle and stitch like this.'

'She's certainly in her stride,' Victoria whispered.

'And much happier now she's using her own scissors, although they look quite lethal.' Louisa shuddered. 'Perhaps we should get her to cut out all the pieces while the others sew,' she said, getting up to suggest it.

'You're certainly a splendid teacher,' she told the woman, who beamed with delight.

'Glad me talents is recognised at last. Felt quite put out when her ladyship commissioned Jane Haydon instead of me to make her things. Still, it's funny when yer think about it.'

'What is, Mrs Somers?' Louisa asked.

'Well, hers trading with the posh people of Salthaven whilst you ladies from the manor deals with the working classes here in Combe.'

'Oh, I see. Yes, I suppose it could seem funny as you say. Now, I was going to make a suggestion. As you are so proficient with those shears of yours, how about you cutting out all the fabric whilst the ladies do the sewing? It would save time and everyone would earn more money.'

'I'da couldn't have put it better myself. And I have a suggestion for you. How about we split them two big tables so I has one for the cutting out and the women can use t'other for stitching?'

'Splendid, Mrs Somers. Shall we do it now or later?'

'No time like the present, unless that magic man of yours is around?' she said, beady eyes scanning the room.

'Oh, you mean Quick? He had some errands to do but will be back later.' Louisa watched as the woman's face split into a wide grin. Well, well, she thought as she resumed her place.

'What's so funny?' Victoria asked.

'I think our Mrs Somers has a soft spot for Quick,' she whispered. 'Careful, she's watching,' she added, picking up a needle and threading it as Victoria tried to stifle her giggles.

With the delicious aroma of Lizzie's stew permeating the room, and under Ida's watchful eye, the women all began sewing.

'Well, I'da be,' Ida crowed some time later as she rose to her feet and walked over to the other table to inspect their work. 'Ida's teaching must be good cos yer work's almost passable,' she cackled. 'Bit of a wonky seam there though, Mary. Give us it here and I'll sort it.'

Flustered, the woman picked up the vest she'd been working on but as she passed it over, the sleeve of her top rose. The women gasped, their eyes widening in horror.

'What the...' Ida began, looking at the open sores and yellow bruising that covered the woman's arm. 'How'd yer get that, as if I didn't know,' she tutted. 'Have yer put anything on it?'

'Ain't got nothing at home,' Mary mumbled, shaking her head.

'Right, my girl, you come with me. Those are festering and want seeing to. Anyone else need help?' Reluctantly, her friend got to her feet.

'Me chest is hurting something dreadful,' she admitted.

'We're going to see Winnie,' Ida announced to Louisa.

'I'll come with you,' Victoria said, jumping to her feet, but Ida was already marching the women out of the door. 'It doesn't take a genius to work out the parson's men are responsible.'

'Sit down, Victoria, Papa made us promise we wouldn't get involved,' Louisa ordered. 'Right, ladies, you can resume your stitching. If you need any help, let us know,' she told the group who were now gossiping about what they'd seen.

'But we can't just leave them… Oh thank heavens, Quick is back and he's going after them.'

'I know it's horrible, but if we break our word Papa will stop us from coming here and that won't help the widows, especially now they're beginning to get the hang of making the vests. Besides, they already rely on the money they've been getting to keep their heads above water.'

'Yes, you're right, of course,' Victoria sighed. 'Wonder how many more of those poor widows are suffering. Evil so and so.'

'I know, but all we can do is tell Papa and leave it for him to deal with.'

***

That Sunday Edwin led his family down the aisle after the morning service.

'We are honoured by your presence in our humble church for what, three weeks in a row now?' Parson Preetcher said, bowing as Edwin reached the door. 'Perhaps you find the service here more agreeable than in the great cathedral of Exeter?'

'It is always good to worship with the people of the village. Although, I have to say I was surprised you didn't give praise for our lads' safe arrival in Gallipoli earlier this week.'

'I do not condone war in any way,' the parson said piously.

'Not even when they are fighting to stop the incursion of the Russian Empire into the Holy Land?' Edwin asked.

'I'm afraid not. I see Lady Farringdon is not with you today,' he said, changing the subject.

'She is indisposed, I'm afraid. And Louisa is visiting her future in-laws. Plans for the wedding and reception continue to be made for when Captain Beauchamp returns,' Edwin said, seizing his opportunity.

'Ah yes, indeed. Perhaps I might have a word when the others have gone?' the parson replied, a gleam glinting in his eye.

'Of course, I need to speak with some people myself before we leave,' Edwin said, ushering Sarah and Maria away from their fascination with the gravestones.

'Quick will take you and the girls home, Nanny, whilst I speak with Gill and his family.'

'Oh, can't we play here?' the girls clamoured.

'No, you can't, you little minxes,' Beatrice laughed. 'You'll be late for luncheon and I understand Cook has made the largest Yorkshire pudding to go with the roast beef. Come on, race you to the carriage.'

'I'll stay with you, Papa,' said Victoria. 'Fend off questions about Step Mama. Where is she, by the way?'

'Your guess is as good as mine,' Edwin sighed, for in truth he was growing weary of Charlotte's histrionics. 'Good morning, Edith, Wilf, Sam,' he said, striding over to where the Gills were making their way towards the cart.

'Good morning, my lord, Lady Victoria,' Edith replied, smiling prettily. 'I see Lady Farringdon is not with you. I do hope there is nothing wrong?'

'Step Mama is a little out of sorts,' Victoria replied truthfully. 'I trust you are keeping well.'

'Oh yes indeed, thank you.'

'And what about you, Wilf, is that leg of yours better now?' she asked.

'It be almost as good as new. That concoction Winnie do keep giving me might be vile but it certainly works. Surprised I still need it, though.' He frowned, as Edith winked behind his back and Victoria struggled to keep a straight face. How lovely it must be to belong to a family that didn't go in for hysterics, although to be fair it was only her stepmother that created dramas.

'And how are things with you, Sam?' Edwin asked. 'I haven't yet thanked you properly for helping catch those poachers.' As Sam nodded, Edith beamed proudly.

'Riding high at the moment, walking out with Miss Haydon, he is. Promised to bring her home to tea one day soon.'

'Ma, please,' he protested. 'And, if you'll excuse us, my lord, Lady Victoria, we'd better be getting home for luncheon. I only get to see Jane— Miss Haydon on a Sunday afternoon and it's a mighty long walk.'

'I think after your prowess up at the deer park, the least I can do is let you take the cart to Salthaven, Sam,' Edwin told him. 'And it is time we were leaving too. Good day to you.'

Just as he had thought, no sooner had they broken away from the group congregated outside the lych gate, than the parson came hurrying over.

'Might I have a word, Lord Farringdon?' he said, staring meaningfully at Victoria.

'I shall go and talk to Lily and Tom,' she said, hurrying away.

'What can I do for you, Parson?' Edwin asked, forcing himself to be pleasant.

'It is more what I can do for you, my lord,' he replied, edging Edwin towards the graveyard. 'You see, I was thinking that you will be wanting your daughter to have a really splendid party… wedding reception.'

'Indeed, I shall,' Edwin agreed.

'And you will probably be wishing to serve the finest brandy and claret.' Edwin nearly laughed out loud for he could almost see the guinea signs flashing in the man's eyes.

'Only the finest will do for my daughter and her intended,' he agreed. 'And, of course, we shall be throwing a betrothal ball at the end of next month,' he added for good measure, crossing his fingers behind his back.

'Ah really? Well, that could be very fortunate timing for you then. You see, I happen to have heard whisper of a special consignment being shipped over from France in the next week or so. I'm sure for a reasonable, how shall I say, recognition, some could just happen to be dropped off via your cellar, if you get my meaning,' he said.

'Well, I can't deny that wouldn't be convenient,' Edwin replied. 'But how could that possibly happen?'

'Ah well, these old tunnels lead off all ways. You just need to be in the know.' The man grinned, tapping the side of his nose with his finger.

'Goodness, well I never. How will I know when and where exactly to expect such a dropping off, as you put it?' Edwin frowned.

'I'll tip you the wink and, don't worry, you can pay me then.'

'That will certainly make my life easy,' Edwin replied. The parson's avaricious smirk made him want to punch the man on his weasel-like nose, and he hurried away before the feelings got the better of him. Making a note to inform Wakeley to keep his ear to the ground and alert the authorities about possible illegal activity in the quarry caves, he made his way out of the churchyard.

Seeing his carriage heading towards him, he hastened his step only to find his way blocked by Winnie. As ever she had the black cat with those piercing amber eyes on her shoulder.

'Hello, Winnie. I believe you have been working your magic on some of those widow's wounds,' he greeted her.

'If yer means sores and lesions, then I has indeed, my lord. And there'll be worse coming. Yer mark my words. Servants of the devil, those men,' she spat.

'I couldn't have put it better myself. However, you can rest assured I intend seeing all will be well.'

'It's action that's needed to put an end to those immoral

goings-on. Those poor women,' she sighed. 'Yer smelt that lavender then?' she said, giving him a searching look.

'No, I can't say that I have.'

'Well, yer should have. And it be a warning. I see danger ahead. Beware a dark big hole,' she cackled, shaking her finger at him.

Oh goodness, she must mean the caves, Edwin thought. How could that woman possibly know of his discussion with the parson mere minutes since?

Chapter 32

As the carriage made its way through the Devonshire countryside, Louisa leaned back against the velvet squabs. Vanny, never one to be idle, was sitting opposite embroidering daisies on one of Maria's frocks. It had been lovely spending the weekend at Woolbrooke House with Henry's parents. Warm and welcoming as ever, they had enthused over the few wedding plans that had already been made, offering their suggestions and telling Louisa she must say if there were any changes she wished made to the house. Yet at the same time they were mindful that whilst Henry's regiment had survived the long sea voyage, their part in the battle against Russian domination had only just begun. When Lord Beauchamp had disappeared to find out if there had been any further news of the war, she had shown Lady Beauchamp the lace sprigs Lily had given her.

Together they had designed the pattern for her veil, which was also to subtly incorporate both families' coats of arms. It was so nice to have her gentle encouragement rather than the ostentatious ideas her stepmother came up with. Finally however, at Louisa's insistence, Charlotte had reluctantly agreed there would be no betrothal ball until Henry returned.

Looking out of the window, she noticed they were skirting the deer park and felt her face growing hot as she recalled their last outing together. Snuggled together in Henry's coach, for a short space of time, they had been lost in their own world of love and passion. If only they could have stayed that way.

'Soon be home, m'lady,' Vanny murmured. 'Just as well, as it is growing too dark to sew any more,' she added, folding the dress and carefully placing it in her bag.

'I do hope there are tea and crumpets waiting,' Louisa murmured, the carriage lurching suddenly as they turned into the driveway. Even from here they could see the lamps had already been lit, smoke curling lazily from the chimneys as it disappeared into the darkening sky. It all looked cosy and welcoming and Louisa was glad to be home.

'I will see that Cookson has some ready when you have changed out of your travelling things.' Vanny smiled but as she looked back out of the window, Louisa saw her frown.

'Goodness, what are all those lights bobbing around over there?' Louisa cried, following the maid's gaze.

'I don't know, m'lady. Seems a bit late for the men to be working on the estate, but we'll soon find out,' she said, as they pulled to a halt outside the manor.

'Oh, Louisa, thank heavens you are home,' Victoria cried, hurrying down the steps to meet her. 'Sarah and Maria have gone missing. The men have been searching all afternoon for them.'

'Heavens, I must go and help,' she exclaimed, but as she turned to retrace her steps, Victoria put a detaining hand on her arm.

'Papa insists we are to stay here. He says we will be of more use when they are found. If they are,' she sobbed.

'Now then, of course they'll be found,' Louisa said, leading her sister indoors and settling her on the chaise in front of the fire in the Ruby Room. 'Where are Papa and Step Mama?'

'Papa's helping with the search. Step Mama cursed Nanny then flounced off to her room.'

'Very helpful,' Louisa muttered, just as the door opened and Edwin staggered into the room closely followed by Ellery. Grey with fatigue and worry, he collapsed into the chair and with a low whine, his faithful dog placed his head on his lap.

'Any news, Papa?' Louisa asked. He shook his head then let out a long sigh.

'And night falling isn't helping.'

'You need a stiff drink, Papa,' she said, signalling to Ferris who nodded and strode over to the sideboard.

'Where's Bea?' Louisa asked, a few minutes later.

'She said she was going to see to Firecracker, but that was hours ago so...' Victoria whispered. 'Knowing Bea, she's probably helping with the search.'

'I can hear you, Victoria,' Edwin told her, draining his glass and wincing as the hot liquid seared his throat. 'And telling your sister not to do something is like telling her not to get on her beloved horse.'

They lapsed into silence, the ticking of the grandmother clock in the corner of the room marking the passing of each interminable minute. Louisa was bursting with questions but knew this was not the time to ask them. Thankfully, the whisky had done its work and she was pleased to note the colour returning to her papa's cheeks, although his expression remained fearful as he absent-mindedly stroked Ellery's head.

'I simply cannot stay in here any longer,' he suddenly cried, but as he struggled to his feet Ellery gave an excited bark and they heard a commotion in the hallway.

'They've been found,' Beatrice cried, as two of the estate workers, carrying two bundles wrapped in blankets, followed her into the room.

'Are they…?' Louisa asked.

'They are both fine. Cold and frightened, but thankfully unhurt. I was searching the grounds on Firecracker and saw Jed and Paul carrying them back,' Bea told them as Nanny, tears coursing down her cheeks, rushed over to check her charges.

'Praise be,' she cried, stroking their cheeks in turn. 'There are pans warming their beds and I'll see they have a hot drink and wash straight away.'

'Take your hands off my babies,' Charlotte screeched, appearing in the doorway. 'Haven't you caused enough trouble, you stupid old woman? I want you gone from my house immediately.'

'That's enough,' Edwin told her, as the little girls whimpered. 'Your first priority as a mother should be to see to their welfare.'

'Well,' she gasped, staring at him outraged. 'See the girls are taken upstairs immediately,' she ordered, clicking her fingers at Vanny. 'And have a large brandy sent up to my chamber. All this worry has brought on the most dreadful headache.'

'We'll help you with the girls,' Louisa said, breaking the stunned silence as she lifted Maria from one of the men whilst Victoria took Sarah.

'And I'd better go and have a bath, I stink worse than when I've been mucking out Firecracker.'

'I'll go and pack my bags,' Nanny said quietly.

'You will do no such thing,' Edwin told her. 'You are not to blame yourself, Nanny. Charlotte is overwrought. Go and get some sleep and we will have a chat in the morning. Oh, and Nanny?'

'Yes, Edwin?'

'I should have a little nip in your warm milk to help you sleep,' he told her, before turning back to the men who were hovering in the doorway.

'Good work, Jed, Paul. Where were they?'

'Down the well. Well, the bigger one was, the other was whimpering on the edge. Miracle she didn't fall in too,' Jed told him.

'But that well is terribly deep,' Edwin exclaimed.

'Luckily, she fell onto a ledge. Didn't know how we was going to rescue her until Sam thought of using the treadwheel. Climbed down and placed her in the bucket then we hoisted her up,' Paul said, shaking his head.

'I can't express my gratitude enough, lads. Now, I must go and thank Sam, right away.'

'Reed and the others are still trying to get him out.'

'What?' Edwin cried. 'Is he all right?'

'We need to get back and find out,' Paul said. 'Brought the girls straight back, see.'

'I'll come with you,' Edwin told them.

'Be quicker without you, with respect, your lordship. We'll send word soon as we know.'

As they disappeared out of the door, Edwin sank back into his seat and prayed that Sam would soon be rescued.

'Goodness, you wouldn't believe those girls,' Bea laughed. 'The monkeys are only demanding ice cream to make up for missing tea. Do we know exactly what happened? Oh, are you quite well, Papa? You look awfully pale.' She frowned, peering closely at him. Not wishing to alarm her unnecessarily, he forced a smile.

'It's been a stressful day and I'm exhausted,' he told her truthfully. 'Go and get some sleep and tell Louisa and Victoria to as well. We'll have a proper chat in the morning. Oh, and Bea,' he added. 'You might be a disobedient little minx but I'm proud of the way you helped this afternoon.'

'Thank you, Papa,' she said, bending to kiss his cheek. 'Sleep tight.'

Some hope, Edwin thought, yet despite his worries, exhaustion must have overtaken him, for the next thing he knew Ferris was shaking his arm.

'Forgive me, my lord, but the men have news,' he said gravely as the little group of estate workers filed silently into the room.

'Is he...' Edwin began, but their haggard faces told him everything.

'We lowered down a bigger bucket and thought we'd be able to haul him up. We heard him say he'd got it and was going to climb in. Then he shouted he'd dropped his glasses. Suddenly there was a loud crack, followed by a terrible scream and then nothing.'

'We shone the lights down and saw the ledge had come

away and the bucket was gone. He didn't stand a chance, poor bugger,' Paul muttered.

'We'll get the crane up from the quarry in the morning and see if we can retrieve his body.'

'Thank you. What about Mr and Mrs Gill, do they know?'

'Wilf was helping,' Jed told him sadly. 'Edith was beside herself and Winnie's given her something to make her sleep.'

'I shall, of course, call on them first thing. I can only thank you for all you have done today. One fatality is tragic enough but without your perseverance, it might well have been three.'

As the men nodded and left, Edwin sank back onto his seat, sickened and saddened by what he'd just heard. Poor Sam, he had been a likeable fellow, hard-working and trustworthy. Far too young to have died, and in such a tragic way, falling down the well when he'd saved his daughters. The well. Of course, that was what Winnie had meant when she'd warned him about a dark black hole earlier. Naturally, having just been speaking to the parson, he'd thought she was referring to the caves. But would it have made any difference had he known? That area was strictly out of bounds for anyone other than staff. But even so, the fact remained that at six and four, his daughters should have been under supervision when they played outside. There was something niggling the back of his mind about that, but however hard he tried, he couldn't put his finger on it.

Going over to the sideboard, he poured himself another stiff drink then paced the floor, going over and over the events of the day until finally, as first light filtered through the drapes and he heard the servants stirring, he knew what he had to do.

He was making his way to his office when he saw Nanny

coming towards him and, to his dismay, she was carrying her bags.

'Oh Edwin, I was hoping to have left before you had risen but as you are here, let me say again how sorry I am about yesterday. I have spent half the night wishing I hadn't gone to visit my friend in Combe, then it might not have happened.'

'Let's discuss this in my office,' he said, taking her bags from her. He was halfway down the hallway when he turned and frowned. 'Did you say you were in Combe when the girls went missing?'

'Well yes, Sunday afternoon is my half day.'

'Of course it is. Come in,' he said, opening the door and gesturing to the easy chair beside the fire. He waited until she was seated then asked, 'Obviously you wouldn't have left Sarah and Maria by themselves?'

'Of course not,' she said indignantly. 'I might be getting old and slow, Edwin, but I'm not stupid. I left them with her ladyship in the Ruby Room.'

'I see,' he said slowly, understanding dawning.

'However, I did a lot of thinking last night and realised things need to change. If you don't mind me saying, I really do feel the time has come for Sarah and Maria to have a governess.'

'I agree,' he said, nodding.

'Well, at least that's something. I really have enjoyed my time here at Nettlecombe,' she began, staring at him fondly as she rose to her feet. But he shook his head.

'And I hope you will enjoy many more years here. Now do sit down again. I've been thinking too and this is what I propose…'

His meeting with Wilf Gill was awkward, not that he blamed Edwin, but grief had taken its toll and the man looked as if he'd aged twenty years overnight.

'Winnie's given Edith some more of that sleeping stuff, so I'll not wake her if you don't mind.'

'I wouldn't want you to, Wilf. I just want to say that in my eyes Sam died a hero. He was a fine young man of whom you should be very proud. I hope you will permit me to cover the cost of his funeral? Let him be laid to rest in the family chapel?' Wilf nodded then shook his head, tears running down his weather-beaten cheeks.

'Edith will want him to placed alongside his grandparents and great-parents in the churchyard in Combe. But a new headstone would be—' He broke off and shook his head helplessly. Blinking back his own tears Edwin could only pat his shoulder. 'Neither of you will feel like working for the next few days so I'll get Louisa to bring over some provisions to tide you over.'

Heart heavy at such a futile waste of life, he strode back to the house, only to meet with Charlotte coming down the stairs.

'For heaven's sake, Edwin, look at the state of you. Surely you haven't been up all night?' she tutted. As ever, she was immaculately dressed, bearing no signs of the previous day's crisis.

'Good morning, Charlotte. How are Sarah and Maria this morning?' he asked.

'Really, Edwin, I have only just risen and have yet to break my fast. However, as you have raised the subject, I want to speak to you about Nanny neglecting her duties.'

'And I wish to speak with you about that too. We'll talk in the parlour.'

'For heaven's sake, Edwin, please remember it is called the Ruby Room,' she retorted, strutting into the room and throwing herself down on the chaise. 'Now, Nanny has clearly been negligent in her duties and I must insist she leave Nettlecombe immediately.'

Edwin stared at her for a full moment, taking in her glacial stare and lips set in a hard line. To think he'd once thought her lovely. She was selfish and self-centred through and through.

'I agree that the person responsible for the welfare of Sarah and Maria has been negligent and that she must indeed leave forthwith.'

'Well, I'm glad we agree on something,' Charlotte said, staring at him in surprise.

'Except Nanny wasn't here yesterday afternoon, was she?'

'Goodness, I can't remember.' She shrugged, giving a brittle laugh.

'I understand Nanny left them in your care, here in this very room. The question is, did you leave the girls by themselves?' he asked, staring directly at her.

'Well, I might have done. They were in the middle of a game. Besides, the house is always full of servants.'

'Did you tell anyone you were going, wherever it was you went?'

'What is this, some kind of inquisition?' she asked, her voice rising.

'As their father, it is my responsibility to establish who neglected their care. And now I know that person was you, Charlotte,' he said, ignoring her.

'Don't be ridiculous,' she retorted. 'I'm their mother, not their nursemaid.'

'And frankly you are a sad excuse for one. What was so important that you had to leave the girls anyway?'

'It is not for you to question my movements, Edwin,' she told him, waving him away like some troublesome fly. He stared at her for a moment, then decided it wasn't worth arguing that as her husband he had every right to know.

'But it is for me to tell you your next one,' he replied, trying to keep his voice level and his temper under control. 'You cannot be trusted to fulfil your responsibilities to this family, so I want you to leave the house right away, before another tragedy occurs.'

'Leave? Don't be ridiculous, Edwin, I am your wife,' she said, her voice becoming conciliatory.

'And a poor one at that.'

'But I've never refused you—' she began.

'Nor given without expecting something in return,' he countered. 'Go and pack what you need, I want you gone within the hour.'

'But where will I go?' she cried. 'And what about the Season? I'm meant to be presenting Victoria in court.'

'Let me know where you are staying and, when I have had time to consider the future, I will send you a letter telling you what my intentions are. Goodbye, Charlotte,' he said, striding from the room and leaving her gaping like a fish.

Chapter 33

'Whatever's going on, Papa?' Bea asked, bursting into his office some time later. 'Step Mama's just gone off in the second carriage. She was in a foul mood, shouting at the servants as they stowed her trunks then, when Ferris insisted young Lewis drove her, goodness, you should have heard her language,' she cried, shaking her head.

'So, she's left then?' Edwin asked, looking up from the report he'd unsuccessfully been trying to finish.

'Yes, but where has she gone? And why was she taking so much luggage?'

'All in good time, Bea. Call Louisa and Victoria then meet me in the parlour in ten minutes,' he said, looking at his pocket watch. 'I will explain everything then. By the way, have you seen Sarah and Maria yet this morning?'

'Yes, and they are well, Papa, a little subdued but that's to be expected. Sarah's talking about being like the pussy cat in "Ding Dong Bell" and insisting Vanny sings the nursery rhyme. She doesn't appear to be overly hot but I wonder if she might be delirious. Do you think we should call the physician to check them over?' she asked.

'I think that might be a good idea. No, on second thoughts,

I'll get Winnie to look at them. She'll be calling on Edith Gill later.'

'Why, is she sick, Papa?' Bea frowned, and Edwin knew he needed to have that discussion with his daughters immediately before they heard from the servants what had been going on. 'Not exactly. Go and get your sisters, there are things you need to know.' Bea gave him one of her old-fashioned looks, then shrugged and did as he'd asked. Sighing, he made his way to the Ruby Room where, as agreed, Nanny was waiting.

'Girls, please sit down, I'm afraid I have some very sad news to impart,' he told them when they arrived. They looked from him to Nanny enquiringly, but did as he asked.

'As you know, Sarah and Maria went missing yesterday and I'm very grateful to all the estate and quarry workers who turned out to look for them. Eventually, Sarah was found in the well, Maria was at the top screaming hysterically down at her—'

'Oh, I understand the "Ding Dong Bell" now,' Victoria interjected, then seeing his grave expression, fell silent.

'Although all the men assisted, it was Sam Gill who actually climbed down and rescued Sarah.'

'Goodness, we must go and thank him,' Louisa cried, jumping to her feet.

'I'm afraid that won't be possible.' Edwin paused and took a deep breath. 'Somehow, he fell and...' he had to stop again to swallow the lump that had risen in his throat, 'and lost his life.'

'No,' Louisa cried, tears welling as she sank back into her chair. 'Oh, poor Sam. Poor Edith and Wilf.'

'Yes,' Edwin murmured, wishing he could somehow soften

the dreadful shock. Having played together as children, he knew how close they'd all been.

'Has this got anything to do with Step Mama leaving?' Bea asked, breaking the silence that had descended on the room. Instinctively Edwin looked at Nanny for support and, just as she'd done when he was a little boy, she nodded her encouragement.

'As you are probably aware, things have been a little strained between us for some time now.'

'Just a bit,' Bea snorted.

'Well, I'm afraid yesterday's catastrophe was the final straw and I told Charlotte to leave,' Edwin told them.

'Good for you,' Bea exclaimed. 'I heard her trying to blame Nanny.'

'I know you think I'm as soft as butter,' Edwin continued, looking directly at them so that they coloured uncomfortably. 'However, even I have a breaking point. Charlotte's behaviour was unforgivable, with catastrophic results.' He paused as if gathering strength. 'We all make mistakes but I will not tolerate a person who doesn't take responsibility for them.'

'And Step Mama always blames everyone else,' Bea muttered.

'Not any more, Beatrice,' Edwin told her. 'From now on, things around here are going to be very different. Firstly, I shall be engaging a governess for Sarah and Maria.'

'But what about Nanny?' they chorused, looking at her in dismay. 'She can't leave.'

'Of course not, Nanny is an invaluable member of our family. Nettlecombe is her home and I hope she will remain here for many years to come. In view of the circumstances, she has kindly agreed to take on the onerous role of caring for us,' he said, smiling at the woman who flushed with pleasure. 'She will liaise with Spick to ensure the home runs smoothly.'

'What about us, Papa?' Bea asked. 'What can we do to help?'

'Well, Bea, until a suitable governess is found, I would like you to assist Nanny with caring for Sarah and Maria.'

'Of course. It will be good practice for when I undertake my nursing training and have to keep patients in line,' she replied.

'Indeed, it will,' Edwin agreed, turning to Louisa and Victoria. 'For the foreseeable future, you may continue to concentrate your energies on the Quarry Crafters. We will discuss plans for your debut at a later date, Victoria. When things have settled down.'

'Yes, Papa.'

'In the meantime, Nanny will be here should any of you need someone to confide in, and I'm sure I don't need to remind you that she is very discreet.' Despite the unhappy circumstances, they smiled wryly, for it was well known that Nanny never broke a confidence, no matter how hard they tried to prise it out of her.

'Will Step Mama be coming back?' Louisa asked.

'I really cannot say,' Edwin replied. 'At the moment I cannot see it being likely but…' He shrugged.

'Thank the Lord she's gone, I say,' Bea muttered.

'I know things have not been easy for you of late. However, the official line will be that Charlotte has gone ahead to London to prepare for Victoria's debut. Now, back to the tragic news of Sam. We all need to help the Gills in any way we can. I've told Wilf that he and Edith will not be expected at work for the next few days and that you would take them some victuals to tide them over, Louisa.'

'Yes, Papa,' she replied. 'Poor, poor Sam.'

'Yes indeed. He will always be a hero in our eyes. I need to go and see how the men are getting on over at the well,' he said, rising to his feet. 'Nanny, I will leave you in charge here, and hope you won't regret taking us on.'

'I'm delighted you have put so much faith in an old lady like me. This has been my family home for so many years, I was dreading having to leave,' she told him.

'You are needed here more than ever now,' Edwin said, patting her shoulder as he passed.

'I'll go with Louisa and pay my condolences,' Victoria told him. 'Then we really should go to Combe and make sure everything's all right with the Crafters. I know you gave Mrs Somers a key and that she will have opened up by now, but there might be some query.'

'They're bound to have heard about the accident by now, so that's probably a good idea,' Edwin replied. 'But please, don't let them enter into any gossip about Charlotte. Speculation is one thing, confirmation quite another. Oh, and remember, Quick is to stay with you.'

Lost in their thoughts, Louisa and Victoria were subdued as the cart trundled towards the Gills' cottage. Winnie was just leaving.

'Yer'd best leave yer basket on the table,' she told them. 'Thems in such a state, I've given them both something to make them sleep. 'Tis a rum do. Told yer father to beware a black hole but of course, he weren't thinking of the well. 'Tis strange nobody smelled the lavender though; it's always foretold the fate of the Farringdon's Nettlecombe before.'

'Oh goodness, I've just remembered,' Louisa gasped, her hand flying to her mouth. 'Jane Haydon mentioned the fragrance of lavender when we were in the Amber Room. But that was a little while ago.'

'Portents arrive ahead of disaster. That's the point of them. They don't keep to timetables.' Winnie sniffed, dark eyes boring into them. 'Corse, makes sense, what with her being so close to young Sam. Poor girl, she'll be out of her mind when she hears. Well, Beatrice sent word your father wishes me to take a look at those girls, so I'd best be off.'

As the woman scurried across the grass, black cape billowing in her wake, Louisa turned to Victoria.

'Poor Jane Haydon. She will be heartbroken.'

'Do you think she knows yet?' Victoria asked, as she climbed back into the cart.

'I'm sure Combe will be rife with the news but we should send her a note of condolence at the very least,' Louisa said.

As they trundled down the driveway, their spirits sank even further when they saw the outline of a crane over by the far field. Even from this distance they could hear the men shouting to each other as they set about their challenging task.

'It's a very sad day, this,' Quick muttered, tipping his hat respectfully. Sick to their stomachs, Louisa and Victoria could only nod and the rest of the journey passed by in silence.

'Oh well, what did we expect?' Victoria sighed, when they pushed open the door to the workshop and saw the women chattering together at the back of the barn.

'Goodness, there are at least eleven here today,' Louisa murmured, as she did a rough headcount. 'Good morning, everyone,' she called, as enthusiastically as she could. As the little group turned to face them, Mrs Somers came scurrying over.

'Oh, it be the worst news,' she cried, shaking her head in despair.

'I know, Mrs Somers. Sam died a hero and will be for ever remembered as such.'

'Yes, that as well. He were a fine young man,' she added, making the sign of the cross. 'But it were them poor widows I was meaning.'

'I see there are more ladies here today – have they all come to work?'

'Well, Jeannie the staymaker has. Her be standing in for Flo cos hers had a real bad time with the baby coming breech. Split her right across… Well, I'm sure yer get my meaning,' she said when Victoria flinched. 'Anyhow, the others are waiting to speak with you, specially her,' Ida said pointing to the fire where Edna was eyeing them uncertainly. 'I told them that being the supervisor I'da needed to get on with the cutting out,' she added, gesturing to the new bolt of fabric lying ready.

'Thank you, Mrs Somers. Perhaps you could get the usual ladies along with Jeannie to begin stitching, the rest can wait whilst I speak with Edna.'

The woman strutted over to the others and began issuing orders. As Edna sidled towards them, Louisa was shocked at the change in the woman's appearance. Gone was the swagger, her eyes were dull while her previously tight clothes hung from her skeletal frame. She didn't even pass comment when Quick passed by carrying more fabric. Clearly something was very wrong and out of the corner of her eye Louisa noticed her compatriots waiting anxiously to see what was going to happen.

'Why don't we go outside and talk?' she suggested, signalling to Victoria to follow. 'I can see you're unhappy—'

'Unhappy! Scared rigid, more like,' the woman howled. 'I suppose yer going to laugh now and I don't blame yer,' she added, wiping her eyes with her less than clean sleeve. Louisa went to offer her handkerchief then realised it was already wet from her own tears and thought better of it.

'Look, I don't know what you mean, but if you're in trouble then I can assure you neither Victoria nor I would dream of laughing.'

'Why not tell us what the problem is?' Victoria urged.

'Well, it ain't me, exactly. That bastard Preetcher promised we'd get given good money and vittals if we was nice to his friends,' she said, stressing the word 'nice'. 'Well, we was, and what they given us? Only the bleeding pox, that's what.'

'I beg your pardon?' Louisa frowned. 'Oh, you don't mean...' she cried, realisation dawning.

'Syphilis,' said the woman grimly, nodding. 'Them last lot of men off the boat must have had it. By then though we'd had enough and was locked in the basement and beaten till we could hardly stand. Luckily, they got stinking drunk on the cognac they brought in and fell into a stupor, leaving the door unbolted. We waited till they was snoring and fled.'

'That's terrible. How many of you are... er, affected?'

'Infected, yer mean.' She gave a harsh laugh. 'Just the three who gave in. Parson went mad when he found out and sent them packing. Rest of us are all right. Still, I don't know why I'm telling you this, yer'll not want us near now, will yer?'

'I don't think any decisions should be made until you've all seen a physic,' Victoria told her. The woman stared at her as if she was talking another language.

'Thems cost money and that's what we don't have. And with the parson not paying us we don't have owt for food neither. Which is why we was hoping yer might let us work for yer. Bloomin' cheek me askin' after I was horrid to yer, I know, but when yer that hungry, yer got no pride.'

'I'm sure we can sort something out, Edna. Now the best thing for today would be for you and your friends to go home. I'll send Quick to the baker to buy some bread and get him to deliver it to you. I'm sure once you have eaten, things will look a bit better.'

'Yer mean, yer'll help us?' she asked, looking incredulous.

'We'll certainly try. However, the children will be coming out of school for their luncheon in a moment so perhaps it would be better if you disappeared before they arrive.'

'Yer, I get it,' she said going over to the doorway and letting out a piercing whistle. 'Come on, you lot, time for grub,' she hollered.

Louisa and Victoria stared at each other then watched as the new women surged towards Edna.

'I shall depart for the bakery, shall I?' Quick said, appearing silently at their side.

'Did you hear all of that?' Louisa asked him.

'I did, Lady Louisa, and believe you me, this will help

your father finish his report. Although, if you don't mind my saying, I feel you should speak with him before doing anything else.' She stared at the footman in astonishment; how dare he suggest what she could or couldn't do?

'Yes, you're right of course, Quick,' she said finally, for, of course, he was merely carrying out her papa's orders to keep her safe. 'Well, perhaps you'd distribute some provisions and make sure they've enough to tide them over. I'll check Ida's happy to run the workshop for the afternoon then go and speak to Papa,' she told him, her voice rising to be heard above the church bells chiming the noon hour and the cries of the children clamouring for their food.

'Actually, whilst the school's closed for luncheon, I just want to return these to Lily and show her the design Lady Beauchamp and I drafted for the veil,' Louisa told Victoria, delving into her bag and bringing out the sprigs of lace.

As they walked down the lane towards Lily's cottage, they met Winnie, Athame perched on her shoulders as usual.

'Hello, Winnie. I'm glad I bumped into you. I wanted to thank you for tending to Sarah and Maria,' Louisa greeted the woman. 'There doesn't appear to be any lasting damage to them, thank heavens. Although, of course, it's tragic about Sam.'

'Happen it were his time,' the woman replied, staring at the lace in Louisa's hand. 'There be a season for everything and autumn won't be yours. There'll be no wedding until the mist lifts.' As Winnie gave one of her knowing looks, Louisa felt a shiver slither down her spine.

Chapter 34

Edwin was sitting at his desk, trying to dispel memories of the harrowing sight of Sam's body being winched out of the well, as he tried to finish his report. Quick informing him of the previous day's events had provided the vital evidence needed about the parson's nefarious activities for him to insist the man be defrocked with immediate effect. But it was his daughters' involvement with the widows that was concerning him most.

'You wish to see me, Papa?' Louisa asked, popping her head round the door.

'I do. Come and sit down, there is something important I wish to discuss with you,' he said, signing his name at the bottom of the page, then putting down his pen.

'Is it about poor Sam? Only I have sent a letter of condolence to Miss Haydon on behalf of us all but if there is anything else that I can do, then say.'

'That was thoughtful of you, Louisa, I can't begin to imagine what the poor woman is going through.' He paused, wondering how best to approach the delicate subject then decided it was better to be forthright. 'Now, Quick has told me something of your discussion with this Edna yesterday and I must admit to being more than a little disturbed at the thought of you and Victoria being involved with such women.'

'Papa, really. Surely you should be the first to show compassion towards those widows, seeing as how most of them lost their men folk in accidents at your quarry. All they've done wrong is try to earn a living in the way they thought best. Albeit I find their way distasteful,' she added quickly, seeing him frown. 'It's Parson Preetcher tempting them with promises of riches then abusing their vulnerability who should be punished.'

'And he will, Louisa. That is why I am sending this report to the bishop straight away,' he said, tapping the sheets before him. 'I will make it my mission to see he is banished from any involvement with the church for good.'

'Thank the Lord,' Louisa said, then smiled at the irony of what she'd said. 'However, that still leaves the issue of the widows needing immediate help and employment in the future.'

'I agree. However, there are official organisations who can assist and—'

'You mean the workhouse?' she snorted. 'I cannot believe you expect me to shy away from this situation because it's distasteful.'

'We'd help with the appropriate arrangements,' he said, trying to be conciliatory.

'You mean stand by and let someone else come to their rescue? Papa, you should be ashamed of yourself. Suppose Sam had done that with Sarah and Maria? By the time official help arrived it might have been too late.'

'That's hardly the same,' Edwin retorted, beginning to feel uncomfortable.

'It is, Papa. It's about offering assistance when it's needed. I intend doing something constructive, with or without your blessing,' she told him.

Looking at the fire in her eyes and the determined set of her chin, he was reminded of his beloved first wife, Beatrice. In fact, he could almost hear her voice endorsing Louisa's proposal.

'You'd better tell me what your intentions are then,' he said sitting back in his seat, and from the gleam in her eyes, he could see she knew that she'd won.

'Thank you, Papa. All I ask is that you release more money from my trust fund so that I can pay for a physic to examine the widows. Those who are well can be offered a job in the workshop, the others will receive necessary treatment.'

'That will cost a fair amount. Always supposing you can find one agreeable to help. Physicians are particular about the patients they treat.'

'You and I both know money speaks volumes, Papa.'

'Very well. I will send word to Hooken, he is known for being discreet. Although, I dare say the whole of Combe, if not Devonshire, will know by now.' He gave a wry smile and then leaned towards her. 'You are sure about this, aren't you? I mean, your trust fund is meant to provide for your future and Henry—'

'Would agree that some of it should be used to help these unfortunate women,' she stated adamantly.

'Then you have chosen well,' he agreed. 'I was just thinking how like your dear mama you are. She would have been proud of you, Louisa.'

'Thank you, Papa,' she cried, jumping up and kissing his cheek.

***

It seemed the whole village had turned out for Sam's funeral with the shops closed, blinds pulled down and curtains closed out of respect for the unassuming young man everyone had liked. As the cortège of carts and carriages followed the wagon bearing the coffin slowly through the village, servants, quarry-men and estate workers, caps in hand, lined the street leading to St Winifred's. To acknowledge the young man's bravery, Edwin had offered to hold the service in the family chapel but Wilfred and Edith had politely declined, saying they wished their son to be remembered in the village church where they'd always worshipped.

Despite Wilfred's leg, still weak from his accident, he insisted on bearing his son's coffin down the aisle along with the men who'd helped in the rescue. As they placed it on the bier, the scent of the wild primroses, bluebells, hyacinths and violets Sam had loved so much wafted around the church.

To the villagers' amazement, the service was conducted by the bishop himself, Parson Preetcher having mysteriously disappeared overnight. As he spoke movingly about the bright young man who'd selflessly sacrificed his life so that a young child could live, even the hardened workers were seen to wipe their sleeves across their eyes. But at the graveside, when

Edith was invited to throw the first sod of earth, she turned and gestured for Jane Haydon to do it, their tear-filled eyes meeting through veils of black, two women united in grief for the man they'd both loved.

'He loved you so very much,' Edith whispered. 'I know we would have been friends, had he…' she choked.

'And he always spoke so fondly of you,' Jane sobbed.

'He were a lovely man,' Millie told Edith, turning away as the diggers picked up their shovels and began completing their job. 'They do say that God calls the good home young. Hey, I bet there'll be a right party in heaven tonight as his grandparents welcome him up there.'

'Thank you, that is a comforting thought, isn't it, Wilf?' When he didn't reply, she turned to Jane. 'I've brought you this,' she said, handing Jane a parcel.

'But, I…' Jane began, then seeing the woman waiting expectantly, she pulled back the paper. 'Why, it's beautiful,' she murmured, staring at the wooden bodkin which had been polished to a high shine. 'Oh,' she gasped, tears blurring her vision when she saw the heart on the handle that he'd carved with both their initials.

'Spent hours making that for you, he did,' Edith told her. 'Said he was going to make another one for when you wed, when you took his name.'

'Thank you, Mrs Gill. I shall treasure this for the rest of my life.'

'I hope it will bring you some comfort and that in time you will find happiness again,' she whispered.

'I don't think so. Sam was my one true love and I'll never

forget him. I shall now devote the rest of my life to my business.'

'You might think that now, but you are still very young with your life ahead of you. Unlike...' She shook her head as grief overcame her.

'Come along, I think it's time we went,' Wilf said gently, as with a nod to Jane and Millie, he took his wife's arm and led her away.

As the mourners began drifting off, Lady Connaught appeared by their side.

'Miss Haydon, Millie, I really don't know what to say.'

'But yous already sent us that nice card,' Millie replied, when she saw Jane struggling to maintain her composure.

'I still can't believe it,' Jane whispered, cradling the bodkin tighter. 'If you'll forgive me, I'd like to return to Salthaven and make sure everything is in order at the *magasin*, although of course it is closed today.'

'At times like this, Miss Haydon, I think a little flexibility is permissible. And understandably you are looking fatigued.'

'Don't yous worry, Lady C, I'll look after her. And Mouse too. That's me new role see, I'm now their housekeeper,' Millie said, proudly. 'I doesn't have time to work in the shop any more.'

'Well, I'm very pleased to hear it,' Lady Connaught replied, giving Jane a knowing look. 'Oh, I do believe Lord Farringdon wishes to speak with us.'

'Good afternoon, Lady Connaught, Miss Haydon and...?' He paused, looking enquiringly at Millie.

'Millicent,' she squeaked.

'Well, ladies, I wonder if you will do me the honour of accompanying me to the Crafters' workshop just up the lane here. My daughters have arranged a wake in honour of Samuel, and before you refuse,' he said, holding up his hand as Jane opened her mouth, 'Louisa has a special surprise which I can promise you won't want to miss. Although Mr and Mrs Gill are understandably grief-stricken, they have been kind enough to accede to our request.' He turned to Jane. 'It is, I hope, something that will bring you a degree of comfort at this very sad time.' Then, to her surprise, he held out his arm for her to take before leading her gently, but firmly, up the lane.

'Blimey O'Reilly, would yous believe that, Lady C?' Millie exclaimed.

'Lord Farringdon is nothing if not a gentleman,' Lady Connaught said.

The barn was packed with well-wishers. Ida was presiding over the large tables which instead of holding the usual sewing paraphernalia now groaned under the weight of sandwiches, pastries and cakes. However, keeping a firm grip on Jane's arm, Edwin led her over to where his daughters were standing.

'Miss Haydon,' they chorused.

'I'm so sorry for your loss,' Louisa said. 'It is obviously a very difficult time for you. Thank you for coming with Papa. I know it must feel like a terrible ordeal but I really wanted you to be here.'

'You have worked miracles since the last time I saw it...' Jane began then stopped, as she recalled the indoor picnic she and Sam had shared.

'I hear you have done well for yourself,' Victoria said, to fill the sudden gap in their conversation.

'I never did get to see your premises in Exeter so I shall be sure to travel to Salthaven soon,' said Louisa, smiling.

'And I will come with you, for I simply must collect that riding corset, the one I'm wearing simply cuts me in two.'

'I shall look forward to seeing you,' Jane managed. Seeing she was still struggling, Louisa turned to her father.

'Do you think it's time, Papa?'

'Indeed. Ladies and gentlemen, if I could please have your attention,' Edwin called. On hearing his voice, the hall instantly fell silent. 'As you know, Samuel Gill was our assistant estate manager and a very fine one at that. I don't need to remind you of the sad event that has caused us to be here today. Sam was a fine man who will never be forgotten. And my daughter Louisa has been instrumental in ensuring he isn't. I will now allow her to explain.'

'Although this is a sad occasion, it is also a significant one for the village of Combe,' Louisa told the expectant gathering. 'As you no doubt know, this building which Sam helped renovate has become the workshop for our Quarry Crafters. However, we have now been fortunate to be joined by other ladies of the village so have decided to rename this barn. From now on, it will be known as the Sam Gill Community Hall.'

A stunned silence was followed by thunderous applause then someone called, 'Three cheers for Sam.'

'I do hope you approve?' Louisa said, raising her voice to be heard against the hubbub as she turned to where Jane was standing beside Edith and Wilf. The astonishment and delight on their faces said it all.

'Thank you,' Edith murmured, tears rolling down her cheeks once more.

'Sam would be so proud,' Jane murmured.

'No, it is we who are proud to have known him,' Edwin told them.

Chapter 35

For the first time in quite a while Edwin Farringdon felt content as, with faithful black Labrador Ellery by his side, he made his way down the sunken lane, where the hedges were now a riot of early summer flowers and the glorious song of a skylark sounded from the nearby fields. At last, it seemed his problems were beginning to sort themselves out.

His meeting with Tom Wakeley had gone well. The quarry workers had responded to his promise of a bonus if they fulfilled the new order received from abroad on time. Parson Preetcher, having heard the authorities had seized the illegal consignment of liquor and his men had been arrested, had fled. Rumour had it he'd been seen cadging a lift to Cornwall. Edwin, a law-abiding man, was pleased the boats his company used wouldn't be implicated in the smuggling.

His heart lifted further as the manor came into view. The elegant symmetry, tall chimneys and mullioned windows bathed in the rosy glow of the afternoon sun looked warm and welcoming. With Nanny's help his home was gradually returning to the haven it had previously been and once again he looked forward to being indoors with his family.

'Life is on the up, old boy,' he said, bending to pat his

faithful friend. Ellery peered up at him through his one good eye and barked. 'And you're happier too now that you can relax in the front of the fire without being shouted at. I really don't know how I put up with things for so long.'

Yet he had wanted to make his marriage work, to sire the son he'd so longed for. Charlotte had led him to believe that it would happen one day but she had other priorities, he could see that now. She was all about appearance and had no depth or sense of responsibility.

That terrible incident with Sarah and Maria had been the final straw, making him realise he could no longer put his family at risk. He would never know if the tragedy with Sam could have been avoided had he insisted a governess be engaged sooner, but that was something he would have to live with for the rest of his life. The fact that nobody had enquired about Charlotte's absence both at the funeral and the naming of the hall spoke volumes as to how little she was regarded in the community. And if gossip was to be believed, the servants were happier now that she'd gone.

With Sarah and Maria safely under the watchful eye of Miss Birkett, he could concentrate his energies on his elder daughters. The Crafters' Workshop was running well and providing employment for many of the local women. With Sal the Sunday school teacher looking after the youngest children, they could concentrate on their work and were now turning out shirts and vests of a quality surpassing anything the visiting hawker could supply.

At Louisa's expense, Dr Hooken had examined those who'd been in the parson's pay and the three women showing symptoms of syphilis had been taken to the asylum where they would be looked after. Whilst there was no hope of a cure, they would at least be made comfortable. He was proud of the way his eldest daughter had thrown herself into the project and few would guess she waited with trepidation for news from the Crimea. It was probably only he who had seen her gripping Henry's uniform button tightly in her hand as she prayed for him. God willing, he would return safely and they would be married. In time, when they produced children, he might even have a grandson to inherit his beloved Nettlecombe. His heart warmed at the thought.

After much deliberation, Victoria had decided she would go to London for the Season after all. Being the most reticent of his daughters, Edwin knew it would give her the confidence she so lacked. However, he had to speak with Charlotte in order to finalise arrangements, a task he was not looking forward to.

Then there was Beatrice who was eagerly awaiting her interview with Professor Todd. He knew she was determined to begin her training with the sisters in Westminster as soon as she could. Being passionate as well as caring, Edwin had no doubt she would make a very fine nurse indeed.

Stopping under the shade of the lime trees that were now in full leaf and humming with the music of bees in the heat of the afternoon, he took out the letter that had arrived that morning.

My Dear Edwin,

It has been some time since we parted and when you are in London next I would appreciate you calling in to see me. I am staying with my sister, address above, and we are busy with preparations for the Season and Victoria and Hester's debut.

We need to discuss our future, if indeed we have any.

Your wife,
Charlotte (Lady Farringdon)

Edwin shook his head. Only Charlotte could write a letter in that vein. He would arrange to see her when he travelled to London for Bea's interview. But what did he actually want for the future? Despite everything, he still questioned if he had the right to deprive Sarah and Maria of their mother. Yet they both seemed to be happy, even after their ordeal, and he certainly appreciated a more peaceful and less tempestuous existence. The bills for new clothes and household paraphernalia had reduced significantly too. What a quandary, he thought, letting out a long sigh that caused Ellery to whimper and brush against his leg.

'Come on, old boy, time to get going,' he told him, striding up the driveway.

As Edwin entered Nettlecombe he could feel its warmth wrap around him. The portraits of his ancestors seemed to be smiling and he knew with sudden certainty that, despite the curse of the gypsies, the Farringdon dynasty would continue. Whether it be through son or grandson, Nettlecombe Manor would remain the family home for some time to come. A thought that made him smile back at them.

Acknowledgements

To Kate Mills and all the marvellous team at HQ who made this book possible during a very testing time. You have gone above and beyond.

To Teresa Chris: Your continued encouragement and support is so very much appreciated.

To BWC: Our monthly meet ups on Zoom during lockdown have been a highlight to look forward to. Hope we can meet in person again very soon.

ONE PLACE. MANY STORIES

Bold, Innovative and
empowering publishing.

FOLLOW US ON:

@HQStories